Once Upon a Dystopia:

An Anthology of Twisted Fairy Tales and Fractured Folklore

Table of Contents

Copyright © 2021

Cover Design MiblArt

ISBN: 9798715824974

Caught in the Siren's Wake

By Audrey M. Stevens

"Veya! Oh my! Wake up!" my mother says excitingly, shaking me awake. This summer has been hot, and my skin sticks to the thin sheets made of plant fibers and wool.

"What?" I ask my mother in a groggy voice as I wipe a few strands of my thick, black hair off my face.

"Look!" she says, pointing her finger at my leaf-stuffed mattress. I slowly sit up on my elbows and look to where she is pointing. Even though my eyes are blurry and adjusting to the rising sun, I can still see the red-soaked stain on my sheet below my abdomen.

I immediately sit up and pull the sheet off my body. More blood sits on my nightgown. I quickly stand next to my mother and see the blood has seeped into the fibers of the mattress. My heart sinks and my stomach ties itself in knots.

"You have become a woman today! I must go fetch Charon!" She turns to leave me.

"Mother!" I call in a frightened voice, making her stop. When she sees my worried expression, she comes back to embrace me.

"Today is a cause for celebration, not remorse," she says, kissing my forehead. "The weather is good and the sea will bless you with good travels." She releases me and quickly leaves my room.

I look back to my ruined mattress and sheet. I stare at the gore and feel a sudden hatred for my body. I don't want to be a woman. Not now, not ever. I strike one fist on the mattress, and then my other, and then hit it again, over and over until I am completely exhausted.

I slowly fall to the dirt floor and lean against my mattress. Tears well in my eyes as I watch the loose particles float in the sunlight. Their happy dancing makes me want to catch each one and bury them deep in the ground. My mother has been preparing me for this day for my entire life, but it won't make today any better.

Through my tears, I see my father enter the room. He stands in the doorway, inspecting the sight from a distance. His body is stiff and he doesn't say a word. I wish he would say something, anything, so that I may speak. Today I'm a woman and I'm no longer permitted to speak to a man unless he interacts with me first. It's almost as if he is testing me now as he stares at me in my most fragile state. I want to break the rules, but being beaten before I'm forced to board Charon's boat will do me no good. I will need my good health and strength.

My mother appears behind my father and waits for him to move. He stands for a few more moments before leaving us to tend to our womanly needs. Once he is gone, my mother enters the room and squats down beside me. "Veya, my dear, what did I say?" She wipes the tears from my face. "It is an honor to become a woman. Today is not for remorse. If you must cry, get out all your tears now. Your father will not tolerate the embarrassment of your emotions outside of our hut." Anger fills my body, but I nod my head in understanding.

"I had your brother fetch a pail of water from the sea. You must bath in it while I dye your gown." She speaks to me as if I don't already know what is expected of me today. She stands and sticks out her hand, offering to help me up. I look to her hand and then to her, not wanting to leave this spot. She sighs. "Causing a delay will not prevent today's events from occurring."

I wonder, for a moment, if she remembers the emotions that went through her head on the day she became a woman. Was she angry and scared like I am, or was she proud and confident like she says she was? I don't know how any woman could willingly want to leave the island. If death wasn't the other option, I would be more defiant.

Not wanting today to be my last, and not wanting to bring shame on my family, I grab my mother's hand and stand beside her. "I need your gown dear." My mother gestures at my stained garment. I lift the thinned wool over my head and give it to my mother. "I'll be

4

back soon," she smiles. "Please be ready when I return," she adds before leaving me again.

As I stand alone in my room, I look down at my cursed body. My flat chest and square hips give me a clear view of my bare pelvis that is stained red between my thighs. Over the next few years I will develop my body hair and breasts, making me worthy enough to rejoin my islanders. Until then, I will wait on the isolated island of Wahine Pono.

I hear my brother in the next room sloshing around my two buckets of seawater. I take in a deep breath and walk toward the sound. When I enter the tub room, I see my ten-year-old brother, Frey, finish dumping the second bucket into the wooden basin. He looks at me, but only sees the stain on my inner thighs. I look at him and envy him. Frey will never know the pain of leaving the island or the family. He will get to stay here once he becomes a man. Once Frey's voice deepens and his body hair grows in, he will gain the respect due a man and will be eligible to wed a woman that has returned from Wahine Pono. His innocent eyes meet my anger filled face for only a moment before he darts out of the room.

I take in a deep breath and step into the saltwater bath. I watch as the blood slowly disappears as if it were never there, causing the water to gain a light hue of pink. I wish the blood wasn't there. I push the wishful thinking aside and submerge my head in the water drowning out all the noises of the village. Is this what it sounds like on Wahine Pono? Like nothing?

Other girls have been sent to the island just like I will be, but are they still there? Will I be sentenced to years in solitude? Or are the other women who have gone before me still waiting for their opportunity to come back?

I can't hold my breath anymore and I'm not brave enough to allow the water to fill my lungs so I quickly sit up, gasping for air. When I have caught my breath, I slowly sink back down, into the tub and rest my head on the edge of the basin. A feeling of hopelessness slowly envelops me as anxiety creeps though my body.

"Did you scrub your hair dear?" my mother asks from the hallway. I don't look up to meet her gaze or answer her as she enters the room. "Here, let me," she says, squatting behind me and running her nails along my scalp. "It's important to lather in the salt," she explains.

"I collected the seaweed for your crown and have Vada braiding it now. Your dress is drying on the line." She stops scrubbing my scalp and kisses me on the forehead. "Everything is ready once you are finished cleaning up." She stands and leaves the room.

I stay until I can no longer bear the chill of the water. My hair has almost completely dried and my fingers and toes are wrinkled. I step out of the bath and slowly make my way back to my room. The sun has risen to the point that its warmth fills the house, but the bumps on my skin and the chill in my back don't go away.

When I enter my room, I see that my stained mattress has already been removed. Instead, on top of the worn, wooden frame, my crown and dyed gown lay, waiting for me. The stain of my blood on my gown has been hidden with the red dye of the berries. Our neighbor, Vada, has taken it upon herself to add palm leaves amongst the woven seaweed. I stare at the pair of them, willing them to disappear, but they stay, taunting me.

I lift the dress and catch a whiff of the soured berries as the gown slides over my head and onto my body. I place the entwined fibers securely on my head. I still feel naked, but I am now ready to be presented to the village as a woman. My feet must remain bare and my hair in its natural state. That's how it is meant to be.

I take a deep breath and enter into the main living area of my father's hut. My entire family is pacing the room, waiting for me. I clear my throat, and all at once their eyes fall on me. My mother looks elated, my brother sad, and my father disappointed.

"Everyone is waiting," he says in an annoyed tone. I nod my head and bite my tongue, not wanting today to become worse than it already is. He gestures for me to exit the house.

I hold my head high and enter into the sunlight. The entire village has lined up, forming a path from my house to the ocean. My stomach feels as if it has twisted in on itself. I swallow down the bile that feels like it may spill out of my mouth and begin my walk to the sea.

As I walk, my family stays close behind, escorting me away from our home. No one speaks, but they all watch. I see the excited looks from the young girls who do not yet understand the curse we are under. Men stare at me, wondering that if I return, if I will be their wife. I try not to meet the eyes of anyone and keep my gaze on the water.

I walk past the muffled cries of my friend, Eva, but I can't stand to look at her. I must stay strong. I'm one of the oldest in our generation, and I have to set an example. We all knew this day would come, but it was impossible to know when. Since it has been five years since a woman was sent to Wahine Pono, I guess we all just stayed ignorant to the fact that my time was getting closer and closer.

We have made our way to the center of the village and I am forced to walk by the statue of the woman who made this tradition possible. I want to spit on it, but know it will bring shame on my family and me. Her presence on this island over a hundred years ago has wasted the lives of many innocent girls.

We've been told the story of the woman of the sea. Before her arrival, women didn't have to prove themselves worthy of living. Men and women married and had children based on mutual agreements or love. Our way of life was simple, but that all changed when she came to our shores.

A large storm had been brewing over the sea and our village was preparing itself for a brutal night. Just before sunset, a beautiful woman came rising out of the sea. She wore nothing except a crown of seaweed on her head. The villagers wondered where she came from and how she had survived, alone in the sea. They asked her many questions, but she didn't utter a single word.

She seemed unaffected by the raging water behind her. The naked woman walked along our beaches, all the while gaining the affection of every man in the village. Her poise, beauty, and silence emphasized all the flaws in the women residing on the island.

Once she had turned the hearts of all the men with her perfection, she returned back into the sea. The storm that was

7

developing suddenly faded as she entered the water. The story says that several men even tried to follow her back into the sea, never to be seen again. The last thing the men saw of the woman was a large fish-like tail following close behind her perfect bust.

Even after the mysterious woman left, the men still yearned for her presence. They despised that their wives weren't like her. In their hatred, many of the men killed their spouses in a fit of rage, finding it better to have no wife at all.

Many of the young girls became afraid of their fathers, worried that they would not live up to the men's new standards. In order to prove that they deserved a husband and a life in our village, the young girls were forced into the sea like the mysterious woman. If the young girls could prove that they could survive on their own, against the strength of the ocean, they would be allowed to return.

Not knowing where the woman came from, the men placed the young girls on a small, deserted island within sight of their own island. The men decided that once a girl became a woman, she would be sent to the island and could not return until her body was developed and ready for a man. The women would not be given any supplies nor help from the islanders. They had to do it all on their own.

Since then, all young girls have been taken to the island. In the five years since the last girl was sent away, only two have returned. It has been said that the journey on the boat to the island takes many hours and that the trek back without a boat can take days.

I keep my body stiff for the rest of the walk, resisting the urge to turn around and run back into my room. Well, what used to be my room. I no longer live there. Even if I do return, my father will immediately pair me with a suitor and I will go live with him. I will never return to my father's hut. For me, love has become a thing of the past. All that is left are standards that must be met.

Charon has a small grin on his face as he watches me inch closer and closer to him. His facial expression resembles that of a proud father, but he is far from it. I already know that if the sea or island doesn't kill me, Charon will. He will kill me if I run now and he will kill me if today I exit the boat too soon. If I don't attempt to return to the island within seven years, he will come to Wahine Pono to hunt me down for shaming my gender.

He is the only man allowed on the island. His role is one of enforcement and is highly respected by the leaders of our island. He is tasked with the delivery of every girl along with the death of every woman who refuses to participate in our traditions. Charon will never marry nor have children. He is a eunuch with the life altering power of a god and the smirk of a demon.

I grind my teeth and purse my lips as we approach him. My eyebrows are furrowed and my fists are clenched as anger rises up within me. I have to force my bare feet onto the hot sand, but I don't show my discomfort from the heat on my soles. Instead, I keep a steady pace, straight for Charon's boat.

When I reach the wooden frame of his vessel, I don't stop to look at him. I lift up my leg, ready to board until my mother grasps my hand. My aggravated expression falls from my face when I feel her touch.

I turn to her and notice her bottom lip quivering. She quickly looks me over, studying each of my features as if she will never see me again. She may not. I may never see anyone on this island again.

"Come back soon, Veya," she whispers to me as she releases her grip. I glance at my brother who has stayed by my father's side. His eyes are glued to the ground, not wanting to upset me further. I suddenly wish I hadn't been so rude to him this morning. This is as much his fault as it is mine; none of us get a say in our future. I want to run to him and embrace him one last time, but I am a woman now and he is a man. I no longer have the right to do as I wish.

Before I step into the boat, I look to my father who seems unimpressed and bored. He doesn't utter a word and looks at me like I mean nothing. My anger boils again under my skin. I sit myself down forcefully, ready for Charon to row us out to his large boat so I may leave this life of unachievable perfection behind me.

***

The water was rough and choppy, but after a few hours of silence, Charon and I finally made it into the reef of Wahine Pono. It is my first time on a boat and I hope it is my last. The rocking and sudden movements made my head ache, my stomach uneasy, and my muscles spasm.

"This is as far as I take you," Charon says as he quickly throws down the heavy anchor and the boat leans to one side. The sharp turn takes me off guard and I almost fall into the water. I have only just regained my balance when he throws a small sack into my crossed arms.

"Basic provisions," he explains when I give him a puzzled look. I peek into the bag and catch a glimpse of a hook, fishing line, sharpened knife, and a small piece of flint.

My jaw hangs low as I shake the bag, looking for more. I'm astonished by the lack of provisions he has provided. "Get on your way. I'm expected back before nightfall," he says, shooing me like a feral animal.

"But…" I begin, gesturing to the island that is still at least a mile away. Charon rears back his hand, ready to strike me for speaking, but stops the motion when I don't continue to argue. I lean over the side of the boat and look into the crystal-clear water far below. I can see the bottom, but know I won't be able to reach it. I will have to swim.

I take in a deep breath and jump into the cool water, clinging tight to my only belongings as I refrain from screaming during my fall. Bubbles dance around me as I bounce back up to the surface. When I open my eyes, I see the boat has already begun its trek back, swaying from side to side as if waving goodbye. My fiber crown floats beside me.

***

The weight of my gown and my one occupied hand makes my swim to shore more difficult. When I can finally stand on the ocean's floor, I catch my breath and curse Charon for not bringing me in closer with his rowboat. It's midday and I haven't had anything to eat or drink. My body is beginning to feel the fatigue of my journey.

The shoreline is now in view. This island resembles my home. The white sand stretches up the beach, following the flow of the rising and falling tides. The sand quickly blurs into rocks and shrubbery before allowing trees to grow tall on the horizon. I catch a glimpse of a few silhouettes on the beach and just within the tree line. I'm not sure if they have yet to notice my presence, or they just don't care.

I wade through the water, carefully observing each step I take. Small fish scurry out of my way as my feet glide through the water. I carefully time each movement so that the waves don't knock me over. The rough rocks and scattered coral could easily break my skin and I don't need to add an injury to my list of burdens.

When I finally make it onto the shore, I notice that a few women have come to the beach to inspect the new arrival. I wring out my soaked gown, trying to release some of the added weight as they walk toward me.

"Veya?" one of them calls, making me look up.

I recognize her face, but she doesn't resemble the girl I once knew. The red gown that she wore when she was taken from the island has since faded to a dull pink. The fabric has grown thin and is covered in rips and tears. The bottom of her dress is tied in a knot, right above her knees. Her braided hair is tied back with a small, ropelike fiber and is frizzed from the roots to the ends.

Her body has fully developed. Her waist is small and her hips are wide. The small amount of fat that has accumulated on her body rests in her thighs, buttock, and breasts. Her arms and legs are toned causing her muscles to be easily defined.

"Anniya?" I ask, after studying her for a moment.

"You remember," she responds with a small smile. Anniya was the last girl I saw leave the island. Her time to return is quickly approaching.

"Yes," I say, returning my attention to my heavy gown. "Even though the men try to make us forget those on this island, it's hard to ignore when it will soon be your fate." My now damp gown feels more manageable as I make my way up the shore.

"How was your ride?" Anniya asks, trying to make conversation.

"Fine. How do I get some of those?" I ask, gesturing to her covered feet.

"Oh," she says, looking at her handmade shoes. "I can teach you. That's how you will learn everything. Each woman tries to pass down as much knowledge as possible before leaving the Wahine Pono. It gives us all a better chance at success." She smiles at me as she guides me inland. I slowly follow behind, watching my step. My feet are rough, but not enough to not be cut on the rocks and sharp sticks on the ground.

We reach a clearing where the ground isn't covered in debris and I can finally look over my new home. Three small shacks are tucked between the trees. They are made of sticks, vines, and palms leaves. Though a strong storm would cause some damage, they seem fairly secure.

A makeshift table and chairs are in the center of the clearing beside a fire pit filled with hot coals. "How many women are here?" I ask, not seeing many others.

"There are five of us currently. You make six," she explains as we each take a seat. "They are all performing their daily tasks. We work together to survive until we attempt to cross the sea to go back home." She pauses, looking at the ground as if embarrassed.

"What is it?" I ask.

"Did Bai or Ragna make it back?" she asks, not meeting my eyes.

"It's been many years since a woman came onto the shores of Komo Mai," I respond, not knowing what else to say.

"Who was the last one?"

"Zen. She was paired with Borke," I state.

She takes in a deep breath and exhales slowly through her nostrils. "That means three of us didn't make it back. We swim almost every day, training to make it back. I don't know what went wrong." Anniya sighs as she rests her head in her hands. "I wish I could talk to Zen and ask her how she did it."

"You want to go back?" I ask, appalled.

"What choice do I have?" she scoffs. "I know you just got here, but life on Wahine Pono isn't easy. We work hard just to survive. Over the years, we have learned how to take care of ourselves. Like I said, the older women pass down whatever knowledge they can before they leave, but with our limited numbers and resources, life here is nothing compared to life back at Komo Mai."

"Even if you do reach the shores of our home, you will immediately be given to a man like a prized hog and be forced to breed with him," I state, still angry with my current situation.

"And the other option is death. I'll take having a family and a husband who provides for me over that."

"I don't ever want to go back there," I say through gritted teeth. "I refuse to be an object that has to prove its worth by risking my life."

She reaches a hand out and places it on my shoulder. "I know you are angry and scared and confused. We all were. But eventually, we must all go back."

"No," I say. "We don't"

***

It took me many days and a lot of persuasion to convince the others we needed to leave. We aren't allowed to live on Wahine Pono permanently and we won't be happy back on Komo Mai. The woman that supposedly visited the island all those years ago ruined any chance we had at being free on our home island. I won't go back to be a slave and now that I've convinced the others, they don't want that either.

There are no other islands in sight. We have looked in every direction from every point on this island and yet, only Komo Mai can be seen even on the clearest of days. That doesn't matter though. There has to be another island we can go to, an island with more resources where we can be free. We have a better chance at survival and happiness together, away from the laws of Komo Mai.

Since my arrival, Charon has only returned to this island once to abandon Eva. However, he stayed off shore, just like he did with me. He will be back again soon for Anniya. It took me a while to convince her, but she is willing to try and escape the island with all of us. If there is another option rather than returning to Komo Mai, we want to take it. Although our ancestors were willing to participate in this barbaric tradition, we are not.

After almost a year of preparation, we are ready to try and leave. Our raft is made of planks and sticks and tied together with fibrous ropes. We used our gowns and the scraps of those who have attempted to cross the ocean to make a sail. The raft is sturdy and holds enough rations for a few weeks if needed. Our coconut flasks hold fresh water from the spring. Palm leaves have been tightly strung together holding dried fruit, nuts, berries, hardened bread, and the few pieces of fresh fruit and cooked fish we gathered yesterday.

"Are you sure this is strong enough to get us past the reef?" Anniya asks nervously.

"No," I admit. "I have never built a boat before, especially not one that can hold seven people, but we have to try. Charon could come back any day for you."

"Alright. Let's give it a go," she says, climbing aboard.

Eva and I push the boat farther into the water, until it completely floats. Anniya helps us onto the raft. It wobbles and rocks from our weight, but stabilizes quickly. I lower our makeshift sail and the wind catches it, thrusting us forward. We all stay silent, keeping our balance as the waves try to push us back.

We make it all the way to the edge of the reef. Calm water, unaffected by the tide is within reach. The last wave is taller and stronger than the others. We brace ourselves for the impact against the front of the boat, but it doesn't help. We tip too far upward and flip the raft.

"Grab the gear!" I yell when I break the surface. We all begin scrambling in the water, looking for anything that came off the boat.

After we collect as much as we can, we slowly make our way back to the shore. The tipped raft follows us on the waves as if mocking our failure. We are all exhausted by the time we reach the beach and lay on the warmed sand.

"I knew we shouldn't have tried!" Anniya cries. "Charon will be here any day for me. I have no choice but to take my chances in the sea."

"Don't do that!" Eva begs. "We can fix this. The boat will float back and then…"

"And then what?" Anniya interrupts. "We already know it won't work!"

"What if we tell Charon that you left? He will just assume you died at sea. You can just stay here," I say.

"No. When he finds out you lied, he will kill us all. Our families will be shamed and our village will suffer from the loss."

"Forget about them!" I yell. "They abandoned us!"

"And that means we should abandon them?"

"Why not? All they want to do is breed more of us anyway! What if you have a daughter? Will you send her over here?" I ask.

"I-," Anniya begins, not knowing how to respond.

"You'll have to, or you will be put to death," I say, answering my own question. "Is that what you want? To continue living your life in fear? To make your offspring live this way? Aren't you tired of being treated like a lesser being?

"Look at all we have accomplished in our short time on this island. We don't need to prove our worth to anyone but ourselves! And I have proved that I don't need them. I can live the life I want." I feel breathless after my rant and notice all the women are looking at me. "We are strong and capable. We don't need a man's protection nor the laws made for a man's satisfaction. We can make a better life for ourselves, together."

"Now who is with me?" I ask.

"I want to be," Anniya admits. "But I'm not sure what other options I have at this point. You all have time. I don't."

I think for a moment, considering our options. We need something bigger, something stronger if we are ever going to get off Wahine Pono. We need a boat like Charon's. No. We need Charon's boat.

***

Eva spotted Charon a few miles off and alerted the rest of us. It's only been a week since our failed attempt to leave the island, so we didn't get as much time as I was hoping to prepare. We dismantled our boat and used our limited supplies to make weapons. Charon is strong, but with Eva, it's seven against one. Surprise and numbers are on our side.

We all grab the weapon we feel most comfortable with and hide among the trees. Charon knows this island, but he has never lived here. He knows how to hunt, but does he know what it feels like to be the prey? Will he realize our plan before we get to him and overpower us? When he can't find us, will he leave and come back with others, forcing us back into submission? We can't allow that to happen.

Eva stays on the shore so Charon won't become suspicious. She will lead him into our small village and we will have to act fast. He cannot make it back to the boat. He must never leave this island.

I hear the crunching of twigs as someone approaches the clearing. Suddenly Eva breaks through the trees and runs into one of the shacks as if taking cover. I immediately lift my makeshift bow and place one of the two arrows I have on the taut string. I place my hand holding the end of the arrow on my cheek and try to keep my breath steady.

Within moments Charon has entered the camp with a machete in his hand. The weapon is raised up by his face, ready to strike down anyone in his way. I take in a deep breath and release it with the arrow. It strikes his neck as blood pools onto his sternum. His face is filled with panic, surprise, and anger as he falls to the ground, searching for the source of the arrow. A smile creeps over my face as the others come out of hiding, ready to attack.

Audrey M. Stevens is an Indiana resident who married her high school sweetheart after graduating from IUPUI. Now a stay-at-home mom to a beautiful daughter and rambunctious pup, she continues to write in the hopes of publishing more books. Find all her current works at:

https://www.amazon.com/Audrey-M.-Stevens/e/B087777W7P

<u>GLASS</u>

By Kathryn Jacques

Mirrors are outlawed. Vanity is sinful. It breeds arrogance and the mirrors breed vanity so therefore, there hasn't been a mirror in the United Republic of Delmar in almost thirty years.

The alarm on my nightstand goes off, but I am already awake, lying on my back on the lumpy mattress and staring at the cracked, stained ceiling of the apartment. I smack the silence button on the alarm with one hand, sitting up to stare out the window. It's been coated in a film to make sure it's not reflective, but I can still see the facades of the other brick and stone buildings outside my bedroom window, the tops of a few sparse trees growing along the curb and the city street beyond that, clogged with cars and buses and bright yellow taxis. People bustle along the congested sidewalks, going about their morning routines, all but oblivious to those around them.

Reaching for my mask, the one I have been required to wear every waking moment since my fourth birthday over thirteen years ago. I secure the straps behind my head, adjust the eyeholes so I can see and allow the hole for my mouth to be exposed. I then make sure the base of the plain white mask rests below my chin so every part of my face from hairline to jawline is covered.

It's been taught that women are more susceptible to the sins of vanity and arrogance. Before the changes thirty years ago, pretty women lavished themselves with gifts and money and fame simply for being gorgeous. They then used that money and fame to surgically alter themselves to continue raising the bar higher and higher toward an unrealistic standard of beauty everyone else was expected to follow. Those deemed ugly were ostracized and publicly ridiculed, sometimes to the point of suicide, all because they didn't fit the ever-changing standards. So now all women must wear masks. A punishment for the choices of those before us.

Aside from bathing or sleeping, the mask is not to be removed. Ever. Doing so is punishable by public whipping outside the city capital building, and then sentenced to a year locked in a metal mask that cannot be removed at all. Those who report violations of the masking laws are rewarded, and with three quarters of the province living in poverty, people are happy to report to the authorities. It feels like a prison each morning when I put it on, but the threats of the punishment are terrifying enough for me to comply.

No one has seen my face since my fourth birthday. Not even my stepmother, Lorette, who married my father when I was nine. I have not seen her face either, nor the faces of my two stepsisters. We've lived together for years, and yet I could not tell you one aspect of their features except for dark hair and dark eyes; a dramatic contrast to my pale hair and blue eyes.

What they look like, and if I'll ever know, are irrelevant anyway. Today is likely my last day in my childhood home and the last day I will see any of them. The idea stabs into my heart again, slowly chipping away as it has been for several weeks now.

Once the mask is secure, I dress myself and wander down the hall, quiet so as not to wake my sisters who are still asleep in their own room. In the tiny kitchen my stepmother serves breakfast; scrambled eggs, fresh baked bread and hot tea. I have little appetite to eat and instead push the food around on my plate.

"You should try to eat something," she says, laying aside a plate for herself and adjusting her own mask.

"I'm too nervous," I say, staring at the food as the little I've eaten congeals in my stomach.

In the opening of the mask around her mouth, I see her lips form into a tight line and I know what's coming next. "It's an honor to have been chosen. Some girls don't even make the first cut."

I've tried to remind myself of this for weeks, ever since we received the letter announcing I made the final selection for this year's Offering. Thousands of girls apply, only twenty-four were chosen this year after the application process and interviews. This afternoon is the official Offering Ceremony, where the twenty-three other girls and I will be put on display and the wealthy elite in our province will bid on us for marriage to themselves or their sons. It's the opportunity of a lifetime to escape the poverty I will otherwise be forced to live in, like the thousands of teenage girls who weren't chosen, if they even applied at all.

But I don't feel lucky. I feel disgusted and terrified and overwhelmed. If it were solely up to me, I wouldn't have applied at all, but I have my younger sisters to think about. They're only twelve. Once my father died, we were left with nothing but the tiny apartment in the city, barely enough funds to pay the taxes for the year and nothing left over for food or clothing or anything at all. Lorette has done her best, but opportunities are slim, especially ones that pay well enough for a single mother to support her family. She could have just turned me out to the streets, but she didn't. She's made sacrifices for my survival, now I must do the same. When the chance to apply for the Offering came up, I reluctantly did so. If I'm chosen today, my stepmother, as my legal guardian, will be paid quite well in exchange for allowing me to marry whomever selects me. She won't need to worry about the next meal anymore or the constantly increasing taxes inside the city lines that make getting ahead shift farther and farther out of reach.

Neither will I to be honest. Which is why I tell myself again this is an honor, and I should be thankful. Most girls are grateful to be chosen.

"Do you need help getting ready?" Lorette asks, but I shake my head, pushing up from the table to head for the bathroom.

Removing the mask to bathe, I spend a few extra minutes letting the lukewarm water of the shower run over my head. If I am chosen today, this will be the last shower I take here. My last breakfast. My last time sleeping in the bed I've slept in every night since I was born. A tear winds its way down my cheek.

The water runs cool, chilling me before I shut it off and step out. Drying my hair, I twist the blond curls into their usual chignon at the nape of my neck because women aren't supposed to leave the house with their hair loose or unruly. Then I resecure my mask. It's only a little longer before the chauffeur arrives to take me away.

***

It's late afternoon by the time I arrive at the Governor's mansion where the Offering Ceremony will take place. The chauffeur of the white limo sent for me remained silent the entire three-hour drive, only speaking once when helping me with the bag now clutched tightly in my right hand; all the things important to me in this world packed into one small suitcase.

"Number?" a woman says at the front door of the massive brick mansion.

"Twenty- two," I reply, the number given to me on my selection paperwork because no one seems to care about my name.

Checking the tablet in her hands, she nods to a guard just inside the main doors that stand open to the elaborate foyer. "Follow him."

Apprehension swells inside me. I take a final look behind me at the street and for a fleeting moment I consider running away, hiding in the city, or maybe farther, getting as far away from the Offering as I can get.

But it's too late for that. I have nowhere to go. No money. No job. Not even a passport or identification to leave Delmar. At least not legally. The only family I have left needs me to be here, to be chosen by someone tonight if they are to have any hopes of a better life. If I can hope for a better life too. Out there in the world, there is nothing else for me. Drugs, murderers, rapists, and psychopaths; people don't survive on the streets here for long. Every day the news reports another body found, dumped in the river or buried in a shallow grave in a park. As far as anyone cares, the dead were nobodies so therefore, nothing is done to stop it. I am not special enough to think I can manage any better.

So I follow the guard into the building and through a maze of hallways boasting lush carpet, polished wood doors, bronze light fixtures and blue damask wallpaper. Arched lead-paned windows overlook the gardens surrounding the home. Beyond, the grey, towering buildings of the city loom over it all, the sunset behind them painting a brilliant backdrop of mauve and cerulean as the sky transforms into twilight.

I'm led into a small room towards the back of the home, lavish in its décor of paneled walls, a coffered ceiling and a sparkling crystal chandelier, but little furniture other than a sofa, two chairs and a round coffee table. Artwork hangs on the walls and just one could probably pay our rent for a year.

A grey-haired woman sits perched in one of the chairs, standing when I enter, her eyes finding mine behind both our masks. She looks me over from head to toe, as if analyzing whether I truly belong here.

"Twenty-two?" she asks, her voice cool and indifferent as she smooths the folds of her conservative dark suit.

"Yes, ma'am."

She dismisses the guard, who shuts the door behind him leaving me alone with the woman. She holds forward a tablet of her own. "Your thumbprint please, to confirm you've arrived."

I place my thumb on the pad and the screen flips to an image of my resume.

Name: Ciella Tremaine

Age: Seventeen

IQ: 132

Personality Type: INFJ

Blood Type: O+

Hereditary markers: Safe

Overall Health: 9

Parents: Deceased

The woman flicks off the screen before I have a chance to read the rest, but I already know what it says. It's the reason I'm here. I've been deemed "enough." Healthy enough, smart enough, skilled enough for men to potentially want me as their wife; hopefully willing to bid high enough that my stepmother won't have to work three jobs anymore just to make ends meet and make sure my sisters don't slowly starve. Perhaps even enough that they can go to school like I was able to before my father died and I dropped out to work for the dry cleaners down the street.

"There's a dress and shoes on that chair there for you to change into," the woman says, pointing to a blue dress draped over one of the armchairs. "A guard will be stationed in the hall if you need to use a restroom. The Offering will begin in an hour, but seeing as you're twenty- two, you'll be towards the end. If we make it that far."

Her final words aren't lost on me as she leaves the room. There's a chance I won't even stand on the platform to be bid upon. If only twenty guests show up to make bids, and twenty of the girls before me are chosen, I'll be sent home with nothing. Worse than nothing. Those selected for the Offering but not chosen as a wife are mocked and outcaste. Too "good" for the normal world, not "good enough" for the wealthy who dictate our entire lives and put on this whole charade each year to give some sort of ridiculous idea of hope to the hundreds of girls in the province believing they are "enough" to be chosen and climb their family out of poverty.

Nerves flip and flutter in my stomach as I change into the pale blue dress with long puffed sleeves and a high-buttoned neckline. Its hemline reaches past my knees and swirls around my legs when I turn. The fabric feels soft and silky against my skin, possibly one of the nicer dresses I've had the opportunity to wear.

I look to the windows in the hopes of seeing my reflection, but they are tinted just enough that I'm nothing but a formless blur in the glass. A blur and a number are all I have become in this world.

Under the chair I find a pair of shoes, heavy and sparkling in the overhead light. I clink them together and realize they are made of glass.

Most girls are glad to be here, all things considered. The see it as an escape. But I am reminded of a young girl several years ago, her name and story displayed on the TV for weeks. Much like me, she wanted nothing to do with the Offering but was forced into it by her father in the hopes she would be chosen and the money would help take care of her six younger siblings. But she wasn't chosen. She wasn't even in the building long enough for the Offering to start before she ran away and disappeared into the city. I guess she felt the streets were better than whatever future awaited her here. Whatever happened to her, I guess I'll never know. She's probably dead and sometimes I wonder if that wouldn't just be easier than all of this.

But because of her, now all of the girls in the Offering must wear glass shoes because they don't know which of us might also try to run. It's impossible to run fast or far with glass on your feet. I slide them on, cringing at how they pinch and squish my toes and wondering how I'm supposed to even walk in them. Forget running anywhere.

***

Well over two hours pass before anyone comes for me. My stomach growls because I haven't eaten since breakfast and it's now past dinner. The grey-haired woman doesn't even offer a courtesy knock before flinging open the door of the room, startling me to my feet.

"Come with me, it's your turn."

My hands tremble as I run them along the side of the dress in an attempt to quell my nerves. My feet ache in the horrible shoes,

25

but I notch my chin higher and ignore the pain as I follow the woman back into the maze of hallways.

She guides me out a side door and along a narrow walkway lined with hedges that veer around the back of the mansion. The heels of our shoes click on the flagstone path.

The soft murmur of voices reaches my ears and as we round the corner of the home, I find myself in the back courtyard. At least twenty people still mill about, mostly middle-aged men and older but a few women appear too, their faces covered by their own masks as they cling to their husband's sides. Those will be the parents here to bid for their sons. A part of me hopes I'll be chosen by one of them. At least there's a chance the son will be closer to my age rather than old enough to be my father.

Tables display an array of foods; desserts, sliced meats, fresh shrimp and hot buttered rolls. My mouth waters at the sight, more food than I've ever seen in one place in my life. Servers wander through the crowd, gathering dirty plates or offering refills of wine and champagne. The Offering, the ceremony that will change the entire course of my life, is nothing but an extravagant party for them. A social function to show off their wealth. A hint of anger burns through me and for once, I am glad I wear a mask to cover the scowl on my face.

The grey-haired woman escorts me to a round platform at the front of the space. I step onto it as she garners the crowd's attention and suddenly every eye is on me as the guests fall silent. I can feel their probing stares, looking over my body, judging my height and weight and anything else they can see that isn't covered by the modest dress or the featureless mask.

My breath comes quicker as my heart pounds wildly. Nausea rises in my stomach and I swallow against it, willing my anxiety to calm and my hands to stop quivering. I can't appear frightened or nervous or no one will bid on me.

"Auction number Twenty- Two," the woman calls, her finger flicking over her tablet as she brings up my resume and calls out the information on my health and intelligence. "Skills; cooking rank 7, cleaning rank 9, sewing rank 10; that's impressive, we don't normally see such a skilled seamstress. Foreign languages; French and German."

She rattles off the rest of the details as the guests continue to ogle me. One wanders behind me and touches my hair in its low bun, his fingers trailing the back of my neck and I resist the urge to shiver in disgust.

"A natural blond?" someone calls from the back.

"Yes. And blue eyes if you're too far away to tell."

"She's pure?" a man to my right asks and my face immediately flushes with the inappropriate intimacy of his question.

"Of course," replies the woman as if it's a perfectly normal question to ask. "All of our girls have been checked."

Yes, we have been. If I could erase that experience from my memory, I would do so in a heartbeat.

"If there's no further questions, I'll start the bidding at $250,000," the grey-haired woman calls and I stiffen. It's a low number. There must not be many guests who haven't already claimed other girls. It needs to at least triple if there's any hope of Lorette being able to pay off our debts and still have enough left over to invest and live off of.

The man in the back indicates he'll pay the starting price of a quarter million and the bidding goes from there.

"$300,000 from Mr. Satyr. Do I have three-fifty? Three-fifty, yes, Mr. Zabbet, thank you."

The number increases, the grey-haired woman confirming each bid and occasionally reminding everyone of my excellent health record and low risk of hereditary diseases that could be passed on to children, both of which are highly desirable traits in the Offering and probably why I'm even here in the first place.

As the bidding passes $500,000 and then $600,000 and eventually $700,000, I feel some of my tension ease. It's enough that Lorette and my stepsisters will be set. Whatever happens from here, at least they will survive and the girls won't ever have to consider entering an Offering themselves. I can make this sacrifice for them.

"$925,000 is the current bid. Anyone for nine-fifty? Once? Twice? Sold for $925,000 to Mr. Tulerno. Thank you, sir."

Almost a million dollars. That is the value I have been given by these people. That is what I am worth.

My eyes scan the guests hoping to pick out the man who has just purchased me. The one I will be marrying before the end of the week. A lump of fear rises in my throat because this is it. I'll go home with a stranger tonight, likely someone forty years older than me. I can only hope he is kind. I've heard so many horror stories. I don't care if he's hideous or old or even dumb, but I just have to pray he treats me well enough.

Moments later I'm whisked away, limping in the painful shoes and looking forward to the chance to change back into my normal clothes. But I'm not returned to the small room I sat in before my auction. Instead, I'm led to a larger space no doubt used as a parlor for receiving guests. It's bedecked in burgundy and gold and dark, heavy furniture.

As I'm guided into the room, I see a man standing at the far end, his back to me as he looks out the windows into the darkness beyond. He's tall and thin, his navy-blue suit well-tailored to accommodate long arms and legs. In one hand he holds a wooden cane tipped in silver, though he does not lean on it for support. Still, I have to wonder what is wrong with him if he is here to bid on a wife because he can't find one on his own. Wouldn't something have to be wrong with any of the men buying us tonight? Why else would they be here?

"Mr. Tulerno," the grey-haired woman says, "I'd like to present Ciella Tremaine, your purchase for this evening."

The man says nothing, flicking a hand over his shoulder to indicate the woman is free to go. Without a single glance my direction, she shuts the door behind herself, leaving me alone with the man. Fear and anxiety swell inside me as the realization of what I've committed to crashes upon me. Dizziness sets in and I wish I could sit down so I don't collapse.

This man, this stranger will become my husband, I will need to rely on him for anything I need to survive from here forward. I take a deep breath and step farther into the room on wobbly, unsteady legs.

"Mr. Tulerno," I say, my voice a squeak as my throat clenches. "It's nice to meet you."

"Kyle," he says, his voice deep. "Mr. Tulerno is my father. He's the one who bid on you for me. You may call me Kyle. If we are to be married, the formalities seem silly. You may take off your mask."

The request causes me to freeze and my eyes dart about the room expecting hidden cameras or to see the police watching from a secret space. "Sir?"

"Kyle. And your mask. You may remove it."

"But, sir… Kyle… it's illegal…" I stammer, torn between obliging the demands of someone who has the power to make the rest of my life miserable and risking the wrath of the government's punishment should this be some sort of test for him to see how loyal I am. I don't know him. I can't trust him. What if he or his father oversee the punishments here? I have no idea who they are.

Then the man turns and I realize he's not much older than me, his dark hair swept back from his thin face. It's his eyes though, that cause me to gasp and now I know why his father was bidding on a bride for him. Now I know what is "wrong."

"As you can see," he says, gesturing one hand to his glassy and unfocused gaze, "I am blind. It seems ridiculous for you to wear a mask when I can't see your face at all anyway. If we are alone together, you may be free of that one confinement. Sadly, it is the best I can offer."

Raised and living in Baltimore, Kathryn Jacques, a graduate of Towson University, is a former classical and contemporary dancer and TV/ Film actress. She starred in the 2016 horror feature Soul Fray, which premiered at the Cannes Film Festival, and she can also been seen on the ID Discovery Network, Veep and House of Cards.

After retiring from performing and film work, she returned to her childhood love of writing. She is the author of the *The Gamble* series, a Young Adult dystopian trilogy which was featured in Girls' Life Magazine and voted Dystopian Ink's December 2020 Book of the Month. She also works with a literary agent in London and plans to publish more young adult dystopian and fantasy works soon.

https://kathrynjacquesbaltimore.wordpress.com/

Big Bad Wolfe and the Three Little P.I.G.G.s

By Jared K Chapman

Four years ago, thousands of alien soldiers armed with advanced technology, far beyond anything we could ever imagine, obliterated the human race in an instant. Well, almost.

A radio beacon called out from the depths of the Brookhaven Institute underground research facility, where hundreds of scientists, engineers, and private soldiers survived the surface attacks. Anyone with an old radio receiver found the beacon calling on every channel. I had one of those old Sony Walkman cassette players. My dad gave it to me as a joke Christmas gift when I was thirteen. In the card, he wrote, "You kids with your easy access to music have no idea what it was like to have your favorite song eaten up by one of these damned things. Merry Christmas, Bee Bee."

I wish he were here now. No one I know survived the attacks. I don't even know how I lived through it ... or understand why. Why did I survive and they didn't? There were so many people out there far more important than me. So many people who could be doing something right now to stop the monsters above. I'm just a twenty-four-year-old former bartender who got lucky because I was hiking a secluded mountain trail, thinking about life and pondering what I should do and where I should go next.

The damn universe answered it for me.

Here in the underground, the scientists and engineers are working on alien tech gathered by the soldiers in above-ground raids. They're all trying to figure out how the stuff works and if we can use it to fight back. Our weapons and tech have pretty much had no effect. And still, no one has any idea how the aliens got here. Or if they even are aliens. I've never seen one, but I've seen their tech and it's out of this world. I've seen sleek silver bubbles that blast violet laser beams and ships glimmering in the sky like they're covered in diamonds. At least, I think they're ships. That's why I call the aliens Lucies, as in Lucy in the Sky with Diamonds. In case you didn't know, that's the third track from the Beatles' Sgt. Pepper's Lonely Hearts Club Band album.

It's one of the three cassettes that survived with me. The other two are Everclear's Sparkle & Fade and Depeche Mode's Violator. These albums contain the only songs I've heard over the last four years. They're my soundtrack for the Armageddon. A perfect playlist for watching the world die.

Some songs I just play and rewind and play and rewind over and over and over. Santa Monica. Enjoy the Silence. When I'm Sixty-Four.

Yeah. These last four years have been a real tough go, let me tell you. I've made mostly casual acquaintances with the other survivors … and one special friend. He was a soldier. He went up and didn't come back. I haven't made that mistake again.

Feelings are hard, especially knowing that they can gut you at any moment. I had already mourned my family. My parents. My brother and sister. Everyone. My dog, Rowdy. My cat, Mr. Mercedes. He was actually Philomena first, but then we discovered he was a boy cat and a freaking psychopath, so we changed his name. All my cousins, aunts, uncles, grandparents. All my friends were gone—wiped out in one fell swoop of a laser light show from above.

Every day more and more soldiers don't come back, so the scientists and engineers have been recruiting from the survivors. I don't have anyone, so I volunteered. I'm still waiting for my first assignment, but if the leadership frantically running around yelling at one another like those stock traders on Wall Street used to is any indication, then my time may be coming soon.

"Bee Bee Wolfe, please report to the facilities manager on the lower-level B platform."

See. Told ya.

***

Now, not to bore you with all the little details, but the situation is stark. I guess we're down to three soldiers, and they're all old, heavy-set men who can't fit into the super-secret suits the engineers have been building. The scientists backward engineered something or other for shielding, weaponry, and transportation, which provided what was needed to design these crazy things. Of course, no one else volunteered. No one is stupid enough to go out there. I really just don't care whether I live or die anymore, just as long as I can take some of these alien bastards out with me.

They want me to climb inside the suit because I'm small, like a child. So what if I haven't grown an inch since I was sixteen years old? There's not enough food in the underground to gorge myself into obesity anyway. I'd already have depression-eaten the hell out of it if there was.

They don't force me to do it, but they definitely coerce me, if you catch what I'm throwing down. The human race is at stake. If we want our planet back, I've got to do something about it. Obi-Wan Kenobi, you're our only hope. Gawdammit!

Of course, I accept the mission and strap up inside the damn thing.

"You'll need to remove the earbuds," the engineer says.

I laugh.

"Fine, you can wear one. We need to be able to communicate with you through the interface."

I nod, pulling it out by the cord, letting it dangle in front of me. Then, the machinery closes in on me like I'm Darth Vader lying on the operating table, watching the mask lower onto my head. It hisses and cracks as the sounds of several latches clunk down the sides. I wince at the stench of fiberglass, ozone, and burning metal. Then, I feel the pain. They warned me about this, but I forgot, so it came as a shock to my system. Needles from various places in the suit entered into my veins and began pumping fluid into me to keep me from dehydrating.

"You won't need to eat," I remember them saying now. "All your nutrients and more will be provided by the suit."

Feeling the cold fluid circulate through my body makes me shiver. The suit shakes with me, shuttering with a clunking, scraping sound that catches the unwanted attention of the engineers. They look at me like I did something wrong, but I just have to laugh. It comes out all mechanical and I want to yell, "Exterminate!"

Fixing a Hole plays in my earbud like a commentary of what is happening all around me. People run back and forth, checking up on me and monitoring machines latched to my suit by umbilical cords. As I stand inside, I think about all the things I never did and all the things I never will do again.

They tell me to take a step forward. So, I do. And with each step I take, my teeth clench and chatter. It feels like they're going to break free from my mouth. That's the first thing I need fixed. At the end of each arm are three metal-fingered claws. The engineers teach me to use them like my hands. The operating system has some kind of psychic interface allowing me to open and close them like I'm using my own hands. They say it will become more automatic as I practice with the suit. Then they show me the coolest feature. The palms of the hands are laser cannons or something. I'm gawdamn Ironman ... or Ironheart as the case may be.

I love target practice. That's my favorite.

It takes some time, but we work out all the kinks in the suit. They fit me with this mouthpiece that keeps my teeth from breaking apart and allows me to suck in water as I need it. They integrate my music from my three cassette tapes into the speaker system to choose songs at will, like I used to do on internet streaming services. And they figure out how to cycle urine and feces out of my suit, so I don't have to exit the suit to use the bathroom. It's a diaper ... a very special diaper.

So, after a few months of training with the suit, I'm ready for my mission. That's when they reveal what I'm meant to do.

"The alien threat enters this world through something we call Pan-Interdimensional Gateways. Three small generators on the ground power each one. We've discovered their whereabouts and integrated those locations into your suit's navigation systems. Travel during the day and rest at night," the lead engineer says to me as she fiddles with things all over my suit. "The suit is solar-powered, as you know, and the battery system will last about twelve hours with limited use. So, you should have no issues in daylight, but make sure you find somewhere safe at night to sleep and try to move as little as possible. You'll want all that battery juice to go into shielding. We've outfitted you with three hydro-cell bombs. The remote detonator interfaces with your operating system. You'll probably want to be a mile or so away before detonating them."

"Just me?" I ask. "What about those other suits?"

"We need soldiers ... or volunteers like you. Good luck!"

And with that, they set me off to find the three little P.I.G.G.s. That's what I call the Pan-Interdimensional Gateway Generators. It's just easier that way, don't you think?

***

In the suit, I run fast. Automatic oscillators and stabilizers, and other technical terms the engineers and scientists threw at me, keep me upright as I run at speeds of sixty plus miles per hour. Though my legs and arms move in the suit with each step I take, I feel like I'm floating, like I'm running on clouds or something. The loud metallic clanking is dulled by the music playing in my ears, and I never get tired. At least, not during the day. I sleep well at night, hidden within my shielding.

With World in My Eyes set to repeat, the synthesized melody plays over and over in my helmet as I fall asleep.

Then I wake up in the morning and do it all over again.

All three P.I.G.G.s are miles and miles away. At my fast pace, it'll still be three days or so before I arrive at the first one in old Nebraska. It may take even longer if I run into Lucies along the way. I try my best to stay off the beaten path as much as possible, but old roads are generally there for a reason.

I make it all the way to just south of Lake Michigan before I realize I'm being followed.

I jinxed myself, I think, reflecting on my stupid belief that this mission would be a walk in the park.

The twinkling diamond vibrating silently behind me almost went unnoticed with its chameleon-like exterior. I probably wouldn't have ever seen it if not for the reflection in the windshield of a broken-down car on the side of the road. Right as I passed, the alien ship glimmered in the sky behind me. I don't understand why it hasn't attacked yet, but I'm waiting for dark. If I'm solar-powered, they probably are too, and they might not have batteries like I do.

I run toward the ruin of Chicago. Until now I've avoided cities, but if this thing is following me, the Lucies may not be occupying the cities anymore. I try not to let it figure out that I'm aware of its presence as I zip through the gridlock of broken-down cars searching for a high tower. If I can reach the top of a skyscraper, I might stand a better chance against Lucy there.

I make it inside the Tribune Tower, find the stairwell, and start climbing.

Yellow, orange, pink, and purple colors scatter across the sky in a beautiful sunset as I reach the top. I only had to use my laser a couple of times to blast open doors. I didn't want to elicit unwelcome company, so I tried to keep it to a minimum. Plus, I need to reserve my energy stores if I'm going to go after that Lucy tonight. I soak in the last rays of the sun and wait.

Just as I thought it would, Lucy searches the sky-scraping buildings around me and then touches down on one, probably to rest through the night. I mark the landing spot on my internal map and race down the stairs. I cut down Michigan to Kinzie, finding the building with a signature name missing a T. I have a good laugh before crashing through the front doors.

The slow and steady buildup of Pale Green Stars plays in my ears as I reach the roof.

The diamond ship hovers with a slow oscillation around some kind of alien pillar. Intestine-like cables extend from the ship to the pillar anchoring it to the roof. No one's around—just a low buzzing sound. I find a dark spot to crouch and keep watch, hoping I won't use up too much of my battery before I have to face this thing. I've never seen one before, so I have no idea what I'm even looking for. I'm just watching for any little movement. For all I know, it could be invisible. If so, then I'm probably completely screwed.

Hell, I'm not even sure if my weapons will work on these alien machines. I'm way in over my head here.

A slithering sound of footsteps echoes nearby. I want to look, but I'm afraid to move now. Then the fear takes hold as I remember my family and friends. They all died. These things killed them. I try to calm myself and regain control of my breathing. It's a lot harder than you'd think in this massive suit. A red light blinks on my display.

"Proximity alert," it chirps. "Movement detected. Possible violence imminent."

Are you kidding me? I think. *I'm having a gawdamn panic attack right now, and this alien can't give me a moment to pull myself together.*

"Play Chemical Smile," I command as I twist around while opening my metal hands. "Lasers ready."

The drums beat fast, and the guitars wail before Art begins to sing the opening lyrics that are somehow so fitting. I burst forward with all my energy, lurching toward my unseen foe. "Take this, you alien sonuvabitch!" I yell as I blast into its backside.

Two chunks of its armor crater inward as shiny shrapnel falls to the floor with a double clank. The massive hulk of a thing turns toward me with surprise in its giant black alien eyes. At least, I think it's surprise. Hard to tell. I've never seen one before with its Cthulhu face—no, more like an Ood with long, slender dangly tentacles like some outer space Duck Dynasty reject. Whatever it is, it's damn ugly. Without hesitation, I blast its wriggling head worms with both lasers.

The headless alien falls into a metallic heap on the ground with a resounding thud. Then, the diamond ship crashes into the ground, and I jump out of the way of flying debris, just in time. *The suit and ship must be connected*, I think, as I inspect the decapitated corpse. Is it decapitated when the head is blown off or just cut off? Either way, I don't see massive pools of darkness staring at me from above a hundred slimy tendrils anymore.

That's when I notice the green dots. Close to a dozen shine like pinpricks around me, closing in and creating a polka dot pattern on my suit.

"What are you?" a voice cries out from the dark. "Human or alien?"

"Human," I yell inside my helmet, which comes out as a distorted vibration of noise through the speaker. I sound like a Dalek. "I'm not a Dalek. I'm definitely human!"

"Well, guys. I don't think an alien would say they're not a Dalek," the voice says, getting closer to me as the green dots disappear. "So, who are you? You big bad mutha—"

"Wolfe. Bee Bee Wolfe."

***

They want me to stay with them to fight the aliens around Chicago. Before I leave, I tell them all about the Brookhaven Institute, their suits built from alien tech, and my mission to destroy the Pan-Interdimensional Gateway Generators.

"So, they're not aliens from outer space?" asks the team leader. "They're from another dimension? Interdimensional beings?"

"I guess so. I'm no scientist."

"We can come with you. Help you take them down."

"You don't have super special suits," I say with a laugh. I can only imagine what the mechanized laughter sounds like coming from the speaker in the helmet.

"If we can't go with you, take this," the team leader says, clamping something to my metal wrists. "They're amplifying bracers. We got them off an alien awhile back but haven't been able to use them with our tech. I bet they'll work with your suit. They should turn those lasers up to eleven if you know what I mean."

I do.

I say thanks, bow my head, turn away, and run from the morning sun.

I stay off the beaten path again, trying not to stop until I reach my destination. It takes about nine hours, but I make it just as the sun starts to fall toward the western horizon. I can't take the time to admire the beautiful coloration in the sky because there is work to be done.

Golden fields of hay lay before me with round bales here and there, but there aren't any diamonds or silver suited tendril-faced Lucies. I don't see anything out of this world at all. I aimlessly walk around the marker on my map for about an hour until I realize that I'm standing in the middle of a crop circle. A friggin' crop circle! The face of Giorgio Tsoukalos of Ancient Aliens fame pops into my head, saying, "I'm not saying it was aliens ... but it was aliens."

Personal Jesus plays like a prophecy in my ears.

I bend down and spread the hay apart, finding the silver top of something that resembles a utility hole cover, except it's almost twice the size and shaped in a nonagon. It's not a typical shape, and I'm not really sure how I know the name. Maybe high school geometry wasn't a waste of time after all.

Intricate alien writing covers the whole thing like an Egyptian sarcophagus. I think, *It'd be cool if I could take a picture*, and then the helmet snapped an image. They didn't tell me it could do that … or did they? Maybe I was zoned out at the time.

Anyway, I open the cover, drop the hydro-cell inside, and get the hell out of there. About a mile and a half away, I trigger the detonator. The explosion throws hay all around.

That's one, I think as I find a place to rest for the night.

***

The next morning, I wake up with the sunrise all alone. Without anyone keeping my attention away from my task, I run. I run like the wind. Well, like a mechanical wind thingamajig. I guess the Lucies must be somewhere else because there was no sign of anyone between the Nebraska hayfield and this sign welcoming me to Yellowstone National Park: National Park Service. The sign's not pristine by any means, but it still stands, and behind it is a massive wooded forest.

The second spot blinks on my map telling me I'm getting hotter. Hotter. Then, it goes out. Cold. Colder. Then, it comes back. Red hot!

How am I ever going to find this thing? I think, as I trample over old leaves on the forest floor. I should rake these things up while I'm here. Don't want to start a fire.

I laugh my mechanical laugh through my speakers.

Then, a red light blinks on my display, chirping, "Proximity alert. Movement detected. Possible violence imminent."

41

Oops, I think, as I try to find cover while searching all around me for the threat.

Then it hits me. Plowing me from behind like I'm a quarterback sacked by an overenthusiastic linebacker, I smack the ground hard. But I'm not hurt. My systems flash a red warning but display no damage. Well, no major damage. My attacker roars behind me, and I turn. The gigantic snout of a grizzly bear slobbers all over me with another menacing roar. Its monstrous paws with razor-sharp claws swipe at my armor.

"Stop!" I yell, as I try to stand up. "Just chill out! I'm not trying to hurt you!"

The grizzly stands tall and roars again, swiping at me with both hands. It knocks me off kilter a bit, but I'm able to replant my feet and stand firm. The poor thing is hurting itself more than it hurts me. Broken claws and bloody paws. I probably startled it with my laugh, or maybe it's a mama bear protecting her family.

"Please stop!" I yell again, trying to stand as tall as possible. Then, I shoot my lasers at two trees on either side of the bear.

It glances at the charred trees, then back to me before it drops to the ground on all fours and ambles away, limping on one forelimb.

Poor guy, I think, examining the area around me. *Why was he here?*

The signal for the location of the second P.I.G.G. flashes on the screen. Super red friggin' hot, like boiling hot lava.

The rooster signaling the beginning of Good Morning Good Morning crows in my ears, while John Lennon seems to impart some much-needed optimism.

Do I feel cool? Yes, I do. I certainly do, Mr. Lennon. And there it is, the familiar nonagonal shape lying at the base of a tree trunk. Isn't there a massive supervolcano or something like that in Yellowstone? If I blow this hydro-cell will it trigger the thing? Can I risk not blowing up this generator?

42

Thoughts flicker away as fast as they come. Nothing can stop this. If we don't blow away the generators, we don't save the human race from the Lucies. If I trigger a supervolcano, then I guess I'll be taking the invaders with us. I'm in a Kobayashi Maru kind of situation, and I'm just not equipped to deal with it right now. So I open up the nonagonal cover, drop the hydro-cell, and run like a bat out of hell.

Just to be on the safe side, I detonate this one around three miles away. Not sure if that's safe enough. When it explodes, I run. I don't look back. I'm not about to be Lot's wife or some Pompeiian sculpture of ash. I run and run and run into the dark, and I forget all about my battery life until the red warning flashes on my screen. *Are you kidding me?* I think as I calculate the time before sunrise. I'm going to have to chill right here and not move an inch for the next eight hours or so, and even doing that might not be enough.

I sit facing Yellowstone. If volcanic lava is headed my way, I want to see it coming for me. So I wait, too scared to sleep. I don't even close my eyes. When the sun starts to rise, I'm filled with surprise. For a second, I think, *here it comes*, but then I realize the light is coming from the wrong place. It's morning, and here comes the sun. But I'm too damn tired today to run.

***

It takes me about two days to reach the mountains, huge mountains with peaks of snow. I find a highway that winds me through the beauty and majesty of it all. I can't believe no one is here anymore to enjoy it. It surprises me that there aren't even any aliens around. I've taken out two of their generators. They've got to know something is happening. They've got to know we're fighting back.

I find a lodge at Chalk Mountain on the side of the highway, and I rest. I can't keep up my speed through the mountains. Up and down. I run faster going down, but the momentum shifts suddenly as I'm going up again. It wears me out.

In the morning, I'm ready to go again.

The first track of Sparkle and Fade jams in my head, like a beacon of sound to guide my way. I think Electra Made Me Blind is a great title, but right now my eyes are wide open.

I start to run because I'm finally well-rested, and once I've made it through this damn mountain corridor, I'll be at the third marker in just a few more hours.

The path clears for a while as I race through the valley with tree-lined mountains on either side of me. The closer I get to the third marker, the closer the hills are again. I decide that the high ground is probably my best bet to find a strategic view of everything ... to assess what I'm up against. So, I climb the mountain directly north of the marker.

In the valley below, a modern city sprawls with quiet streets, but just north of it, between me and the city, is some kind of village. It seems old. The buildings don't look modern at all. In fact, they look like the ancient adobe houses I read about in fourth grade for Indigenous People's Day. And in the sky above them, something shimmers in the evening sun.

I didn't expect the place to be empty like the other two but seeing three diamond ships tethered to pillars like they are hot air balloons waiting for the Albuquerque International Balloon Fiesta to begin is quite unsettling. I'm not even sure how many Lucies can fit into one of those things. I could be heading straight for an ambush.

I need to attack at night for the best odds of winning, so I sneak closer to the marker, finding a sign that says Taos Pueblo. This P.I.G.G.'s in a gawdamn UNESCO World Heritage Site with thousand-year-old buildings made from mud bricks. These aliens suck! I mean, come on. I don't want to destroy this ancient architecture. So much of our world has already been destroyed by these damn alien invaders. Why would they put their generator here?

Probably to make me think twice about blowing this damn thing away. Dammit!

Darkness reaches the old town as I creep through in search of the Lucies. *They have to be here somewhere*, I think, muting the music and turning up the outside volume to listen for anything out of the ordinary. I don't hear anything weird, and nothing is pinging on my screen. I can't help but think that I'm in grave danger as I continue to approach the marker.

And then I see it in the middle of the village. Surrounded by three pillars with diamonds hovering overhead is that familiar nonagonal form. To destroy this P.I.G.G. and the gateway these Lucies use to enter our dimension, I'm going to have to obliterate some Native American heritage. That's the last thing I want to do, but I have no choice. The human race depends on me.

So, I ready my lasers, place my arms next to each other, and blast the crap out of the pillars. The bracers amplify my lasers as they form into a single giant beam, one by one shattering the pillars into millions of metallic shards. An otherworldly scream echoes as metal suited aliens drop from the diamonds above. *Yup, this is an ambush*, I think, counting the half dozen Lucies with their wriggling, tentacle hairs on their chins.

Well, if this is the end of me, then I'm going to go out with a bang. Play the Sergeant Pepper album, I command, as I start blasting the Lucies.

Lasers fire at me, knocking bits and pieces of armor away. Red and yellow lights flash on my screen with warnings of danger and imminent violence. I'm certain I take a few of them out before they knock my shields into oblivion.

"Reroute all battery power to shields," I cry, as I huddle crumpled in a heap.

The Lucies slither around, coming closer. Maybe three left. Maybe less. I'm not sure how successful I was. I've failed my mission. I've—

Lasers blast into the chest armor of the Lucies. All three of them fall backward with shattered pieces of shiny metal scattering all around them. They wail with their disgusting tentacled faces, trying to reclaim their ground and fight back against whatever is attacking them. I can't move. I can't see anything, but the second track from Lonely Hearts plays through my headphones, giving me a clue.

If you don't know, the song is With A Little Help From My Friends.

Reroute power to movement and screens, I say, hoping I'm not blasted while my shields are powerless.

The three Lucies retreat, taking laser hits to their armor. One drops to its knees—
maybe knees. I'm not sure if it has knees, but it drops down anyway and takes a laser blast to the face. Buh bye, Lucy in the sky.

I turn toward the volleys of laser fire to find four super-secret suits march my way, blasting the Lucies into dust. I'm not Catholic, but I crossed myself. Who were these fine saviors of mine arriving just at the nick of time?

"You okay, Big Bad Wolfe?" the familiar team leader's voice spoke into my earbuds, commandeering them right when Ringo was giving a possible answer.

"I'm okay. How do you have the suits? How are you here?"

He blasted the last Lucy's head clean away before answering.

"You told us about Brookhaven and the suits. We figured out how to use the alien's suit to power up the diamond ship, flew to Brookhaven, and suited up. They gave us the coordinates for this generator. Thought you might need some backup."

"Perfect timing."

"Now let's blow this little Piggy up so we can get the hell out of here!"

"I've got another idea."

46

Thankfully, the boys placate my little annoyance about wanting to relocate the generator before blowing it up. We remove the nonagonal cover, attach the cables from each diamond ship to the generator inside, and strap the shiny metal Lucy armor over us. Then, we psychically command the vessels to lift the generator out of the ground.

"Where to?" the team leader asks me.

"A few hours south of here is a place called Roswell. Seems like the perfect spot to me. Make this a real full-circle kind of thing."

"Sounds good. And when this is over, we can start searching for the other Pan-Interdimensional Gateway generators around the world."

"Well, I've always wanted to travel. I guess this is my chance. This Big Bad Wolfe is ready to blow up some more P.I.G.G.s!"

Jared K. Chapman is an author, filmmaker, and educator. He is a native Californian who spent his formative years at school in frigid Alberta, Canada with his father and summer vacation in arid central California with his mother. He holds degrees in psychology & religious studies and is currently a doctoral candidate studying the social psychology of extreme groups. He lives in a little oasis just east of Los Angeles with his wife and three sons. 2HVØRHVNØT is his debut novel. You can find him at: jaredkchapman.com

Twisted

By K. R. S. McEntire

The Studer Kingdom is known as the "Land of the Immortals," and my mother has ruled the kingdom for 500 years.

Long before I was born, we were the poorest of the Three Kingdoms. Now we were the most prosperous. Mother built the wall surrounding the Kingdom to keep the evil ones out; she built the castle to host the Realm's best and brightest, and she built the castle's tower for me, her eldest daughter and heir, simply to keep me safe.

Those who call the Studer Kingdom home age slowly, and my mother looked as young and as beautiful as the day I was born. Her desire to step down and let me take the throne was a choice, not a necessity. But I am more than ready.

You see, I've spent my whole life inside the castle. My curse makes it risky to go out. It's the eve of my eighteenth birthday, and I am ready to reign. I'll celebrate tonight, and tomorrow I'll claim my crown.

***

Prince Marius of the Bahkiah Kingdom was the most handsome man in the ballroom. There was something about the way he carried himself—like he owned every room he walked into. Every time he stole a glance at me my pulse sped up and my stomach tangled. His eyes followed me as I moved about the room. He wasn't trying to be coy about it—when I met his stare his lips would twist into a crooked smile.

It was the same smile he had two years ago when we first met. Though his shoulders were broader and his muscles were toned, he had the same effect on me as he had when I was a young teen.

I'd danced with dozens of men throughout the night, my full-skirted white gown flowing behind me with my every move, all the while wondering if, or when, he would make his way over.

The sound of harps and flutes drifted over hundreds of dancing bodies, all dressed immaculately. The men were eager to dance with me, but they didn't make conversation while we moved. Their feet were unsteady and their hands trembled. Did I make them nervous?

I'd daydreamed about this day all my life, but I'd never anticipated the somber ambience that clung to the room. The men watched my feet rather than my eyes as we danced, they held me as if I might break under the weight of their touch. Their odd behavior made me eager to talk to Marius, to rest in familiar arms.

Marius's family first visited my castle when I was 16. We'd become fast friends. He told me all about his life in the Bahkiah Kingdom—he'd shared stories about sword duels with his father's army and studying at a prestigious academy. He'd let me wield a katana and read through his textbooks about the Three Kingdoms.

I'd never stepped foot outside of my parent's castle. In fact, it was rare I left the tower my mother built for me. I definitely had never held a weapon or been to a school. His world sounded like such an adventure.

He was a flirt, even at sixteen, and had given me my first kiss during his parent's trip. I knew what he could do with a word, a glance, or a touch. I remembered the way the world seemed to pause when his lips met mine. If only he'd come over. I wanted the universe to freeze as I melted again.

My heart swelled in my chest as he finally made his way to me. I tried to play it cool as I adjusted my dress and the awful corset mother insisted I wear beneath it. My mother and sister added gold jewels and white flowers to my hair, and the dainty gold necklace that accentuated my collarbone glistened. Golden eyeshadow highlighted my honey brown eyes before blending into my almond skin. My satin dress was pearl white lace with gold trim, and I'd twisted my long, coily, gravity-defying hair so that it fell down my back. I'd styled it in a way that hid my ears. I didn't want the world to focus on my curse today.

I didn't look like anyone else in the Studer Kingdom, and I was okay with that. My mother always told me that girls who focus on fitting in rarely rule kingdoms. I knew it was silly for a princess to worry about one man when I would soon have my pick of them all. But as a cursed princess who'd never left home, seeing Prince Marius again was the highlight of my year.

He walked up to me, and from the corner of my eye I saw both of my bodyguards move closer. They wore chainmail armor despite the fact that everyone else was dressed for the ball.

I'd been in the shadow of my guards forever. They stood outside my bedroom as I slept. I'd promised myself that when I became queen, my first rule of command would be to tell them to let me sleep alone. I wanted to be the type of queen who could slay her own assassins.

"May I have this dance?" Marius's voice was just as I remembered it—low and throaty. His eyes were a deeper brown than mine, almost black, and his skin held a deep golden tan. But there was something in his eyes that wasn't as familiar. They were wide, shifty, and fearful, much like the other men I'd danced with.

"I thought you'd never ask," I said, shooting my bodyguards a pleading look. Couldn't they give me just one moment alone?

They seemed to get the message and backed off. I knew the semblance of privacy they were offering was not real, but I'd take whatever I could get.

Prince Marius took my hand and a jolt of electricity shot through me. His dark eyes sparked, and his grin was devilish. I let out a sigh of relief. This was the Marius I knew.

He led me away from my bodyguards, to a quiet corner of the ballroom. I looked over my shoulder and saw the guards eyeing me. I knew we wouldn't have much time alone, but a small moment would be better than nothing.

Marius danced elegantly, his body in tune with the slow music. He pulled me closer, and his embrace felt warm. His lead was soft but not subtle as he invited me to mirror his steps, his eyes drifting from mine to the ballroom behind me. I giggled as he spun me in his arms.

"Rapunzel," he said. "It's been a while."

I could see him looking over my shoulder, distracted by something. I glanced back and saw that he was watching my guards.

"Indeed." I moved closer, wanting him to focus on me. "What took you so long to come and say hello?"

"I was waiting for the right moment." He pulled me closer, finally looking at me. "You looked so bored out there, dancing with those men. I thought I'd come and save you from your misery."

He reached out to touch my necklace, then traced his fingers up towards my cheek. I held my breath as his fingers moved to my hair, which he pulled back, revealing the point of ear.

I stepped back, suddenly embarrassed, and quickly put my hair back in place.

"I'm sorry," he said.

"It's okay." I didn't want to make a fuss about it. For my entire life, everyone would peak at my ears when they thought I wasn't looking. The sharp point was a tell-tale sign of my curse.

"No, it's not okay," he said. "It's just... when I first met you, I assumed you were Akalik, because of your brown skin. I didn't know you were Aziza. I wanted to be sure."

I blinked up at him. I'd never heard the term 'Aziza' before. What was he talking about?

"You shouldn't be embarrassed about what you are," he said. "You, and your ears, are beautiful."

He leaned in closer, tracing his hands down my dress.

"Do you trust me, Rapunzel?"

I laughed nervously. "I suppose I trust you more than this room full of strangers. If I'm honest, they are all acting very odd. It's my eighteenth birthday celebration, but everyone is so quiet. No one is speaking with me or looking me in the eye. They almost seem afraid of me."

"It's not fear." He glanced over his shoulder as he spoke.

"I will be queen of the most prosperous nation in the Realm tomorrow. You'd think they'd all be vying for my favor."

Then he leaned in closer, laced his fingers into mine, and pulled my body against his. My face warmed. Marius had always been flirty, but I didn't remember him being quite as bold as he was tonight. I was glancing around the room, worried that someone saw his sly advances when his lips brushed against my cursed ear. "Rapunzel, I didn't come here just to dance with you. I came to deliver a message."

I pulled back and blinked up at him. "Pardon me?"

"A warning," he clarified.

I raised an eyebrow. I expected him to whisper sweet nothings like he'd done when I was sixteen, but his words only brought questions and fear.

"I know why the men are acting strange," he said. "No one wants to dance with a dead princess."

My eyes grew wide. "Rest assured that there are no dead princesses here."

"Trust me, Rapunzel," he whispered. "I'd love to dance with you again someday, so it would be best if you left the castle tonight."

I shook my head and stepped back. "I can't sneak away. My ceremony is in a few hours. You are not making any sense." As the words left my lips, I saw my bodyguards approaching from over Prince Marius's shoulder. Marius followed my glaze, turning to look over his own shoulder.

"You should run," Marius whispered.

As my bodyguards rushed over, he slipped his hand away from mine and rushed off, leaving a crumpled sheet of paper in my palm.

***

Prince Marius disappeared into the crowd like a phantom. I clasped my fist tight in front of me, hiding his mysterious gift from the guard's gaze.

"Rapunzel, are you okay?" Ade, my guard of Akalik Kingdom heritage, inquired. He was the only person in the palace with a complexion like mine, which led some hecklers to say he was my true father. As a child, I wondered if that could be true and began to see him as such. But he didn't have my ears, and I knew I must have gotten my curse from someone. The true origin of my father would remain a mystery.

My mind was whirling. "I don't feel very well. I'm going to head up to my room and rest my head before the feast." I finally said, raising my palm to my forehead for dramatic effect.

"You can't leave," Ade said.

"This celebration is for you," Rowan, my guard of Studer heritage, added quickly.

I turned up my nose. "If it's my party, then I can choose to take a break from it."

My guardians exchanged glances but said nothing as I pushed past them towards the ballroom exit to the grand hall. In the grand hall, a spiral staircase leads to my tower. Mother said the 300 steps between the castle and my bedroom keeps me safe. My bedroom, located in the highest tower of the castle, was the only room that the guards let me enter alone, and I needed to be alone to read this note.

His words echoed in my ear as I rushed past the large, purple "Studer Kingdom" banner hanging above the marble stairs.

No one wants to dance with a dead princess. What could Marius have possibly meant by that?

I could hear my guards trying to keep up, but they were not as spry as me in their chainmail armor. Despite my sedentary life, I'd always been nimble and quick. In another life, I imagined I'd be a dancer or a warrior.

I locked the door as soon as soon I made it inside my room, and ignored their desperate knocks.

"Rapunzel?" Rowan called from the other side of my door.

"I'm undressing! Leave me be!"

My room wasn't large, but it had the best view of all the rooms in the castle. I could watch the kingdom from my tower window. Even though I'd never stepped foot outside the castle, I knew the commoners' daily routines.

I'd watch the townsfolk walk from the tailor, to the inn, to the stable. The Studer Kingdom was built on a peninsula, so the docks surrounded most of the city. I'd watch the ships come in and imagined sailing to faraway lands. The only other exit was blocked by a heavily guarded wall, but caravans would carry shipments in and out. When I watched the townsfolk, I made up stories about their lives.

Most nights I'd dream of leaping from my window, sprouting wings, floating to the ground, and exploring the world below. When I woke up, I'd touch my back to feel the wings, praying they were still there. But this was not a time to daydream. I opened the crumpled sheet of paper with trembling hands and saw Mother's perfect handwriting in neat black ink.

We have secured Rapunzel's replacement.

The ceremony will take place as planned.'

I frowned. What did Mother mean by "replacement?"

"Rapunzel!" Ade called through the door. "Your ceremony is starting soon."

"One minute," I called back. Another message was scribbled in the corner of the paper in messy, unfamiliar handwriting

'The stables.

The red caravan.

Run.

Now.'

I looked out of my tower window at the stables near the city gates. Was Marius trying to sneak me out of the city?

I could hear a key rattling in my doorknob, so I placed Prince Marius's note under my pillow. My bedroom door flew open, and Mother stood beside her guards with a key in hand. She twisted her raged expression into feigned concern.

"Rapunzel, I was worried sick! Why aren't you at your party?"

"I wasn't feeling well. This corset is too tight." I pulled at my corset.

"Well, you are in luck, you don't need it for your ceremony," she said, walking over to me and fixing my hair. "No need to wear a corset with your robe."

"Robe?" I questioned.

"Why yes, it's customary to wear a robe to your ceremony. You'd usually change right before the ceremony, but since you are already in your room, how about you put it on now." She turned to Rowan. "Be a dear and fetch Rapunzel her robe."

He bowed and stole a quick glance at me before he scurried off to do mother's bidding. When he returned with the robe, I saw that it was a ghostly white, and made with the finest silk and lace. It wasn't as flashy as my ball gown, but gold thread embroidered ancient symbols into the silk. I recognized some of the faint markings as a language that I'd only seen in mages' spell books.

"You didn't tell me about this part of the ceremony," I said.

She nodded. "Yes, well, there's a lot of things about the ceremony you don't know. You'll find out as you go."

"Did you wear a robe?"

Mother tilted her head in confusion.

"At your ceremony. Did you wear one?" I asked again.

"Oh, Rapunzel, that was 500 years ago! I don't remember all the details." She dismissed my question with a swipe of her hand, then grinned. "I remember what came next. After the party, the dinner, and the ceremony, I fell asleep with the knowledge that tomorrow I'd be queen. I remember putting on my crown for the first time. And most of all, selecting my king. I knew I'd help lead this Kingdom to greatness, the same as you will."

I tried to read Rowan's expression as he handed me the gown, but though his face was pointed towards mine his eyes seemed to look past me. Through me.

I put the gown on my bed, then followed my mother's gaze to my hands. They were trembling.

"I'm sorry," my voice cracked as I spoke. "I didn't want to show any weakness on the day I was to become queen, but I'm a little scared. I'm not accustomed to being around so many people. I came up to my tower to catch my breath."

Mother pulled part of my hair over my ear. "You've always been a brave girl. I *know* you can do this. The ceremony will start after dinner. Hurry down," she said as my sister, Rachel, joined her at my bedroom door, cradling something large in her arms.

At first, I thought Rachel was carrying a doll, though at the age of fourteen I hadn't seen her play with one in years. It cooed and lifted an arm. My heart swelled with excitement. I ran over to take a look. I hadn't seen a baby since Rachel was one, but when I took a closer look I gasped in shock. This baby had brown skin and sharp ears like mine. Could we have the same father?

"Isn't she cute!" Rachel smiled at me, but my mind flashed back to the words on the note.

We have secured Rapunzel's replacement.

"She looks like me." I watched Mother's face for answers. "What kingdom is she from?"

"She's from our kingdom now," my sister interrupted. "She's going to stay here with us."

"Why?" I asked, still watching my mother. "Does she have the same father as me?"

"Rapunzel, we don't have time for this. You are late to your ceremony." There was a challenge in her ice-blue eyes. "I need you to start behaving like a queen. Get dressed. Come down. Address your people."

I felt conflicted. Maybe Marius was wrong, or worse, maybe he was trying to sneak me away for selfish reasons. My mom worked hard to shield me from my enemies, but maybe one had found his way inside.

"I will," I promised. "Let me change."

As the door finally shut, I let out a sigh. It felt nice to take off my corset, but I left my garter intact. I found the tiniest blade I could, not much larger than my index finger, and tucked it sheathed inside my garter. I didn't own any proper weapons, but this was better than nothing. Then I slipped on the robe and grimaced when I saw that it was translucent. It left little to the imagination, and my blade was noticeable.

I untwisted my hair and let my long locs crown my face like a lion's mane, my cursed ears were visible and proud. I removed the small blade from my thigh and hid it twisted in my long, thick coily hair.

I questioned whether I should trust Marius or mother, but a queen didn't run from her kingdom. I didn't know who my enemy was, but I was ready to fight.

***

When I walked into the dining hall, with my big hair out and pointy ears visible, the crowd finally looked at me instead of my feet. I found my place at the table, across from my mother. A big fat ham sat between us. There were six people on each side of the rectangular table, with my mother and me at each end.

"Rapunzel, what did you do to your hair?" Mother snapped. She knew this was how it looked more often than not.

"I let it down." My tone was light as I looked around the room.

Representatives from all three kingdoms were here: kings, queens, princes, and high lords. Marius sat to the right of mother, and was the only man to not stare at my hair or ears. He looked down, his hands fidgeting with a napkin on the table until he finally placed them in his lap.

My mother and I were the only women in the room, and I thought about the fact that when I selected my king he'd be the first King that The Studer Kingdom had in 500 years. Even though we were a matriarchy, I felt pressure to choose a perfect match.

"I like it out," a man from the Akalik Kingdom said. "I can see her ears." But his honey-brown eyes looked dark and greedy as he said it, his voice mocking.

At that moment the big, heavy, wooden dining room doors swung open and a priest and two mages came in.

I glanced at my mother, who smiled sweetly at the mages as they started chanting in an ancient language that neither of us could understand. As they spoke, the gold thread on my gown started to glow. I caught Marius watching me again.

"Run," he mouthed before turning to watch at the mages with mother.

The ham sat untouched as a server passed out wine to all of the guests, skipping over me.

If it were any other day, if I hadn't just been given proof that my mother was planning to replace me, I'd have jokingly asked if I was old enough to drink yet. My throat was parched, and wine would have been nice. But at that moment, I felt too terrified to speak.

The priest carried me a drink in a tall golden goblet, holding his arm outstretched as he took it to me, as if he was afraid the drink might explode. Dragons with beady red eyes and detailed scales were carved into the gold. The dragons reminded me of the hilt of Marius' katana.

When the priest placed it before me on the table, I looked at the blood red liquid and gulped. Why was my drink separated from the rest? Was this a normal part of the ceremony? The mages stopped chanting. They stood at the doorway, next to the priest and my two guards.

My mother offered me an encouraging smile. Her eyes were alight with excitement as she stood to make a toast.

"Rapunzel has the power to grant the Three Kingdoms another 500 years of peace and prosperity. Drink to the wisdom of the Bahkiah Kingdom, to the strength of the Akalik kingdom, and to the eternal reign of the Studer Kingdom!" mother said. "We offer blessings to Rapunzel as she leads us to greatness!"

They lifted their glasses off the table, and after a second of hesitation I did the same. Marius' eyes were wide with concern, and my mother's grin was eager. She gave me a slight nod, encouraging me to take a sip.

I looked around the table. Whenever my eyes met one of the men's gazes, they looked away. Marius was fidgeting in his chair now, and his father was staring at him now. I could all but see his father nudging him under the table.

"Drink Rapunzel," mother insisted.

"Rowan," I said instead.

My mother's gaze narrowed, her lips forming a tight line.

"Y-yes, my Lady?" Rowan asked.

"Take a sip from my goblet first."

He gasped and traded a concerned look with Ade, who looked away and held a deadpan expression.

"What?" Rowan asked, breathless.

"Rapunzel…" my mother said, but I interrupted her.

"Rowan's job is to keep me safe at all times. He should be able to handle testing my wine."

"That's not how the ceremony works," my mother said through gritted teeth. "It's tradition…"

"I'll be queen tomorrow. I'll make my own traditions." I stood up from the table and carried my goblet over to Rowan. He looked at my mother.

"Do as she asks, Rowan," my mother said with a sigh.

"But Your Highness…"

She slammed a fist on the table. "Do as she asks or I'll have Ade slit your throat right here and now."

Rowan swiftly took the goblet, raising it to his lips with shaky palms. The red liquid splashed about, falling down his fingers, dropping to the clear marble floor. I could see sweat forming on his brow, all but dripping into the drink. He took the tiniest sip, then held his breath as he waited for my approval.

"More," I said.

He glanced at mother again.

"Tomorrow I'll be your queen," I said. "You'll need to get accustomed to taking direct orders from me."

A tear slipped down his cheek as he took two big gulps of the wine. He handed the goblet back to me with trembling hands, but he was standing upright and seemed healthy. It looked like he was full of nerves rather than poison.

"Now can we please get on with the ceremony, Rapunzel?" my mother asked. "Quickly. You have guests here waiting."

I carried what was left of my wine back to the table and took my seat, unsure of what to believe.

Maybe Marius had been lying to me all along. I sighed and lifted the goblet to my lips as my mother smiled in approval.

A large thump echoed through the room. I dropped my goblet when I saw that Rowan had fallen to the ground. He was clawing at his neck, ripping at his armor, and taking labored breaths. He coughed up blood and mucus as he whimpered on the floor. The people in the room looked alarmed, but not necessarily surprised. They looked to my mother for guidance, and gaped at me in fear.

I looked at my mother, wondering if she'd try to give some explanation. I didn't want to believe that the woman who had raised me for eighteen years was trying to kill me—at a public dinner party no less. But she offered no explanation. Instead, she turned to Ade.

"Seize her," my mother called, and the guard who had protected me my entire life, the one who's been the closest thing I'd ever had to a father, lunged at me with his blade drawn.

***

Ade was strong, but I was quick. I pulled the blade from my hair and stabbed it in Ade's gut, right beneath his breastplate. Blood gushed onto my white gown as he fell to my feet. If I paused and gave myself even a moment to think about what I'd just done I knew my heart would break. So I didn't pause; I ran.

The mages tried to weaken me with spells as I pushed my way out of the dining hall. The priest dashed away from me as if I were a demon, not the blessed savior of the Kingdom they said I was a second ago.

I made my way out of the dining hall back to the grand hall. Dozens of guards were waiting at the palace exit with weapons ready, and I realized that my guards hadn't been hired to keep me safe, but rather to keep me prisoner. My tiny blade would be useless against their broadswords and war hammers, so rather than fighting my way through an army I raced up the spiral stairs. If I could just make it to the peace of my room, I could at least spend a few extra seconds alive. Maybe, just maybe, I'd find a way to escape from the window like I'd done in my dreams.

I could hear the army behind me, their loud graceless steps no match for my nimble ones. I resisted the effects of the mage's spells as I made it to the top of the staircase. Rachel stood in the hall outside my room, rocking my replacement to sleep. The baby played with my sisters long, blond hair. I wondered if my sister knew what was supposed to happen to me tonight. I considered grabbing her, or the baby, as collateral to barter for my life. But mother knew I'd never hurt Rachel, and the baby might be my own blood. The army was close behind me. I locked myself in my room, but I knew mother would have a key.

I was raised to die today. All eighteen years of my life led to this moment; the moment the only family that I ever knew would betray me.

I glanced out my window to the town below. The people looked like insects from up here. I studied the castle to see if there was any possible way to climb down. I remembered my dreams of growing wings and talking off in flight. It would take a miracle to stay alive today.

I could hear the click of a key in my door as it swung open, and I could feel the mages weakening me. The gold thread on my gown was glowing black. My body felt heavy, like weights were attached to my limbs.

I willed myself back towards the tower window, glanced down the 200-foot drop, and decided I wanted to die on my own terms. Right as Abe pointed his sword at my throat, I leapt from my window to see if I could make my dreams come true.

***

I didn't sprout wings, but what happened was just as magical. My body drifted to the ground as if I were a feather. My heart raced with aw and excitement as the sea breeze teased my hair as I made my way down.

What type of sorcery was this?

I glanced up to see if a mage was helping to slow my fall. I looked towards my window and saw my mother looking down at me. A guard stood beside her aiming his bow and firing an arrow at me. I caught his arrow and smiled at Mother as I drifted to the world below.

The tips of my toes touched the ground first, and my heels followed. I'd never been outside the palace before, and I wanted to take it all in—the sun felt brighter and warmer than it ever felt from my room and the Kingdom looked so full of possibilities. But I didn't have the luxury to explore. The second I was free; I took off running.

I wondered if I could blend in with the townsfolk and live the rest of my life as a common girl, but my ears were a tell-tale sign that I was different. I found my way to the stables and peeked inside. The horses were twice as beautiful as they'd looked from my tower, but they were three times smellier than I'd imagined.

I leapt into the back of a red caravan, grateful for a curtain to hide behind. As I caught my breath, pain shot through my legs and my arms. I gasped for air as I took in my surroundings. The shipments, food, and supplies were in boxes and under blankets. I knew the guards searching the city would kill me on sight if they found me, but there were plenty of places here to hide.

I briefly wondered how the townspeople would respond to the news that their princess was murdered, before I realized even that aspect of my life had been a farce.

The townspeople didn't know of my existence because Mother had never intended for me to be queen; that title would probably go to Rachel one day.

"Don't scream," an unfamiliar voice said from behind me. Before I could think of a reply rough hands grabbed me and pulled me down, covering my mouth with cloth to muffle my scream. A strange scent filled my nose and made my head woozy. Suddenly, I was falling again, slipping away from the known world. My body grew weak as my mind fell into darkness.

***

"Did you see a baby?" a voice called through the darkness.

"She's out cold," another voice said.

"I saw her eyes blink," the first voice insisted. He had an odd accent that I couldn't place. "She's waking up."

Was I waking up? I willed my heavy eyes to open and looked into the warm, brown eyes of a boy of about fourteen years. His long locs were pulled back from his face, revealing the point of his ears.

"Did you see a baby?" he asked again.

The tree I was pressed against was uncomfortable. Despite my pounding head, I tried to sit up straight. But my arms were met with resistance when I tried to push myself up.

I glanced over my shoulder. A sailor's rope tied my wrists to a tree, but I didn't see the sailors, or boats, or sea that I'd watched from my tower window. The Kingdom was long gone, and I was in some type of makeshift settlement. The ground was covered in sandy brown dust, and the sun's rays were hotter than I'd ever imagined they could be.

The caravan I'd hidden in was nearby, but so were hundreds of others. Could this be some type of town for nomads?

"Let me go." My voice was weaker than I wanted it to sound. A girl with red hair and freckles walked to the boy's side. She looked about my age and wore loose fitting, wrinkled, dirty clothing.

She grinned. "Hello, Rapunzel."

I looked around and saw people from all three kingdoms in this community, but they weren't like any of the people I'd met before. They were thin, and their skin was covered in scars. The children played in the dirt with no shoes.

"What is this place?" I asked.

"I'm sorry if it's not as nice as your gilded kingdom," the girl said. "Welcome to the real Realm."

"We must have traveled far," I said.

"Actually, we are just outside the wall." The boy pointed, and I could see the wall of my kingdom in the distance. But how was that possible? The environment was completely different here. How could a wall divide a temperate climate from a dried-up place like this?

"This is what most of the world is like, Rapunzel. Dunes. Wastelands. Desserts," the redhead said. "The Three Kingdoms are the only places in the Realm with grass and rain and shade."

"How is that possible?" I asked.

"How is it possible for one woman to rule a kingdom for 500 years?" she asked. "It's possible because of people like you."

"Why are you all camped out here?" I asked.

"It's how we get our clothes and food," she explained. "When they dump their trash."

I wanted to ask if mother knew about this, but of course she did. How could she not know about the thousands of starving people living right outside the walls of her kingdom? Mother told me that the people who lived outside the wall were dangerous and evil. So much of what I knew about the world had been a lie.

"Please tell me if she's okay," the boy asked me.

"Who?"

"The baby. My sister."

I looked at his ears. "You are cursed too."

"Cursed?" He twisted his face in confusion.

"Mother said people would hunt me down because of my cursed ears," I said. "That's why I never left home. But after today, I don't think I can trust much of what my mother said."

"We are Aziza," he states. "The fourth Kingdom of the Realm. A displaced people, sure, but definitely not cursed. Your mother has ruled for 500 years Rapunzel. People don't live that long without a blessing."

My forehead creased as I took his words in.

"That's why they take us. When our natural magic is harvested, others can live long and prosperous lives."

"Hey, you're up," a familiar voice called from behind me. I twisted my neck to see Marius approaching. He had not abandoned me after all, and a warm sensation swept over me. Even though he was no longer wearing his suit, he looked out of place here. Something about the way he carried himself hinted at his royal upbringing.

He walked up to me and pulled out a dagger. I gasped and recoiled back.

His eyes softened. "I'm going to free you, Rapunzel."

He gently took my wrist and started sawing the rope with his blade. "I'd never harm you."

"Why did you tie me up in the first place?" I asked.

"We didn't want you to wake in the night and run off before we had a chance to talk to you."

I rubbed my sore wrists once they were free. "They drugged me," I said.

"To get you out safely. Would you prefer the drug your so-called mother prepared for you?"

I rolled my eyes. "What did you want to talk about?"

"The kingdoms."

"Why are you helping me? You stand to benefit from my death like everyone else in that room." There was a question on my mind I dreaded asking, but I needed to know. "What were they going to do with me when I died?"

"The Aziza have powerful, natural magic. Their blood has been used to make potions and elixirs for years. They don't hunt Aziza. Not anymore, at least. I guess to make themselves feel better about kidnapping and killing people, they made it into a type of religious ceremony. They call them Tributes—children taken from Aziza tribes. They tell themselves they are doing the Aziza a favor by allowing you to live in their palace, raising you like a daughter, treating you like a queen. They wait till Tributes are eighteen to harvest their blood. Every eighteen years, they do it again."

"That's twisted," I said.

Marius shrugged. "In your kingdom everyone has long and prosperous lives. A lot of times, to create a perfect, utopian kingdom for some, the rest of the world needs to suffer. Outside of the Three Kingdoms, life is hard for everyone. When I saw what the world was really like, I wanted to be a part of rectifying it."

"How long have you known about this?" I questioned.

He gave me his familiar crooked grin. "I've been helping in the dunes for the past couple of years now. I met Amare." He gestured to the boy with ears like mine. "He told me they'd kidnapped his sister, and I … remembered you. I knew what they were going to do on your birthday, and I wanted to stop it. To help him. And to help you."

I shut my eyes as I tried to process everything. Mother wasn't my real mother. Rapunzel probably wasn't even my real name. I'd been stolen as a baby; a perfect kingdom had been founded on the blood of people like me.

"I have secured passage for you to a safe place. You'll stay with Amare's family as we work to retrieve his baby sister. They live in a small community of Aziza. You'll be able to meet others with magic like yours."

"So your plan was to hide me away?" I asked, clenching my fists and I stood up. I felt like I'd discovered the world for the first time. There was no way he was going to leave me now.

"My plan is to keep you safe as we save his sister's life."

"You can't just kidnap the baby," I protested.

"We can," Amare said. "We have to."

"There will be more babies—girls like me, just waiting for their death day. Let me come with you, stand up to mother, and take my rightful place as queen."

Marius moved closer and took my hands.

"I want you safe, Rapunzel," he whispered. "You promised me another dance someday."

"I woke up this morning thinking I'd be queen tomorrow," I said. "I'm not going to hide away. Not while there are babies who are raised to be murdered. This all has to stop. If I really do have natural magic, I can help."

"You don't know how to wield your power yet," he spoke through gritted teeth.

"If I needed to know how to wield my power, I wouldn't be alive right now," I said. "The kingdom needs a new queen."

Marius was silent for a second, but eventually he sighed. "Okay."

I blinked at him. "Okay?"

"Yes, Rapunzel. Come with us. I saw you race up those steps, I saw you float through the sky like an angel. I want to keep you safe, but you'll probably end up being the one that rescues me."

The redhead rushed to the back of the caravan. She grunted as she pulled out a large wooden chest of weapons. I smiled as I picked a larger Broadsword and deposited my tiny blade from home. This wasn't how I expected to claim my title, but a queen doesn't run from her kingdom. It was time to take my rightful place on the throne.

K. R. S. McEntire lives on a healthy diet of fiction and tea. She loves art, photography and travel because, like books, they allow her to explore new worlds. She lives in Indianapolis with her husband and runs the Facebook page Diverse Fantasy and Sci-Finds, where she shares book recommendations with other bibliophiles.

Find her at: https://krsmcentire.wordpress.com/

While They Sleep

By Heather Carson

"Mom, tell them they made a mistake." Emma shakes as the chill of the room creeps up the back of her thin hospital robe. "Please mom, I'm begging you. I don't want this to happen."

"Shh, my darling." Bethany kisses the top of her daughter's head before tucking a long lock of blond hair behind her ear. "I promise this isn't a bad thing. It's for the greater good. I was honored with this blessing too. I'm so proud of who you are and what you will accomplish."

"No." Emma clenches her teeth to stop them from chattering. Tears burn hot streams down her cold cheeks. "This isn't fair. I don't want this. Tell them to sterilize me."

"I can't do that sweetheart." Bethany smiles brightly for her daughter, willing the fears to dissipate like they did when she was a young girl. One reassuring smile was all it took for a brave Emma to dust herself off and continue to play. "The tests are never wrong. I always knew you were special, and the doctors just confirmed it. This is the highest honor a woman can have."

"I still don't understand." Emma's face contorts in anger. "I don't want this. Why does everyone else get a choice but me?"

"They don't get to make their choices either." Bethany swallows down sympathy for the entire world with a sip of water from the paper cup. "You're a woman now. Women have a special job of protecting and caring for our way of life."

"Mom. Stop." Emma grasps Bethany's arm and digs her perfectly shaped fingernails into her mother's skin. Every word she speaks is punctuated and slow, "I don't want this."

"Every woman who goes through this is scared. You'll be completely safe. They care for all the girls here. You'll be treated like a princess." Bethany pulls her daughter close and hugs her. "I need you to be strong for all of us."

"How can you say this to me?" The heat of rage vibrates through her skin and stops her from shaking. "Are you even going to miss me?"

"Of course I will, sweetheart." Tears well in Bethany's eyes. "But it isn't the time to be selfish."

"And what if I lose fifty years like you did? What then?" Emma spits. "You'll be dead. Dad will be dead. I'll be lucky if Bryne even remembers me."

"It won't be that way," Bethany whispers as the deep throated sound of male laughter and giggles from a little girl echo down the hall.

"I was a first trial run," she rushes to explain. "The time is getting shorter, but I need you to put on a brave face. Please don't scare your sister."

Emma clenches her teeth and turns to stare at the clinically white wall. Those words are the only ones her mother could speak that would stop her from causing a scene. She won't run. She won't fight. Not if it will tarnish Bryne's reputation. To hell with her mother and father who would willingly let her go. Bryne is the only one worth fighting for.

"I got you a doughnut," Bryne says she climbs up on the hospital bed next to Emma. "The lady at the counter gave me two for free." The little girl's sticky sweet face gazes adoringly at her older sister. She holds the doughnut with melting glaze out to her like a prize.

"Of course they would." Emma smiles as she wipes tears from her face. "I bet they would have given you twenty free doughnuts if you asked."

Bryne beams as Emma takes the pastry, but her little eyes shift downward in sadness when Emma takes a bite.

"You know, I'm not really that hungry." Emma studies her sister's expression. "Would you eat this one for me?"

Bryne's eyes brighten. "Sure! I can eat it."

"It went well?" Henry asks as he kisses his wife on the cheek. Emma listens to their conversation in the corner as Bryne happily chews on the sugary treat.

"She's perfect." Bethany sighs. "The doctor will be back shortly."

Emma grips the thin sheet that covers the bed. The window is open. She can jump through it. Death on her own terms sounds much better than a life decided by them.

"There's jelly inside," Bryne squeals. "Emma, try a teeny tiny bite of this. It's so yummy."

Emma shudders, letting the thought of freedom dissipate into the ventilated air of the room.

"Is it blackberry jelly?" she asks.

***

"Everything is perfect." Dr. Briar smiles at Bethany and Henry. "She is a perfect specimen."

She is right here, Emma thinks. Bryne crawls into her lap and Emma wraps her slender arms around the child. Ever since Bryne was born, she'd always preferred the company of her older sister. Most nights the girl climbed into her bed after all the lights in the house were out. Emma never minded. None of her friends had any siblings.

"I am a little concerned about the timeline of this." Henry scratches his head in thought. Hope rises in Emma's chest as a relieving sigh. Maybe her father can fix this.

"Don't worry about a thing." The doctor smiles and the white whiskers of his mustache raise with the expression. His liver spotted thumb swipes up across the device in his hands.

"We've made remarkable progress." He speaks these words theatrically, putting on a show for her parents. "I remember when we woke our darling Bethany up. What was it, seventeen years ago now?"

"Nineteen." Bethany blushes and Emma fights the urge to gag. "The year before Emma was born."

"Nineteen years," Dr. Briar continues, "but it seems like only yesterday."

Bryne lays her head on Emma's shoulder and softly begins to hum. She hugs her sister tighter. Despite the melody, her ears focus desperately on the doctor's every word.

He stretches his back and neck, scanning the room for a swivel stool. It sits beside Emma's feet where Bryne left it when she used it to crawl onto the bed. Without so much as a glance at Emma, he pulls a stool over and plops down upon it in front of her parents.

"Where were we?" He adjusts his glasses as he stares at the screen. "Oh yes, data. When Bethany went in, we were expecting 40 to 60 years. With a decrease in the world population accelerating as fast as it is due to this natural phenomenon, we've been able to reduce that time to 25 years."

"Think of that." The doctor slaps his thigh and laughs while Emma suffocates under the weight of the words that hang in the air. "In just your lifetime, Bethany, we've been able to cut wait time in half."

But it isn't in her lifetime, Emma wants to scream. *She should have already been dead by now.* Bryne continues to sing and Emma smooths the golden hair on her little head.

"I still don't understand." Henry chews his lip. "If you've been able to reduce it that drastically is there even a need for this program anymore?"

"Unfortunately, yes." Dr. Briar removes his glasses and rubs his eyes before replacing them. "The world population is not at manageable levels and the rate of infertility is still increasing. This biological reaction to our circumstances concerns us. With the slow to change genetic human system, we could see the end of our species in the next 200 years. Thankfully we have the foresight to stop this unlike many of our extinct mammal cousins. With Bethany, and now remarkably Emma, as our outliers to this phenomenon we can save humanity."

"You might have to walk me through this again." Henry shrugs. "I still don't understand why you need to freeze my daughter."

Thank you, Daddy, Emma struggles to keep from crying out loud as Bryne drifts into sugar tainted dreams in her arms.

"We prefer not to call it a freeze here." Dr. Briar stands from his stool and winks. "There is no other option. With the alarming rate of female and male infertility, we need to preserve perfect female specimens in case we never get optimal rates back. It's really a simple system. We put our fertile girls to sleep until population levels drop enough that we can allow them to wake and start families of their own."

"Like I said," the doctor continues, acknowledging Henry's nod of acceptance and ignoring the burning rage on Emma's face. "She'll be out of here in no time at all."

***

"Just put your finger here." The nurse smiles at Emma as she holds the screen in front of her.

"And if I don't?" Emma glares at the nurse in defiance. The woman casts a confused glance over her shoulder toward Emma's parents.

"She's just playing," Bethany giggles nervously. "Do you mind giving us one more minute?"

The nurse arches her eyebrow as she steps quietly into the hall. Emma stares unblinking at the door. The saline running through the IV port in her arm is cold, but she doesn't feel it because she is numb. Bryne snores on the chair beside the hospital bed.

"I know this is hard." Bethany sits on the edge of the thin mattress and lowers her head as she speaks.

"This was hard for me too. My world was so different when I went to sleep. There was fighting and fear and confusion. When the first batch of us fertile girls were set up here in the hospital, they televised the event. It gave a lost world hope that things weren't going to be as bad as they seemed. And guess what? It worked. I had a lot of pressure to deal with, but so do you. You are the beacon for future generations. You are the salvation to this way of life. Everyone will know if you fail. They'll blame you. They'll blame all of us. And since you think that my sacrifice was for nothing, at least think of Bryne and the life she will live if people hear that her sister refused to do this."

Emma blinks as she stares at her mother's face. It's beautiful and kind. The face she remembers comforting her when she came home from school crying one day after the group of southside old women teased her about her expensive clothes. She doesn't understand how that gentle face can be so cruel right now.

"Bryne wake up." Emma nudges her little sister. Bryne stirs and rubs a tiny fist across her sleep crested eyes.

"I love you more than anything," Emma says, kissing the top of the child's head and ignoring her mother's tears. "I have to go away for a while, but I promise I'll come back to you."

"Is it time for you to go to sleep?" Bryne yawns.

"Yep." Emma smiles.

"Okay." She wraps her arms around her older sister and kisses her forehead. "Go to sleep. I'll see you when you wake up tomorrow."

"We are ready." Henry's voice is flat as he opens the door to the hospital room. The nurse comes shuffling back in, annoyed at the inconvenience.

"I need your fingerprint here." She pushes the tablet forward. Emma's eyes never leave the harsh woman's face as she lifts her arm with the taped IV needle and places her finger on the screen. She refuses to look at her parents. Instead, she clings to Bryne's tiny hand as the nurse releases the button for the medicine into her veins.

Then there is only blackness.

***

"Hey Charlie, I've got to go." Bryne downs her tequila in a single gulp and slams the glass back onto the counter. The techno beat thumps throughout the crowded nightclub.

"Why?" Charlie whines as he grips her arm. "You promised you'd wing man for me tonight."

"No," she laughs. "I promised I'd come have a drink with you. That was two. I have to be up early tomorrow."

"For what?" Charlie turns and raises his arms as his hips gyrate to the pulsing beat. He points around the VIP section and down to the floor packed with bodies dancing below them. There's no difference between the elites in the balcony and the ones who party downstairs. They all move with vacant eyes and wandering hands searching for a comfort they'll never grasp. "What is more important than this?"

"It's my sister's birthday tomorrow." Bryne shrugs. "I don't want to be late."

***

"Mom, wake up." Bryne smooths down the pleats of her skirt as she stands at the side of her parents' bed. "It's almost time to go."

"Go where?" Bethany mumbles. She gives her mother a minute to register where she's at. The bottles of pills on the nightstand the doctor prescribed make her groggy in the mornings.

Bethany forces herself awake and sits up against the mahogany headboard. She fumbles for the eye mask and pushes it up. The elastic band causes her hair to tangle. Bryne clicks the remote allowing the sun to filtrate the room of their high-rise apartment.

"We need to go see your daughter on her birthday." She rolls her eyes. "Don't tell me you forgot."

"Oh honey." Bethany stifles a yawn with the back of her hand and shuts her eyes against the light. "I thought I told you that we can't go see her today."

"What?" Bryne's smile falters. "Why wouldn't we go see her? It's her birthday. They always allow visitors on her birthday."

"Not this year." Bethany blinks as her eyes begin to focus. "Dr. Briar is running some sort of test. He had to move her to a different facility temporarily."

"Are they waking her up?" Bryne shrieks in excitement.

"No, no. Not yet." Bethany glances toward her sleeping husband. "Your dad had a long night. Keep it down so he can get some rest. We will go next year for her birthday. I promise."

Bryne begins to protest and Henry groans as he reaches for the pills on his nightstand.

"Shh." Her mother places a red painted fingernail over her lips and motions for Bryne to leave.

***

"To Red Pine Hospital," Bryne directs the automated taxi system as she slams the car door behind her.

"Music, Miss?" the automated system asks.

"Yes," she answers. "Classic rock and please make it loud."

The taxi whips through the northside streets, winding through the posh neighborhood of elites. The homes owned by the generation of families still fertile and able to have children of their own. Red pine hospital is in this district, but the car rolls close enough to the outskirts where slums sprawl like rivers from the city.

Aging bodies slump against doorways of the red-light district. They pass the club Bryne was in last night with Charlie. It's supposed to be one of the more reputable establishments. Its back door faces the slums. The front of the building is painted white with gold leaf trim. They want it to look pleasant, not like the rest of the world. It's supposed to look like it isn't in the red-light district.

Isn't every place here red-light? she thinks. *Everyone is just sleeping around with one another hoping something will stick.* But the building is supposed to not offend children. This whole neighborhood was designed to give children a wonderful childhood.

That might have been true once. There were bigger kids when she was a young girl, kids Emma's age, but it wasn't like that when she went to school. She and Charlie were the only ones in her class. Even her fertile mother couldn't have more than two children. Now the whole world is wasting away, lost in their own personal pity devices just like the expensive pill bottles on Bethany's nightstand.

The music quiets just as a guitar riff reaches its crescendo. "We are here, Miss. How long should I wait?"

Bryne slides her credit card into the meter and leaves it there. "I'll be back after I see my sister."

***

"Good morning, Miss." The front desk guard looks up from a stack of papers. The muscles of his biceps flex under his steely gray uniform. His size would cause anyone to shrink into themselves, but it doesn't bother Bryne. He'd always snuck her pieces of candy on every yearly visit.

"Have you forgotten me already Frederick?" She bats her eyelashes. He studies her face for a moment.

80

"Little Miss Bryne." Frederick finally smiles. "You've grown so much since last year. Where are your mother and father?"

Bryne moves closer to the desk. "My mother said they moved Emma to a different facility for some sort of test. I'd like to know where she is so that I can visit my sister for her birthday."

"Hmm." Frederick scratches the top of his head, running his fingers against the salt-colored fade stubble. "I've never known them to move anyone. Where else would they go?" He turns his attention to the computer screen.

"Here she is." He taps the digital file. "Right where she's always been. I wonder why your mother thought that. Maybe there was a miscommunication somewhere."

"Probably in her drug riddled brain," Bryne mumbles under her breath.

"Are we good then?" She smiles brightly. "Can I get my pass?"

"Are you eighteen already?" Fredrick looks up from the screen. "How did I get so old?"

"Not yet." Bryne's cheeks flush as she remembers the need for adult supervision in the stasis rooms. "But I will be in a few months," she hurries to add.

"I am sorry," Frederick says with genuine concern. "Why don't you see if your parents can make it down here after all, now that you know she is still here?" Bryne mentally calculates the amount of time it'll take her mother to get ready.

"Visiting hours will be over before they can come." Frustrated tears well in her eyes. "Please Frederick, this might be the last time I'll get to see her before the final test."

"The tests have been positive for you?" he asks hopefully and then coughs in embarrassment. "I'm sorry, that's none of my business."

"No, it's okay." She smiles. Everyone gets excited when they hear of more fertile women. "I've been acing everything so far. We'll see what the final test in a few months has to say." Frederick chews his bottom lip.

"Take it," he whispers sliding the pass into her hand as easily as he did the peppermint patty when she was five.

"Thank you so much," she beams as she slips the lanyard around her neck. He presses the release switch on the steel door behind him.

***

The heels of her shoes click down the linoleum floors of the long and empty hallway. Fluorescent lights give an eerie glow to this silent portion of the hospital. When Bryne was younger, she'd clung to her mother's warm hand as they walked this hall. Now that hand was as cold as the sterile hospital air flowing from the vents.

It was the pills that did it, Bryne thinks bitterly. *She couldn't have another healthy pregnancy and she lost Emma to this place. She'll lose me too and she can't cope with this shit world we live in.*

The hall turns sharply left and heads deeper into the underbelly of the building. At the end is the basement freezer where they keep the fertile girls in cryogenic sleep until it's time to be awakened.

Where I'll be soon, Bryne sighs as she slides the guest pass key against the entrance lock.

Emma's container number is 22. It's near the back of the room. Bryne passes the familiar faces of the girls locked tightly in the clear glass tubes, frozen and floating in their blue liquid sleep of death.

Not death, Bryne reminds herself to calm her anxieties. *Just sleep. If Emma is strong enough to do this then so am I.*

She passes by the container holding the girl with floating braids who has been there longer than Emma. Then she pauses as she recounts the numbers of the tubes. There is no mistake. Number 22 is empty. Emma isn't asleep where she should be.

Bryne stands horrified as she stares at the empty stasis tube. There is no clear blue gel, no preservatives keeping her sister afloat as it has been for the past fourteen years. Emma isn't there waiting for Bryne to sing her happy birthday. *Where the hell is she?*

The sound of clicking heels echoes from the far corner of the room. Out of instinct, Bryne dives behind tube 21 and curls herself into a ball. The footsteps come closer.

Holding her breath, she peeks out from behind the fluid filled glass to find a young doctor with a wart on her nose running temperature checks on the capsules. Bryne pulls her head back and tries not to make any noise as she holds her legs tightly against her chest.

When the doctor gets to tube 22, she passes without a second glance. Anger clouds Bryne's vision. *Either that clipboard or that doctor knows where Emma is.* She inhales deeply, standing upright, but the footsteps suddenly fade from the room as they exit through the back door.

Bryne races across the room to follow the sound. She catches the closing door before it shuts and holds it still in her hands for a moment. The hallway is empty. There's no sign of the woman doctor that was there moments before. It's as if she vanished into thin air.

She counts to three to steady herself before opening the door wide and walking down the hall. Her heels echo loudly against the fluorescent lit walkway so she kicks them off and laces them around her wrist. There are no doors and no windows, just white walls of empty space. The hall takes a sharp incline upward and seems to go for a mile until it reaches a set of cement stairs.

The stairs are as empty and abandoned as the hall behind them. The cold cement floor slaps quietly beneath her bare feet as she climbs the steps two at a time until she gets the top.

"Who are you and what are you doing here?" a large woman wearing a nurse's cap barks at Bryne when she reaches the landing. The window shows the entire city beneath them in this uppermost portion of the hospital.

"I'm looking for my sister," Bryne stammers. "She's not in her stasis tube."

The nurse's eyes bulge in terror as she reaches for the girl. "Who let you in here?" Her breath is fiery hot again Bryne's face.

"No one." She stands her ground refusing to be escorted down the steps. "Like I said, I'm looking for my sister."

"Well she's not here," the nurse spits, tugging roughly on Bryne's arm. "You need to leave now."

"I don't think so." Bryne peels back the woman's fingers. "I want to see my sister. What's behind that door?"

"Nothing." The nurse glares at her. "Turn around and go back the way you came, or I'll drag you back there myself."

"No." Bryne stares in outrage at the woman. "Move out of my way so I can see what's behind that door."

The nurse folds her sunburnt arms across her chest. "Get out of here now. I'm not making a suggestion."

"Neither am I." Bryne doesn't budge. "Move out of my way."

"You have no power here," the nurse sneers. "All you elites are the same, thinking you are better than us just because you can breed. You're no better than animals. We should keep you in stalls like pigs."

Bryne isn't fazed by the insult. She's heard much worse in her life. Her family has always been treated differently because her mother had not only one, but two kids. Even the other mothers stopped talking to Bethany when she had Bryne. Everyone wants what they can't have and no one in this world gets a choice anymore.

Her mother didn't, Emma didn't, and she won't either if she passes the final test.

"Move," she sighs. "I'm going to see what's behind that door and I'm not playing this game anymore with you."

The nurse reaches her meaty hand to grab Bryne by her neck, but she dodges it and drops below the woman's heavy arm. The nurse lunges forward again and manages to grab a handful of Bryne's hair.

Bryne cries out and tries to twist away, but the woman tightens her grip, pulling her back from the door and toward the steps. Bryne swings her arms blindly. The heel of her shoe connects with the nurse's back.

The nurse screams and releases her grip from Bryne's head as she tries to dislodge the pointed tip of the shoe from her skin. Bryne looks up just in time to see the woman trip over the landing and stumble down the top step. She doesn't hesitate. Bryne rips the lanyard from the nurse's throat as the large woman crashes down the staircase with a sickening bone crunching thud.

She races to the security door and unlocks it. Her heart beats rapidly in her chest as she eases the heavy door open and looks inside.

Another empty hall. This one is lined with windows overlooking the slums of the city behind the hospital. Bryne quickly closes the door behind her and begins to search the patient rooms on her right. The steady hum of machinery covers the soft steps of her bare feet. Each room is empty, but the sound of machinery grows louder.

The elevator doors at the end of the hall *ping*, jarring Bryne into a panic. She quickly slips into one of the empty rooms and maneuvers herself quietly behind the door. The click of heels reverberates down the hall. She holds her breath as she peeks through the crack in the door hinge. The young doctor from the stasis room is walking to the security door.

When the heavy door slams behind the doctor, Bryne lets out a ragged breath and anxiously resumes her search. She ignores the open patient rooms and instead focuses on the sound of machinery. It grows louder until she reaches the last room in the hall.

"What is this?" Bryne cries in revulsion as she enters the room.

Emma lays stark naked on a hospital bed as a host of machines pump her legs and arms in various directions. Her knees bend and are pulled straight again. Plastic suction bags compress her extremities. Tubes stick out of her mouth and nose as IV lines push a mixture of fluids into her veins.

The color drains from Bryne's face. In the center of the contraptions, in the middle of her sister's body, Emma's belly is overstretched and purple. The skin ripples as movement comes from inside.

"What the hell did they do to you?" Bryne screams as she races to her sister's side. Emma lays unresponsive as the machines continue to contort her body.

"Stop it!" Bryne cries while searching for the plug to end this suffering. She yanks the cord from the wall and the machines go blissfully silent.

"Wake up Emma." Tears streak Bryne's cheeks as she gently pulls the tubes and needles from her sister's body. "Please wake up. I need to figure out a way to get you out of here." She ignores the movement in Emma's stomach and searches for a sheet to cover her up.

"Please, please wake up." She brushes the long blond hair away from Emma's face and kisses her forehead.

Alarms sirens blare through the hospital causing an ear shattering screech in the quiet room.

"Where am I?" Emma croaks in a hoarse voice and instantly begins to cough.

"Oh, thank goodness," Bryne cries. "Listen to me. We need to get you out of here. I don't know what they did to you, but we need to leave now."

Emma runs her hands over her body, her eyes widening in shock. "Who are you? What is happening?"

"It's me Bryne," she cries. "You weren't in the stasis tube and I had to come find you. They did this to you. Now we need to get the hell out of here."

"Okay." Emma nods earnestly through the tears streaming down her cheeks.

"Can you stand?" Bryne asks as the sirens continue to blare around them.

"I'm going to try." Emma forces her weak legs to move and clings to her sister as she pushes herself up from the bed. Bryne groans under the weight but manages to keep them both upright as they head to the elevator.

"I'm going to be sick," Emma whispers before vomiting yellow liquid all over the linoleum floor.

"Let's just get out of here and I'll find someone who can help us." Bryne punches the button for the elevator and the doors slide open.

"Wait!" the doctor in heels emerges from the security door and screams at them from the end of the hall. Bryne raises her middle finger as the elevator doors shut.

"Now I'm really going to be sick," Emma groans as she begins to dry heave.

"Just a few more floors," Bryne reassures her.

"Miss Bryne!" Fredrick calls out as she exits the elevator and heads across the lobby to the front door, keeping Emma supported and moving forward. "What is going on here? I can't let anyone leave."

"Please." Bryne turns to face him. Tears blur her eyes as she begs, "Look what they did to her. You have to let us go."

Fredrick stares in amazement at Emma's protruding belly. His face hardens.

"Don't let those girls leave the premises!" The female doctor comes bursting through the steel basement entrance door. Old Doctor Briar stumbles breathlessly from the opposite hall.

"My God," he gasps as rage overtakes his body. He points a shaky finger at Bryne. "What have you done?" Bryne inches backwards toward the exit pulling Emma along with her.

"Don't let them leave," the young doctor screams her command to Fredrick. He removes his taser from his guard belt.

"You stupid girl," Dr. Briar spits. "Those babies do not belong to you. Security guard, I order you to detain them."

"I don't know what you did to my sister you sick bastard, but I promise you that you will never touch her again," Bryne screams at the decrepit old man.

Emma clings to her arm, swaying as she tries to stand tall. Her voice is dry and cracked but it rings loudly through the waiting room, "You promised nothing would happen to me. You promised to take care of all the girls."

"You spoiled breeding cows don't know the first thing about science," the female doctor continues advancing toward them. "Security guard, escort them to Doctor Briar's office."

"These two women are free to go." Frederick steps in front of the doctor with his taser level at her heart as the glass doors slide open letting Emma and Bryne escape. He turns to give Bryne a slight smile before gripping the doctor by her arm. "As for you two, you'll sit right here until the authorities arrive."

***

"Feeling better?" Bryne asks Emma as she steps out from the bathroom.

"So much better." Emma ties her robe and slips her feet into the fuzzy white slippers. "Thanks for watching them for me. I really needed a shower."

The twin boys coo at their Aunt Bryne from their playmat on the floor as she kisses each of their toes again. Emma smiles at them fondly. She never wanted to be a mother, but she's adjusting to the role.

"Anytime." Bryne smiles. "If you want, I can stay the night and help with a feeding or two."

"You are amazing." Emma falls onto the sofa and pulls a pillow across her lap. "Hey, I know we aren't supposed to dwell on it, but I keep thinking that I wish we could have gotten the other girls out."

"We did all we could. Dr. Briar and his whole team are in jail. They won't be able to run tests on infants anymore." Bryne whispers these last words hoping her nephews won't hear them.

"It's not just that," Emma sighs. "It worries me to think of what could happen to all the girls that are still asleep. I don't know how you did it, but I am so glad you ended up failing your tests."

Bryne fingers the ancient plastic compact containing pills that Charlie scored for her from the black market in the slums. It never leaves her pocket now, but she won't need to cheat the system anymore. "I'm really glad I failed them too."

Heather Carson is the mother of two feral little boys by day and an author by night. When she isn't working on a new book, you'll probably find her running away to the wild somewhere.

Her love for literature pushed her into writing and her crazy dreams give her inspiration for new story ideas. She loves the dystopian/apocalyptic genres because of the thought-provoking conversations that come from reading them.

Her current works include the *Project Dandelion Series, A Haunting Dystopian Tale* (trilogy), and *City on the Sea Series.* To find out more, visit: www.heatherkcarson.com

The Fairest Blade

By L. B. Winters

"Deep within the hidden folds of despair...strength lives."

Eve thought of her father's words as she stood in the middle of the elevated platform like a queen standing on the balcony of a mighty castle. Behind her, strands of thick, dark, silk hair cascaded down her back creating a reflective waterfall that flowed against her thin frame. She stood tall, chin lifted with the confidence of a ruler. But in her kingdom, it wasn't the faces of loyal subjects that stared back at her. A thick and twisting sea of thorny branches extended as far as the eye could see. This place was nothing like the beautiful lush woods of her childhood. This was a cold, colorless world of muted browns, where silence reigned and sharp branches surrounded her "throne" like swords pointed at the neck of a criminal being led to the guillotine.

She closed her eyes and tried to remember what freedom felt like. The taste of her favorite summer berries, the smell of jasmine and rose carried on the evening breeze. The image of her friends gathered in the center of the western fields dancing to the hypnotic pulse of a drum beat echoing from the forest's edge. She could picture their faces. The smiles and the laughter as they twirled in circles, the woodland creatures watching their movements from afar.

She turned abruptly, black hair sweeping up into the air as she tried to get as far away from the memory as she could. She couldn't think about these things, couldn't think about how much time had passed. Not when all signs pointed to her never making it back to those people again.

The paper-thin coating of calmness that usually kept her panic at bay was beginning to dissolve.

She could feel it as she moved, cracking and falling, piece by piece, like broken shards of glass from a shattered mirror. As the pieces fell the world spun, rotating faster and faster.

She fumbled for the railing, clutching to it for just a second before finally collapsing, her tear-stained cheek landing on the rotting wood of her palace. As the light faded, she was pulled deep into another realm that she had come to rule. Darkness…

***

Eve shot up from the hard ground, a blood curdling scream erupting from her mouth. She panted, her body struggling to pull in air as her heart beat frantically below her breast. She sat like this for several minutes as the fear slowly subsided and her surroundings came into focus.

She was in the Capitol Forest, the last perimeter before the waterway. She squeezed her eyes shut, repeating the words that were meant to bring her peace in moments like these. "You're not there anymore. You're free."

The doctors had said the nightmares would come. They warned her from the very beginning that this was a side effect of her torture. "Nobody can be trapped in a mental prison for that long and not be affected, Eve."

Mental prison, she repeated to herself. That was the perfect description of what she had endured. For three years she was kept in an isolated room, strapped to a bed and pumped full of medications meant to keep her in a state of permanent hallucinations. And now…she was irrefutably damaged, filled with trauma that had driven its roots deep into the farthest corners of her subconscious. The worst part was that everyone knew it. A wave of nausea hit her, then another. She felt like she was losing her strength. Losing her ability to survive this.

Reaching for the bag beside her, Eve opened the main compartment and pulled out the last of the bread wrapped in cloth. The bread was stale and tasteless but it calmed her stomach which was a twisted knot. As she chewed, she surveyed the forest around her. *How ironic*, she thought, *that the government left a forest for themselves.* They'd stolen the beauty from everyone else, but made sure to keep a piece for themselves.

The Andrews Corp, aka the government, had targeted the forests first. Hundreds of thousands of acres of trees were torn down after the initial take over, their resources used up and replaced with large concrete towers that dotted the horizon. These machines were named "The Breathers" since their purpose was to filter the air, create oxygen, and sustain life.

Eve scoffed at their tag line. "We don't need to be concerned about what nature is doing, when we have science to counterbalance its changes."

In the 25 years since their takeover, the Corp had taken control of the waterways and the skies. They'd wiped out huge populations of animals and filled the world with a thick black haze that seemed to infiltrate every surface and hidden crevice in the land.

The worst part was that this all had been done under the "watchful" eye of the people. Corp ads would run on TV, their propaganda printed in newspapers and journals. Commentators would debate the pros and cons of their mission. Why worry about the loss of resources when scientifically there would always be a way to replace them?

These days The Corp no longer needed to spin anything, now they controlled everything and their success was necessary for human survival.

But there was hope. Year after year more people grew tired of bowing to the will of the Corp. There was a growing willingness to fight back, to join the other side and use influence to deal major blows to the capital.

Eve finished her bread and tossed the cloth back in the bag before pushing herself up from the ground. She picked up the satchel and threw it over her shoulder. As she started forward, she once again thought of her father's words. "Deep within the folds of despair...strength lives."

**

The 10 Board members sat quietly at the massive conference table glancing nervously at one another. Something was different today. Vie Andrews stood in front, her back turned to them as she surveyed the grand expanse of factories, rail lines and billowing steam pipes that stretched on just outside the window. Her long white hair ran down the back of her silk black suit creating a jarring contrast. Nobody said a thing.

They'd been sitting in silence for almost 30 minutes, anxieties high as they waited to hear why she had called an emergency meeting. When she finally spoke, there was an eerie calm to her usually hate filled voice.

"The one who finds their leader will become vice chancellor." She kept her back turned as she talked.

A collective gasp filled the room as the chancellor's words hit them hard. *Vice chancellor?* Heads moved from side to side as coworkers looked at one another. The realization of what this could mean slowly dawned on them and their expressions changed from confusion to ones of possibility.

"Oh... and I almost forgot," she said as she turned around. "For the ones who prove to be useless in this matter. I have already made arrangements for you to be taken to THE CAMPS where you will spend your last days with the rebel Filth." With that she turned and walked out the door leaving a sea of colorless faces behind.

*****

There was no going back. A heavy lump sat in Eve's throat as she stared down the dock and into the organized chaos of activity that filled the port. A million moving parts that somehow came together to move people and supplies across the River.

Behind the commotion a giant cityscape loomed in the distance, a thick blanket of gray smog puffing out from the hundreds of factory stacks that filled the sky.

Eve moved down the dock dodging ropes and large stacks of supplies being carted about by camp workers who were assigned to the port. Thin, brittle humans moved about the deck in groups, supervised by the security agents who stood with their guns at the ready. The sight sickened her.

There was nothing to be done. Nothing she could do to help these people. They were casualties of war, their names a tiny drop in an overflowing bucket of loss.

As she made her way onto a boat, Eve moved to the stern and sat next to a pile of crates. When she was settled, she opened her bag and searched the contents until her warm fingers came in contact with the cool steel of her blade. She ran a finger along the sharp edge, pressing just hard enough to feel pain without breaking the skin.

She needed to remember the pain. The pain those prisoners felt. The pain her father felt. She carefully slipped the knife out of the bag, the sun illuminating the words intricately carved into the metal handle of her father's knife. She traced the loops and curls of cursive, something she had done countless times since his death.

"Harris Andrews." It was barely a whisper.

***

The chancellor stood in front of the waterfall that cascaded down the side of the concrete and into a large man-made pool below. On the walls, green vines hung like tapestries, while soft moss carpeted the entire floor of her office.

The rebels were beginning to turn the tide of the war. Everyday new intel came into the capital of major supply centers that had been targeted and destroyed. The group had captured high ranking members of the capital army and successfully completed a series of tunnels that bypassed known checkpoints. Her eyes darted to the windows. They were out there right now, hiding in the shadows. Plotting.

Her fist tightened, sharp nails cutting into the paper-thin skin of her aging hands. She needed to crush them. To deal a blow so devastating they would never be able to bounce back.

95

A click at her office door pulled her from her thoughts, and she turned to find her head of security moving into the office with a stack of folders.

"Place it on the table and leave" she growled.

Once he was gone, she tore open the folders and scanned the thick packet of papers that held the names of the capital soldiers who had fallen and the locations of warehouses that had been hit in the last 24 hours. She let the causality list fall to the floor and instead focused on the names of the high value spots that were raided.

She crumpled the sheets between her hands and threw them onto the floor, a loud scream erupting from her mouth. "God, damn it!" she yelled.

"I'm sorry that your plans are failing…"

Vie spun around at the sound of the soft words spoken behind her, her body suddenly freezing in place as her eyes fell upon the ghost of her daughter. A daughter who was supposed to be dead.

"You figured you took care of this problem," Eve said louder, as she pointed to herself. Vie stared back, her confusion visible. Eve continued, "Unfortunately for you I am very much alive."

"How is this possible, you're dead," Vie stuttered, the last remaining color draining from her face.

"You chose someone to kill me, but little did you know you chose someone that still had a heart. Still had a conscience." Eve took a step closer to her mother's rigid frame. "Someone who could never justify killing a young girl."

Realization dawned on her mother's face. "No, it's not possible," she cried. "He is my captain; his loyalty is unwavering."

"Oh, he was loyal," Eve spit out the words, as thoughts of her time in captivity came flooding in. "In the beginning… But in the end, he was more loyal to his conscience."

Eve stepped closer. "You tried to get rid of me, the same way you got rid of my father." Inside her anger was boiling over. "You didn't want any of us alive. You knew father was going to pull the plug. He was going to try and fix what you both had done."

Vie stumbled backwards as her daughter advanced. In Eve's small hand sat the knife she had promised herself she would use to rid the world of her mother's cruelty. Vie's eyes widened as she looked down at Eve's clenched fist.

"This was father's knife." Her eyes glanced down at the blade in her hand. She flexed her fingers feeling cool metal against her sweaty palm.

"Eve, this is your inheritance. This is in your blood. The Andrews blood that runs through your veins."

Eve knew there was no use in discussion. No use in hearing her mother's lies or trying to change her mind.

She moved forward with purpose pushing her mother further back until she was pressed against the glass of the massive floor to ceiling windows.

"You can either jump," Eve looked towards the window, then she lifted her hand and pointed the blade at her mother's throat, "or I can gut you. Bleed you out as you have our land, our people."

Her heart ached as she thought about her beloved forest friends that she had spent her childhood watching. The ones that were slaughtered. Inside her chest, her heart pounded against her ribcage as images quickly flashed in her mind.

Friends, family...*they were all gone.*

Eve took one last look at her mother, the defiant tilt of her head and the cold sneer on her aging face made everything easier.

"Dad didn't get the chance to stop you, but I will." Suddenly, Eve's arm shot forward, her knife penetrating the delicate skin of her mother's neck.

As blood poured from the wound her mother's face grew pale, her cold hard gaze quickly melting away to a set of lifeless eyes. Within seconds her mother's body fell to the floor, her white hair splatter with blood.

Eve immediately turned, no hesitation, no sudden feeling of regret.

"It's done," she whispered, as she wiped the blade on her pant leg.

As she walked from the room, she moved towards her bag that she'd hidden in the shadows. She bent down, pulling the burned phone from the front pocket and powered it on. When the screen was lit up, she flipped the phone open and dialed the number she memorized.

It rang for several seconds before the line connected and she heard the deep vibration of her captain as he answered.

"Go ahead," he said

Taking several steadying breaths, she finally spoke, her voice strong, her message filled with purpose.

"Friends, we have fought long and hard for this. For a chance to end the suffering. A chance to fix our mistakes and hold those who willingly lied to us accountable. That day has finally arrived. The chancellor is dead."

Silence.

With that she closed the phone and slipped it into her pocket. A single tear formed as she glanced back at the still form of the woman who had given birth to her all those years ago. The woman who had condemned her father to death and stolen everything from generations and generations of people who would long feel the effects of her assault. With that she turned and left, leaving behind her anger and hatred and instead moving towards a future of hope.

***

98

Eve moved carefully through the building, peeking around corners and artfully dodging cameras that she was given advance warning about. She moved like a shadow, sliding up and down the walls as she made her way closer to the large wooden door at the end of the hall.

She slowed as she approached, her hand coming to rest on the metal handle. She didn't walk through right away. She waited, taking several steadying breaths, as she listened to the words she had just broadcast repeated behind the door.

She slowly pushed on the handle and moved into the dark room as her words echoed louder now from a speaker in the corner.

Across from her a lone figure sat staring out into the night sky, a glass of amber liquid and a half empty bottle beside him.

Her breath caught in her throat as she took in his large muscular frame slouched back in his chair, his sleeves rolled up to his elbows revealing a splattering of dark hair along his tan forearms.

He turned towards her as she moved further into the room, a mixture of anger and relief etched on his face. "So it's done," he said carefully.

She didn't speak, only continued to stare as a heavy feeling of sadness came over her. He drained the rest of the liquid back in one motion and slammed the glass down before standing and moving towards her.

"Hunt, please…" her voice cracked as she said the words. This had been the plan all along. One he hadn't been willing to go along with but now as she stood in front of him, she knew more so than ever that this was meant to be.

"You are the reason we've been successful. You've given us the information. You've given us codes and access…"

"And now you're asking me to let you do this?" he cut in sharply.

She didn't reply, she simply waited, knowing there was nothing she could say to make this better. Hunt stared down, his intense gaze taking in the angles of her face.

It had been so long since he was able to look at her. She looked older but still exuded the gentle innocence that had captivated him from the moment he kidnapped her and brought her to the prison camps.

The thought of that day still haunted him. He had done as much damage to her as her mother had. Maybe more.

He moved forward, suddenly wrapping his arms around her shoulders and pulling her tight against his body. She tensed, fighting to maintain her strength, but as the seconds clicked by he could feel her beginning to relax into him.

They stood like this for several moments, neither of them speaking or making a move to separate.

Finally, Eve pushed away from his body and backed up. As she did, she dug into the front pocket of her black jeans. She pulled a tiny bag from her pocket and held it up. Inside two red pills sat within the confines of the plastic.

His stomach clenched as she pulled out the red pills that had been given to him years before. The ones he had not been able to use on her.

She slowly opened the bag and dropped the contents into her small hand. There was fear pulsing through her. He could feel it flowing from her as if it were his own. there was something else as well. Strength.

She made her way over to the black couch in the far corner of the room and sat on the edge of a cushion balancing the pills in her hand. She glanced towards his desk, her eyes settling on the bottle of liquor.

Understanding, he moved to the desk and filled the heavy crystal glass before carrying it back over to the couch. He took a sip and placed it next to her on the table.

Without warning she popped the pills in her mouth and reached for the glass, emptying its contents in one large gulp. The liquid burned as it went down, warming her from the inside.

When she finished, she placed the glass back on the table and turned to face Hunt. She moved into him, wrapping one of her arms across his chest and placed her head against his shoulder.

"Thank you for saving me," her soft voice cracked as she spoke.

"I was the only reason you ended up in that prison," he said staring up at the ceiling.

She looked up, his eyes coming to rest on her face. She couldn't help but see the man that rescued her.

"You are the only reason I escaped."

A heavy lump sat in his throat, as he tried to speak but stopped.

"Bring my body to the committee. They'll hold true to her promise about bringing in the rebel leader." Her voice grew soft. "With Vie dead you will be made Chancellor. You were her most trusted advisor. Nobody is going to forget that."

"Okay," he said through a constricted throat.

The pills were already taking effect. She could feel it. Unable to keep her eyes open any longer she slowly let her lids fall.

She relaxed into Hunt's warmth, his hand making slow lazy trails up and down her arm. She breathed deep, inhaling the intoxicating mixture of aftershave and soap. The scent calmed her. It was the same smell she had noticed when he had rescued her. When she had been "saved."

Eve finally opened her eyes as warm beams of light touched her face. Inside a feeling of peace moved through her, a feeling she had not known since childhood. As she looked around, she noticed a brilliant glow that seemed to flow out of everything. Like a thin gold coating from Midas himself.

In the distance a small grouping of deer grazed, while two young fawns pranced playfully about. As she watched the beauty of the scene unfold, her mind drifted back to her friends at the camp, to Hunt, their true leader, and to the future she knew he would build.

L. B. Winters grew up in a small town in upstate New York where she spent the majority of her early days reading, writing and exploring the beautiful forests surrounding her home. After living in NYC for a couple of years she moved back to the country, a place she still loves to explore. Laura currently works as a registered nurse and spends her free time running her book blog "Balancing Books and Bottles" and pursuing her lifelong dream of becoming a full-time author. You can find her on Instagram at
www.instagram.com/ellebwinters

HETEROCHROMIA

By Mikhaeyla Kopievsky

Ella shoved her fists into her pockets, fighting the itch to claw out the coloured contact lens that felt like sandpaper against her right eye. Her blue eye; the one that marked her as Primi. As hunted.

The streets of Anders weren't crowded, the deep snow drifts and biting cold enough to keep most people home, but the EyeSpy drones still hovered overhead, so she endured the discomfort and kept walking. In the early evening light, with the sky a swathe of grey and purple, the city seemed softer. Gentler. Like a muted, slumbering beast hulking down against the snow and easing into hibernation.

A deep, low rumbling grew too close. Ella looked over her shoulder as a dark truck sped along the road, skidding over the ice and splashing freezing water over her uniform. Curses sprung to her lips, but died on her tongue—the truck was long gone and she was as much to blame for her icy, muddy clothes as the idiotic driver. Civi ears would have picked up the sound of the truck advancing much earlier, Civi reflexes would have been quicker to jump out of the way, Civi disposition would be more resilient against such a minor inconvenience. And maybe, for a Civi, it would be a minor inconvenience—their engineered biomechanics designed to be invulnerable to changes in temperature and minor injuries. But to Ella, it felt as though dead, cold hands gripped her calves and talons of ice dug into her skin.

She rushed the rest of the way home, past the empty concrete playgrounds and utilitarian brick buildings plastered with posters of Civi soldiers and their 231 insignias, no longer caring that the snow sploshed around her ankles and further drenched her pants. She was miserably cold already, the only thing that would help would be the rickety old oil heater that Papa turned on as her shift ended—enough time to make their apartment toasty without wasting precious fuel.

"You're early," he exclaimed as she entered the apartment and banged the door shut. "And wet."

"Has it arrived yet?" she asked, ignoring his fussing, and heading to their small laundry. She stripped off her uniform and threw it into the sink. The artificial lens scraped along her eyeball as she plucked it out, her fingertip appearing brown under its flimsy polymer, before she deposited it into the compact of saline solution. Out in the living area, Papa had turned on the radio and the sound of old-time waltzes floated through the flimsy walls.

Washing her face in the small porcelain sink, she turned away from her reflection in the cracked mirror, from the defect that would always put her and Papa at risk. Her faded blue jeans and soft, cotton pullover were already stacked on the benchtop, warmed by the hot water bottle Papa had hidden underneath. She dressed quickly, her skin tingling at the warmth and the smell of spiced oranges and chlorine.

"It's too soon for a reply," Papa said, handing her a mug of steaming kaf as she stepped into the kitchen. "Our last communication was only a week ago. Things take time. And we need to be careful."

She took a sip of the kaf and sat down at the table. The hot liquid was sweeter than the sludge they served at the factory; Papa always made it with extra milk. That was the difference when you were more than just a number to someone—they spent more than they could afford on you; time, effort, money. Spent more. Risked more.

"We're running out of time," she said quietly, not bothering to voice what they both already knew—the last artificial lens was rapidly losing its integrity and once it failed, there would be no hiding her true nature, or hiding from the execution chamber. "Why do we have to wait? Why can't we just go to them?"

"Because we don't know who they are anymore. Or where they are." He was more patient than she. Always so much calmer.

Maybe it was his Civi nature. "Jonas will contact us when it's safe. For now, we must wait."

***

The concrete slab of the factory floor pushed the chill through Ella's boots and up her calves. Her fingers, stiff and sore, struggled to manipulate the steel screw into place. Surreptitiously, she rubbed her hand on the stiff cotton of her uniform, trying to warm it and restore enough dexterity to get through the rest of her shift.

"Worker 43," her supervisor yelled across the factory floor. Quickly, she dropped her hands back to the bench. "Your output is slipping."

Ella turned and looked up at the small monitor above her workspace, her output number flashing angry and red in a sea of green around her. Carver would think she was being lazy or insubordinate. She was neither of those things, she just lacked the fine-tuned capabilities of her Civi colleagues, with their bodies engineered to optimal effectiveness.

"Sorry," she mumbled, pushing her numb fingers to work faster.

"Sorry does not erase the past four incidences of sub-optimal performance," he said, scribbling away in his notebook. "This is your last warning."

The threat of performance management would be uncomfortable for anyone, but for Ella it was a fire brand to her chest. "Yes, sir," she stuttered, eyes cast down and finger painfully threading bolts onto screws. Carver nodded, returning the notebook and pen to his shirt pocket and walking away.

Around her, the factory continued humming along in its regular rhythm of activity. Massive conveyor belts pushed steel behemoths from one end of the floor to the other, grey-clad workers hauling oversized gears and plates to the assembly line, golden sparks flying where metal clashed with metal. The war effort on the northern front showed no signs of slowing down; for decades it had proven itself a titan with an insatiable appetite—for resources, for bodies, and for perfection.

The cramps in Ella's hands intensified, pulsing like the lights in her and Papa's apartment when the electricity supply became patchy. She ignored them, and the cold, and the deadened muscles in her legs from standing too long. *Pin, fasten, screw, tighten, push. Pin, fasten, screw, tighten, push.*

The blades of the fan shone bright under the factory lights. Wicked things with sharpened edges to cut through the metal of the enemy's artillery. Until the enemy's technology evolved again, and the factories stepped up production of the next defence system.

An unexpected sensation of warmth at her fingers sharpened her attention. She stared at the blood dripping onto the metal blade, and then at the index finger on her right hand where the tip had been sheared off.

"Medic," the worker next to her yelled.

Carver looked over, his eyes widening at the blood still dripping to the fan and workbench. "Medic to section 4," he patched into the transmitter at his shoulder.

"I'm fine," she mumbled. "It's—" The pain hit like a suckerpunch. Her knees threatened to buckle and she grabbed the bench to steady herself. The pain flashed bright and hot, stealing her breath and clouding her sight with ink stains. Pressure was building in her ears, a low whistle growing more shrill.

Stay upright. Stay upright. Stay up—

***

Bright light broke through the darkness, like pins pressing into her brain. Ella blinked open her eyes, squinting against the harsh whiteness.

Someone hovered nearby, their footfalls lost amongst the beeping and whirring of strange machines.

She blinked again, bringing the room into focus. The infirmary was a small space; barely large enough for the three beds pushed up against one side and a long white credenza awkwardly positioned against the opposite wall and cluttered with medical supplies.

Belatedly, she looked down at her hand, a thick wad of gauze in the place where her fingertip used to be, a catheter jutting from her wrist and leading to a thin, clear tube.

"Don't pull at it." A nurse stepped into view, his white uniform as bright and clean as everything else in the room. The machine beeped as he pressed buttons and flicked tubes. "The doctor is on his way now to assess you." The machine beeped again. "If I could just get this stupid machine to work," he muttered.

Ella laid very still. It wasn't the machine that wasn't working properly.

"The doctor is on his way now?"

The nurse mumbled something, fixated on the diagnostic machine.

"I need to go to the bathroom," she said louder. "I think I'm going to vomit."

"Here." He grabbed a metal bedpan and handed it to her.

The machine continued to beep. Ella, light-headed and queasy, flitted her gaze from the pan to the nurse to the door. There were no good options, but some were better than others.

Gripping the pan in her hands, she brought it up closer as if she were about to heave, and then smashed it into the side of the nurse's head. He stumbled a little and she struck again, wincing at the blood that spurted from his nose. There was a brief sting as Ella pulled the catheter from her wrist and leapt from the bed. The nurse stared up at her in horror, his hands dripping blood as he tried to staunch the flow from his busted nose and lip.

The bed pan, still gripped tightly, hung heavy in her hands. She should hit him again—it would give her more time—but her gut twisted with guilt. With his hands still up around his head, his keys and transmitter dangled in full view at his waist. Indecision was not a luxury she could afford. She advanced quickly with the bed pan and yanked at his belt, the transmitter dislodging easily, but the keys stubbornly resisting her grip, snagged on something she couldn't see. Swearing, she dropped the bed pan, and ran.

The space outside the infirmary was empty. Ella switched off the transmitter and tossed it in the nearest bin. She could hear the nurse begin to yell, his hoarse shouts warped and mangled. Ignoring the hammering of her heart, she raced to the fire exit and pushed open the heavy door gummed closed by years of grime and inactivity.

Her hand was throbbing as she exited the building two flights down. The fire escape had led her to the back of the factory, away from the street. She used it to her advantage, avoiding the drones and darting across the car lots of adjacent residential buildings with her hand stuffed into her uniform to avoid leaving a trail of blood in the snow.

***

"Early again?" Papa exclaimed as she barged into their cold apartment. The little heater sat silent and frigid in the corner. His eyes dropped to the growing dark patch at her midsection, where her injured hand lay hidden, and his calm demeanour finally slipped.

"Ella!" He rushed to her, his fingers gentle as he unbuttoned the shirt and pulled her arm free.

"I'm okay," she said. "Papa, I'm okay—just a flesh wound. But they know something is wrong with me, and they'll be looking for me."

He nodded sadly and peered deep into her eyes. With a gentle press of his lips against her forehead, he slowly lowered her hand to her side. "We must hurry, then."

It took them not more than ten minutes to get what they needed; Papa grabbed their meagre savings from the air vent, a few handfuls of dirty notes and the gold chains left behind after his mama had passed. Not that she had been his biological mama—like all Civis, he had grown up with guardians, not parents. Not like she had.

The money and jewellery he stuffed into a secret pocket of his briefcase, her Civi papers and a change of clothes for the two of them placed neatly in the main compartment. Ella changed quickly, her jeans and pullover from yesterday still clean. Papa wrapped her hand more tightly with a strip of cotton towel and gave her an analgesic to help with the pain.

"Jonas will help us find the surgeon," Papa whispered as he ushered her out of the apartment. "Everything will be alright."

***

The car rattled along the backwater streets, the snow chain clinking loudly as the car hit uneven patches of road and struck debris lurking under finer layers of snow. The air conditioner and radio stayed switched to their off positions to conserve fuel, so the two of them shivered in silence as the icy wind snuck through the vents.

"I wish we would have had more time to prepare," Papa murmured.

"We have what we need."

"I wanted to stockpile more painkillers for you. And now with your hand…"

"It will be fine, Papa."

"Perhaps the surgeon will have something, to stave off any infection. Perhaps even something that can serve as a prosthetic…"

She stayed silent. Her father was a smart man; he knew that the cornea transplant was not a guaranteed success and was always cautioning her of the same thing. He would know that even a successful transplant would not be a reset button. There could be no return to the little apartment; no going back to the factory, no living the simple dreams of just surviving as part of the war machine so she could go home to her Papa and the small comforts of warm clothes and spicy-sweet kaf.

She stayed silent as a small mercy.

Let him have his hopes. They will be dashed soon enough.

"I'm sorry," she mumbled. If she had been more careful, more focused…

"No, Ella," he said vehemently, shaking his head. "This is not your fault."

"I was too distracted, too clumsy, too reckless." *Too Primi.*

"It is not your fault." He rested a hand on her knee and patted it, smiling sadly. "It is mine. And your mother's. We were the reckless ones."

Ella startled. It had been years since Papa had spoken of her mother; some cuts stayed deep no matter how much time passed.

"But," he said firmly, "I would not change it. Not for anything—not the promise of one more day, not for *anything.*"

He turned back to the road, his knuckles white on the steering wheel. Eventually he sighed, and his body seemed to slump about him, as if the icy coil of stress inside had collapsed into a pool of melted snow. "You see, you were our act of defiance and rebellion."

"When I was little," he said, "younger than you are now, the war was only a decade old and the idea of a Civi-only generation was, for many people, unthinkable. Before then, Civis like me were something to prop up the natural population, foisted upon good patriots like my guardians to raise. We were meant to supplement Primis, not replace them. When the Government floated the idea of a sterilisation program, it almost divided the nation."

Resolution 234. The government-sanctioned eradication of Primis. Their first step in creating a race of invulnerable superhumans designed to win an unwinnable war.

"My great-grandfather hated everything about it. I was old enough to know him before he died; they say that Primis are inferior, built to break early, but he lived to one-hundred-and-two. In the months before he died, he would argue with my father constantly about Resolution 234. 'Humanity can only be borne of love,' he'd say. 'Robots will only create robots.' He never agreed with my father's decision to raise a Civi, but the thought of anyone voting for a sterilisation program incensed him.

"After the resolution passed, he would sit with me at his kitchen table, like we do now, and tell me about the old ways. The old world. He would point to scars, long spidery lines on his wrinkly skin, and tell me how he got them. And he would say to me, 'these scars aren't flaws, Henry. They aren't something ugly to be wished away or erased. They are stories, evidence of our choices, signs of our humanity. They are beautiful.'"

Ella stared at him, mesmerised by the story and the love and melancholy that ran through it. Papa never spoke about the past and she had never pressed him on it.

"On the night before my sterilisation, he met me after school. He and my father no longer spoke—*'politics divides families'*—so he would find me in the park or playground just to see me, to ask about my life. 'Tomorrow is a big day for you, Henry. Are you nervous?' I was worried he was going to start another argument, pick up with me where he and father had left off. But he just handed me some boiled lollies. 'For tomorrow morning, before you leave the apartment,' he said. 'They'll help with the nausea.'

"He didn't have to tell me not to tell Father, I'd always kept our visits secret. And he was a pharmacist as a young man, had always given me home-made remedies, even though my Civi body didn't need them. But that was the thing about him, he was always so

112

good to me—supportive, gentle, earnest—taking his remedies was a kindness to him."

"He stopped the sterilisation?"

Papa eased the car to the side of the road and switched off the ignition. Without the hum of the engine or rattling of chains, there was only the sound of their breathing. It was a while before Papa looked at her, and when he did, he did not meet her eyes.

"No," he murmured. "That is the ending I wanted for this story. What I wanted to be able to tell you. I've told it to myself for years, have almost come to believe it, even though I've never spoken it aloud until today." He looked up at her. "The sterilisation worked as it should. The only thing my great-grandfather changed was my understanding, my perspective. He made me compassionate, he made me appreciate our humanity, he made me understand that true beauty comes from our flaws, that we are perfect in our imperfections."

Ella pressed a hand to her stomach, trying in vain to hold back the sudden nausea and claustrophobia. "Papa?" she whispered.

He smiled sadly. "I *am* your Papa. I'll always *be* your Papa, just like my father will always be my father. Our connection is a bond that will never be severed. But it is not a genetic bond, Ella. And I am sorry—" His voice broke and he scrubbed at his eyes. "Oh, Ella, I am so sorry I never told you. You have been the best thing to have ever happened to me. I have loved you from the moment your tiny hand gripped my finger. I had planned on telling you when you were old enough to understand, but…"

But there is never a good time to tell someone you are not their father.

"And Mama? Did…" *Did you lie about her too?*

"I knew her only for a short time. She was not much older than you when I found her hiding in the basement of our old apartment building. She had run away from a secret commune the objectionists had set up somewhere in the mountains. You were only a few weeks old and both of you were weak and sick…"

He lapsed into a silence she didn't break. There were no more questions; she knew the rest of the story. A few months later the Government had picked her mother up, her growing chest infection too noticeable to be hidden. There were two types of Primis they hunted--those born before the Resolution and those with a fatal error, an RNA malfunction that remained hidden until something triggered its manifestation. Not knowing about the commune, they had assumed she was RNA defective. And they had killed her.

Just like they would kill Ella.

"I couldn't save her," Papa said, his voice grown tired and soft. "But I will save you Ella. I promise. I will save you."

***

They met Jonas in an abandoned shed a half-mile down a dirt road off the highway hidden by trees. Papa had left their car two miles away in a hospital carpark, and he and Ella had trudged through snow the rest of the way. By morning, the fresh snow would cover their tracks.

"You shouldn't have come here." Jonas' eyes twitched nervously and his hands pulled and smoothed the frayed ends of his woollen jumper. The three of them sat on wooden pallets stacked in the middle of the room and covered with scratchy hessian sacks, Jonas on one, Papa and Ella sharing the other.

"We have no time left," Papa said. "We need to see the surgeon."

"I told you I would contact you. Things need to be in place before it can go ahead." He looked from Papa to Ella, scratched at his arms, shifted on his pallet. "We don't know if she is compatible."

Papa reached down and grabbed Ella's hand. He squeezed it gently and didn't let go. "She will die in any case. The surgery is our only hope."

"The surgeon will not like it. She is not one to be told where to be and when to be there. These are dangerous times. We need to be more careful."

"But it can be done?" Ella asked.

"It is too reckless. The surgery is never in the same place. There are government raids every other month. We haven't tested you for the anaesthesia. You should wait."

"We don't need to involve you, Jonas," Papa said gently. "I understand that you have already risked enough. Just tell us where the surgery was the last time and we will go alone."

"But it may not be there."

"It's a risk we'll take."

Jonas sighed loudly, spittle flying from his lips. "Fine. But you will need someone to go with you. Someone the surgeon trusts. I'll send Thadeus with you."

***

The makeshift surgery was only a block away from the hospital. Thadeus walked ahead of Ella and Papa, his gait awkward and self-conscious. He was younger than she had expected, only a year or two older than herself, and just as twitchy as Jonas. He paused briefly at the entry of an old apartment building and then ducked inside so quickly it was as if the building had swallowed him. With its cancer-ridden façade and rusted rebar poking out at strange angles, it could not be long before it was condemned.

Ella recalled memory fragments of the first building she saw demolished. It had been summer and crowds of people lined the lake, the water uncontaminated and still blue under a cloudless sky. There had been a fair—clowns walked on stilts, carrying coloured balloons that floated in the breeze, and hawkers meandered through the crowds with their paper bags full of hot popcorn, the smell of salty butter and charred corn making her mouth water. The cloud of smoke had appeared without fanfare and she had been disappointed

115

to think this great spectacle had been reduced to a small, grey puff of dust. And then the noise exploded around her, rippling across the lake in waves and sending birds squawking from the trees. Debris had rained down from the sky, launched like so many stones from the slingshot she kept under her pillow. Except they were not stones, but chunks of concrete and metal. Three people died that day, struck down by an obliterated past. Papa didn't take her to demolitions after that.

"Are you feeling okay?" Papa murmured to her as they climbed the stairs of the dilapidated building.

"Yes," she lied. "Just a little cold."

He shrugged out of his jacket and handed it to her. "They won't let me be with you in the surgery room. The risk of infection is already too high."

She nodded and pulled the jacket tight around her, relishing its warmth and the scent of her Papa that lingered in the threads.

"Ella?"

"Yes, Papa?"

"I will miss your one-brown-one-blue eyes."

She paused on the stairs and smiled at him, letting his arms wrap around her and hold her in a fierce embrace.

"It will still be me afterwards."

"I know." He relaxed his embrace, his arms lingering for a few extra moments before they fell limp at his side.

Ella reached up and pulled the coloured lens from her eye, blinking a few times to relish the feeling of freedom and comfort that came from removing her armour. He looked up and brushed a hand over her temple, staring into her mismatched eyes.

"I love you, Ella."

She smiled at him, secured the lens back into position and pressed a kiss to his cheek. "I love you too, Papa."

***

It was eerily quiet as they walked the final two flights of stairs, their footsteps thudding too loud no matter how slowly they ascended. The corridor's plaster walls were water damaged; dark patches and bulging sheets cast strange shadows under flickering lights. Ella glanced at Papa; he had aged a century since they'd left their little apartment in Anders Central.

Halfway down the corridor, Thadeus stood waiting for them beside a plain brown door with its handle on the left side instead of the right.

"Have you got the money?" he asked Papa.

Papa nodded to Ella and she pulled the envelope of notes from his jacket pocket and handed it to the boy. "There's extra in there," Papa said, "to pardon the inconvenience."

Thadeus grunted and gripped the envelope tight, turning it into a grotesque paper bowtie in his meaty grasp. With his free hand he rapped on the door.

She didn't hear the door behind them open, only saw her papa swivel around. Before she could turn to see what had caught his attention, something heavy collided with her, pushing her off-balance and slamming her into the wall.

"You Civi bastards can't do this to me!" Papa yelled.

Gasping for breath on the linoleum floor, Ella could see him surrounded by four uniformed officials, each of them throwing punches to try and subdue him. Papa was transformed; his mild demeanour shed like a tree's leaves in autumn, something rabid and feral unleashed. Sickening blows rained down on him, bending him over and splitting his skin. He swung back almost lazily, hiding his Civi superiority in an effort to appear Primi. She scrambled to get up and go to him.

He knelt on the floor, holding himself up with one arm while his other covered his face to avoid more blows. She looked around for Thadeus and caught the final glimpse of him running to the stairs. Her chest tightened at the betrayal. Had this meeting always been doomed?

She pushed away from the wall, her heart a heavy rock in her chest. As if knowing she was close, Papa turned and looked at her, his eyes wild and bright and his busted lip forming one simple syllable. *Run.*

Her mind rejected the silent order. She would not leave him, would not let these brutes damage him any further. And then logic caught up; only her presence would condemn him. Without her, they could not convict him of anything—he was no Primi. If she left, he would stop fighting and submit. He would live.

The same panic that had assaulted her in the factory's infirmary clawed at her insides. She fixed her mismatched eyes on her father one last time—*I love you, Papa*—and she ran.

***

The car was still in the hospital carpark when she arrived. Her hand trembled as she pulled the key from Papa's jacket and jammed it into the ignition. The car roared to life with a vitality that mocked her, and through eyes blurred with unshed tears, she pulled out onto the street. In the rear-view mirror she watched the ugly apartment building grow smaller and smaller until it had disappeared completely from view. Only then did she allow the sobs to escape from her chest; strangled, tortured wails that rained hot tears down her cheeks and set fire to her right eye. She pulled angrily at the offending lens, the polymer tearing under her rough handling and triggering a fresh avalanche of tears.

She drove for hours until the car gasped its last breath; both she and it were spent—it of fuel, her of tears. For the longest time she stood there, her legs growing numb in the cold, her eyelashes setting like concrete with the residue of tears turned to ice. Leaving the car behind was a final farewell she was not ready to utter.

The light had disappeared in the overcast evening and the mountains on the horizon loomed like monsters ready to devour her. In the growing darkness, the car appeared to her as any other, and finally she was able to turn from it.

There was no sensation of cold as she trudged through the snow. Cold had lost its power hours ago; like eyes that grew accustomed to the night, her body no longer felt the pins and needles of the biting chill. But, every few minutes, like a nervous tic, her hand flew up to her face and pressed against her right eye. From her earliest memories, the coloured lenses had been her armour, and for just as long, Papa had cultivated a healthy fear of forgetting them.

'They itch, Papa.'

Papa looked over at her from the sink, his hands soapy and cradling a chipped plate. 'All things that restrain us, itch. All people chafe against the rules of someone else.'

She clenched her hands under the table. 'But, the lenses itch.'

'Do you know what itches more?'

She shook her head; in that moment she couldn't imagine anything itchier than the flimsy polymer lens that felt like a shard of glass embedded in her eye.

'Handcuffs, Ella. A hangman's noose. Scabs from where the skin has been whipped into a bloody pulp. Those things are itchy. Your lenses are a safety net.'

Her knees were wet. Belatedly, she realised she was kneeling in the snow. Her brain yelled at her to stand up, and she could see herself doing just that—pressing her palms into the drift, forcing her muscles to contract and spring, lifting herself from the frozen ground—but the sensation rolled away from her; like a dream about waking, real and yet not real at the same time.

Her mind was drifting. She caught it slipping away from her and tried to pull it back, but it ran like one of the fish Papa had hooked on his fishing line that time at the river.

'Why is it swimming away, Papa?' Her skin was warm under the sun and her pinafore smelled of the vanilla ice cream that had melted and dripped down her chubby, childhood fingers.

'Because it doesn't want to get eaten.' He held the rod securely, but looked away from his battle to flash her a smile. His skin was golden and his eyes sparkled blue like the sun-bathed river. She wished, not for the first time, that her lens was for her left eye; that, in her pretense, she had two blue eyes just like her papa.

'Then why does it come so close to your hook?' she asked.

'Because it wants to eat.'

The snow caressed her cheek, the drift like a pillow. Her body was shivering, but not the rapid shivers that came after a cold shower or stepping into a cold wind. It shivered like the fish had shivered that afternoon on the riverbank; in slow, laboured gasps, scales glinting as its gills flared open in search of water that lay just out of reach.

'But there is food all along the river! Midges and minnows. Why does it risk your hook for the promise of a measly worm?'

'Nothing can deny its true nature forever. It can ignore it for a while, avoid it, fight it. But chasing the hook is not so much succumbing to temptation as it is living a truth. Even if that truth is fatal.'

***

Warmth tingled in her bones. She tried to open her eyes, but they were still so heavy with exhaustion. Around her, she heard the shuffling of feet and murmured voices. The panic that gripped her chest wasn't the sharp, bright blade she had felt in the corridor outside the makeshift surgery; it was dull and colourless. Weariness and defeat had robbed her of what little fight she had left.

"Kill me."

Something prodded her chest, blunt and insistent. She flinched in anticipation of the gunshot.

120

"Mama! Mama!" a shrill voice called. "She's waking up!"

"Fallon, leave be."

"But there hasn't been a new one in forever. And she's the prettiest of them all."

A hand pressed against Ella's forehead. "Easy there; you're safe, now. Can you open your eyes for me?"

Curiosity pricked in the darker corners of her mind, but she couldn't prise her eyelids open. A wet, rough cloth wiped away the sleep that glued her eyelashes together. There was nothing keeping her eyes shut now. Nothing, except her fear.

"It's okay. Rest now. When you're ready, we can talk." Soft hands brushed away the hair on her forehead. "You don't need to be scared, here; we've stayed hidden from Civis for years. They can't get you here. You don't need to hide who you are."

***

Ella drifted in and out of consciousness; at times waking to strange noises and hushed conversations, at others to nothing but a deep and unending silence. There was no way to tell how much time had passed, or whether she lived half-conscious in a fever dream.

When she finally opened her eyes, the world was not the one she knew. Candlelight flickered in niches carved into cave walls, and pallets, like the ones at Jonas' shed, lay tied together in makeshift beds. A small girl, no older than five, sat nearby, regarding Ella curiously. Her red hair fell messily about her dirt-stained face, and her hands fidgeted clumsily in her lap, the left hand missing two of its fingers. She was flawed, more flawed than Ella, and she was beautiful.

"Primi," Ella whispered.

The girl startled and leapt up, racing from the cave.

On shaky legs, Ella stood to follow her. The cave was small and the scent of wet earth filled her nostrils, recalling memories of walking with Papa to the cemetery to lay daisies beneath the headstone of his mother and father.

Papa. The thought of him flicked a switch in her mind, making everything seem too small, too vast, too loud, too empty.

She pushed on through the cave network, bare feet tingling at the touch of the cold stone floor, searching for glimpses of the girl and getting lost in the maze of possible pathways.

Ahead, the light shifted from the soft flickering of candles to something brighter and warmer. The sound of rushing water echoed against the rock walls, calling her forward. Without preamble, the cave opened up to the sky as if the hand of God had punched through its ceiling. A river carved its way through the dark rock, twisting and glittering under a rare moment of unclouded sky.

In the circle of light, a lilac tree grew tall and spindly, its boughs bending to water that pooled and fell calm in an oxbow lake. She sat under its branches and dangled her feet in the icy water. So still, the lake was a mirror, and in it she saw her true reflection; her one-brown-one-blue eyes shining with sadness and gratitude. She shivered and raised her head to the blue sky above, whispering with exultation in her heart, "I am safe, Papa."

Mikhaeyla Kopievsky is an Australian speculative fiction author who loves writing about complex and flawed characters in stories that explore identity, loyalty, betrayal, and rebellion. She is the author of the *Divided Elements* series, a dark dystopian trilogy set in a future Paris where identities are engineered and assigned. Her short stories have appeared in anthologies and longlisted for the EJ Brady Prize.

Born in Sydney, Mikhaeyla now lives in the Hunter Valley with her husband, son, two rescue dogs, four Australorp chooks, a hive of cantankerous bees, and the occasional herd of beautiful Black Angus steers.

Sign up to her newsletter for exclusive content, early access to works in progress, and amazing giveaways. You can also follow her on bookbub to get alerts on book sales and new releases.

Wings

By Emily Pirrello

"Claramond, it's time to get up."

As she rolled over, her ancient mattress springs whined in harmony with her sigh of exhaustion. Wrapping herself deeper into her threadbare duvet cover, Claramond responded with a groan. Her wooden door creaked. Her mother's heavy steps pressed down on Claramond's patchy hardwood floor. Martha circled around the bed to draw back the curtains. The residents of Abaddon never experienced sunshine, when they looked up all they saw were stagnant grey skies. Reaching for the security of her duvet, Claramond was met with warm callused hands.

"Not today Claramond, you know how important this day is for your father."

The mention of her father caused her to turn rigid. Suddenly triggered, she could no longer enjoy the innocence of her worn-out bed. Claramond's father was the leader of their small commune. Daniel Demagogue was both feared and worshiped by the occupants of Abaddon.

The residents of Abaddon never could quite look Daniel in the face. He didn't have an off-putting appearance per say, but those who have more than glanced at Daniel shudder at the blueness of his features. His eyes were cold. Not his irises, those were dark as coal, but it was his sclera that was shaded blue. His curt thin lips resembled those of a man six feet below the earth.

"Be ready in fifteen minutes, I ironed that nice dress Mema made for you. It will look so lovely with your new chapel veil I picked up in town this week."

Great. Who doesn't love sporting overelaborate attire in front of the entire populace of Abaddon?

124

Her morning temper did not justly express her true spirits concerning her Mema's creations. Claramond quite enjoyed her Mema's personal handiworks.

After washing her face and completing the rest of her hygienic morning practices, Claramond retreated back to the solidarity of her barren bedroom. She stood in front of her fractured full-length mirror to add the final touch of her Sunday garb, her mother's newly purchased chapel veil. The currency of Abaddon was avarus, circular hammered bits of silver. The majority of the population lived in poverty but the Demagogue's were able to afford certain superfluities due to Daniel's title. Claramond analyzed her reflection. Her golden hair hung in loose ringlets down past her thin frame. The intricate ivory crochet hem of Mema's emerald green cotton dress accentuated Claramond's fair skin.

She was quite tall for her age of fifteen and surpassed most of the boys in her division long ago. Though, Momma did say it would be soon enough when the neighborhood boys would shoot up like beanstalks and Claramond would no longer feel so out of sorts. For Claramond, it wasn't just her lanky appearance that made her feel so disconnected from her peers. Her father being the leader of their community made it so none of the other children would speak with her.

She couldn't blame them; everyone knows what happens to those who cross Daniel Demagogue… they never show up for church the following Sunday.

Claramond, admiring the craftsmanship of her Mema's design, held each hand on either side of the dress and did a slight twirl. As she turned her lanky shoulders showcasing her backside, she stiffened. She could see the red welts peeking through the top of her dress.

She sorrowfully sauntered over to her favorite item in her room, her Papa's old reclining chair. It had been the one thing Claramond had pleaded for after her grandfather's ascension. They were extremely close; Mema used to say that they were "cut from the same cloth." Her grandfather always looked after her when she was a child. When she was growing up, Abaddon was practically in full lockdown. She was too young to remember the severity of the communities' dismay, but within four months seven adolescent girls had disappeared. Curfews were set, children were exercising the buddy system to walk to and from lessons, and for a brief time the town was in shambles.

Claramond's father, being the pastor of the only church in Abaddon, held candlelight vigils and hosted search parties for the young girls. Claramond's grandfather had physically endured many injuries during his time in The Great Severance, so he was the one left with Claramond while her mother and father were working together with the town to find the girls.

Their quaint community, as conservative and pious as it was, had an unusual amount of missing children cases. The majority of the missing were adolescent girls, which allowed the Deistic Department a simple explanation when their investigations turned up empty: "apostasies." In private the residents of Abaddon had their own theories, all of which involved fornication as motive. Whether they left in shame of their sins or ran off to be with "the devil's advocates," there wasn't any evidence of possible foul play to continue investigating.

So as the town of Abaddon did with all of its unorthodox history, these cases were swept under the rug.

Claramond's mother never spoke up to her husband in their thirty-nine years of marriage, except right after her father's passing. Martha saw how desperate her daughter was to obtain her father's timeworn chair. Luckily, Claramond's father had spent one too many nights that week at the local tavern and had no choice but to oblige his mourning wife.

As she ran her long fingers across the tattered upholstery, her heart warmed to the thought of her Papa. She plucked her favorite knit cardigan off her grandfather's chair and covered up her insecurity, not ever wanting her scars to be seen. Claramond went back to the mirror and adjusted her newfangled veil to shield only the crown of her porcelain forehead.

"Claramond, it's time to go!"

"Coming, Momma!" she called back as she bent over to secure the buckles on her ivory Mary-Jane shoes. Claramond quickly gave herself a final onceover in the fractured mirror before heading out.

***

Claramond's pale grey eyes scanned the congregational crowd as her father addressed them.

"Good morning my dearest disciples, I hope you are all having a blessed Sunday morning."

The congregation praised and responded in unison. Although it was just past dawn, Claramond could feel the heat pulsating through the stained-glass window panes. Her cheeks began to flush as she inhaled and exhaled the warm chapel air. Using her program for a fan, she instantaneously earned several *tsks* from the elder women in the pew behind her. As she turned around to give her sincere apologies to the Weldman sisters, she was met by a subtle, cool, gust of wind. Claramond murmured a quick, "I'm sorry," and immediately turned to the source of the crisp breeze.

In all of her years of spending time in this run-down building, she had never felt external air run through the chapel. Generally speaking, the atmosphere inside the cathedral was rather stuffy. From a young age Claramond was told that when you open a passageway, whether it be a window-frame or a doorframe, you never know who will walk on in. Those in Abaddon believed that the devil would have the audacity to walk right on in if it seemed as though he was given an invitation. Which is why she was instantly alarmed by the coolness of the air.

In truth, Claramond was not as superstitious as the rest of the inhabitants were, but she couldn't help but feel on edge as goosebumps budded atop her skin. To her astonishment, she could not find the source of the breeze, and the stranger thing was that no one else seemed to be experiencing the temperature drop as she was. Beads of perspiration dripped down the foreheads of the mass of the

127

congregation. Claramond crossed her cardigan snugly across her chest as she felt a chill run down her spine, the hairs on the back of her neck shooting straight up.

"As much as I would like to keep this sermon light, today is not a day of cheerfulness but a day of unease. There is a new plague threatening the lives of our children."

The rather lighthearted mood that momentarily ago occupied the congregation promptly dissipated. The aged chapel was laden with silence. Claramond, accustomed to her father's ranting sermons decided she was not in the mood to hear which serpent threatened the innocence of the children this week and quietly left her pew to head towards the washroom. As she made her way towards the back of the church she was met with numerous disappointed eyes and murmurs.

Yes. What a sin, the preacher's daughter visits the restroom in the middle of Sunday Service.

"Our precious children are in danger. As you know, since The Great Severance decades ago we have not had contact with the miscreants beyond our borders. Our noble Deistic Department recently spotted movement outside our walls…"

Almost to the back doors, the pews erupt with cries and shrieks of terror. Claramond herself is startled as she feels a brash clamp clinging to her right arm. Looking to see who has grabbed her, Claramond meets the eyes of an elderly woman with a pinched face. "You best watch out child, the devil would love a pretty little number like you to call his own."

Releasing herself from the startlingly tight grip on her lower arm, Claramond stumbled back. Uncertain of an appropriate response she simply pressed her weight frontward onto the hefty timber doors to make her way towards the restroom.

The air is less dense in the parlor allowing Claramond to relax once more. She continues to head towards the unnerving basement stairs. In her younger years, Claramond would run down the decrepit staircase as quick as gunpowder. Although she is no longer that six-year-old girl with a vivid imagination, the church basement still gave her the heebie-jeebies.

The basement was deemed "off-limits" in prior years supposedly due to its unsecure foundation, but Claramond believed her father simply wanted his own private dwelling. She had seen him venture down into the cellar many times through the years. In truth, they did have an outhouse constructed once the basement was no longer accessible terrain, but she disliked the outhouse even more than the basement due to its taboo location. They built it adjacent to the crowded ascension grounds. She decided that the basement was the lesser of the two evils and continued onward. Reaching up to pull down on the metal string, an eerie glow illuminates the stairway. Exhaling deeply and placing her hand on the well-worn, unstable banister, Claramond descends into the cellar.

After using the antique restroom, she washed her hands in the deep, rusty barn sink. As she peered up into the dusty mirror, for a brief moment, Claramond could have sworn she saw movement behind her. Her heart rate began to quicken. Gripping onto the old vanity for support, she closed her eyes and counted to ten.

"I am okay. It is just my mind playing tricks, I am alone."

While stating her mantra, Claramond feels the mysterious cool breeze that she had experienced upstairs once more. Unable to keep her eyes pressed shut any longer, Claramond opened them and looked back into the mirror. Behind her stood a shadowy figure, similar in height and stature. Although she felt as though she were paralyzed, it was more so a feeling of shock that consumed her, not fear. She turned to face the figure, but the apparition swiftly vanished.

"Hello? Who are you? Where did you go?"

The bathroom door creaked open with no aid from Claramond. Tentative of what to do next, she turned off the faucet sink and followed her intuition. She searched the basement for any sign of movement for a few minutes, but all was still. Feeling as

129

though her supernatural encounter had come and passed, Claramond departed towards the run-down staircase.

"Do not leave us."

As a child, Claramond had always felt as though shadows were following her. The first time she brought it up her father beat her. After the same turnout each time, Claramond gave up defending her unusual sounds and sights. She only confided in her Papa, who shared with her that in a world so unsighted, she was one of the few who would truly "see." She never quite knew what to make of her Papa's declamations. As Claramond aged, her experiences lessened and she concluded that she simply had an over-active imagination and that her beloved grandfather was just trying to console her childhood qualms.

Removing her hand from the banister, Claramond turned around yet again was left wondering if she was delusional. As her eyes scanned the cluttered basement, light from a singular tiny window caught her attention. From a protruding nail hung a chain. Venturing over to inspect the glimmering item, Claramond realized it was not only a chain, but an ornamental skeleton key. She cupped the ominous trinket in her trembling hands and studied it closely. Although almost unnoticed at first glance, there seemed to be a crimson staining on the key. She pressed her dominant thumb into the cold worn metal, but was unable to remove the discoloration.

"Claramond! Is that you down there?"

She could hear the displeasure in her mother's distant voice. "Get up here right this minute, before your father realizes you defied his rules!"

"Coming, Momma!" She unlatched the necklace from the rusty spike and quickly sprinted upstairs.

"Claramond. You know how your father feels about anyone going down into the cellar."

Securing the door shut behind her, Claramond met her mother's anxious eyes. Martha placed her arm around her daughter's shoulders, and led them outside onto the front lawn where everyone was gathered to say their goodbyes.

Her father approached forebodingly.

Placing a firm grip on her left shoulder, he sneered through clenched teeth, "Where were you, Claramond?" The vein that ran across his stern forehead throbbed slightly, his jaw stiff.

"She was just tending to the lilies around back. I had asked her to make sure the garden was well watered since we've had quite a heat spell lately," Martha spoke hesitantly.

"Alright, make sure you inform me next time you give our daughter busywork. I want to follow up and make sure she doesn't do a sloppy job."

"Of course, Daniel. I am sorry."

As her father walked away to bid farewell to the people of Abaddon, Claramond stared up into her mother's blue eyes quizzically.

"Your father doesn't need to know about your little adventure this afternoon. Just be sure it doesn't happen again."

Claramond silently thanked her mother as her father found his way to those who wished to speak one-on-one with the pastor. She watched him go, moving her thumb against the key held tightly in her palm, but was still unable to remove the discoloration.

A sudden urge compelled her to wear the trinket herself. Her clammy hands undid the clasp and without difficulty she was able to put the necklace on. She felt a brief surge of energy spread across her chest and deep within her bones. The wind moved past, ruffling the crisping autumn leaves.

***

Hours later, sitting down at their dilapidated wooden table, Claramond and her parents ate their late breakfast in silence. The bland oatmeal and grits satisfied only her hunger, not her taste buds. Still frazzled by the confrontation in the morning, Martha accidently left the breakfast biscuits on the stove for too long. Though they typically resembled the color of fresh harvested corn, today they looked more like the dark and foul manure used to fertilize the local farms.

After Claramond finished washing her family's filthy saucers and silverware, she sat down at the table and fiddled her fingers around the trinket that adorned her neck.

"That is a lovely necklace darling, where did you get that? Was it an early budding gift from Mema?"

"I found it today, Momma."

"What do you mean you found…"

For the first time since reprimanding her outside the chapel, Daniel laid eyes on his daughter. His dark expression intensified as his eyes fixated on Claramond's neck. Her father's body went stiff, his large shoulders and chest pressed outward, just as a wild animal showing their dominance. He slammed his blue-tinted rough, monstrous hand onto the table with such might the overhead ceiling-fan shook. His fuming voice dominated their miniscule dining room.

"I told you to *never* go down there!"

Startled by her husband's roar, Martha's glass of homemade lemonade shattered into several pieces as it hit the unsympathetic black and white checkered tiles.

"It is as if the devil has been whispering in your ear since you were born."

Claramond was accustomed to the harsh lip her father was giving her. However, it generally came after a few drinks were in him. Her cheeks flushed crimson. Claramond was muzzled by the thick

132

raging hand of her father. Too familiar with the sound of her father's belt unfastening she grimaced. Clenching her teeth, she took the eight thrashings with a sense of acquaintance.

***

Claramond lay unclothed in the sanctuary of her bed. Although her wounds ached dreadfully, she felt a sense of enlightenment, she no longer felt so desolate and isolated. She spent hours alone in her bleak bedroom, soaking in her own sweat and blood. She dreamed of angels. She knew they were angels, though they looked nothing like her Sunday Service instructor had described. These girls were coated in dirt, their hair in knots pressed against their scalps with a dark red paste. They were battered and bruised; their faces were hallowed. Yet, she felt no fear by these new acquaintances, only an overwhelming sense of peace.

***

"Daniel, please, she has been running a fever for three days now. We have to take her to Dr. Herman!"

"Martha, there is nothing Dr. Herman can do to heal that child. Our Lord and Savior cannot even prevent this, Satan has already claimed her."

***

As the night went on, Claramond's mother sat fretfully at the bedside of her lethargic daughter. With her sacred writings clenched between her hands, in the wee hours of the night she was finally able to drift off to sleep.

Her mother awoke to the blood curdling sound of her daughter's screams. These piercing cries woke Claramond's slumbering father. Martha's screams soon joined the demonic shrieking. Unsure of what he would encounter, Daniel, cross in hand, swung open the door of his daughter's bedroom.

"What the…"

Claramond hovered over her blood-soaked bedding. Her exposed bare body was unnaturally arched and contorted. Where the once fresh whipping wounds sliced her juvenile back there were two

133

protruding wings. Blinding white feathers coated them, color so white and pure a radiant glow emanated from them. Surrounding Claramond's bed were seven adolescent girls, all of which bore diverse abrasions and gashes. Though these girls wore these injuries, they were luminously shimmering. They too sported wings of various shades of opal. The children reached out with their nimble hands, alleviating Claramond's agony.

An enraged invisible narrator filled only Daniel's ears. His ears began to bleed as he pressed his hardened hands against either side of his inverted blue body. Claramond's mother reached not for her husband, but her ascending daughter.

"This child shall no longer suffer under your coercion. You will no longer inflict pain on others. I am claiming, sweet Claramond, just as I prematurely had to claim all those girls. You shall no longer hide your demons Daniel Demagogue. The Brothers are coming..."

Emily Pirrello is a recent graduate of Montclair State University, where she obtained a B.A. in English with a Concentration in Creative Writing. Since childhood she has had such a strong passion for literature and the arts. She has always loved creating, from illustrations to iambic pentameter, Emily enjoys expressing her imagination through multiple mediums.

When she doesn't have her nose between the pages of a book, she also enjoys sunshine, spending time with her family, and 10-year-old papillon, Gizmo.

You can find her on Instagram at
www.instagram.com/emilypirrellowriter

The Bridge

By Ginny Young

"It's not going to work, Billie."

"Of course it will," she said from her place beside him, belly down on the gritty ground. "Have a little faith."

She peered over the pile of rubble at the bridge below. The hundred-foot expanse of metal and concrete was the only one left standing for a hundred miles. It spanned the chasm that ended in the inky blackness of the swift-moving river below. Every so often the surface of the water caught the light to reflect the rainbow swirls of the oily sheen floating on the surface, its colorful beauty mocking the fact that it was poison. No one knew what havoc had been wrought upstream to render it that way, but one thing was for sure: nothing that went into that river came back out again.

Kid wiggled between his two siblings, propping himself up on his elbows. "Yeah, Buck. They look stupid enough to me. It'll totally work."

The guards were stupid, yes, but deadly.

"Friggin' trolls." Buck toggled the dial on his binoculars but the men milling about on the bridge were clear enough with the naked eye from where Billie and the boys hid amongst the ruins at the top of the ridge.

Six today. Ugly, mean, muscled-up-thugs toting guns as ugly as their faces. Yesterday it had been four, but they'd been scouting for more than two weeks now and she knew the total was closer to twenty. Anyone not on the bridge was tucked underneath it in the makeshift shelter that housed the guards. Probably drinking, and fighting, and cleaning their guns. Billie watched the biggest man of the group convince one of his comrades to vacate the seat atop the barricade with the threat of a fist. He had to be the leader. Being a foot taller than the other men and at least a foot wider would be enough to set him apart even without the grizzly scar cutting down his face. He was the one they'd have to target if this was going to work.

"Come on." She shimmied far enough back to push herself up without being spotted before standing. "Our friend looks grumpy today, let's get out of here."

"You don't have to tell me twice." Buck stuck his goggles in the holder at his side and mimicked her retreat, pulling Kid to his feet after him. Watching her brother brush himself off and straighten his clothes was like watching herself. His sandy brown hair and tan skin matched hers exactly, and though his features were beginning to take on the hard lines of a man they still shared the same steel grey eyes, tinged blue today as they reflected the high clear sky. They'd often been accused of being twins, though she was two years his senior. Kid, the eleven-year-old cookie-cutter version of the two of them, pawed at her worn backpack for the water bottle. Ignoring the dust on her own tongue she let him drain it before they set off.

Her stomach growled as she led them back through the winding path that snaked through the Eastern blast zone. A picture in her mind of the stacks of food they'd gathered back at the hideout made her mouth water, but they couldn't eat that stuff. It was too important. It would be Mare's slop from the Chophouse again. Hopefully, the mediocre excuse for a meal would have something other than canned ham and oats in it today. Yesterday's bowl had been less than satisfying.

"Can we go to the Row tonight to eat? Maybe they'll be doing the dice game again!" Kid said.

She reached out to tousle his mussed hair. He was probably as hungry as she was. Although, she wasn't about to let him gamble even if he loved to watch. "Sure, bud. It'll be fun."

Buck snorted behind her but she ignored it. *Let the kid be excited about something. Heaven knows, there's not much to get excited about anymore.* She ran her hand over her pocket, feeling the outline of the coins nestled deep in the fabric of her tattered jeans. Not enough to last. Her plan had to work if any of them were going to survive. And it had to work soon.

The street that held the Chophouse was already crowded and bustling when they arrived. Warm light filled windows and spilled out of doors to paint the cracked pavement beneath their feet. The swathes of yellow on the ground brightened as the red sun sunk below the line of the mountains, ushering in another turbulent summer night in the cramped length of buildings that made up the Row. The half market, half housing domain was the core of the city, drawing the miserable inhabitants of the surrounding sector to it like moths to a porch light. Drunken laughter floated on the air, but most of the faces they passed were hard and grim.

Equal parts empathy and dread slashed through Billie's heart at the sight of a mother crouched in the gutter, attempting to comfort her dirty-faced toddler. The Row was full of hopeless people like that woman. Not everyone had it so bad. This part of the city had electricity and the shabby buildings lining the street provided better housing than most, if you could afford it, but not everyone could. She suspected the woman was one of the less fortunate, the ones who lived on the street. Makeshift shacks and lean-tos filled the spaces between buildings, housing the inhabitants too poor and afraid to venture out into the derelict parts of the city for shelter.

"Hey, what's going on over there?"

Kid's question pulled her attention away from the gaunt faces peeking out from the shadows of a nearby alley and back to the street. A crowd was gathered around a crude corral thrown up in the middle of the road. Her stomach dropped to her toes when she realized what was happening inside of it. Two naked women fought each other with blunt weapons, surely to the death. Why did it have to be tonight? Jeering laughter came from a cruel face standing above the crowd, egging them on. One of Kane's guards, she'd seen him at the bridge before. Just another brutal asshole having his fun at the expense of the inhabitants they held prisoner in this dirty excuse for a city. Things like this happened way too often, it was getting harder and harder to shelter Kid from seeing the horror.

As she grabbed his hand to pull him away from the nauseating sight a body came crashing between them. The man who had parted them jumped up as quickly as he'd fallen to return the punch that had knocked him over, swearing and swinging wildly. It was probably just drunkards fighting over a bet, but it took only seconds before the two men fighting had turned into four, then eight. Within moments the street had erupted into chaos.

Heart thumping in her chest, she searched for her brothers. She fought the panic rising in her throat as she locked eyes on Kid being swept into the blood-thirsty crowd. Pushing a pair of grappling bodies out of her way she snatched him from the current. One hand gripping Buck's shirt and the other wrapped around Kid's wrist, they ran in the opposite direction and ducked into the relative safety of the Chophouse. The commotion outside threatened to spill into the dingy gathering place but Mare was already at the door barring it behind them. The old woman's wrinkled brown eyes looked sad as she fastened the locks and positioned the heavy metal crossbar. An angry yell preceded the heavy thump of a shoulder being thrown against the door, but it held fast. Ignoring the tirade of voices on the other side, the old cook shook her head and wiped her hands on her apron as she turned back toward the counter.

"No one else gettin' in 'til things calm down. Can't have 'em busting everything up again." Mare's gnarled hand gave Billie's arm a squeeze as she hobbled past on her way back to her place behind the counter. "Sit down, darlings. I'll get you fixed up."

They tucked into a cracked leather booth in the back corner and sat in nervous silence as the sounds of violence escalated outside. Billie chewed half her nails off before she caught herself, a nervous habit she fell into when things got rough. That was too close for comfort. They were all going to die here if she didn't go through with her plan. It was the only way for survival. That thought took away a bit of the sting in her heart when she thought about what she was going to do to her brothers. *It's the only way.*

The bowls Mare brought them were full of yesterday's strange ham stew, but it was hot, and they were hungry enough to eat it anyway. For a moment she focused on nothing but filling her belly.

But the satisfaction was short lived as the sharp crack of gunfire sounded outside, sending a shot of dread coursing through her that threatened to bring everything she'd put down back up again. Not good. It was bad enough they were throwing their fists out there. When the guns came out, things always got ugly. Anyone stupid enough to shoot a gun in the city was pronouncing their own death sentence. Kane's boys would be out to claim it in minutes flat, likely leaving its previous owner's lifeless body laid out in the street for everyone to see. Must be a newcomer. Everyone knew that any weapons found in the city went to boost Kane's personal collection, adding more firepower to the barriers he used to keep everyone inside. Just like that stupid bridge. She wrapped her arms around Kid to quiet the soft sounds of crying at her elbow. He didn't deserve this garbage. Maybe they were all better off dead.

It was an hour before sunrise when they made it back to the derelict old factory building they called home. Kid had slept on the bench in the Chophouse, curled into a ball, his blonde hair falling over his peaceful face. But she and Buck had stayed awake, listening to the fighting outside until the sounds of the angry mob had lessened to the sounds of a busy street and then finally faded into silence. When the street was quiet, they'd made their way back out into the night, stealing into the darkness to avoid anyone who might still be looking for a fight. She wanted nothing more than to get home and collapse onto their old mattress, but she halted them across the street from the stark facade of the factory building looming in the dark. They must not be followed. If someone found their hoard the plan would be ruined and months of work would be lost. They'd never be able to gather that much stuff again. Caution was critical. When she was satisfied they were alone, they raced across the street and down the concrete stairwell that led to their shelter.

The abandoned electronics factory they sheltered in was a dark and empty maze of machines and wires that would have terrified her in simpler times, but she found herself sighing with relief once she'd bolted the door behind them. When did this start to feel like home? The boys were asleep the moment they were tucked in together, but her head whirled with thoughts despite her exhaustion. This wasn't a life. She knew what she had to do, even if it would hurt them. A single tear rolled down her cheek to sink into the scratchy top of the bare mattress. *It's the only way.*

Billie woke with a start, surfacing from a fleeting nightmare she did not attempt to remember. The sun was up but her sluggish mind and heavy limbs told her it was still early. Dust motes danced in the shaft of clear morning light streaming through the only window, a tiny glass square nestled into the top of the wall. The gentle breathing of her brothers told her they were still asleep. After last night they probably needed the extra rest, but she had things to do. Silently she slipped from Kid's side, careful not to wake him. The last element in her plan was so close to completion, but it had been days since she could slip away to work on it. If her brothers found out, she'd never be able to go through with it. Better to surprise them at the end. It would hurt less that way.

When she returned two hours later she could sense the frustration coming from Buck at her extended absence. His brows were drawn and his mouth was a hard line, his posture rigid where he sat forcefully turning the pages of a magazine he wasn't really reading. The bundle of papers slapped the table as he stood to face her.

"Where were you? You can't be sneaking off like that. You could disappear!" He scolded her like a parent, a burden usually reserved for herself.

"I had some stuff to do. I didn't even leave the building. I'm fine," she said.

"Whatever. Just don't do that, okay?" He scowled as he said it, but he slumped back down onto the metal chair, indicating that the fight was over.

Kid wandered over to wrap his arms around her. "Do we have to go out today? I'm hungry."

His eyes lingered on the stacks of boxes and cans piled in the corner. Maybe it was worth dipping into the pile today. Things were always tense in the city the day after a riot, and they didn't need any more trouble.

"Let's stay in today." She squeezed his shoulders. "Go pick something from the pile. Anything you want, bud."

He danced and whooped on his way over, putting a smile on her face. The box he chose was a sugar-laden travesty of the modern age but she didn't scold him. Let him have it. Who knows if it would be the last thing he ever tasted? Her choice from the pile was more sensible but she savored it all the same, rolling the granola around on her tongue before biting into the tangy crunch. They lounged the day away in their dingy basement storage room resting and talking. Inevitably the discussion came around to the plan. No matter how many times they'd gone over it there were always questions.

The folding chair beneath her whined when she shifted her weight to rest her forearms on the rough surface of the table. She was tired, the stress of past events and things to come weighing her down equally until she wanted nothing more than to cover her head with a dark blanket and never resurface. But it was only for a little longer. She had to be strong. Her brother's jaw flexed and he squeezed his threaded fingers together as he voiced the biggest flaw to the plan.

"Okay, say we do make it across. What's going to stop them from just killing us on the other side. You know what happened to Josh," Buck said.

She did know. The sight of his severed head stuck on a pole was burned into her memory forever. It was Josh who had given them the idea: pay the trolls for passage. Give them enough money or food and they'd let you slip out. They had huddled in their scouting spot above the bridge the day he had made his attempt. Everything seemed to be working, he had given the guards a sack of money, a pretty substantial sum by any account. They'd let him pass. He knew she and her siblings were watching and he'd given them a jaunty wave once he'd made it to the other side. Everything had gone perfectly, but the next day his tortured face adorned an eight-foot pole at the mouth of the bridge.

"I have a plan for that." She tried to make her voice sound confident. "Besides, you guys are fast. Josh probably didn't even think to run or hide. We've got that all worked out."

Lying to them was harder than anything she'd ever done, but they had to believe it would work or she'd never get them on that bridge. Buck thrust his legs forward and ran his hands through his hair.

"You keep saying you have a plan but you won't tell us! What the heck is it?"

She could hear the frustration in his tone. A stinging pain like a needle bit into her insides. They would never forgive her for what she was going to do, but she was elbow deep now. There was no way out of it. Pushing down the regret and sadness she gave him a reassuring smile. "Just trust me okay? I promise it will work."

It was a testament to their loyalty that he and Kid both nodded and the questioning stopped. She didn't deserve them. How could she go through with something that would hurt them so much? Stopping to think about the reality of what was going to happen made her insides twist and her stomach roil. She pushed the image from her mind and replaced it with a silent pleading for forgiveness to the boys at her side.

As she lay staring at the ceiling that night fighting tears, she made a decision. The anxious waiting had to be as bad as the real thing. It was time to do it, if only to stop the constant burning in her chest every time she thought about it. Besides, they weren't likely to find much more to add to the pile anyway. They'd searched every nook and cranny of every empty building within a ten-mile radius. Any farther out and they'd have to use the truck, and if they got the truck confiscated they'd never get all that stuff to the bridge. They would go tomorrow. Stuffing her emotions behind a brick wall, she ushered in the peaceful apathy that can only be found in total acceptance. The price for survival was high but it was worth it. She repeated those words in her mind, willing herself to believe them until she fell into a dark and fitful sleep.

They did not argue when she announced to them the following morning that the time had come. Maybe the waiting was torturing them as much as it was her, although for different reasons. It took no time to pack their meager belongings into their backpacks. Loading the truck took longer. Sweat dripped from her face and her legs ached by the time they got all the supplies up the stairwell. They loaded everything into the back of the old moving truck, including the flatbed carts they would need to transport everything once they got too close to drive. Everything was ready. Just one last thing to grab.

"You guys get loaded, I've got one last thing to grab!" She called as she darted back into the building and up the stairs to the room where she'd been working the last two months. She'd been going over and over in her mind how to hide her little surprise, not only from her brothers but from the guards too. In the end, she snuck it under a cardboard box and tucked it into the truck bed amongst the others. As long as she was the one to move it to the cart they wouldn't suspect. Buck and Kid were already buckled into the cab, groaning at her to hurry up, when she pulled herself into the driver's seat.

Within an hour they were parked on the outer fringes of the Eastern blast zone. Buck looked at her as she killed the engine, his green eyes serious.

"This is it. We could still take the stuff, and the truck, and run. But once we unload, that's it. No turning back."

They couldn't run. The roads out of the city were as heavily guarded as their current route, but at least they knew there was life on the other side of the bridge. She'd seen the twinkling lights herself, a sure sign of civilization. No one could confirm there was anything more than desolation past the western border. It was a chance she wasn't willing to take.

"No turning back," she said, forcing a smile, "let's get busy."

Loading the goods onto the carts seemed to take far less time than loading them onto the truck had. Or maybe it was her dread of the things to come speeding up her perception of it. Either way, they were trundling up the path toward the bridge before she knew it. She watched as Kid's little muscles strained with the effort of pushing the heavy load over the uneven ground. With a sigh, she took several of the boxes from his cart and put them on her own. What her plan would do to him broke her heart the most. Pain or not, it was the clear path now. Somebody had to make it to the other side.

When they came in sight of the bridge, they ducked low and rolled their carts as close as they dared to the sheer drop off on this side of the chasm while staying hidden behind the wall of rubble. The river roiled and spat a noxious smell into the air, looking extra menacing today. With a hand, she halted them. If she'd calculated correctly, they would become visible to the men on the bridge by rolling the carts to the break in the wall six feet from where they stood. Her stomach tensed as she peeked over the rubble to the bridge below. Seven. More than there had ever been. *Damn it.* But the boss was there, sitting on the barricade, looking as surly as ever, and he's the only one that really mattered anyway. If he didn't take the bait, no one would.

Leaving Buck with the two larger carts, she and Kid quietly pulled the third down the winding path that led to the mouth of the bridge. Stopping a few steps from the road she dropped to her knees and held his face in her hands. He was shaking and pale, rightfully terrified by the task before him.

"Do you remember what to say?" she asked.

He nodded, his blue eyes wet.

"Tell me!"

He took a deep breath before reciting the words she had drilled into him for days. "This is payment in exchange for crossing the bridge. If you let me pass, my brother will bring you another cart with twice as much, but if you hurt me he'll push it into the river."

"Right. Then you point so that Buck can show them the cart. When they let you pass, you run hard to the other side, okay? Get as far up the road as possible. Don't wait. Do you remember the rendezvous point?"

He nodded again. "The red roof building."

Despite the lead in her stomach, she gave him a confident smile and pulled him in for a tight hug. "Good job. You're ready. Everything will work out, okay? I love you, remember that, no matter what. Give me time to get back to the top before you go, okay? Count to one hundred."

He squared his brave little shoulders and nodded. Oh sweet, precious, Kid. How could she do this? *It's the only way.* The words pounded in her brain like a mantra. Gravel skidded beneath her feet as she sprinted back to the spot where Buck waited. Chest heaving, she squished up beside him to watch from between the tilted slabs of concrete. The moment the men on the bridge spotted Kid was obvious by the commotion as they jumped to their feet, pointing and squinting at the approaching figure and his burden. First alert, then amused, the men's body language changed as Kid neared, pushing the heavy cart in front of him at a comically slow pace. It felt like sending a lamb to the slaughter but she knew he had to go first, he couldn't be threatening even if he tried.

The big one rose from his makeshift throne on the barricade and inspected the items on the flatbed, casually rifling through what was more food than most people saw in a year. Kid's lines ran over and over in her mind, willing him to remember and say them correctly. Equal doses of fear and relief washed over her when she saw him point to where they hid, seven faces snapping their gaze to follow his finger.

"Now!" She shoved Buck but he was already moving.

Weak light from the shrouded mid-day sun glinted off the metal cans stacked amidst the wealth of supplies loaded onto the cart as he pushed it into the opening to hover only feet away from the deadly drop into the black water below. He pulled himself out of sight just as quickly. No need to catch a bullet in the head. The men were passing around a pair of binoculars. When they were satisfied that the load was worth more than the child, they let Kid go. Like a wild rabbit, he was gone in seconds, across the bridge and sprinting down the road on the other side.

She nodded at Buck. "He's across! You're up!"

"Okay. I got this." He bounced up and down, shaking the jitters from his limbs. "See you on the other side, sis."

Her eyes burned but she hid it with a smile as she pulled him into a desperate hug. "Yeah, on the other side."

The weight of the cart practically pulled him after it as he started down the path. Every second seemed a lifetime as she waited for him to come into sight again. When he finally surfaced on the bridge the men were standing taller, warier of this lanky youth that looked almost like a man. More than one had a hand on their weapon. She held her breath as she waited for him to speak his line.

'This is the payment my brother promised. If you let me cross my sister will bring you another cart with even more than this one. But if you hurt me she'll push it into the river.'

Hopefully, they hadn't overestimated. Maybe the guards would be happy with the two loads within their reach and not bother with the deal for the third? No, men like this were always greedy. They would take the third cart and when they had it, they'd still chase them down and kill them for crossing. But not if she had anything to say about it.

Buck's arm pointed, giving the signal. She pushed the last cart into the opening to display its splendor. It had everything anyone could want, food, drinks, even medicine. They had to take it. She braved the risk and peered around the chunk of wall to see if they would let him cross. For a moment it seemed they would keep him there, but with a shove from the big one, they parted ranks to let him pass. Once his feet hit the pavement on the other side she started moving. Her feet tangled in her haste and she fell, scraping her knees on a jagged rock. Ignoring the sting, she righted herself and started again. *Keep it cool, girl. It'll be worth it. Everything comes with a price.*

The metal handle was slick under her sweaty palms and her limbs shook with hidden terror as she pushed the cart over the threshold of the bridge. Smug sneers painted the men's ugly faces as she approached them. Unless a fourth family member was hiding in the hills they had no reason to let her pass. She was just another piece of the prize. Several yards from them she stopped. The leader was gloating, his shirt now covered in the beer he had guzzled before flinging the can off the bridge. He took a step forward, laughing.

"And why should we let *you* cross? You got another cart up in those hills? No, I think we'll keep you, *and* the goods, then fetch your little brothers and gut them in front of you for good measure."

Cruel laughter from his cronies filled the air but she blocked it out. Without speaking she moved to the cart and lifted the box that held her salvation and placed it at the top of the pile. Calmly, she removed the cardboard box to display the bomb she had built and picked up the detonator. Judging by the looks on their faces they had not yet realized what she had uncovered.

"Yeah," spat an unshaven man, laughing as he brandished his large pistol at her, "you really thought we'd let you cross to the other side?"

"Oh," she said with a chuckle of her own, "I'm planning on crossing to the other side, alright. And I'm taking you assholes with me!"

The most brilliant light filled her vision as she pressed the button that would blow them all into oblivion. Agonizing pain blasted through her body but her mind was peaceful, thoughts of her brothers filling her heart even as the life was ripped from it. No one would chase them. They were safe now. She did it. *It was the only way.*

Ginny Young is a world-traveled writer and artist. When she's not nose deep in a book or covered in paint, she enjoys camping, hiking, and rock crawling around her Utah home. Find her on www.ginnyyoung.com to get updated on her latest projects.

<u>The Frozen Eye</u>

By Harry Carpenter

Once upon a time, in a land far away, the kingdom of Windvale was cast into darkness. A once-prosperous settlement, Windvale had come upon the curse of a powerful witch. This witch, you see, had a dark curse upon her. Her curse, which none of the townsfolk could understand, was the power to manipulate water and ice. This power came at a price. The Queen had to be locked away atop a frozen mountainside, with her palace resting upon a perpetually frozen lake. If she left her fortress, she would soon feel the heat of the sun upon her flesh, causing her to melt.

For ages, The Queen stayed in her castle, overseeing the kingdom. Windvale was unaffected by her rule at first, allowing her to attain more and more power. Before the kingdom knew what had happened, she had seized the ruling class's power, killing them within her frigid fortress. The townsfolk knew this did not bode well. Reality set in as the ice crept further from her frozen moat, down the green grassy mountainside, into the bustling town square. The fountain froze in place. Windows shattered. Those that were unwise found themselves trapped in a thick layer of ice. The ones that were smart enough to stay indoors, such as young Alma and her parents, found themselves spared from the frigid death that encroached upon the land.

Years had passed in the kingdom of Windvale. People learned to work around the ice sheets but were generally displeased by the situation they found themselves in. Alma, now practically an adult, began to wonder exactly what she could do to spend her day. She had completed her chores in the home. Ever since her mother passed from a terrible fever, she picked up the household tasks, helping her father as often as she could. Her father was once a fit and robust lumberjack. He could fell any tree with his bare hands and a trusty ax. Now, he could barely get out of bed. A terrible sickness and sadness had come upon Windvale.

Alma stepped outside of her home, gazing up at the gray overcast sky. Every day was bleak and drab. The mood was reflected on her various neighbors' faces as they moped along, trying to complete daily chores.

"This is absolute madness!" Alma yelled out to nobody in particular. "I recall the sun, the grass, the rolling hills."

Alma did remember. As a child, she remembered playing with the neighbor child, Ella, in a vast field of daisies and other beautiful flowers. A fleeting memory, but vivid nonetheless. A blast of cold air snapped Alma out of her daydreams and fantasies. She was greeted once again by the cold, uninviting wasteland that was once her beautiful home. Another blast of cold air snapped at her cheek. She turned to see The Ice Queen, hovering gently above the ground, encased in a whirlwind of snow. She floated toward the town square, which Alma crept around to view.

"People of Windvale! It has come to my attention that I, your beautiful, wonderful Queen, have failed you in a way," The Queen announced. Her voice coming through clear over the howl of the winds.

Townsfolk began to gravitate toward the town square. Most never saw The Queen or her power. They heard stories, and that was enough for them. Here she stood, addressing the nation she reigned over.

"I come to you, my people, urging you to cheer up! Have I not given you protection from enemy ships? Invading armies? Barbarians who would surely do unspeakable things to your women and children?" The Queen boomed across the town.

There was a moment of discussion amongst the townsfolk before their queen raised her hand once more to stifle the crowd. The sound instantly went away.

"People of Windvale! I fear that it is your mood that brings this town and its morale down."

One man stepped forward. "Our mood? My Queen, are you insane? Take a look around! It's miserable here! Everything is gray and white. We 'avent seen the sun in ages, m'lady. Pardon my speech, but this is why morale is low."

The Queen floated toward the ground, seating herself on the edge of the fountain. She seemed to be in deep thought as the townsfolk looked at each other with confused expressions. Muttering amongst the town began to drum up once more before The Queen raised her hand again to silence them.

"I have a solution to our situation. It appears you are not happy, and I can recognize that. You live in a beautiful part of the land, adorned with the finest and purest of snow," The Queen bellowed. "You should smile more. Believing in this kingdom as I do will help you feel pleasure and love as I do!"

The townsfolk once again muttered amongst themselves while Alma watched on. She was curious about what was happening, so she moved in a bit closer.

"From this moment forth, everyone in Windvale shall be happy! Smile! Be merry! Delight in your existence!" The Queen smiled as she waved her hand in the air, creating a blue glow of ice and snow around it.

Alma watched as the butcher, Mr. Pederson, stepped out of the crowd. He took a knee in front of her, removing his winter hat as he did.

"What is it, my subject?" The Queen asked.

Pederson looked up to meet The Queen's gaze. "My ladyship. I haven't had game through these woods in ages. Each day we venture further and further into the tundra, searching for wildlife. How do you expect us to smile more with empty bellies?"

The Queen stepped forward from the fountain to stand in front of Pederson. She held his chin in her hand, smiling down at him. Gently, she caressed his bearded cheek with the back of her hand. Mr. Pederson seemed uneased yet relaxed at the same time.

"I see. Perhaps you did not hear my words; were they unclear? I demand that everyone be happy!" The Queen screamed as she floated once more in front of Mr. Pederson. "Unhappy? Are you not finding food? Are you not eating at all? I'm sure you are, look at you! You oafish, over-bloated buffoon! What do you take me for?"

Mr. Pederson stood up, gripping his hat in his hands nervously. "I meant nothing by it, m'lady! Swear!"

A smirk twisted onto The Queen's face. "So be it. I have told you what to do. My instructions are simple. Now, I shall demonstrate the consequences!"

The Queen waved her hand over Mr. Pederson's face. He quickly screamed as he shielded his face with his hands. Alma tried to see what had happened to the poor man. As Pederson writhed around on the snow, the townsfolk watched in horror. Slowly, Pederson dropped his hands from his face to retrieve his hat from the ground. Several onlookers in the crowd fainted. The gasp exhaled from the rest of the group made Alma move closer to see. Mr. Pederson's eyes were now glazed in ice. It took everything she had to not scream. There they were, clear as day! Grey and blue, frozen over with ice! She couldn't believe it.

"That was my warning. Should I find any of you are not in absolute delight- frowning, or complaining, I will inflict the same consequence upon you!"

Another town member stepped forward. This time, it was Mrs. Birk. "How exactly will you know, my Queen?"

The evil queen smirked. "Oh, I'll have my eyes. If that fails me, I'll be able to watch you with some help."

She waved her hand in the air across the open field beside her. Dozens of snowmen began to form.

"This is absolutely insane! You cannot do this!" Mrs. Birk shrieked.

With the flick of a wrist and a cold smile, Mrs. Birk received the same fate as Mr. Pederson. The process seemed painful as she writhed on the ground in agony. Alma glanced over at Mr. Pederson, who was now standing back in line with the townsfolk with a smile ear to ear. His eyes, now an empty hollow full of reflective ice, placed his expression in a somewhat uneasy tone. Alma dashed off to her home at once and closed the door behind her.

As time passed, Alma became more adjusted to the new lifestyle. In town, people would pass her by with the largest of smiles. It was obvious which of those scowled, even for a slight moment. Their eyes were replaced with reflective sheets of ice. The ghostly hollow void that once was a beautiful set of eyes sat eerily centered on various faces of the townsfolk. Overall, Alma was glad The Queen hadn't killed them. Things could have been worse. Much, much worse, in fact.

As Alma passed by Mr. Pederson's butcher shop, she peered inside to see what she could see. Beyond the doorway, a dark shop sat ahead of her. The counter was covered in strange meats, while other cuts hung from the various hooks on the walls. Mr. Pederson must have been in the back as the storefront was empty. Alma decided to step inside to take a better look. The smell was off. There was something about this meat that was not the traditional smell of venison or boar. This was a whole new stench.

"Alma, dear! Welcome to my happy little store! Can I help you with any wonderful selections of meat today?" Mr. Pederson called out as he emerged from the shop's rear, carrying with him a large slab of prime cuts.

Alma backed away slightly, trying to maintain her false smile. "Oh, no, thank you. I just wanted to stop in and say hello."

"Shame about your father and all. Oh well! Would you like some of this meat for the road?" Mr. Pederson said as he gestured his armful of meat at her.

Alma took another step backward toward the door. "Oh, no. I'm fine."

"Cheer up, sweetie. I'm sure your father is with us right now. He'd be proud of the young lady you've become."

Alma thought about the word choices of Mr. Pederson but quickly brushed it off. The memory of losing her father began to trouble her mind, and she didn't need to be seen upset in town. She wiped away a quick tear that started to well up in the corner of her eyes and turned to face the cold outside. She was nearly knocked over by one of The Queen's patrolmen.

"Oh, sorry there!" Alma said, picking herself up with a smile.

The snowman leaned in. The coal for its eyes stared daggers into Alma, practically reading her soul. She almost believed they could read her soul at one point. Without a word, the patrolman began its route once more, gliding gracefully through the snow. The world she knew as a child was becoming less and less what she knew, fading into a memory of times she would never regain.

Her boyfriend, Hansel, waived to her from the doorstep of her home as she returned.

"Alma, sweetie! What a great day, right?" Hansel exclaimed as he picked her up in his arms. "It's almost magical!"

Alma tried to hide her sarcastic smirk before replying, "Whoopie, magical!"

Hansel's expression changed. "Hey, hey now. Don't do that. You know what they'll do to you, right?" Hansel shifted from his slightly serious expression back to a smile. He erupted with a boast of laughter before continuing. "You'll have a great day, that's for sure. So buck up, kiddo!"

Alma hated how fake this town was. She was tired of seeing the dead, void filled eye sockets of her friends and neighbors. Those that hadn't been converted were living in such fear that they were shells of their former selves. She had been planning to leave ever since her father unexpectedly passed away a few weeks ago. There was nothing for her in this town. Nothing that is, except perhaps Hansel. He could be convinced to flee with her, indeed.

Alma quickly took Hansel by the arm and pulled him into her home. The walls were still adorned with hunting trinkets and trophies from her father. He used to hunt with Mr. Pederson until he fell too ill. Hansel was pulled further into the home, deeper toward the kitchen near the fireplace. Alma quickly lit a roaring fire, glancing around to ensure the coast was clear.

"Ok, listen. I have a plan to get out of here," Alma whispered under the crackling of the fire logs.

Hansel dropped the smirk from his face. "You're kidding me. You want to risk leaving?"

Alma paused momentarily. "I don't think anyone has tried. They're too afraid to. And if they did make it, we'd likely never know, right?"

"Right."

"So, what if we packed a small number of rations and headed out of town. We don't stop running until we see beautiful hills of grass, flowers, and trees."

Hansel smiled at that thought. It was one of the first times he'd worn a genuine smile in a long time. "I think we could do it."

Alma used the dirt on the floor to map out their route. She detailed to Hansel that they would travel on foot. If a horse made a noise, they'd surely be captured. Hansel agreed to that. The plan seemed to make sense as Alma went on. The two of them would leave in the cover of night, tonight. A small bag would be packed for each, nothing metallic. They wanted to ensure stealth was on their side. If any of these patrolmen heard them, frankly, they'd be done for.

Alma and Hansel broke up their plans, quickly rubbing out the floor of anything that could incriminate them should they be captured.

"Ok, I'll meet you near the back of the butcher shop. We'd need to run from there to the main gates. There's barely any cover," Hansel asserted. "We'd have to run as fast as we can. After we're past the gates, we'll dash into the woods."

Alma nodded. This was going to work; she was sure of it. She gave Hansel a final hug before plans were in motion. He set foot out of her door with the most enormous smile on his face. Usually, this would be suspicious. However, in these times, it was just what they needed. His genuine smile and happy demeanor would undoubtedly blend in with the falsities of this town. Alma took a small nap to prepare her body for the grueling journey through ice and snow ahead.

As she awoke, the world was a bit quieter. The town has gone to rest for the evening. She peered out of her door slowly, as she noticed the stillness of the night. The sky was black, covered in an overcast created by the evil Queen. A gentle snowfall drifted through the atmosphere, coating the ground with a fresh layer of powder. Quietly, she exited her home, closing the door gently behind her. Taking one last hard look at the structure, she shook out the memories attached to it, pushing herself to move along in the shadows across town.

Alma passed one house, then another. Each one seemed more manageable than the last. The Snow Patrolmen were clearly busy somewhere else. Either they were engaged, or she was just lucky. Swiftly, Alma dashed toward the next home and crouched below an open window. Taking great care to not make a sound as she crawled on hands and knees around the opening, she quietly moved to the opposite side of the home. Her hands now stinging from the cold, frozen snow. She clenched her fists for a moment, knowing time was a fleeting gift. She needed to hurry along to the butcher shop.

Rounding the corner, Alma's heart skipped several beats. One of The Queen's patrol passed directly in front of her. Their snowman bases skidding gently across the fresh powder. They didn't seem to notice her as she relaxed her body against the building. Alma waited a few more moments to ensure the patrol was long out of her sight. She was about to make a mad dash across the main road toward the butcher shop. She'd use the fountain for cover if needed but wanted to make the sprint in one movement.

Alma felt as if she'd been running for hours as she tore across the open road. Crouching, she quickly and swiftly made it to the fountain. Hastily glancing around, Alma checked for anybody in sight before moving toward the other side of the road. As Alma made it across the two buildings' threshold, she dove for cover behind several barrels. She squinted her eyes tightly, hoping nobody had seen her.

"Oh god, oh god, oh god," she muttered under her breath while trying to breathe normally again.

Peering slightly over the barrels, she glanced down the main road. Once again, as before, it remained empty and quiet. The darkness helped paint an eerie shadow across her once beautiful home in the distance. Her moment of relief was jolted out of her as she felt a hand on her shoulder and another across her mouth as she tried to scream.

"Shh, calm down. It's me!" Hansel grunted through his teeth, trying to be as quiet as possible.

Alma felt relief wash over her body as she saw her true love. She gazed into his beautiful dragon scale green eyes. She could still see the fierceness within them, even in the blanket of nightfall.

"Ok, let's move," Alma said, with Hansel nodding in agreement.

The two gently moved from building to building, making their way to the end of the row. Each dash across the open air was no less terrifying than the last. Alma could hear her heartbeat in her head as she rushed across each structure. Soon, they were upon the last building on the left.

"Butcher shop," Hansel whispered as he pointed to the front of the building.

The two of them swiftly moved along the side of the wall, pressing their bodies as close as possible. Inch by inch, the two crept closer and closer to the end of the shop. As they reached the corner, Hansel peered around.

"Clear. You ready?" he asked.

"Ready."

Hansel tightened up the straps to his pack. He knew the two of them were about to sprint to their finish line. Ahead, he could see the gates practically glowing. Hansel gripped Alma's hand and stepped out into the open road. He glanced back to Alma one last time, who shot him a slight smile before the two of them made a mad dash for the gate, hand in hand.

Alma spotted that the door to the butcher's shop was ajar, but paid it no mind as she hurried to keep up with Hansel. He was much stronger and faster than she was, practically dragging her along. The gates grew closer and closer as they ran. Alma could almost picture the flowing rivers, the songbirds chirping, and the children's laughter. She began to run harder than ever before, inspired by her thoughts.

As the two approached the gates, Hansel pushed himself even harder, yanking Alma along for the ride. They passed under the arches of the kingdom entrance, into the wooded area beyond. Hansel ran several meters from the trail until he felt the coast was clear. He slowly let go of Alma's hand, leaning against a tree to collect himself. Alma decided to lay on her back and catch her breath. Her heart was pounding so hard.

As they recovered, Hansel felt uneasy. Something wasn't right. He shook the feeling off and grabbed Alma's hand, moving along in the wood line toward the edge of the Queen's reach. Alma began to suspect they were not alone in the woods, either. She continually glanced around at every angle and bend in the dark woods for the hint of something moving. Nothing was out there. She focused her attention forward to see the trees beginning to clear ahead.

"We've made it, Alma! We've made it!" Hansel cheered as he stopped at the edge of the wood line.

Alma stepped forward slightly to see what Hansel was able to see. Ahead of her lie the edge of the snowline, just meters ahead! It was only in reach. Beyond that, she could see darkness on the ground.

"Grass!" Alma exclaimed. "I see grass!"

Hansel smiled at her. She looked deep into his piercing green eyes as he gazed into her large blue ones.

"Look up."

Alma adjusted her gaze to the sky. She wandered around in dismay and wonder as she was able to see the stars for the first time in ages. All the constellations, the galaxies, the heavens! They were there for Alma to take in. She held her arms out as if to reach for the stars herself. She felt a warm glow wash over her as she wiped away several tears that had formed. Alma could hear the hoot of an owl and the buzzing of insects. The sound of the buzzing grew louder and louder. She turned to face Hansel. As she looked upon his face, something was wrong. His once beautiful green eyes were now replaced by hollow, reflective ice shards.

"Not the bees!" Alma screamed as she saw crystalline wasps float away from Hansel.

She immediately went to her lover.

"You see, my dear? I have eyes all over. You cannot escape my grasp," Hansel said.

"I don't understand!" Alma replied, shaking Hansel.

"My eyes, loyal subject. Did you think you'd go unnoticed?" Hansel replied.

From behind several trees, dozens of townsfolk, each with their eyes encased in frozen sheets of ice, stepped into view.

"NO! No!" Alma cried out as she was subdued by Hansel and the others.

The next morning, the village resumed its everyday hustle and bustle. The butcher was laying out his freshest cuts while the tailor stitched trousers for the youngsters. The town square was busier than ever before as Alma stepped into the crowded marketplace to purchase goods for the home she and Hansel shared. She walked to the merchant, buying spices to season her stew for the evening.

"What a wonderful day it is!" Alma said, paying for her goods.

"Yes, it really, truly is, isn't it?" the shopkeeper replied.

As Alma collected her purchase, the shopkeeper tried his best to not stare too hard into the icy, cold eyes that sat in Alma's skull. The reflection of his face staring back at him as a reminder that, in fact, the Queen is always watching. Her eyes are everywhere.

Harry Carpenter, writer of "Tales from an Ex-Husband" and the "Fubar" series, is a fan of horror, science fiction, and suspense. Born in Baltimore, Maryland, a city full of illustrious authors and performers, Harry began writing in elementary school. He formally pursued his passion, releasing his first book "Tales From an Ex-Husband" in 2019.

Harry has since won the "Best Short Short Story" award from the Veteran's Administration writing contest and was featured as the bestselling author in local bookstores. Using his experiences in the United States Army, various retail and fast-food establishments, childhood encounters, and chaotic first marriage, he has developed a mind for creativity.

He is a huge fan of cats, video games, and quirky science fiction and horror movies. He also films an internet web series called "The Web-Pool" on YouTube, as well As volunteers with the "Charm City Ghostbusters," a charity organization out of Baltimore who, as the name dictates, dress as the Ghostbusters 1984 movie. Harry now lives in Baltimore with his wife and cats.

www.hcarpenterwriter.com

Goldie Bear

By Emily VanOverloop

Destroyed. The Guardians told me my family had been destroyed. Some accident left me without my memory and my only remaining relative was some uncle twice removed. I was supposed to live out the rest of my life in the Chew with him. Like hell.

"Goldie, don't be too late," my uncle had yelled at me one day as I closed the door on my way to the market. That was the last time I'd seen him. He was a shit person—verbally, physically, and emotionally abusive to every person he encountered—it was no wonder why he ended up in the Chew. I decided living on the streets of the Chew was better than living with him. That was three years ago.

Oh, the Chew. The Guardians and everyone in the Colony regarded the Chew with so much disdain, it had become a threat. "You don't want to end up in the Chew," they'd warn their children.

The Chew and the Colony were separated by a hill. While the Chew was desolate, dirty, and poor, the Colony was the exact opposite. I often climbed to the top of the hill and looked down on the Colony. Every house looked the same. Every house had one man, one woman, and one child. The Guardians distributed three meals a day to each house. Every day, the children went to school learning the ins and outs of how to succeed and prosper in the Colony. The men went to work, making sure to uphold the Colony standards. The women stayed home. I wasn't sure what they did all day, but they only left the house to go get essentials from the market. Other than that, every member of the Colony went to the same church on Sunday mornings. Attendance was mandatory.

If I'm being completely honest, I hated everything about the Colony. Who wanted the same thing day in and day out? They didn't have any kind of entertainment or fun that I could see. The Chew at least had some variety—the kinds of people, the kinds of entertainment, the kinds of food. I thought life was much better in the Chew than the Colony gave it credit for. But there was something to be said about having a home and three meals a day.

I was sitting at the top of the hill, looking down at the orderly houses as the sun started to set. I'd never been able to shake the feeling that I was missing something. Part of me felt like it belonged in the Colony. A cool breeze blew across the grass and I watched it ripple down the hill. Hopefully, my task tonight would cause beautiful ripples, too. I breathed in the fresh air and closed my eyes, knowing that it might very well be my last sunset.

"You coming, Goldie?" my best friend's high-pitched voice startled me. I turned and saw Lacey had dyed her hair bright pink this afternoon. *Subtle.* I stood and dusted the grass from my pants.

"Promise me something?" I said as we started the trek down the hill. "If I get wiped tonight, do not let anyone name me 'Goldie' when I come back." She laughed but nodded. My uncle had started calling me 'Goldie' based on my hair. He said he despised the color. I despised him.

I used humor to cover my fear. If I got wiped tonight, I wouldn't even care about the name 'Goldie.'

While the Guardians insisted I lost my memory and my family in an unspecified accident, there were a remarkable number of similar stories in the Chew. Eventually, someone had the good sense to question this and had us all gather in an old war bunker below the hill. Twenty-five people showed up that night, including Lacey and me. We'd been best friends ever since. The group decided to call themselves "The Chew-sers." I rolled my eyes every time someone said it.

The twenty-five Chewsers were all younger than thirty. Casey, the oldest of the group, was the one that found me within a week of me leaving my uncle. He had found all the others with the same story and convinced me to come to that first meeting. He knew Zach and Isaac from the market. Supposedly, they were brothers, but they couldn't look or act more different from each other if they tried. They were good friends, though.

Casey had set up the bunker with all kinds of supplies. Most of them were smuggled in from the Colony. Casey claimed he'd been working on getting everything for years but didn't ask all of us to join until he was sure there was enough evidence of something wrong. I wasn't sure how much I believed him—it almost seemed like he knew too much—but staying in the bunker was a lot warmer at night than staying alone on the street. Besides, what did I have to lose? Lacey was the only other girl my age, so I clung to her. Zach and Isaac trained everyone, but were a few years older than us. Casey was older than them and acted as the group's leader because he'd found everyone. I didn't know many of the others, but considered them all my family. Everyone was friendly because we were all after one goal. Our memories.

The theory was that the Guardians would wipe memories clean. For some reason, we'd all had our memories wiped clean from our lives before. Recently, we'd discovered we all had a faint scar along the base of the neck. It wasn't an ordinary scar, though. It was blue. Casey's father had just passed away. Out of curiosity, he decided to cut his father's scar open. He found a mechanical chip in his father's skin. When he put that chip into a screen, a video of sorts played showing all of his father's memories. Turns out, he wasn't Casey's father at all. His last memory had shown him questioning his boss about some sort of business transaction that didn't make sense to him. Instead of answering him, his boss called the Guardians. Before going black, "wipe him," was heard coming from a Guardian.

"You're not going to get wiped," Lacey said as we finally made it to the entrance of the bunker. "You're the best fighter we have. Casey wouldn't send you if he didn't think you'd make it back. You're too smart for him to let go."

That was true. Zach and Isaac had been trained for hand-to-hand combat sometime in the past. Casey's other theory was that muscle memory couldn't be wiped. So, I trained with them as much as I could. Physical exertion felt better than the mental exertion I put myself through when left alone.

I let her boost my ego before going in because I didn't want Casey, or anyone, to see how scared I really was. If I succeeded tonight, we'd all get our memories restored. If I didn't, I'd either wake up without a memory again, or die. I took a deep breath and Lacey pushed the door open.

"Finally, the woman of the hour," Casey said at the front of the room. I was only sixteen or seventeen, hardly a woman but still one of the oldest in the room. They pressed me forward with a round of applause.

"I haven't done anything yet," I said. At the same second I stepped up to Casey's table, a knife whirred past my head. I shoved Casey out of the way and ducked as someone's fist came toward my face. My training took over.

Duck. Dodge. Punch. Duck. Dodge. Punch. I wasn't even sure how many people I was fighting.

"Enough," Casey yelled. "We don't want to wear her out before she leaves."

The fight stopped. Zach and Isaac removed their hoods and smiled. Zach had a slit over his left cheekbone. "Impressive," he said. I didn't know if he was just being nice because of what I was about to do, or if I should actually be proud that I got a punch in on one of our toughest fighters. I smiled anyway.

"Anything new?" I asked Casey as Lacey brought me over some water. Fresh water was hard to come by in the Chew, but we had a barrel of water that Casey had smuggled in from the other end of the tunnel attached to the bunker. I was going to take that same tunnel to sneak into the Colony and get back our memories. I tried not to choke on the water.

"We've got it narrowed down to three houses," Casey started, opening a map and pointing. "Once you leave the tunnel, you'll go four blocks straight and then turn left. Follow that street—Prosper Avenue, I believe—until it dead ends. Then turn right onto Forest Lane. There are only three houses on that street. It has to be in one

166

of those. It'll either be in with the Bears, the Foxes, or the Toads." I stared at him. *Seriously?*

He put his hands up in defense. "Hey, I didn't name these people." He looked at his watch. "It's just about time." I nodded. Lacey and Zach started handing me supplies—flashlight, gun, knife—and I strapped them to various places on my body without even thinking. Thank goodness for muscle memory.

"And it's in a security box. Likely under a hexagon." The hexagon was the shape of the Colony's flag. Casey had done some serious work finding all of this out. He'd kidnapped a Guardian from the market not too long after he'd discovered the chip. The Guardian answered all his questions, but Casey still killed him.

"Why don't they want us to have our memories, again?" I asked, my fear getting the better of me. I rubbed my palms along my shirt. I hated sweaty palms.

"Hey, hey," Casey turned my face toward his. "You can do this. You will free us and once we all have our memories back, we can go join the Colony. We all deserve to be sheltered and fed." He tried to smile but I knew he was too bitter. I nodded and made my way to the door.

"Wait!" Lacey grabbed my arm. "Wear the goggles. Maybe we can help." The goggles were set up to stream my view back to the screen. They also had speakers attached to the earpieces. We'd never tried them outside of the Chew though. Lacey strapped them to my head and turned them on. Her smile filled the screen in front of Casey.

He just shrugged. "Worth a shot."

I turned back to Lacey and hugged her as hard as I could. She sniffed and I knew she was holding back her sobs—she was always overly emotional. I turned to hug Zach and Isaac. Hopefully, I would make them proud.

"Why does she have to go alone?" Zach suddenly demanded of Casey. Casey was as shocked as I was—Zach hardly ever showed an opinion about anything-- and fumbled for words.

"It's risky enough with just me going. We don't want to risk our memories being destroyed. If I'm found, they can't trace anything back," I explained. Rationale always calmed me down. "All of these supplies were once theirs. Nothing will expose you all." I swallowed. "I want to keep you safe."

With that, I refused to make eye contact with anyone else. I walked out the door opposite of where Lacey and I had come in and entered the tunnel. I clicked on the flashlight. For some reason, I thought the tunnel was going to be the worst part, filled with dirt and bugs and all kinds of things I didn't want to see. I was pleasantly surprised to find a cement floor with brick walls. It was just like the bunker.

"Can you still see me?" I couldn't remember if the goggles had microphones or not.

"We see you," I could hear the buzz from the bunker and Lacey's excited voice. "I knew these were a good idea!"

"We'll see how long they last. You guys will need to be quiet though. Who knows how far the sound will carry?" The buzz quieted. I could picture them all surrounding the screen, watching my progress. I knew Lacey was proud of me, so I pictured her smile the rest of the way through the tunnel. I was doing this for her. And for me. I wanted to know what destroyed my family.

The tunnel went on much longer than I thought it would. I was about to ask Casey how much longer when I finally saw the wall at the end. I ran the rest of the way, eager to get out. I climbed the ladder and pushed the button by the opening in the ceiling. A hexagon started slowly moving to the right.

"Kill the light!" Casey whisper yelled. I turned off the flashlight and waited a minute before climbing out.

I poked my head out slowly and looked around. All I could see were bushes and trees. I pulled the rest of my body out but kept low to the ground. I crawled toward a tree and slowly snuck around it. The street was right on the other side. It was too dark to make anything out, but I wasn't going to use the flashlight again.

"Go forward. You'll see streetlamps soon," Casey's voice came over the earpiece. Apparently, the goggles still worked.

I recited the instructions in my head for the billionth time and forced my feet to move. The street was smooth, like the floor in the tunnel. There were no streets in the Chew, just dirt paths. My boots almost felt too heavy to walk on it. Their thud was sure to wake anyone nearby. Stepping lightly would take too long. I had to risk it. I crept along the street. Casey was right. By the time I reached the second block, streetlights lit up every doorway. How many times had I stared down at the Colony and not seen these? Luckily, the street between the rows of houses was still fairly dark in the middle. That's where I decided to stay.

There were no signs of life—human, Guardian, animal, anything. I knew I'd left late in the evening, but how early did these people go to bed? Granted, my sense of time was currently skewed. I felt like I'd been out here for hours already.

"Forest Lane is coming up on your right." Casey's voice startled me so much I jumped. I stopped for a second to take a breath. I had to admit that the air did feel cleaner down here.

I saw the street sign for Forest Lane and felt my heart rate increase. I picked up my pace. The Bears, the Foxes, and the Toads. I rolled my eyes and decided to start with the farthest house from the street. If I needed to run, at least I could shave off some time trying to get back.

All three houses were identical on the outside. White brick with black shutters and a black door. There wasn't a trace of light coming from inside. It was almost disorienting.

"Can you hear me?" I whispered.

"Yes. And see you," Casey answered. "See the number pad below the doorknob? Type in 7-8-1-7." I did so and heard the release of the lock with a beep. It was deafening in the silence from the house. "That's the risk you'll have to take," he said.

I tiptoed in and quietly shut the door behind me. I'd always wondered why the crime rate was so low in the Colony. The threat of the Chew couldn't be that bad. But looking at the almost empty house, I could see why. Nothing to steal when everyone had the same things.

"He said it would be on the bottom floor. There's no underground floor on this row of houses," Casey informed me. At least that narrowed it down a little.

Casey had asked the Guardian he kidnapped why they kept something so important inside a civilian house. "Easier to wipe one house than a whole building." I still got chills when I thought of the Guardians flippant answer, as if it were no big deal. Anger started pushing me forward.

There was a white couch with a white coffee table. There was a screen on the wall opposite of the couch, but nothing else on any wall on this floor. The kitchen was the same. A solid metal table and chairs next to metal appliances. It was stark and cold. It even smelled sterile. I couldn't understand why anyone would want to live in this house. I checked under the coffee table but already knew the box wasn't in this house.

I tiptoed back to the front door and made it outside without a problem. *Phew.*

"One house down, two to go." There was a little relief in Casey's voice. "Try the Foxes next. To your left."

"Who did I just do?"

"The Toads."

There wasn't a lot of space between the houses, so I was exposed the whole way to the Fox's front porch.

"1-2-3-4." Casey was on top of it. "Original, I know." I smirked but didn't dare make a sound.

If the Toad's house was cold, the Fox's house was…hot. There was stuff everywhere. My flashlight shined on so many different odds and ends just to get through the door, I had no idea how I would find a box in here. I shuffled through some stuffed toys and made it to another white couch and coffee table in front of a screen. This couch, however, was no longer white. It was stained in so many places. There was even a small orange handprint on the center cushion. I smiled at the thought of a happy child. I forgot that these people didn't know about the workings of their government. I wondered if it was better to remain blissfully unaware or to know what was wrong and not be able to do anything about it. It was better for me if I pretended they didn't know any better. Because how could they have let this happen to anyone, let alone to someone like me? No. It was better if they were unaware.

"This isn't it. It's gotta be the Bears. Get going." Casey's directions made me jump. I hurried back to the door trying not to trip on anything. As soon as I shut the door, a light flicked on in the house. I ducked below the front windows and prayed my black clothes were enough to keep me hidden.

The shadow of a figure appeared in the window. "Thought I heard something," a man's muffled voice sounded right above me. If I hadn't been hiding under the window, I wouldn't have heard him at all. I held my breath, sure that he was about to open the door and attack me. As I reached for my gun, the light went out.

I nearly cried with relief as I gulped in air. Adrenaline coursed through me. I knew this quest would be risky, but I still wasn't prepared. I shook my head, trying to regain some composure.

"Get it together, Goldie," Zach said in the earpiece. "You're almost there. You got this." It was no secret that I liked Zach. Casey

171

was smart to put him on. He knew I'd probably step up to show off for him. Bravado.

I stood and took in another deep breath. Besides that little almost-incident, it had all been too easy. Where were the Guardians? I thought they patrolled the streets at night. I crept to the Bears front door.

"2-8-7-5." My brow furrowed. There was something familiar about those numbers, but I couldn't place it. Oh well, no time to think of it now. I'd ask Casey when I got back. There was a lot I was going to ask Casey, actually.

The Bears house was neat, but not as neat as the Toads. It was easy to walk through. There was a teal, knitted blanket folded across the top of the white couch. It made it more inviting. I risked sitting on it. *Oooh.* I'd never felt so comfortable. It was like sinking into a hug.

I heard Casey saying something in the earpiece, but a decoration on the wall caught my eye. It was a wooden bear painted the same teal as the blanket. "The Bears" was written on it in white, though not written well. It must have been done by a child.

I stared and stared at the bear. I knew I was wasting time, but I couldn't look away. I got up to get a closer look and caught a whiff of vanilla and honey. That's what my home had always smelled like. It was so comforting. It reminded me of my mom making cookies… I nearly tripped over the coffee table. I had memories?

"Casey," I said, breathless. I walked over to the bear on the wall. I reached out and felt the smooth paint. "I made this." I closed my eyes. I could picture it all so clearly. "My dad had just shown me how to use a saw and we cut it together. I wanted to paint it my mom's favorite color. He had me add on 'The Bears' so we could call it a decoration." I opened my eyes, but my vision was blurred with tears. "This is my family."

"It's you." A woman's voice came from the stairs. I spun around grabbing my gun, blinking away the tears.

172

"Get out! Get out! Get out!" I could hear everyone screaming over the earpieces, but the woman was staring at me, unarmed, and crying. I dared looking longer. Her hair was the same gold as mine. Her eyes were the same blue. It was almost like looking in the mirror, except for the age. She was old enough to be…my mother. I lowered my gun.

"They kept telling me I was crazy," she sputtered, coming closer. "They told me everyone only ever had one baby. But I knew I had a daughter. I love my son, but I knew. I knew I had you." She was standing in front of me now. There was a constant buzz in the earpiece. "Can I hug you?" she sobbed. I nodded.

She put her arms around me and hugged me tighter than even Lacey had before I left. I breathed in her vanilla scent. It was overwhelming. I closed my eyes and hugged her back. I felt the tension leave my shoulders and as soon as it did, all my memories were back. Waves of emotion rolled over me.

"Mom," I cried, finally wrapping my arms around her. She was real. She was here. I was holding her. She wasn't destroyed. "Are Dad and Dylan here, too?" She was still sobbing and hugging me but nodded her head. "You're all safe?" She nodded again, not able to form words. My heart was exploding. I would never let anything happen to them again.

"They sent me away because I was the second child." The memories were all coming together. "They did a reform and altered everyone's memories. I don't know how they all just came back but we must find a box. It's hidden here somewhere. That's why I'm here." She finally let go still nodding her head.

"Everything makes so much sense. I think our connection brought my memories back," she said, making her way over to the couch. "All they let me do here is clean. There's a hexagon seal over here that drives me crazy. All the dust and dirt get stuck there and won't come off."

She shoved the couch a foot to the right and revealed the hexagon. There were all kinds of whoops and hollers in the earpiece.

"How do we get it out?" I asked, hoping either my mom or Casey knew.

"You don't." I whirled around and found myself staring down the barrel of a gun.

"Honey, no. This is Julia. This is our daughter. I told you I wasn't crazy." My mom walked over to the man wearing the Guardian uniform. She put a hand on his arm. I took a step back and looked at the Guardian's face.

"Dad," I almost started crying again, but he didn't lower his gun. "Dad, it's me."

"I don't have a daughter," he said. He'd schooled his face so it showed no emotion, but the bitterness was radiating off him.

"Yes, we do!" my mother insisted. "She's here. She's here and we can be a whole family again. The Colony owns us because you sold her. They offered us food and shelter and a job if we moved with just one child. They promised you that they would take care of her, but they just put her in the Chew." She was crying and pulling at his sleeve. *Sold?* "But this is it. We can get away. We just have to get this box--"

BAM!

The sound of the gunshot reverberated through my skull. But nothing hurt. I felt down my body, but there was no sign of injury.

"Goldie! Goldie! Are you okay?" the shouts through the earpieces were getting louder. I looked up to see my dad—no, that man would never be my dad—holding the gun over my mom. She was on the floor, eyes and mouth still open, blood streaming down her face through the hole in her forehead.

I stumbled back and fell on the couch.

"Goldie, get out now!" Casey was screaming through the earpiece.

"How could you?" I tried to sound angry, but I only sounded as broken as my heart. "She was everything." I shook my head. How could so much have gone so wrong in such a small amount of time? Now my family truly was destroyed. I needed to get out. I started to stand and heard the familiar cock of the gun.

I stood tall and took a steadying breath.

"If something happens," I started, looking at my dad but speaking to my Chew family. "Just know that I loved you all. So very much."

My earpiece fell silent. My dad scrutinized me, but I could tell he was still looking at a stranger. Even if he had *sold* me to the government, we could've gotten past it.

"Just tell me why," I said, putting both of my hands in the air. We both knew I wasn't getting out of this alive.

He shrugged. "You know too much."

Emily VanOverloop is a nurse turned homeschool teacher that has always loved writing—almost as much as she loves reading. Her favorite genre to read and write is fantasy but she also loves the mind-bending realities founded in dystopian societies. When not reading or writing, she is attempting to wrangle three children and a husband in West Chester, Ohio.

https://www.emilyvanoverloop.com/

Atlas: The Tale of Hanna and Greta

By A.K. Harris

Our history books told us after The Great Fall in 2030, the earth was ravaged with disease and famine. Citizens were disarmed systematically until weapons were scarce and most people simply gave up, gave in, and became extinct. Some saw it coming, most did not.

Those that remained banded together under the rule of The Great Master and worked to build up the city of Atlas. Strict protocol was enforced to ensure a quality life for the perfect citizens, but even Atlas faced consequences from those who wished to do it harm. At the end of the year 2146, the walls of Atlas were permanently closed to shut out The Beyond.

We had names, of course, but The Elders referred to us only using our assigned numbers. I am 2147-1. Each generation was assigned a number corresponding with their birth year. 2147s were the first to be born inside the walls of Atlas. In the hierarchy that is high school, First Gen's were the alphas. Our elite social status solidified solely based on the fact we were the first. We were also on the verge of our Ranking Ceremony; the mere thought sent shivers of trepidation through my body.

"Hanna, wait up," Greta said while hurrying toward me.

Greta was my best friend even though it was discouraged to form tight bonds with other girls. She lived in my pod under the sure tyranny of our house mother, Madam Hunt. Greta was a sprite of a girl with dainty features, but what she lacked in size, she doubled up for in personality. She was rather plain looking, although her sunset locks were the envy of the whole pod. The color starkly contrasted to my own raven waves. We could not be more unalike, her light to my dark, my serious nature to her fancifulness. In spite of our contrasts, or maybe because of them, we were inseparable, and she was my only friend.

Whether the Elders approved or not, friendships were formed within the female population. The boys, on the other hand, were encouraged to gather, do sporty type things, and generally congratulate one another on their testicular fortitude. I glanced back over my shoulder at my joyful companion waiting for the unavoidable interrogation.

"So, Madam President, I am dying to know why I was told that Master Heston was spotted taking a stroll with a student last night. Honestly, Hanna, how could you not tell me?" Her brow was furrowed in an exaggerated fashion, reminding me of the dramatics capable when Greta did not get the scoop from the source, mainly me.

"Please stop calling me that. There is nothing to tell. Heston walked me back to the pod and that was it," I said flippantly, a little annoyed that she had not yet abandoned that silly pet name. She used it whenever possible as a jab at my status of being firstborn inside the walls and my all-business character.

"Heavy is the head that bears the crown." She giggled and I rolled my emerald eyes so hard they should have stuck to the back of my skull.

It was quite commonplace for the older men to court the last-year girls, although I would not categorize Master Heston as old. He is a 2138. Aging him at twenty-five to my eighteen. Heston was a pleasant man as men go, meeker and more sweet-tempered than the laborers. It was an honor really to be pursued by an academic, or that is what I kept telling myself. It didn't matter what I thought anyway, I would be chosen or I would not. The women have no say in the matter. It is rumored that The Great Master chooses a wife from the last-year girls, although no one ever sees his wife or wives, whatever the case may be. Then he discards them into The Beyond when he is through with them, throwing them away like yesterday's trash. I definitely do not want to draw that proverbial straw and think it may be suitable to be Heston's wife.

There is no such thing as the love I have read about in the forbidden books, books that have found their way to us from a different time and remain hidden in plain sight within the walls of The Great Library. What it would have been like to fall in love with whomever you wanted, to become whatever you wanted; a writer, an actress, or even a doctor. The Great Before sounds like a wonderfully free place.

"You need to get your head out of the clouds. It would be an arrangement, nothing more. It can't be anything more," I said although I did not want to believe it.

"I am just saying that he is not the worst man to look at and, who knows, maybe we can learn to love our partners, I have heard of it. Look at Mr. and Mrs. Smidt, they are always grossly over-affectionate. They seem quite happy."

She was right though, theoretically, it could happen. She was also correct in her appraisal that Heston was actually quite stunning with his inky curls and lanky limbs. I could fall for him, theoretically, of course.

For the time being, I had to concentrate on final exams of every nature, not theorize about Heston and his long fingers that fit perfectly into my own as I discovered on our stroll last night.

"Rianne told me Master Heston's first wife died in childbirth along with the child. He was so devastated that he went into The Great Beyond for a whole year before coming back. Any man that is capable of that much remorse has to be capable of love, I say," Greta remarked.

"Well, first of all, stop listening to Rianne. She is a pot-stirring gossip and likely to be cast out on that merit alone. You would be wise to stay away from her if you value a warm bed and food in your belly," I balked back even though I knew there was a speck of truth within the speculations just from looking into Heston's eyes.

When you really looked at him close-up, a perceptive person could see the feelings just below the surface of his hazel orbs. I could see pain and possibility, mixed together in a peculiar dance for

179

dominance. He had experienced life, its hardships, its triumphs and he had seen firsthand The Beyond. Surely, if anyone was capable of love it would be him.

"I will see you tonight, Greta, I have reproductive testing today, so I won't be back to the pod until after meal service," I said as I turned toward the medical building that I would be spending a great deal of time in over the next few months as part of final exams.

Greta pulled me in for a brief hug after checking that no one would see. I could detect the anxiety from the force alone without having to look up and see she did, indeed have tears in her pale green eyes. She would be undergoing the same trials and tests.

I tried to look neutral as if all this was just an everyday check-up. Although it is routine and normal for us, it still feels ominous. We don't ever know the results until Ceremonies. If you are deemed unable or unworthy to bear children then you are cast out or sent to work the gardens and forbidden to socialize or marry. The girls speculate that The Undesirables are forced into sexual servitude, although I can't find a difference between that and being obliged into marriage to serve your husband and bear children as your near only function. Regardless, it has to be better than The Beyond.

***

After thrashing about all night, I felt disconnected the following day as I sat for what would be a butt-numbing four-hour lecture on the dangers of The Beyond.

"The Beyond is to be feared. I know this, I have been out there," Master Heston began.

There was an audible collective intake of breath from the student body. I glanced at the blonde boy next to me, 2147-5, who looked as if his eyes may dislodge from their sockets and plop monstrously onto his desk. This was the lecture we all were looking forward to, as last-years we were promised some truths as we were on the precipice of being deemed adults.

Master Heston continued, speaking of a tribe right outside the walls, cannibals scarred and deformed from battle and led by a monarch. He referred to her as The Queen of the Lost. Although he had never personally encountered her, he made no hesitations in his assessment that she was as cunning as she was lethal. Disbelief danced in my ears at hearing this, cannibals, but more than that. This leader was a woman. Women do not lead. The lecture dragged on into hour four as Master Heston told of surviving ultimately by turning back to Atlas and the walls that seem so much like a prison to me.

"A word, 2047-1," Master Heston called out as we dismissed.

The rest of the students with their knowing faces filtered out of the lecture hall leaving us alone. Heston allowed his hand to graze my cheek before settling on my shoulder. A staggering, yet not unwelcome, heat found my cheeks and flushed them a healthy rose.

"I just wanted you to know that I will be stepping forward to claim you at the Ranking Ceremonies and that you have nothing to fear. You have been deemed A Perfect, although I had no doubts. You cannot tell anyone that I have shared this, Hanna, it is imperative. I could be cast out for even encouraging you." He was saying the right words, yet his eyes deceived him. There was a depth of pain that I did not understand.

***

Over the course of the last months leading to the Ranking Ceremony, Heston and I had spent many nights walking the grounds. We spoke of our relentless obligations to Atlas, of our hopes for the future, and our fears. He fortified my ambitions to be more than his subservient wife and ensured me that within the four walls of our home I was free to speak and conduct myself as his equal. Our relationship began to resemble what I thought love to be from my limited knowledge of the subject.

The night before the Ceremonies most of the girls in our pod were fast asleep, content that they would be chosen and have a peaceful existence. However, Greta was fretting her hair into balls around her fingers, a nervous tell she had always had. I was also restless even with the knowledge I had. We decided to take a walk. It was encouraged for us to stay physically fit so no one stopped us as we strolled.

We kept walking silently toward The Great Wall. It was further than we had ever ventured before and certainly well outside the free zone last-years were allowed to explore. It grew darker and more foreboding as we approached. Standing in the shadows of the wall, we seemed so small, so microscopic, so finite as we craned our necks up at the monstrous architecture. It had to stand fifty feet tall. One could not scale the wall as the ego impressed boys had thought. At the very top, curls of wire caught the moonlight and glinted off what appeared to be barbs. Sounds from the outside filtered through, I thought I heard human voices. I walked along the wall running my hand over the cool stone. Greta followed. We were nearing the farthest edge of the complex when Greta screamed.

"My leg, my leg is in a hole," she rasped out through tears.

Assessing the situation in the fragile light was difficult, but she had indeed toppled into a hole. Not just a hole, a tunnel. The tunnel stretched under The Great Wall. It was filled with loose rock, for cover presumably. My mind stored this information if I would ever need it. There was a way out, but what was out there was indubitably more dreadful than what was in here.

I assisted Greta out of the hole and shared her weight back to civilization where we arrived with little time to spare to begin preparation for Ceremonies. Greta needed medical attention, as quietly as possible, so we found our way to Master Heston's home via the back rows of picture-perfect manicured yards.

His home sat alone in the far north end of town, just before the trees began, and well past where we were allowed to roam. I rapped faintly at the back door. Heston appeared moments later with an impeccably rumpled bed head and I smiled in spite of myself, peering around him to catch a glance at what would be my residence in a mere few hours. My eyes scanned the room and landed on a knife peeking out from under a book on one of the many book cases. Perplexed, but pressed for time, I quickly explained our debacle. He assured me that he would get her to medical and brushed a light kiss on my cheek. I started on the long walk back in the morning light to prepare for the day, all the while pondering why a teacher would have or need a knife. Weapons of any kind were reserved for The Guard.

***

The night's events and the lack of sleep did not at all squelch the nervous energy zipping through me as the preparations happened. We were bathed, shaved, and dipped in beautiful smelling lotions. Each of the twenty 2147-girls were adorned with jewels and dresses of white. The hair we were never to cut above our buttocks was identically braided into two tight pleats that sprawled down our backs. Our husbands would be the only persons allowed to see us with our hair down. Baby's breath was woven into the pleats and light color dabbed on our cheeks. When we were deemed appropriate per Madam Hunt, we were lined up numerically. I was first.

As we were paraded down the center aisle the available men took their leering appraisals although Heston told me all matches were made and assignments coordinated beforehand. I tried to keep my head raised and sought out Heston. He would be near the stage as he was our teacher and would lead us up the steps. The Ceremonies served not only to get our assigned role but as our nuptials. By the time I descended the stage, I would be simply Mrs. Heston Grim. I hoped Hanna would remain. As I waited to ascend, with Heston holding steadfast to my arm, I realized I had not seen Greta.

"Where is Greta?" I whispered through clenched teeth.

"She broke her ankle. Hanna, don't panic, but Greta was deemed an Undesirable. She is to be assigned as a house servant for The Great Master," he hushed back.

With that body shaking news, we ascended the stairs and made our way across the stage. Rage boiled inside of me. Heston repeated the process until each of the eighteen other girls were standing awaiting their assignments.

183

The Great Master welcomed the men and made his speech about the importance of the Ceremony. He was a rotund thing, the poster child for gluttony, with lustful eyes ogling the girls. The bile rose in my throat threatening to spill out. My only saving grace was knowing I was going to Heston. My thoughts rounded back to Greta as my number was called and I was asked to step forward. She was going to be alright. She was not going to be his wife, just a house servant.

"2047-1 is quite remarkable. She is the first child to be born within the walls of Atlas and has an IQ of 189, which makes her profoundly gifted. Any children would indeed inherit intelligence. She is fully capable and fertile. She has been deemed A Perfect. Gentlemen, she has been spoken for by Master Heston Grim. Master Heston, do you wish to step forward and claim your bride?" the Great Master questioned.

Heston made his way to me without breaking eye contact. The pronouncement was made and sealed with a kiss; we were a married couple. I felt sick, not because of Heston, but because the whole atmosphere was suggestive of lambs being led to slaughter. Most of these girls were not going to be as lucky as I was.

The Ceremonies continued through the remaining eighteen. Nine girls were deemed Undesirable and assigned to work as house servants for the higher-ranking officials or sent to the gardens. They were sent immediately to their assignments, but The Perfects, and now wives, were invited to feast in celebration of our nuptials. There was food and the finest wine which several of the men were pouring liberally for their betrothed. They groped their wives and laughed drunkenly at each other. We, of course, were not allowed to leave until after the first dance, keeping steadfast with the archaic rules.

Led to the dance floor, all the couples swayed as expected. Heston was incredibly gentle in comparison with his counterparts. It was not at all unenjoyable being nestled against him. He bent so his cheek rested lightly against mine being no easy task as he was a stretched six-foot-two versus my five-foot-seven. I felt safe. When the music stopped, Heston excused us.

We strolled at a good pace; I was anxious to be behind the walls of our home to inquire more about Greta. Heston unlocked the front door and led me inside. I let out an audible sigh and he chuckled.

"That bad?" he asked.

"No, it's not that. I am just worried about Greta."

Being the sweet man I had come to know, Heston tried to assure me that she would be fine in the care of The Great Master. I nodded and allowed my eyes to wander the massive shelves of books covering the dining area as I sat at the table, books I would undoubtedly read. Heston bent and kissed my shoulder as I was freeing the head numbing braids from my hair. I knew my obligations, of course, but Heston insisted that we wait until I felt ready. What I did feel was exhausted and although nothing more than sleep was going to happen tonight, I was still looking forward to being in the same bed as him.

***

Three months passed before I saw Greta again. Most of the married girls were already showing signs of pregnancy and I had just now felt comfortable sharing my body with my husband. I felt happy, as happy as I could in the circumstances. As Greta had once said, maybe we could learn to love our partners. I think I did, although the knife still bothered me. I had not seen it since becoming Mrs. Grim.

Late at night, I heard a light knocking from the back door. Heston answered it and quietly carried Greta into our house. She was rail-thin, dirty, and looked as if she had been beaten every day for the last three months. The shame and guilt gnawed at my belly. Here I was being happy and my best friend was suffering. I immediately drew her a bath as she wept about how sorry she was for coming here.

"Hush now. This is not the same kind of home the others have. Believe it or not, I have a say here," I told her.

185

She told me unspeakable things as I washed her hair. She was beaten, her body violated, and was near starvation, as I could tell from her protruding spine. The exuberance that normally emanated from Greta was drained from her like the filthy tub water down the drain. The tales were true. The Great Master kept a collection of girls and when he tired of them, they were cast out with nothing. Not only that, most of The Undesirables never even made it to their assignments. No one knows where they went. Greta's story got progressively worse as she told of overheard conversations that there was not enough food for everyone inside of Atlas and that is why more and more are being tossed into The Beyond. Being within the walls of The Great Master for three excruciating months, Greta had been privy to all types of classified conversation as she went about her daily chores.

The terrors compounded with each sentence. I could hear the floor protesting as Heston worried the wood outside the bathroom. Men had gone missing in the night, whole family units vanished. We were told that they had simply left Atlas in pursuit of some unknown dream, but the truth, as Greta told it, was that people were being executed so as not to overpopulate the compound.

When we had finished getting months of grime removed from Greta's now feeble body, we settled in around the dining table where there were no windows. Heston's face wrecked with disbelief, mine with disgust. It did not make any sense, if we were overpopulating to the point of food scarcity then why would we also be encouraged to procreate.

Heston appeared to have the answer. I had heard his story before, but in light of the new information, it seemed that perhaps there was more to it. The rumors that his wife had passed during childbirth were lies. She was cast out for something Heston was not yet ready to disclose. He had attempted to follow her, convinced they would fare better together, as he told it. His first wife had not been deemed A Perfect, she was an Acceptable, a practice that had since been eradicated. Theorizing, he told us that during his teaching training he read a book penned by The Great Master that spoke of a population in which only Perfects procreated, at the time Heston had given it no more than passing suspicion.

186

We decided collectively that Greta must remain hidden, it was grounds for being cast out if she was discovered. I fixed a bed in the basement for her. It was crude yet clean and comfortable. Heston and I retired to our room upstairs.

To see a man weep is an otherworldly experience. My poor gentle husband was sobbing. I was his comforter that night and for many to come. We stayed up well into the early morning hours rehashing, speculating, and formulating plans. He confessed that he had a weapon held over from his time outside the walls fashioned from bone and that he had smuggled it back into the compound. At one point, we had a map spread out over our bed showing the details of the sewer system.

"And, this over here by the South wall..." he said indicating on the map the location.

"Is a tunnel under the wall," I finished.

We both looked at each other shocked. I explained how we had discovered it the night before Ceremonies on pure accident.

"How did you know it was there?" I questioned.

"Because I am the one who put it there, Hanna." He described how he dug the tunnel as a means back into Atlas after his year in The Beyond and they had to allow him to return because he had insider knowledge that could reflect badly on the Elders, maybe even cause a revolt.

"What are we going to do? We can't send Greta back to be cast out, and we can't keep her here forever. Oh, God Heston what if they mean to execute her? We don't get enough rations to feed her properly either." And suddenly, I was the one weeping.

Early the next day, strategies were set into motion. Greta would use the tunnel to exit the compound during the day and return after dark. Heston gave her specific instructions to stay near The Great Wall because the tribes out there were fearful of coming too close to the wall. She was to keep the coveted knife in the tunnel and carry it outside the wall.

A month came and went with our arrangement in place. The color returned to Greta's cheeks and her ribs became less visible. Evenings passed in the protected dining room with laughter. Even Heston could not resist joining us. He entertained us with his precious coin collection passed down from his grandfather from The Great Before. Greta was fascinated by them, turning them over and over in her hands.

This time of uneasy happiness, made more poignant by knowledge it could not last, continued until one blistering late summer night. The heat never did break and even the windows protested with humidity, streaking the panes of glass as if proclaiming sadness. We waited through the night with no signs of Greta. When the sun broke over The Great Wall at dawn we discovered why. A commotion was taking place in the square. Everyone was being steadily drawn to the noise of a woman's scream. I recognized it immediately. It was Greta.

Heston and I rushed toward the square. The guards held Greta firmly by each arm as she thrashed violently. The Great Master was also present and making a proclamation.

"2147-8 has been accused and found guilty of abandonment of her duties and is hereby ordered to be cast-out," he boomed triumphantly.

Heston held me firmly to his side. He knew I was writhing in anger, and given half a chance I would scratch that filthy pig's eyes out. I would be cast-out right alongside her. With a sinking resignation, I reluctantly allowed myself to be lugged home. The front door had no more than closed when I started spewing profanities, something that I had never done before. Heston held me.

"Shh, darling. I have a plan. Tonight, we will leave," he told me.

"But, how Heston, how can we leave? We will be in danger every day and surely starve. I can't leave all the others behind either," I protested.

As it turned out Heston did have a plan, and one that would benefit the whole community.

That night, after the sky was as dark as a blackbird's tail, we headed to the south wall and through the tunnel to The Beyond. We would camp near the border until daylight and then continue our journey.

When morning arrived, I stretched out the kinks from sleeping, tucked away in Heston's protective embrace, and picked the twigs from my loose unruly locks. It looked so much different than I had pictured. I had an image in my head of wastelands filled with angry assassins, but what I saw was lush vegetation and sprawling woods. Heston warned me to be on guard, some of the people we would encounter had been made desperate by circumstance and were very dangerous.

We were just starting out when I saw, on the ground and placed with intention, what looked like copper twinkling in the sunlight. I leaned down and picked up the object in question and a smile bloomed on my lips.

"That clever girl, look Heston, Greta has left us a trail to find her. Your coins from the collection, look there is another one," I exclaimed.

The trail of coins led us deep into the woods. It was then that we encountered our first person of The Beyond. We approached carefully and quietly. When the woman turned, I recognized the light blue eyes under the grime of the wilderness.

"Rianne?"

It was indeed Rianne, the pot-stirring gossip. We quickly explained our intentions and showed her that we were not armed, or so I thought. The months spent fighting for survival had matured her. Loneliness had swallowed her innocence, the lost child's eagerness to be amongst the familiar had her yearning to join our voyage. It was made understood that our first priority was finding Greta and I hoped we were not too late. Rianne told us she had seen the guards pushing her deeper and deeper into the woods.

Some of the people we encountered were not at all like Rianne, they had turned feral, animal-like and pledged allegiance to The Queen of the Lost. But we were able to outmaneuver them easily as our bodies were still fed and our pace was quick. Our group continued to grow as we trudged along. Fueled by fear of becoming the next meal and visualizing an opportunity at a better existence, the lost joined ranks without convincing. In hushed tones it was implied that we might overthrow The Queen and her tyrannical rule.

We found many lost faces in our travels. Most had bits of useful information, such as The Queen had captured Greta. By the time we arrived at what appeared to be a fortress and undoubtedly The Queen's lair, we were two hundred strong and some even had crude weaponry forged by hand from the forest's abundance.

We had to be crafty if we were to save Greta's life and tackle phase two of Heston's plan. We could not just storm the castle. Strategically, we assessed the weaknesses in the perimeter and determined that burrowing beneath the barrier was the best option. It was laborious work, but this time we had help. The narrowness of the tunnel did mean, however, that the army we had engaged would have to stay outside. They were to act as the fall back if or when the guards discovered our presence.

Heston placed his knife into my boot as we exited the tunnel and searched for Greta. Sticking to the shadows, we came upon large rows of cages. The rudimentary cells were littered with bones appearing to be human and there, tucked in the far back, we found Greta. I quickly grabbed a finger bone and picked the lock to her cage. Then freed her rope-burned limbs from the hemp restraints and ungagged her. She was whispering repeatedly, "The Queen." It was a warning.

I turned toward Heston who was now face to face with a beautiful and terrifying woman. He motioned for me to stay back with a slight wave of his hand.

"Blair?" he asked, his voice laced with sorrow and disbelief.

"Yes, Heston, it is me. You should not have come. Did you not get the message when I left you with a knife in your arm? I see you have brought my replacement. Maybe she will buy into your foolish obsolete notions of love and family and bear those children you want so badly. How very thoughtful. She will make a lovely meal for my kingdom," she cooed.

"Not even a fleck of dust will be thrown her way, do you understand me?" Heston barked back.

"Who is going to stop me? Surely, not you. You couldn't even keep me in your bed, let alone protect me and you certainly cannot protect this child bride. My guards are disarming your merry band of misfits as we speak."

"How can you be so sure Blair? I am not the same man you left wandering the woods years ago." Heston's eyes hardened.

She heard enough. The Queen lunged at him with her knife drawn, wailing like the rabid banshee she had become. Just as the tip of her blade touched Heston's cheek, I intervened.

"Blair, is it?" I asked.

Intrigued, she inclined her head to me.

"I think you misread my intentions in coming here," I continued.

"And just why did you come here, with our husband in hand, if not to free your little friend?" she asked stepping closer to me.

"I admit, at first, it was just to free Greta, but after hearing you talk about Heston and how I am just a means to breed, I feel every bit the silly child I am." Blair continued closing the gap between us until she was just out of reach.

"I don't want that. I truly thank you for opening my eyes. Perhaps in exchange for Greta I could offer Heston as a replacement. Would you consider letting us stay here with you as your subjects? There is clearly so much I could learn from you." My voice was almost unrecognizable as I heard myself.

Considering my offer, The Queen extended her hand to me and I took it.

"I think we have come to a suitable agreement, child," she said, still shaking my hand.

At that moment I pulled her into me and sank Heston's knife deep in her chest cavity. With a sickening rupture of skin, the blood painted the ground grotesquely. One turn of the blade and she dropped where she stood. As did I, being caught by the two people I cherish most in this world: Heston and Greta. We had no time to fixate on what I did because a whole chain of events had been set into motion and this was just the first obstacle. We made our way back outside carefully checking for the guards Blair spoke of, but not before arming ourselves with The Queen's huge stockpile of weapons. No guards were found. Instead, we found our rag-tag group of malcontents in high spirits.

The next phase of what had become a movement fueled by the rage of injustice took us into the unguarded sewers under Atlas. The women and men mixed together in a way I had never seen, prepared to fight alongside one another. The people of Atlas deserved to make their own choices. The only way to do that is to cut off the head of the beast so freedom might replace fear. There was no going back. We would take on his guard as well if the need arose. We had to see this through or surely a bleak fate awaited us.

Again, our band stood guard, able and ready to assist if we were discovered. Greta, Heston, and I snuck into The Great Master's bedroom. He was caught unaware in his slumber waking to the barrel of a gun pressed against his head. Greta led him outside at gunpoint into the town square. Our army followed closely behind. Every citizen and official in Atlas gathered as we passed. We outnumbered them, we out weaponed them, and we had outsmarted them. No one challenged us.

"This man stands accused of rape, murder, abuse, genocide and malfeasance in office. Does anyone have a statement to the contrary they wish to give?" I asked the crowd.

No one stood up for The Great Master.

"I have led you all and kept you safe and fed and this is how you repay me? No one is willing to bear witness for me? Everything I did, I did for the betterment of Atlas. We could not have some inbred half-wits running through the streets. The girls found to be wanting were cast aside by righteous action. They were the lowest of the gutter trash, harlots!" he screamed.

A gunshot echoed through the silent streets.

Greta was on the bestowing end. Tears streaked her face. I ran to her.

It was over or just beginning, depending on how you looked at it.

We learned so many difficult truths the year of our Ranking Ceremonies, many about the corruption and sheer lies The Great Master was poisoning us with. There was not a food shortage. Just on the other side of the wall was lush forest littered with the possibility of farming and wildlife. I learned, when necessary, I will do anything for the people I love. We had set things right, declared everyone free, women and men stood as equals and first on the agenda was a democratic vote for who should lead us.

"So, tell me Madam President, what is the first order of business?" Heston chuckled in my ear.

"I think it might be to convince my husband to finish painting the nursery before his child is born," I said as he bent down for a kiss, gently rubbing the barely visible bump in my belly.

Greta smiled knowingly from across the porch, secretly saying she told me so. Real love did exist and it existed inside the walls of Atlas.

A.K. Harris was born and raised on a farm in the rural Midwest and continues to live the small-town life in her hometown with her two active children, husband, and her exuberant dog, Roxy. Her love for reading drove her to her current job as Director/Librarian of her local public library, but ranks as a close second to her true passion of writing. When not enduring numbing bleacher butt from her kids' many sporting events she enjoys cooking and running amuck outside, a self-proclaimed wanderer who thinks adventure is just around the next corner. She is currently working on her debut novel *The River Hears.*

Contributions to editing of Atlas: The Tale of Hanna and Gretel by Tom Alston

Find out more at: https://akharrisauthor.com/

My Own Skin

By Sherri Cook Woosley

It doesn't hurt to peel off our outer layer – *pelli* – but tonight when we do, we are nervous. They pronounce our skin "pelts" and call us "selkies," something from their home world. That was one of the original misunderstandings when they came from the stars to our home. That is not what we call ourselves. And our *pelli* is more than skin, more than a shell, more than fur, it is the part that connects our emotions and thoughts to our physical form.

Tonight, we come ashore together, threading through the black rocks that jut out like teeth in a ring that encloses this island. Then, we take off our *pellis*. Two moons light the beach in a soft pink glow. Big Sister pulls at the tides, regular and uniform. Little Sister is the troublemaker. Her skin is pockmarked with volcanoes, her crown is a red corona in the sky. Her flight path is erratic: when she is angry, she yanks at us, causing peaks in our oceans, and eroding shorelines.

We are a pod, so we act together. We set our *pellis* on the black sand in little piles, some transparent and some taking on a soft gray hue as if to match the sand. Tonight we do not want to let go of it, but we are resolved. One of us is missing and we will get them back. We choose a form – some like the newcomer females and some like the males and some with attributes of both or neither. This is funny to us because with our *pelli* we take whatever form we want whenever we want.

This isn't the first time we have shifted so we know how to wiggle our fingers and toes. Some have already begun the dance. It is so different on land than in the sea. Gravity makes us teeter as we stretch away from the sand, arms extended for balance, and then fall to the forgiving beach. And when one comes over to help another up, perhaps they become a tangle of limbs.

The feel of wind is so different than water, but dancing keeps us warm. We know the pattern and soon we flow. And as we create harmony, as we are together, so does our bliss grow. In our *pellis*, our

196

thoughts are open to the pod. By taking them off, we separate and open ourselves to a new way to create beauty through movement.

We sense the newcomer. Awareness passes among us, a resolve, and we hold tight to the dance's form until tension breaks us. We scatter. Grab for our individual *pellis* so we can change form and dive into the friendly water, hide behind the rocky teeth that dash the newcomers' boats.

The newcomer, alone, steps from behind the dune where they'd been hiding, form enveloped in a giant hooded coat. They are done watching our dance. Now their legs pump as they run toward the beach.

We all get away but one.

There is a breaking inside, a ripping as if a leviathan from the deep had bitten us, taken one away, leaving wounds inside of the survivors. Water splashes against the rocks.

We are gone.
No.
They are gone.
I am here.

The newcomer is shoving my *pelli* into a sack and I cannot move. I am a woman, now, and this body feels strange. I reach for my pod with my mind, but there is an absence. I am trying to wave an appendage that doesn't exist in this form. My breath quickens, my torso expands and I am afraid. I have never been separated from my pod and this body does not talk to me. A moment ago, there was harmony in our dance, but now this newcomer has stolen from me. My mind, this woman's mind, knows words, but I don't have the concept.

I try, "Please?"

"You must be cold," he says. How do I know it is a he? This body knows.

I touch my head. Hair grows there, and under my armpits, and where my legs come together, but nowhere else to keep me warm. I shiver.

He is not ungentle as he wraps me in a blanket, my arms held down by my sides, and then scoops me up, carrying me up to the buildings the newcomers built. Alone in my mind, I repeat that this was the plan. That one of us had to be captured. We made the decision and I must carry it out. Over his shoulder I see the moon sisters. Red streams down Little Sister's face and makes me think of tears. I know what tears are now. This body has taught me.

We took their form because we could and they couldn't take ours. We took their form because this is a planet of water and they do not have the right bodies for it. We took their form because we felt sorry that these newcomers had no fur for the cold.

But we did not misunderstand when they stole our *pellis* — and our people — like the leviathans from the deep. Leviathans do not mask their intent. Their jaws open wide and their breath smells of death. They – the newcomers – came with mouths full of teeth, but they hid them behind smiles.

Inside the building, he sets me down and puts something over my head that covers my body. Clothing. Table. Light. The words rush at me. We've—no, I've—experienced this expedited learning when changing forms before, but this human body is complicated.

The table is too large for the two of us; it is solid and made for many people. We do not have this thing under the seas. His metal lantern casts a ring of light and shadow, but my lanterns, the sister moons, hang in the sky. I can see them from the windows behind this man: Big Sister edging out of sight, Little Sister moving into frame. I feel the sea creep up the island in push-pull increments and imagine the sound increasing as water slaps at the black rock teeth.

"You'll live with us now. It will take some time, but you'll get used to it here." He speaks with such authority that each statement traps me in this human body; my bare skin hurts. "This will be a good life for you."

"I do not belong here." I lift the dress that he put over my head and slap at my legs. The fabric is coarse and I long for my sleek skin and warm fur.

"They call me Flicks." He leans forward. "What's your name?"

What do I call myself? I don't know how to answer this so I shrug my shoulders.

"We can help each other. Your pelt-sy," he mangles the word, "is the most amazing bio-aril we've ever seen. The lab is trying to figure it out. They think maybe a gel that holds stem cells of amniotic fluid --"

"Please," I say, as if being polite will persuade him. "Return my skin so I can go home." If he would cooperate, if he would listen, then we could be on the same side. I understand "we," that is how our pod thinks and solves problems, but this man wants something and it is different than what I want: to bring our stolen member back to the pod.

He rises, hands clenched by his side, pacing. His boots beat the floor. "I chose you," he says, finally. "You are beautiful. Your eyes are kind. Not like the other humans on this outpost."

Does it matter whether he chose me or whether my skin was merely the closest? My hands clench into fists, unconscious echo.

"But it's more than that." He faces me, forces his hands to unclench. My body sees that this is hard for him. "This place is my last chance." He swallows. "I'm a soldier. Everyone in this outpost is. We put in our time for a meaningless war and then we're allowed to retire here." He shook his head. "Even if I left, others will come, figure out how to recreate the pelt-sy. How to live on this planet. But we can figure it out together, if you'll help me."

My mouth moves, but it is so dry that it's hard to urge words out. "We tried to help you, we said your bodies were too fragile."

"Right." He sits down across from me, grabs one of my hands, but he did not ask permission. The touch is overwhelming, the way this body responds. We do not do that.

"Who knows how long the labs will take figuring out how to make the pelt-sy? Some of us thought that we could create it another way. That the offspring of," he rushes through, "one of you with one of us would have the best of both worlds. You know?"

The human part of me tries to parse meaning from his words, but the animal in me recognizes desperation. He reeks of a rotting fish.

The kitchen faucet bursts to life and I stand from the chair, rush to the white froth pouring out. "Saltwater." I dip my hands in, splash my face, and gulp at the stream so the familiar taste is on my tongue when I announce, "The sea comes for me."

"No. That's ridiculous." He pushes past me and turns the faucet knobs one way and then the other, but the water won't stop. "Stupid equipment. Maybe a bad pump? I'll check the well head and the casing. They gave us outdated equipment when they dropped us off on this rock."

He leaves the room, it's called kitchen, I know, and does not tie my hands. Why should he? This body, like his, is too fragile to go outside.

I go to the sink, stand there watching with a sense of satisfaction.

"You shouldn't be here." The voice has too many emotions for my limited experience in this body. The statement is, somehow, a command and an entreaty at once. Not something that someone born a human could produce.

I turn toward the speaker. They look like an older human female in a dress that hangs too large on her gaunt frame. Her skin is brown like sediment that clouds the water when the tentacled *dreer* rise from their hiding places. White hair interlaces down the back. A braid, my mind supplies. Her eyes are blue and sad. I imagine that she cries a lot. Her hands have calluses, flesh building up from repeated actions, not from swimming in the sea. Not from playing in the waves, not from dancing in the rosy light of Big Sister and Little Sister.

Something new flutters inside of me like butterfly wings tickling my ribs. I have never seen a butterfly, but this memory of a form with colorful membranes is exactly what I mean. I would like my pod to experience being such an amazing amalgam of scales and hairs and beauty. They would like the harmony. No, we would like the harmony.

Distracted by my mistake, I take a deep breath.

"I'm here," I say, and that butterfly sensation startles me again, "because of you. We didn't forget."

Their chin, her chin, who is she now, anymore?

"You waited so long," she says, "I didn't think anyone would come."

"We have missed you every moment and we sang for you." I swallow because I am happy and I am proud. "And now you can come home."

"They took away my *pelli*." She makes the right sound with the human mouth. "They sent it to a lab. I can never change form again."

Steps announce Flick's arrival with enough time for her to slip into the adjoining room so he does not see us talking.

The sound of the water running is a constant *shhhh* in the background. This is soothing to me, but he is frustrated. "I've put in a work requisition. Hydraulics aren't my specialty, but someone will be here in the morning." He kneels to open the cabinet, using a wrench against the pipe.

"What is a lab?" The word was too foreign. He'd said it earlier and then she/they said it, but the image that fills this mind makes no sense.

"You've been talking to Lucy." It takes me a moment to realize that this set of syllables has been assigned to the woman in the other room. He puts his hands on his hips. "Fine. Scientists. They have to figure out what the pelt-sy was made from and the only way to do that was to cut it open. Our survival on this planet means understanding alien technology and then replicating it. But it's taking too long." He scoffs. "We're not exactly a priority for the off-planet labs."

My stomach drops and I feel dizzy, reaching out a hand to the chair. This body shocks me with picture after picture of what the lab is doing, destroying, desiccating. Our *pelli* is so integral to our being and these newcomers stole it and allowed, no encouraged, other newcomers to rip our *pellis* apart.

I look through the doorway. Lucy is there. She is watching me with her hands clasped together and her chin wobbling. This is why she has given up.

"We need a new plan." He is still talking. "I need my children to have selkie blood so they'll understand the sea. No worries about being drafted in the never-ending war. This is the only way that my family survives. I need our future. That's the only thing that's kept me going through the Hell I've been through."

Little Sister winks in the middle of the window. I look over at Lucy and see her eyes widen as she begins to understand why I was captured tonight.

"Listen, I know that you don't understand, but you're so beautiful. The color of your skin, the shape of your mouth, the size of your eyes. You could save me." Dropping to his knees, the soldier grabs at my dress. "Please. I love you."

This is yearning and it is not something I knew before. The force of it makes me want to give in, to agree to whatever will make him stop asking. I think of my mission and that allows me to feel sad for him, but also to shake my head and pull my dress away from his grasping hands.

"Lucy learned to love her husband and she had a child. It didn't survive, but we know more now. Trust me, I'll take care of you if you do what I say."

I can't meet his eyes.

"I'll see to your room." Flicks leaves and I turn to the woman who had her skin stolen, was married to a stranger, and then forced to have a child.

"Do you want me to embrace you?" I ask.

She nods and I hug her, letting her clutch back at me.

"I'm sorry we had to wait so long."

She steps back. "You had to wait for Little Sister."

"Yes."

"It's too late for me. This body has trapped me and I've grown old." She holds up her wrinkled hands. "But I know where he put your *pelli*."

She scrambles onto the countertop and reaches up high to pull out the sack. She drops it down to me and I pull at the cord wrapped around it.

My skin. Saltwater falls from my eyes. Soft as I remember, pliable and jelly-like. It has not dried out. I bury my face in the fur and inhale the musky, wonderful scent. This close, I hear the echo of my pod and know they are dancing beyond the black teeth, making a plea to Little Sister. Each moment Little Sister is moving away. Soon we will not have the power of the water to help us.

I think about her words. There are no other voices to talk to about this decision. No pleasure in consensus. She is more experienced on land than I am, knows more about this situation, and she tells me to go. And inside me there is an eagerness to leave, to rush back to safety and to the pod.

But I cannot leave without the pod member that he calls Lucy because she is my sister, my mother, my aunt, my daughter. That's why we agreed that one of us would be captured.

She releases a long moan when I replace my *pelli* and hand the bag back to her.

"I will not leave you," I say. "Unless we can both go."

***

He takes me to a room for sleeping. There is a narrow cot and a desk with a chair and a dresser against the far wall. When he closes the door, I wrap my arms around myself and sink to the floor. It is so hard and so cold and so lonely. I have never been alone like this. No sounds of the ocean lull me into dreams, there is no music, there is no comforting mental touch of the other pod members.

A sound on the door makes me look up.

Lucy is there. "May I come in?"

When I nod, she closes the door and comes closer. "May I embrace you?"

Again, I nod.

She helps me to the cot and pulls a blanket up to my chin, she makes soothing sounds that mean nothing in the newcomer's language, but could be the clicking claws of a *caer* or the cheerful screech of a *porphin*. She pulls the chair next to the cot and sits beside me as Little Sister, and our plan, drown in the deeps.

***

In the morning he takes me to the lab. This is the first time I've been so close to their camp. There are several small metal buildings like the one we were in last night and a larger one in the center. That is where we are headed. Clouds shift overhead and the wind sweeps my hair. The crash of the ocean is there, the water calls to me.

Inside the large white room are large machines crewed by five more newcomers. Immediately their needs and wants hammer at my mind. We teach our children not to do this, but these creatures are emotional toddlers, undisciplined with their pain and their demands. They give no thought to the group, only to themselves.

"Is that one of them?" A female with yellow hair cut short. She wears the same clothing as the other newcomers, but her frame is smaller and her voice is higher. The violence in her tone grates against me.

"Nice, Flicks," another one says. He, this human body tells me, has glasses that sit on scars racing down his cheek to disappear under the collar of his shirt. His leg is different, a curve like part of a shell, but he uses it to move around with what appears to be little hindrance. We would do something similar with our *pellis*. I think these changes must be from the war that Flicks told me about. "Is she friendly?"

"Does it matter?" says the yellow-haired one.

They choose silence, but their secrets pulse at me. Embarrassment, gratitude not to be me, implicit us versus them. I am the them.

Flicks holds up the sack with my *pelli*. "I thought we could test it against the ones we've been synthesizing."

205

"Great," the one with scars and glasses says. He moves to a tank, places his hands into over-sized gloves, and then plunges them into the tank. Then he holds up what looks like the body part of a tentacled *dreer*: clear and slippery and the size of a human's torso. "We've grown this so far, but if one of us tries on the real *pelli*, then we can compare." He looks to the yellow-haired girl. "Abby, you're the smallest."

"Yes." She makes a fist and pulls it close to her side in a celebratory move. "Thank you, Cap."

I double over in pain as my stomach cramps. Abby's searing sense of pride, Cap's biting curiosity, Flick's hope all swirl around me like phantom touches. Human words ricochet around my mind and I grasp at them as if I had fins instead of fingers.

Flicks takes out my *pelli*. The edges are curling up. It needs saltwater. He offers it to Abby. "Try it on."

My mental fins turn into claws to snatch up words. I've never had to do this before, to push back against these overwhelming wishes, but I do it now.

"No." I straighten against the cramping in my middle. "No. You will not give away my *pelli*. It is not yours to give. It is mine."

I feel the shock from all directions, but I don't care. I dismiss their feelings. This is unheard of in our colony, but I cannot think about it now. Worse is the violation that these newcomers propose.

"Give it back now." I step forward and hold out my hand. It shakes as my heart bangs against my ribcage so hard that the internal sound muffles my hearing.

"Oh. She's angry." Abby shrugs one shoulder as if I don't matter. "Lucy's never done that before."

"They are different creatures of the same species," Cap says, as if he has any idea. "They will have individual reactions to stimuli, but each interaction brings new information."

206

Flicks looks at me and shoves my *pelli* back in the bag. "We can discuss this later," he says to me. He smiles and his teeth gleam white.

A sound from one of the machines breaks the standoff and the crew returns to their devices. There is a cone-shaped alarm on top that swirls around three times and then quiets. A series of long and short sounds follow, like a *caer's* six limbs tapping against a rock at low tide.

"Ugg," Abby says when the tapping stops. "Typical check-in." She shakes her head. "No reaction to any of the reports we've sent."

Cap places his hand on her shoulder and squeezes. "As soon as they know that human life is sustainable on this planet, they'll send more settlers."

Which means that if human life is not sustainable, then they won't? I keep my face blank. These humans are so insensitive to the emotions of another that they don't notice. Maybe Lucy and I will not be able to escape. Maybe my mission is changing.

Anger stings me inside as if I'd wandered into the tentacled *dreer*. I don't know what to do with it so I feed it until Flicks says it is time to return to our building. The wind blows stronger than before and the light is red. Lucy and I both turn to the place where the seawater strikes the rocks. Our pod is there, standing in a line, buffeted by the water, making themselves seen in order to deliver a message. They stretch their forms to reach toward Little Sister. Lucy and I stare at each other as we receive their message and butterfly wings unfurl inside me. I recognize the sensation. It is my courage. If Flicks asked again, I would say that I'd named myself Butterfly-Wings.

Once we are inside, Flicks says, "Now you understand. I need someone to help me on this forsaken planet. It's a matter of survival. And it helps that you're beautiful. It is easy for me to love you."

Lucy stands by the open door. The pod's chanting has grown louder, welcoming the storm. Rain comes at an angle, blown by the wind. Seawater invades the house, kissing Lucy's feet and then retreating, creeping farther each time. Little Sister must be listening, her volcanoes erupting as she swings close.

"You love the idea of a selkie," I say. He speaks of love but sprinkles his phrases with "me." "A woman who has no past, no needs, no demands." I push him away and he falls into the water covering the floor, soaking the back of his clothes. "But I have my own story."

He stands up, furious. I see the violence in the narrowing of his eyes as he sees the water. "This stupid planet. Flooding again. How can the tide come up so high?" He kicks at the water as if it were alive and then pulls a hunting knife from his hip. The kind used to peel sealskin away from meat and blubber. He holds the blade toward my throat, hand shaking with anger because he is being thwarted. "You can't –"

He doesn't seem to know how to finish. Instead, he wants me to say that I won't leave because his needs are more important than mine. Understanding chokes me. All I can do is stare back at him.

He tosses the knife to the table and exhales as if disappointed. "Shut the door, Lucy. I've got to get sandbags." Flicks stalks away.

Lucy ignores him and grabs the sack with my *pelli*. She rips it open and lowers my skin into the seawater before handing it to me.

Fingers tingling, I strip off the human dress and thrust my feet into the skin. I pull the skin, shimmying it over my hips, forcing my fingers down the sleeves. It feels so good, but then I look at the woman he called Lucy. Being in this human body has changed me, but I choose to think of "we."

I meet her eyes while I hold the knife to my *pelli* and I make the first cut.

It isn't easy but I hold with one hand and I cut with the other. When one of our *pellis* are torn, we gather around and sing to our injured friend. Sometimes one of us will offer blood to help it grow. Growing a *pelli* large enough for two bodies has never been done before. Maybe we will sing songs about it, if we can escape.

I'm taking too long.

She comes over to help me.

Saltwater is up to our knees and Little Sister moves higher in the window. Oh, she is gloriously angry tonight.

I help Lucy slip into half of my skin. It's tight, won't fit. She's been in this body so long, life changed at the whim of a stranger.

"Leave me so you'll be safe," she says.

"Nope." The word feels fierce and defiant. I love it.

I retrieve the hunting knife.

The blade stings. I release his disappointment that I won't stay. Crimson flows down my arm and onto the outer layer of skin surrounding my friend.

The layer absorbs my cells and grows until I can pull it up to cover her shoulders. Now she takes over, massaging and singing to the skin, encouraging it to grow.

I hunker down and work my own portion of skin, kneading and grabbing with my teeth to make it stretch. The soldier and crew changed me, confused and battered me with human feelings and demands. But they will not keep me here.

The soldier returns, carrying sandbags. He splashes to a halt when he sees me with the knife, sees the woman whom he knew as Lucy changing into a sleek, gray-colored creature so similar to his home world's seal. She has dreamed of this moment while lying in the human bed night after night. The images communicate through our *pellis* and I feel her wild joy. She slips out to join the pod, to be the "we."

She can return, but my portion of the *pelli* is not large enough. I am both part of my pod and still a single voice in my own head.

"Don't come closer." I am desperate enough to saw through human flesh and bone in order to return to the sea. My body knows how to show him this truth: my lips pull back in a snarl. It is unnatural to a selkie but feels right to a human. "Am I beautiful now?"

He flinches and looks out the window to avoid my question. His eyes widen as the whole island shakes. He grabs the counter.

I slice again — cutting away my sympathy for his return to a never-ending war or his future children.

Little Sister moves past the window leaving only a red light shining through.

An alarm blares from another building in the human's outpost. He turns to face me, and I see dawning realization. "The storm. Is the island going under? Are you doing this?"

From my *pelli* I hear my pod singing a triumphant chorus as seawater churns.

His shoulders slump. "Please," he says, as if being polite will persuade me. "I didn't mean to hurt you."

Third cut. This time along my ribs. I flick the knife to clean the bit of human skin, hurling away his expectation that I will learn to love him if I have no choice.

"But you did. Your selfishness changed me." This assertion hangs in the silence between us. "I would run for your boats, now, because there will be nothing left here." I smile at him. "It's a matter of your survival."

"No." I see his dawning realization a moment before he stumbles past me and through the door, making his way to the lab with the boats and the manufactured *pellis*.

The knife falls from my human hand and the heaviness in my chest breaks apart, beaten by butterfly wings, as I lower into a watery embrace. Thick green skin -- a leviathan's -- slips over my shoulders as my *pelli* alters my form to match my mind. My eyes, newly large, have no trouble seeing in the dark. My claws are sharp and I am not afraid. I cannot join my pod's chorus but I can swim through these ruins. I can watch for more newcomers and tell them 'no' with my long teeth.

Sherri Cook Woosley holds a master's degree in English Literature from the University of Maryland with a focus on comparative mythology. Her short fiction has recently been published in *DreamForge, Pantheon Magazine,* and *Abyss & Apex*. Her debut novel, WALKING THROUGH FIRE, was published by Talos Press and combines her experience of being a mother of a child with cancer and Sumerian mythology. The novel was long-listed for both the Booknest Debut Novel award and Baltimore's Best 2019 and 2020 in the novel category. www.tasteofsherri.com

Lieutenant Red Hood

By Jordyn Kieft

Leaving the settlement was risky and rarely necessary. It was safer to stay within the walls of the settlement where there was no chance of Shifter attacks. But then harvest season failed. And failed again. And again. People were starving. Each day more and more settlement members were dying, their bodies left out for the Shifters to consume since no one had the energy to bury them. The O17 Council was left with no choice but to send a military team out into the lands beyond the walls with hope of reaching the nearest neighboring settlement. This settlement was known for their aid due to their continual, plentiful seasons. The team's goal was to return with food and resources for potentially better harvest outcomes in the upcoming years.

The nearest settlement is only a few days' travel away through the dense forest surrounding O17. The team should have returned within a week of leaving. But then a week passed without a sign of the team. Then another week passed. Red knew that the possibility of any of the team members being alive was slim. The journey between settlements was a dangerous one as the pathways often bordered the Shifters' feeding grounds. Even providing extra travel time for poor weather conditions, or Shifter sightings, the team should have been returned home by now. There were speculations of a Shifter attack, although no one contained any sort of proof besides the missing travelers. Members of the community were concerned about being able to survive the winter without the aid of the other settlement.

Red did her best to ignore their talk, not wanting to let thoughts of her grandmother, one of the team members on the mission, potentially being dead enter her mind. Commander Hood's vast knowledge of Shifters and the world outside made her an asset both to the team and the settlement in general. She was almost as precious as the cargo - at least in Red's opinion. But Red could not mourn her grandmother right now. Not when she was so close to graduating from her training in the guard. Grandmother would not want her death to get in the way of Red achieving her goals.

The Council discussed how to proceed for three days, causing alarm within the settlement. The Council had never needed to discuss what to do when a team did not return. Team members knew the risks of leaving the settlement and were informed there would be no rescue attempts. But this mission was different. The survival of the settlement depended heavily on its success.

Red's training increased in difficulty in the following days, and she caught wind from a group of Commanders that they were readying all trainees. Some of them would be needed for the potential rescue mission. Hope flitted through her chest at the thought that her grandmother might still be alive and might even be rescued. If her grandmother was still out there, then Red wanted to be the one to make sure she arrived back home safely. She could not lose the only family she had left, and she did not trust others to prioritize her grandmother the way that she would.

Red used this hope to push herself harder in her training. It was the only way she could keep her heart and mind in check. She had never before felt hope this strongly, and she refused to let it consume her thoughts and prevent her from being picked for the mission. Instead, she channeled her feelings into her training, honing her physical capabilities and attempting to exceed them. Although she was not scheduled to graduate from her trainee status until next month, she wanted to make sure she got the chance to be chosen for the rescue mission if the opportunity arose. If they were to pick a trainee, Red wanted to be their top choice.

She knew she stood out as a potential candidate because of her relationship with her grandmother. After all, her grandmother had been teaching her about Shifters and their world since before her parents died. Her grandmother's knowledge put her on the team for the most important mission in O17 history, and Red hoped her learned knowledge would put her on the team for the second most important mission.

Being on the guard kept Red fed as well as possible, but the lack of sustenance along with her already small nature, put her in a weaker position than she wanted. Red saw the wariness in her fellow trainees as well and hoped her enthusiasm the past few days would make her the top candidate.

On the fourth day after the Council first met to discuss the next course of action, Red's training was interrupted by a call for the Commanders around lunchtime. While the Commanders took leave of the training yard to meet with the Council, Red forced herself to eat what little food she was given despite her nerves. She knew she would need her strength no matter what decision they came to. The meeting was not long; the Commanders returned by the time Red and her fellow trainees had finished with lunch. But instead of ordering the trainees into another drill, Commander Logan began calling out names.

"Jax, Weston, Hood," Commander Logan shouted, his voice echoing across the yard. He was a tall man whose burly stature commanded the attention he now held. "Come with me." Red looked up from where she had been re-lacing her boots. Excitement filled her body when she heard her name being called, but she had to keep her composure.

Commander Logan did not wait to see if Red and the others were following, he just turned back in the direction he came from and began walking, his feet kicking up dust from the dry ground. Not wanting to fall behind, Red shoved her untied laces into her boot and jogged to catch up to her peers. As they walked away, Red heard the remaining Commanders order the trainees to get prepared for an after lunch run.

Commander Logan led Red and her peers to the leader hall across the courtyard of the settlement. The leader hall was the biggest and most elaborate building within settlement O17. As the place where all matters pertaining to the settlement were attended to, the leader hall had to be big enough to hold all members of the guard as well as all six Council members. Though most buildings within the settlement were made of plain wood and simply put together, the leader hall was made of a grey limestone that had been carved by hands some time ago. Even the floors were paved with stone. Built in a large square, the walls of the hall were constructed much higher than the walls of the settlement in order to allow lieutenants to overlook the lands beyond for signs of danger.

Red had never been in the leader hall before - only those with rankings could enter - but her grandmother had described the interior to her before even going as far as to teach her each of the Council members' names. Despite her best efforts, however, Red could still not mask her astonishment upon entering the enormous, metal double doors. At the entrance as she drew in a breath. When she released it, her nose filled with a slightly musty scent. A shiver ran along her spine as the cool air inside the hall hit her warmed skin. Within the leader hall was a massive stone table with enough seats to accommodate all members of the Council and the guard, if not more. The ceilings were high, with large chandeliers casting a dim glow upon the room. Red followed the others to the far end of the table where the Council members and what appeared to be two members of the guard sat waiting. Her shoelace fell out of her shoe as she walked, and the sound of it scraping the ground made Red cringe. She hoped she did not appear unprepared.

Councilman Rainne, a short and stout man with a greying goatee, instructed Commander Logan and his trainees to take a seat. Red sat at the end of the row of people next to trainee Jax, quickly tying her shoe while her feet were under the table. While waiting for a Council member to speak, Red peered at the sunken eyes and hollow cheeks that the Council members had hidden behind their stone-faced expressions. Even the most important people in the settlement were suffering from the effects of a slow starvation. Red turned her gaze away from the Council members to the other two people sitting at the table. She noted that they were in fact members of the guard based on their uniforms and ranking patches. One was a Commander with a neat auburn bun on her head and a poised face, but she did not recognize the other member's ranking patch. He commanded attention though, his chest broad and back straightened with time on the guard.

Councilman Rainne looked over the trainees before nodding to Commander Logan. "Great selections, Commander. I think they will work sufficiently for the mission."

Red froze. *So, there is going to be a rescue mission. And I was picked to go!*

"Thank you, Councilmen," Commander Logan responded. "They are the best of our trainees."

"Well, let us begin, shall we? I am sure you are wondering why you were brought here today," Councilman Rainne addressed Red and her peers. "First, I must say, congratulations. You all are officially members of the guard and have now earned the title of Lieutenant." The other Council members stated their congratulations and Commander Logan handed Red a patch signifying her rank. She velcroed it to her uniform after removing her trainee patch.

"Now, with this rank also comes responsibility," Councilman Devan continued for Councilman Rainne, his thick mustache muffling his words slightly. "You three have been selected to join Commander Logan, Commander San, and Captain Johnston on a rescue mission to try to recover the whereabouts of the previous mission."

Red examined Captain Johnston across the table, berating herself for being unable to recognize the patch of the Captain. The Captain's hair was blonde and longer than most of the men in O17. He wore it past his ears, and his bangs often moved into his brown eyes. Red had not met the new Captain yet. It seemed that Commander Johnston took over for the last Captain, who was one of the missing team members from the last mission.

Councilman Devan proceeded, drawing Red's attention away. "As you know, rescue missions are not sent for the recovery of missing team members. This still holds true even with this mission. The only reason for this mission is the recovery of the cargo. The survival of our people relies on the arrival of the cargo to our settlement. Therefore, you must prioritize the recovery of the cargo over the recovery of team members."

"We are only informing you of this as a formality," Councilwoman Yahaya says. "The likelihood of any of the team members still being alive after all this time is practically nonexistent.

If not attacked in the first place, our team members have likely succumbed to the hands of the Shifters." Councilwoman Yahaya clears her throat, her small lips pursing. "That being said, let us remind you of the dangers you face going on this mission."

"Shifters can take the form of any living creature, including humans," Councilwoman Ellen explains. She takes a moment to tuck her gray hair behind her ears. "All Shifters have to do is see a living creature before they can take that exact form. When on your mission, do not assume any person you see is just that, particularly the members that were on the cargo mission. As I am sure Lieutenant Hood already knows, the more recent the sighting, the more realistic the Shifter appears." Councilwoman Ellen looks at Red with her cold gray eyes before turning to Councilwoman Olya.

"There are three ways you can tell the difference between a Shifter and a human," Councilwoman Olya, a tall and narrow woman, begins. "First, behavior. Observe the way the potential Shifter is acting. Do they appear to behave differently than a normal human or the human you know? For less experienced Shifters, the ability to mimic the behaviors of humans is harder to achieve." Councilwoman Olya counts on her fingers. "Look at common human behaviors such as itching a nose, blinking, and walking. If any of these behaviors seem abnormal, then you are encountering a Shifter."

"Second, appearance. Like Councilwoman Ellen just mentioned, the more recent a Shifter sees a human, the more realistic the Shifter appears. Try to notice discrepancies in the appearance of a normal human and the appearance of a Shifter impersonating to be a human." Councilwoman Olya gestures to her arms and face. "One of the main aspects of appearance that Shifters are unable to get right is bodily proportions. Keep an eye out for larger than normal appendages and facial features including the eyes and ears." Councilwoman Olya nods to Councilman Tron.

"Third, voice." Councilman Tron's deep voice echoes around the room, his green eyes narrowing slightly. "Shifters are not able to mimic voices. They can mimic speech and speak to you if experienced enough, but they are unable to sound exactly like

218

another human. This one is particularly important when seeing a human you are familiar with." Councilman Tron meets Red's eyes. "If, by some rare chance, you encounter a team member and they try to speak to you, make sure they sound normal. If there is any sort of discrepancy with their voice, then that 'human' is likely a Shifter."

Red nods in understanding, trying to get the Councilman's piercing gaze off of her by avoiding eye contact. She knew the Council members would be skeptical about her position on the rescue mission team. The look on Councilman Tron's face said everything. They are worried she might fall for the illusions of a Shifter because of her love for her grandmother. Love, afterall, is one of the most blinding aspects of human nature. But Red is a trained member of the guard now. She is not some easily confused farmer or healer. She would not be fooled into mistaking a Shifter for her grandmother. She was better than that.

"Remember, Shifters stay within a ten-mile radius of their nests, so all we have to do is stay on the path and we should remain safe on our mission," Captain Johnston adds as the Council members rise from their chairs. Red and her fellow guards bow their heads as they make their exit. Captain Johnston waits for the door to close before speaking again. "But that does not mean you can let your guard down. Just because our pathways have remained safe thus far, does not mean the Shifters will not evolve in their habits or move nests from time to time." Captain Johnston rises from his seat and everyone follows.

"You have tonight to pack your things," Commander San addresses the group, her voice short and clipped. "Pack light. We must assume that our only wagon was damaged or destroyed during travel. So, we will likely be carrying back what supplies we can carry on our person."

"Rest early tonight," Commander Logan says. "We head out at sunrise."

***

The winds of autumn blew Red's long, ginger hair into her eyes, forcing her to pause for a moment to pull her hair up under her cap. The rescue team had been walking for a few hours now, but the chill from the morning still lingered. Not wanting to hold up the rest of her team, Red forced herself to walk while she messed with her hair. Red was directly behind Commander Logan, third in line in the formation the team maintained as they walked. Red was instructed to keep her eyes on the left side of the pathway, her gun always ready to shoot should the need arise.

Besides the rustling of leaves and Red's stomach complaining of hunger, the morning was quiet. There were no signs of Shifters in the trees off the path, but there was also no sign of the missing wagon or team members. The team remained silent as they walked, not wanting to attract Shifters to their location. Having never been outside of the settlement before, Red did not mind the lack of conversation. She was able to fully soak in her surroundings and wonder what it must have been like for her people before they had built the walls of O17.

Shifters were rarer back then and could be avoided easily. Only the most obscure areas of the O region were known to have Shifter sightings, and for many centuries Shifters were unknown to most of the population. Attacks by Shifters - which were few - were often written off as attacks from other animals. But that was before the Shifters adapted and evolved. No one knows how this occurred, only that it must have happened over an extended period of time, much longer than one person's lifetime. Shifters became faster, braver, and hungrier for animals other than those that resided in the forest. Their hunting ranges doubled in size. As more people were attacked and killed, more Shifters survived and expanded their populations, building more nests in new areas. That was when the colonizers of O17 began to build the wall.

Red's grandmother told her O17 had existed long before the evolution of the Shifters. O17 was a colony in the O region, although it went by a different name in its previous life. When Shifter attacks became nearly impossible to avoid, O17 turned into the settlement that it was now. Families that lived outside of O17 flocked into the lands that would be protected by the walls. Everyone was moved into the leader hall with their belongings so that the stones and bricks used for their houses could be used for the construction of the wall. People worked hard both day and night to build the wall, while others cut trees to rebuild the deconstructed houses, and even more stood guard to protect the workers.

Red could not imagine the life of terror the first members of settlement O17 must have felt knowing they were no longer safe outside the walls. Shaking her head to clear the realization that she was now in a similar situation voluntarily, Red rights her focus to the goal of the mission as well as her own personal goal. Red did not care if the Council members told her to prioritize the cargo over the team members. If her grandmother is still alive, Red would prioritize her safety and rescue over anything else. Her people could figure out a different way to survive. They could not replace the valuable knowledge her grandmother contained.

The team walked for another hour before stopping for a quick lunch of some dried fruits, nuts, and jerky. Red forced herself to eat slowly, attempting to trick her stomach into thinking she had eaten more than she actually did. She took a swig of her water to wash the remainder of her meal down and stored the bottle in her bag so she would not be tempted to drink anymore.

Captain Johnston quietly reminded the team members that there would only be short rest breaks with two team members taking watch in order to minimize travel time from and to the settlement. Commander Logan and Lieutenant Weston would take the first watch when they stopped again at nightfall if they had not yet reached the missing team. With the sun now directly overhead, Captain Johnston led Red and the other team members for another hour or two before instructing a harsh stop with the raising of his hand.

Red took her eyes off of the trees to see why the Captain had halted the procession before the sun had fallen below the horizon. Her lungs constricted in her chest and hope made her stomach flip. Up ahead, only a yard or so off of the path, was the settlement O17 wagon.

"Approach with caution," Johnston whispered. "Everything appears quiet now, but this wagon is off of the path. We do not want to draw attention to the Shifters if they are not already there."

Red and her fellow guards inched their way toward the upturned wagon while staying on the path, heeding the words of the Captain. As they approached, Red drank in the scene, looking for signs of any life. The wagon with their settlement's name lay on its side, various crops now aging with decay bursting from the back like spilled intestines. The way the wagon lay made it appear as if it had been pushed from the side, rolling over itself once, before settling as it is now. The fabric of the wagon was ripped either by Shifters or the tumble - Red could not tell. The cords that hitched the horses to the wagon were pulled from their loops, the horses long gone and most likely eaten.

After confirming no signs of movement, the group split into teams. Commander San, Weston, and Jax watched the trees while Red, Commander Logan, and Captain Johnston gathered what they could from the wreck. Red, being the smallest member of the group, cautiously made her way inside the overturned wagon, sifting her way through the contents so she could scavenge the two large crates at the back that the others could not reach. Approaching the first crate, Red worked as quietly as she could to pry off the side. When the boards came loose, Red gently pushed them over the backside of the crate, causing a groan to erupt from whomever or whatever was on the other side.

Red felt her breath hitch. *She was not alone in the wagon.* She could hear her fellow guards pause in their movements outside of the wagon, listening for further noise to indicate the source of the groan. Red shifted ever so slightly toward the exit, and gently took a step backward, her foot squishing into a rotten tomato. The wet sound that came from where her foot met the tomato, alerted the person or thing on the other side of the crates.

"Hello? Is somebody there?" a familiar but groggy voice whispered from behind the crate. "Captain Liam? Commander Forest? Is that you?" Red held back a cry that threatened to escape her throat. She could not believe it. Her hopeful heart urged her to run toward the sound of her grandmother's voice, but she resisted. She had to make sure she was not being tricked first.

"Grandmother?" Red whispered, skipping the behavior and appearance signs since she could not see her grandmother from where she stood.

"Is that you my darling grandchild? Are you truly here?" Her grandmother's distinct honey-sweet voice filled Red's ears. Red could recognize that voice anywhere. No Shifter could imitate her grandmother's voice down to the twang that accented each word so perfectly. The hope that she had fought against for the last few days overcame her and filled her with relief. Her grandmother was *alive*.

"Lieutenant Hood, what is going on in there?" The Captain's voice entered through one of the rips of the fabric on the wagon.

"It is my grandmother, Captain," Red replied, peeking over the top of the crate nearest her to make sure. Grandmother's angelic face stared back at her, her appearance and behavior normal from what Red could see.

"Are you sure?" Captain Johnston asked, his voice light and breathy.

"I am sure." Red would not let the hope fully consume her before she could properly assess the situation and use the training Grandmother gave her. Red examined her grandmother for wounds, but besides the large crate that was settled on her legs and the other one that was on her arm, she appeared to be unscathed. "She's trapped under some crates. I'm going to attempt to get her free to see if she can still walk." Not waiting to see if Captain Johnston approved of her choice to prioritize her grandmother over the cargo, Red turned back to her grandmother. "Can you feel your legs at all?"

"I can barely feel them, the area is very numb," Grandmother replied. "Oh, my sweet child. I am so glad you are here." Grandmother lifted her free arm to grab Red's hand. Red squeezed her grandmother's hand, noticing how it was much more swollen than usual.

"Grandmother, your hand!" Red examined her grandmother's hand in concern, looking for a reason for the swelling. Besides its larger than normal size, her hand appeared to be in good condition.

"Do not worry, my dear. It is only a result of my lack of food. I have not been able to eat in so long." Pain shot through Red's heart. Swelling from malnutrition was not unfamiliar to her. Most young children back at the settlement experienced similar swelling. Red's position in the guard was the only reason she had not succumbed to malnutrition herself. She hated that her grandmother had begun to experience its effects.

"What happened?" Red asked, setting her grandmother's hand down so she could assess how best to remove the crate from her arm first.

"I honestly do not remember. One moment we were traveling along the path and the next I woke up trapped under these crates. I must have hit my head. I've been alternating between states of unconsciousness and consciousness ever since." Grandmother captured Red's gaze and tears formed in her eyes. Red blinked back tears that began to form as a result. She could see her grandmother's eyes increase in size behind her dilated irises. *She must be so afraid.*

"Don't worry. I'm here now. I will figure out how to free you and we'll get you back to the settlement where you will be safe. I promise." Red got a good stance on the crate, and with all the strength in her arms and legs, she lifted the crate just enough for her grandmother to remove her arm. A sigh escaped Grandmother's lips as she flexed the trapped hand, testing its mobility. Red watched her spread her fingers and wiggle them while twisting her wrist in a circular motion.

"Can you sit up? I am going to need your help to lift this other crate," Red whispered as she talked, keeping the conversation quiet to avoid making more noise than she already was. Red watched her grandmother ease herself into a sitting position. Grandmother twisted from side to side to allow blood to flow throughout her body again. In this movement, her disheveled hair fell back away from her face to expose her puffy cheeks and rather large ears.

"Grandmother! What happened to your ear?" Red cried. Surely the malnutrition did not affect the ears as well.

"Oh, my love. I am not sure. I must have hit my ear in the fall. Perhaps that is what caused me to lose consciousness." Grandmother quickly brushed her hair forward again. Red frowned. Perhaps her grandmother was more injured than she appeared.

"If your head is injured, Grandmother, I need to assess it." Red reached toward her grandmother, but Grandmother grabbed her wrist before she could make contact.

"I am fine, my dear," Grandmother hissed. Her nails dug into Red's forearm so sharply Red gasped in pain. She had never known someone's nails to be so sharp. Blood prickled on her wrist.

"You are hurting me," she whispered, her voice pained. She could not believe her grandmother could be so hostile toward her. Grandmother's grip lessened and Red pulled her hand to her chest, covering the wound.

"Almost done in there, Lieutenant?" Commander San's voice entered the wagon. Red turned her head toward the opening so her voice would carry more easily.

"Yes, Commander. We only have..." Red's response was cut off by the crash that sounded behind her. She whipped her head around to find the crate had been removed from her grandmother's legs and Grandmother now stood facing her. "Wha-? Grandmother, how?" Red was barely able to lift the other crate on her own; she had no idea how her grandmother could have lifted the other crate without any help while also being trapped beneath it.

Instead of responding, Grandmother grinned at Red. Her lips spread over teeth longer than Red's fingers and sharper than spikes. Grandmother's mouth seemingly enveloped her whole face, spreading out much farther than humanly possible. Red suddenly felt sick.

"What a big mouth you have, Grandmother," Red whispered breathlessly.

"Yes, indeed," Grandmother replied.

Red could not withhold the choked scream that tore from her lips as she watched her grandmother's skin begin to peel from her flesh. She stood frozen as the skin melted off of her grandmother's arms, face, and legs. Skin was replaced with mangy, black fur. The putrid smell of burning flesh filled Red's nose and she gagged. Her grandmother's ears grew pointed and her fingers morphed into claws. What skin and clothes that did not immediately melt away was torn from her grandmother's bones as her body and limbs doubled in size. Something made a horrible tearing sound, but Red could not tell if it was the fabric of the wagon or the skin on her grandmother's back.

The creature doubled over on all fours, its bones protruding disgustingly from beneath its skin. Its back became flesh with the fabric of the wagon as it stretched its limbs to work out the kinks that had formed while the creature held a human form.

No one truly knew what Shifters looked like. Most people that came in contact with one did not live to tell the tale. Despite this, Red knew she was staring at a Shifter. She desperately fumbled for the gun strapped to her back, her hands shaking uncontrollably. Her team members were screaming outside of the wagon, telling Red to run or hide. She knew they would not shoot blindly inside. The Shifter grinned at her again, its mouth growing even wider than before. Its solid black eyes did not indicate where the creature was looking, but Red knew it was looking at her.

"Do not fret, my child," the Shifter spoke, its voice sounding just like Grandmother still. "Grandmother is here now."

Red opened her mouth to scream, but no sound came out. Everything she knew about Shifters was now obsolete. Shifters could mimic voices perfectly. *They are evolving.*

226

Freeing her gun from her shoulder at last, Red pointed the barrel at the Shifter's chest and put her finger on the trigger. But her team members never heard her let off a shot. Instead, all they heard before they began to run was a growl so deep they could feel it in their soul and a piercing scream that was cut short by the crunch of what could have only been teeth on bone.

Jordyn Kieft was born and raised in Bloomington, IN. Growing up, Jordyn was obsessed with reading; she was often found to be reading multiple books at a time. Never to be trusted in libraries or bookstores, Jordyn realized in middle school that not only could she read stories, but she could also write them. From then on, Jordyn knew that she wanted to be an author.

Jordyn is currently attending college at Indiana University Bloomington where she is working on her Bachelor of the Arts degree in English with a Creative Writing concentration. Upon graduating in May of 2021, Jordyn plans to get involved in the field of editing while she works to further her career as a published author. "Lieutenant Red Hood" is her first published work.

If you would like to contact Jordyn, you can find her on Instagram under @Jordy829

Forever Young

By Haleigh Diann

They say he comes in the dead of night because that's the time of dreams.

But that's not true.

He comes at night because most sleeping children don't fight. They fold themselves into his arms and think the car ride to the Second Star Hotel is merely a dream. Cool night air, glittering stars, and the floating pleasant sensation of being carried through the empty streets surrounded by bombed skyscrapers and crumbling brownstones belongs in the bewildering world of unconsciousness.

That's what I thought when Peter took me.

I woke up in the basement of the Second Star Hotel and assumed that I'd been saved. No more dealing with the angry, hungry adults at the gas station. No more rules, shouting, or starving, which at seven years old had seemed to be the really important aspect of the whole venture. Being kidnapped never crossed my mind. I was free. A Lost Boy residing in the Second Star Hotel. Nothing bad would ever happen to me, because I was with Peter, and everyone knew that entailed a life of sweets and no rules and no war.

But that's not what happened. Not for any of us.

***

"Simon," I hissed and shoved my fingers against his ribs, a little unkindly.

Simon groaned, rolling over on his bunk and cocooning himself inside his fluffy blanket. I could make out the tuft of his dark hair like a patch of faded grass at the top of the purple blanket but little else.

229

"Simon," I said again, and this time pinched what I thought to be his elbow.

He sat up with a jerk, still encumbered by the blankets, and glared at me. With the blankets wrapped around him, he reminded me of a ghoul. Nothing but narrowed, hard, golden eyes in an expanse of black. He was thin and tall like a ghost, but nowhere near as white.

"Callie," he said.

"Happy Birthday," I replied with a grin, though my voice came out strangled.

Simon's glare hardened even more and he jerked the makeshift blanket hood off his head and looked around the room. It was unnecessary, since I wouldn't have said anything if someone else had been in the basement, and once he realized we were alone, his tense jaw slacked.

"Not so loud," he mumbled, rubbing his palms against his cheeks the way he always did after waking up.

I didn't respond. Birthdays in the hotel weren't the celebrations they were supposed to be. In the Second Star Hotel, birthdays meant you were one year closer to getting booted out onto the war-torn streets. To fend for yourself in the smog-covered city, scrounging and fighting like junkyard dogs for any scrap to survive. Avoiding the feral adults that sucked everything dry.

At least, that's what Peter said. And since Peter was the one that told us everything that happened in the world outside the locked front doors, we had no choice but to believe him.

But Peter also threw one of his legendary tantrums whenever someone slipped up that they were one year older. Especially if, like Simon, that now put him one year older than Peter.

Sixteen was a dangerous year in the Second Star Hotel.

"Callie, stop looking so morose," Simon said.

"Fancy word," I said, fighting to shrug off the feeling.

He pointedly looked at the dictionary sitting on my bed. I grinned and shrugged. Reading was my thing. I had gathered up every book or scrap of newspaper from the rooms and devoured them. The dictionary was the only one I had yet to get all the way through twice. Simon learned by osmosis, meaning he picked up some words when I read out-loud definition after definition in the late hours of the night.

"No one else knows, it's fine," Simon said around a yawn, "It'll be okay."

I rubbed my finger against the side of my nose, mumbling noncommittally. Simon was a year older than me, but I'd been listening to him for years not only because of that. Simon had a stern demeanor, a solidness to him not many of us had. The sort of strength that made him immovable and yet trustworthy. Everyone knew exactly where he'd be.

"It's not just it being your…" I broke off and Simon stiffened as someone's shrill yell echoed in the hall outside the door. The door to the basement bunkroom stayed shut but I finished on a whisper, "You know. But he's called a meeting. That's why I woke you."

Every few weeks, whenever he didn't return with another kid plucked from the chaos of the outside world, Peter called a meeting. They were meant to be gatherings of all the Lost Boys, a get-together to unite us. Most of the time, they descended into madness within the first five minutes since there were no rules.

I hated them. I was always afraid something bad would happen. Something worse than the general mess that came from everyone doing whatever they wanted. What that was, I didn't know, but I waited for it with bated breath the entire time. Every time.

"Of course," Simon groaned and detangled his legs from the blanket. He swung his bare feet over the edge and then brushed his dark hair off his forehead. "Ready, Cal?"

I shook my head but stood up anyway. Simon jerked his head towards the door and I followed behind him reluctantly. When we stepped into the hallway, the shouting from earlier rang out louder, echoing off the torn wallpaper. The storm of footsteps through the stairwell was a low hum that intensified the closer we got. Like a herd of elephants or wild buffalos stampeding through a river. At least, that's what I imagined it would sound like.

"Wonder what it's about," Simon said, shoving open the stairwell door.

Confetti punched us in the face. I spluttered, jerking back as pieces stuck to my lips and eyelashes. Someone cackled high and peeling. Simon sighed wearily and brushed the glittering residue out of his hair.

"Hey, Joseph," he said.

I spat out a piece of confetti and arched a brow. Joseph grinned, waving the empty plastic cannon he'd assaulted us with. His wild red hair was messier than usual this morning and as dirty as the rest of him. He was seven years old and like the rest of that age group had decided showers were too much of a hassle.

"Callie! Simon! Ha! I got you two *good*, didn't I? Betcha didn't even see me coming before BLAM!" He karate-chopped the air and threw his head back with a cackle.

I wanted to tell him to take a shower, but I was afraid he'd go digging for a stink bomb to place in my sheets if I did. Instead, I shook my head and said, "Yup, you got us. Scared me to death."

Joseph grinned wide and gap-toothed, he'd lost another front tooth in the time I'd last seen him, and barreled down the stairs.

232

"Come on! Peter found a whole buncha toys! From that abandoned store in the scary section." Joseph's voice bounced in time with the slapping of his bare feet against the steps. "Ya gotta hurry before all the good ones are gone!"

"Kinda thought it was all scary," Simon mumbled, but his lips were twitching.

I laughed despite not wanting to and headed down the stairs. The Second Star Hotel was an old building from the time before the outside world had devolved into the messy and violent landscape that made the Hotel one of the only safe places, and the only place for children.

It was drafty and beat-up, years of abuse from kids was etched into every corner. I had done the same as Joseph and all the others that age. My art was slathered over the second story bathroom, nail polish and acrylic paint would forever stain the porcelain sinks. Simon had left his mark on a utility closet on the fourth floor. Every single item inside it was broken in increasingly erratic ways.

The only room that had escaped that fate was the Cabinet Room.

We only called it that because it was on the gold-plated plaque screwed to the wall. The younger ones had a hard time saying it, so its other name was Peter's Place.

Plush carpet stretched from wall to wall and the overhead lights looked opulent, though none of us had ever seen them lit. The lights dangled in glittering shards of glass. Tables with thick white cloth circled a small lifted stage where a thickly padded leather recliner sat right in the middle.

When we stepped into the Cabinet Room, Peter was already there.

He sat sloppy, one leg thrown over the side of the chair and one arm tucked behind his head, pushing the headrest and his hat lopsided. His vibrant blond hair was actually combed today, but the ends were still straggly where they rested upon his shoulders.

His grin, however, was as mischievous as ever.

Peter's smile was equal parts boyish and something sharper, something that made my heart pound whenever I saw it. Not in an unpleasant way but a lilting lurch that made it hard to meet his green eyes and impossible not to feel like everything I did was wrong.

Today was no different and when he saw us enter, he waved lazily. My cheeks burned and I slipped behind Simon, my toes nudged against his heel three times before we both stopped at an empty table.

"Cal," Simon said, leaning towards me. "Does he look weird today to you?"

I shrugged, glancing at Peter too quickly to really take him in. "No?"

He looked the same he always did. Young, sprite-like, and full of energy even as he sat motionless. I risked another glance and came to the same conclusion. Peter was the kind of person who could move in seconds, and he always looked ready to do so.

Simon rubbed his eyes and then squinted, lips curling. Like he was trying to see through thick glass. I frowned and elbowed him, motioning for him to sit down. He lagged behind a second and then collapsed with a sigh.

"Maybe I'm going blind."

"You are *not* going blind," I flicked his ear and then sat down as well. "You're still sleepy."

"Ah," he said.

I ignored the way that sounded like an appeasement. Tucking my boot heels against the edge of the table, I set my chin on my knees and studied the gaggle of children yelling and pushing each other around on the floor. So carefree. And dirty.

I didn't envy Peter's close proximity to them but he watched them with a small smirk.

Simon rubbed his eyes and muttered unintelligibly. I brushed my hair out of my face and followed his gaze to Peter. He didn't look different, but he did look odd. Off. I'd say weary if it wasn't for the fact that I'd never seen Peter tired.

Sometimes, when Peter didn't think anyone was looking, he looked old. Not just older than me but aged. Like he'd seen too much and all of it resided behind his eyes until the green of them was something hard to look at. The depth in them was too much. Disturbing.

Today, I noticed it more intensely and my stomach dropped.

"Boys!" Peter's voice rang out over the chatter and I jumped, nearly smacking myself in the face. Simon squeezed my elbow and I set my hands flat against the table. My nerves were weak, always had been, and right now I felt jumpy.

It was his eyes. They weren't just aged. They were *ancient.*

Suddenly, a terrifying thought slammed so hard through me I wanted to throw up. I clenched the edge of the table until my fingers burned. Sweat dotted my forehead.

"I need help. Get to go outside with this one, so bigger kids only please," Peter said, standing up to better project his voice over the grunts of a group of four or five ten-year-olds wrestling. "Any volunteers?"

Going outside was rare. The last time he'd ask was over six months ago, and it hadn't ended well. I was surprised he offered it now. But not as surprised to see hands get raised with abandon, shouts echoing.

"How long has Peter been here?" I asked, whispering against Simon's ear.

He fidgeted, his shoulder rising to combat the hiss of my voice. "I dunno, fifteen years? He's fifteen years old."

I huffed, "But wasn't he fifteen last year?"

Simon's mouth opened and then closed. And then opened and then closed. I swallowed hard, grabbing onto his wrist to stop my hands from shaking. How had I never noticed it before? All the signs were right there. Had I ever seen Peter look any different? Ever seen him grow an inch? He'd looked the same from the time I arrived at six years old to now.

The impossible stared me in the face and made my stomach hurt. My heart raced alongside the whirring thoughts of my brain. There was no way...and yet...

"How long has he been fifteen?" I asked.

Simon elbowed me, hard. "Stop. Stop. We'll talk about it later. Not right now."

The fact that he didn't contradict me made my heart thud harder. My hands gyrated against the tablecloth, jerking it up in small wrinkles. Simon placed his hand over one of mine, his fingers tight against my knuckles.

How had no one noticed?

And more importantly, how did he do it? What did it mean?

"Okay, I need two more," Peter called, jumping over the still twirling mess of wrestling kids. They didn't seem to notice.

I jerked my hand in the air, the one Simon still had a hold of.

"Callie!" he hissed.

Peter's smile was wide and inviting. "Perfect."

***

The outside world had descended into chaos not long after my birth, or so the story went. The city had eaten itself up, riots and violence strewn through it for reasons no kids could recall and the few adults had either been afraid to tell us or couldn't agree on what was wrong. All we knew for certain was that the world was dangerous and we were the lucky ones.

Peter and the Second Star Hotel was the only place that existed that didn't use kids up and spit them out dry. The one spot we could exist as utterly free as anyone could be and as children should be.

Or so Peter said.

The idea of going outside never appealed to me. Why would it? We had everything we wanted in the Hotel. But with the night falling around us, darkening the halls, I felt that feeling even stronger. I didn't want to go outside.

Something about the way Peter bounced and skipped up the stairs set my nerves on edge.

Following him and the two other kids that had volunteered, Morgan and Jacob, up the stairs to the roof did nothing to sate the turmoil in my gut. I held onto Simon's hand so tightly I wasn't sure he had any circulation, but I couldn't let go and he didn't make me.

"What are we doing?" I asked, glad to hear my voice stay steady.

Peter flashed a wide smile, but it slanted sharply. "What else? Something fun."

There'd been a time that would've made me have the same reaction that Morgan and Jacob did, giggling and giddy. Something fun *and* the outside world? But now, with the question still burning through my brain, it just made bile rise to the back of my throat.

"Awesome," Simon said, sounding the same way he always did. Cool and collected.

Peter pushed the rooftop door open. The outside air rushed in, blowing through all of us with a sharp chill. My teeth clanked shut and I winced, expecting a rancid sweet smell reminiscent of old meat. The scent I associated with decay.

The air from outside was the opposite. Clean, fresh, and with a hint of something that reminded me of peppermint.

The night sky was black. Thick and shadow-filled, I couldn't see anything as I waited for my eyes to adjust. Spots of light from the moon and stars and heavy smearing shadow was all I could make out. Peter's voice and Simon's tug helped me up the last step and out onto the roof.

"Let me say, thank you, children. This is never easy."

Something in his voice grabbed my heart and stopped it cold. The thing I'd been wondering, I was about to find out. I could feel it in my bones. For one desperate second, I thought about never opening my eyes again. Ignoring all of it.

"What is?" Simon asked, sounding as wary as I felt.

I blinked hard and my eyes finally adjusted to the faint moonlit night. Peter stood in front of us and in his hand, he held a long, flat, shining blade.

I backed up, jerking Simon with me.

The closed rooftop door handle punched my back.

Peter's smile was bright, and yet subdued. "I know. I know how it looks, but I *will* not grow up." He stomped his foot and gestured with the blade to the city stretched out across the horizon.

"I will not end up out there! One of those mindless hungry things. This place is mine and always will be!"

His shouting was loud, always was, hard and resonant and demanding. It froze me to the spot and froze my breath in my lungs. His face reddened. The beginnings of his legendary temper. I couldn't move. Couldn't breathe.

Peter wasn't our savior.

"So, you're going to kill us?" Simon asked, nudging himself in front of me.

"No," Peter said, his head jerking back. "No. I mean, it happens sometimes. But I don't mean too!" He lurched forward and the four of us jumped backwards, lumping together. "It's always an accident. Always! I just need your blood. That's it! Nothing awful, I promise."

He sounded like Joseph with the confetti. Like he announced something funny and couldn't understand how we didn't get it. Like he spoke about a joke, a prank gone wrong, instead of stealing our *blood*.

"I swear, it'll be fine. You won't feel a thing," Peter said, voice sliding on a whine. He pouted and his bottom lip poked out petulantly. "Plenty of the others don't even remember."

The others. Blood. My stomach fell to my boots and ice curdled in my veins.

"You're a vampire," I said.

Peter sighed, throwing his head back to glare at the moon. "I hate that word. Don't say it. Hear me? Don't say it again!" He stomped his foot once more. "I have to do this! Don't you understand! To keep this place open for kids, I need to be here!"

"Because without us, you'll die." Simon's voice was shaky.

Peter grimaced. "No, no. I can't die. This is necessary."

"Peter," I said, scrambling for something. For words to put to the plea burning my gums. I had to do something, say something, because he was scaring me.

"This is my fun. Don't you realize that?" Peter said, peevish and with narrowed eyes. "Don't you want me to have my fun? I let you have yours."

Simon charged. He stood next to me one moment and the next he was throwing a fist that connected with Peter's chin. I yelped, lungs too strangled to scream. Peter tossed him back effortlessly with a snarl.

The agedness I'd seen before flourished beneath the moonlight. Peter stood braced, angry, and monstrous. Something old and ancient made childish through lack of progress. I realized then that all the kids he claimed to care for were there for one reason. To keep him the same as always. Unchanged and young.

Simon grabbed me by the arm. I jerked my arm free and raced forward, knowing that Peter wouldn't expect it from quiet and unassuming Callie. My hands wrapped around the hilt of the blade, right next to Peter's impossibly cold hands.

He snarled, shocked, and I smacked my head against his nose.

Warm blood gushed over my forehead and I gasped. Simon jerked me back by my collar, choking me. Morgan and Jacob were screaming and pounding on the door. It rattled in the door frame, sounding like a rock thrown across gravel.

"Help! Help!"

I knew no help would come.

Peter roared deep and angry, inhumanly. The blade----I knew it had a real name, it was as long as my forearm but I couldn't remember it---was still in my hand. Peter seemed caught between watching us scream for help and lunging for us, eyes glittering and body tensed. But I knew what I had to do.

I took the blade and jammed it into his chest.

I screamed when I let go, stumbling backwards into Simon's arms. Peter looked down at the blade sunk deep in his middle and laughed.

It was a bone-curdling sound, deep and throaty. The kind of laugh someone gave when they thought of something other people didn't. Like he knew more than we did.

Peter smiled wide and sharp and yanked the blade from his chest.

Morgan and Jacob tried to open the door, scrambling against each other and screaming. I couldn't make out what they said over the pounding of my heart and the sound of Simon's staggered breathing.

The Second Star Hotel and Peter had never been a sanctuary. The world was dead and we were living on borrowed time.

Peter's time.

Simon growled low under his breath and then launched himself at Peter. They fumbled over the blade, both warring for control of it and I stood there frozen. Thinking, stunned, scared.

Peter used us? Raised us to slaughter when he needed to? Had any kid ever left the Hotel? Or were they all part of him now?

The fear warped into anger and then I was beside Simon, slapping and scratching whatever I could reach. Handfuls of Peter's hair tangled around my fingers. He tore the front of my shirt and then screamed when Morgan and Jacob entered the fray.

As we four clobbered him down, shouting nonsense full of rage and betrayal, Simon wrangled control of the sword.

"Do it Simon!" I shouted, motioning to Peter's head. "Hurry!"

The Lost Boys were Peter's. That's how the story went and how it was told. But what made us Lost?

Simon flung the sword above his head. I wanted to close my eyes but didn't.

The Lost Boys takeover of the Second Star Hotel started and ended with the swing of a blade and the rush of blood.

Haleigh has been a longtime lover of words, coffee, and dogs. She can be found in Northeastern Oklahoma dreaming about her next story. You can find her on Twitter @HaleighBaker7

HOOD: A Grindhouse Robin Hood Tale

By Jared K Chapman

Fat pink maggots wriggled, and bulbous black flies buzzed around the rotted hams at the base of the welcome sign on the outskirts of town. Homeless hands hunted through the decay while covering their nostrils and mouths as best they could, so not to add to the myriad puddles of vomit, in hopes of discovering an elusive pristine canned ham to quench their everlasting hunger. The once beautifully colored sign above, now dented from years of cans and hams bashing into it, bore a spray-painted red R over the N.

WELCOME TO *R*OTTINGHAM.

Beyond the makeshift tents of homeless people scattered around the sign were the homes of Huntington Court. Signs littered the small suburban development with the face of real estate developer, Johnson King, now Mayor King. JOHNSON KING WILL MAKE THIS HOUSE YOUR VERY OWN KINGDOM. RE-ELECT YOUR FAVORITE MAYOR, JOHNSON KING. Either way, his face was selling you something.

Brunette sisters, Robin and Randi Locke, dressed in their high school cheerleader uniforms with backpacks slung over their shoulders and bursting with books, raced one another home. Robin wore the sleeveless varsity uniform, while her sister wore the more modest frosh-soph version.

"Another one?" Randi commented, pointing to a FOR SALE sign with Mayor King's face upon it. "I think everyone's moved out now."

"Everyone but us," Robin said, skipping toward their two-story home in the center of a cul-de-sac, the only one without a sign.

Robin reached the door first and rushed inside, dropping her backpack by a table in the entryway. The click-clack of her father's fingers pecking at the computer keys echoed off the walls and the marble floor of the halls and entryway. As she followed the sound to her father's office, a beeping emanated from the kitchen.

"That's dinner!" her father shouted from the office. "Please take care of it. I'm finishing up some work."

"Okay, Dad," Robin replied, spinning on her heels. From the corner of her eye, she spotted Randi sneaking inside the front door. "Dinner's ready. Set the table."

Randi plopped her backpack down in a huff and stomped toward the kitchen.

Just as they set the table and were ready to serve, their forty-something widowed father, Roland, joined them, carrying a stack of papers and file folders. He placed them on the table next to his seat, patting them as he gazed distractedly at the large ham at the center of the table. Robin sliced through it, allowing the honeyed-ham aroma to escape with the steam within. Randi licked her lips as her sister placed a slab onto her plate. Robin snapped her fingers at her father when his plate didn't appear next. He shuttered and passed her the plate with a pensive smile.

"Hard day, Dad?" she asked.

He nodded, withdrawing the plate. Then, with a broad smile, he reached his hands out to his girls. They each grabbed one and then crossed the table to hold each other's hands before bowing their heads.

"Please bless this meal, for we know not when we may have another. Please bless this house, for we know not when we may be uncovered. Please bless this family, for we know not when we may again be with one another. Amen."

"Amen," the girls repeated in unison, dropping their hands and stabbing the meal with their knives and forks.

Roland only stared at the paperwork next to him.

"What is it?" Robin asked, noticing her father's lack of appetite.

"Nothing, love. My job is overwhelming me right now. That's all."

"You're a great man, Daddy," Randi said, placing her hand on top of his. "It takes someone strong to deal with the low-lives and druggies you have to deal with every day."

"That's not even the worst of it, dear," he said with a warm smile, squeezing her hand. "At least with those folks, you have some idea where you stand. When the cops are corrupt, that's when—"

Sudden loud rapping at the door startled them, but Roland most of all. Sweat beaded around his forehead as he swallowed an audible gulp. He grasped hold of Robin's hand and squeezed.

"Stay here."

"Who is it?" Roland shouted as he ambled toward the pounding door. He stopped at the table in the entryway, opened a drawer, and pulled something out. "I have a gun!"

The pounding stopped. Robin snuck a peek out of the dining room door, glimpsing her father grapple the stainless-steel Eiffel Tower paperweight he brought back with him the last time they had traveled with their mother. He put it in there after their mother passed. He could not bear to part with it, but he couldn't bear to look at it daily either. The heavy thing now served as some kind of protection.

He peered through the peephole before reaching for the knob, keeping the chain latched. As he turned the knob, the door burst open, breaking the chain lock and knocking him to the ground. He squealed in pain as he covered his busted open nose, spraying blood all over him. Through his fingers, he counted eight boots stomp inside, marring his precious marble floor.

"What do you want?" he asked, trying to stand.

"Oh, I think you know what we want, Mr. Locke," answered a tall man, wearing a black ski mask and staring at Roland with piercing, blue eyes.

Robin watched the whole thing from her vantage point in the dining room. Her eyes widened and breath quickened. She slid out of view next to her sister. Randi shivered, holding her arms around her knees. Robin placed a tender hand on her knee and whispered, "As quietly as you can, go up the back stairwell and call for help."

Randi nodded and crawled away, creeping out the backdoor of the dining room. With her sister safely away, Robin stood and retrieved the knife she used to cut the ham only moments earlier. Then, she snuck out of the dining room, trying to make a better assessment of the situation.

No guns, she thought, examining the four men. They all wore the same black clothes and masks. One of them held a chain, another had a 2x4, and another had a black bag in his hands. The leader had one hand on her father's shoulder and the other around his right wrist. He seemed to be questioning her father, but she couldn't make sense out of the noise in her head. Then, the man smashed her father's face with his fist, and she ran.

She rushed the first man in her way, stabbing wildly as she screamed, "Leave us alone!"

KARAACK. Everything went black.

As she came to, she discovered herself to be tied to a chair, facing her father. Two of the men scoured the room, knocking things over and making a mess. Her father's eyes filled with regret and guilt gazed at her. Behind him, the tall man stood facing the front stairs.

"Found it, Guy," echoed a voice from the hallway.

"What did I tell you about names?"

"Sorry, Guy," he apologized. "Sorry. I mean. Sorry."

"Well, they've heard my name now," Guy said, spinning around with her knife in his hand.

Without any warning, he lunged forward, yanked Roland's head back by the hair, and ran the blade across his neck. Robin screamed as her father's warm blood sprayed upon her. One of the men bashed her head from behind again. Everything darkened as her eyes glazed over.

"Check this out, Rowdy," a voice from behind her said to the other, tossing him a framed photo. "There's another one."

"Ya know what that means, Flicker?"

"What?"

"You can have this one," Rowdy snarled. "I'm gonna find little sister."

Robin wrestled against her ties, trying in vain to stop Rowdy from stalking toward the stairwell. Flicker's warm breath sent prickles down the back of her neck.

"RUN!" she yelled. "Randi, Run!"

"Crank, go!" Guy ordered, grabbing the stack of files from Crank's hands.

Rowdy bolted up the front stairs, while Crank rushed back down the hall to the back stairwell.

"You bitch!" Rowdy hollered from upstairs. "She's got a phone."

"Well, I guess the fun's over, boys," Guy said, sauntering toward the door. "Time to light'er up."

"Bummer," Flicker whispered into Robin's ear, tugging back on her hair with one hand and cupping her breast with the other. "I was gonna show ya some fun."

Randi screamed, but it stopped abruptly.

"Leave her alone, you sonuva—"

Flicker kicked her head, knocking her to the floor. Then, he grabbed a bottle of lighter fluid out of the black bag and sprayed it all over the room. Crank barreled down the steps, shaking his head.

"He didn't hafta do that," he muttered as he retrieved another bottle and headed to the dining room.

"Rowdy!" Guy called, taking out a final bottle from the bag. "We gotta make moves, big guy!"

"Coming. I'm coming," he responded, making his way to the top of the stairs. He stood there with a blood-splattered shirt, buckling his pants.

"Here," Guy said, tossing the bottle up. "Cover that area."

"You sure he's gonna be cool with this?"

"I'll handle it," answered Guy. "Just do what I say."

"Catch you later, sweet thing," Flicker said, sliding back over to Robin. He kissed her cheek before standing up and stomping on her head. Darkness came again.

The burning flames burned bright behind her eyelids. She fluttered her eyes open, rolling them around, trying to regain consciousness. The heat seared, and fire crackled all around her. It spoke to her in a foreign language, like it was alive. A reeroo-reeroo of a firetruck siren blared, coming nearer and nearer. She closed her eyes again as burning smoke filled her lungs.

When she opened her eyes, she found herself in the arms of a firefighter carrying her out of the inferno. She rolled her head back, catching sight of the fiery stairwell.

"Randi," she coughed.

The firefighter placed her on a stretcher and returned to the blaze. Paramedics attended her, measuring her vitals and applying oxygen, but she kept her eyes on the front door of her home. No one brought her sister out.

***

"Welcome to Sherwood Home for Girls," the monstrous giant with the mountain-man beard said to Robin as he opened the door for her to enter. "You can call me John, or Mr. Little if you're formal."

Still in an opioidic daze, Robin nodded hello, handing him her chart. She spent weeks in ICU and months in recovery before being placed in a group home. John reached out to touch her shoulder. She recoiled.

"Don't worry, Jane," he said, glancing at her chart. "You're in the right place."

Jane? she thought, trying to grasp memories of her recent trauma, but it only came to her in bits and pieces. *My name's... what is my name? Why am I here?*

John guided her through a large room where several girls sat around doing homework. Then, they entered a hallway with numbered doors lining either side. He opened the one marked 4. Inside the room, a tall, waifish brunette and a slender ginger sat on separate beds with an empty bed between them.

"Mary. Scarlet. This is Jane. She's your new roomie. Please make her comfortable."

"Sure thing, John," Scarlet said, saluting John and jumping to her feet. "We'll show her the ropes."

"Thanks, girls," John said, closing the door.

"So, Jane. Where'd John find you?"

"The hospital."

"Which one?" Mary asked. "He picked me up at St. Martha's... a drug rehab."

"I'm not sure. The big one."

"The big one?" Scarlet cut in. "Like Mercy? Were you sick?"

"Head trauma," Robin answered, tapping her forehead. "I can't remember who I am, but my name isn't really Jane."

"Crazy," Mary replied with greater interest, sliding off her bed. "Maybe we can help you figure out your name."

"Maybe," said Robin. After a few seconds of silence, she asked Scarlet, "Where'd John pick you up?"

"He saved me from sex traffickers."

"Whoa! How old are you?"

"Fifteen or sixteen, I think. I'm not really sure."

"So, he's a good guy?" questioned Robin.

"He's the best," they responded in unison.

With a few more months of therapy and physical recovery at the Sherwood Home, Robin finally regained her memories and confided with her roommates. After hearing the gruesome details, Mary said, "You need to come to art therapy. It's not an official program for Sherwood, but most of the girls do it."

"Art therapy? I'm not good at drawing or painting or anything like that."

"Not that kind of art," Scarlet clarified. "Martial arts. Self-defense training. Weapons use. He says we were victims once, but he's going to teach us how to never be helpless victims again."

"You're right, Mary. I do need a little art in my life. I'm in."

***

A frazzle-haired, unkempt homeless woman lounged on a park bench, tapping a syringe filled with bright pink liquid. A black-suited man stood in front of her, carrying a black bag.

"What is it?" she asked.

"Merriment," he answered. "It's brand new. It'll make you euphoric."

"You what?"

"The world will be all bright and beautiful. You'll feel better than you ever have before."

"HAH. Beautiful? Look around."

The man surveys the tents sprawled out in the park and the many homeless men, women, and children wandering around. Everything was dirty and old, and everyone was tired and sick. White vans bearing an NP logo circled the camps, dispensing food and drugs.

"Did I mention we'll pay ya for trying it out and giving us feedback?"

"Well, that's different. Where do I sign up?"

***

Months passed by, Nottingham re-elected Mayor King, and more people lost their homes, moving into tents around the town. Signs with the mayor's face covered lawns all over town, as houses sat empty. Men wearing all black herded the people like cattle into overcrowded slum neighborhoods and camps while distributing Merriment to one and all.

Over time, the free trials ran out, and the poor people needed to pay for their fixes. Unable to afford the price but unwilling to live through withdrawals, they negotiated with all they had left. So, every day, the men in black recruited volunteers from the camps and ushered them into the white NP vans. Some never returned. With their parents gone, children ran wild, looting and vandalizing the area.

"This is awful," Robin said, peering out the window of John's truck. They were on their way to the grocery store to get supplies for the Sherwood home.

"Gets worse every day," Scarlet replied from her middle seat.

They passed a Sheriff's car with a deputy inside, drinking coffee and eating a donut.

"Why don't they do anything?" Robin asked.

"The Sheriff's bought off," John answers to Robin's surprise.

"How do you figure that?"

"I used to be a deputy."

The answer didn't beg for more conversation, and neither did John. As they drove by Huntington Court, Robin stared wide-eyed. The homes were leveled, and barbed wire fences surrounded the neighborhood, bearing a logo she had never seen before, an N and P smashed together with signs saying, PROGRESS IS COMING SOON.

"NP. What's that?"

"What? Nottingham Pharmaceuticals?" answered John. "Some new outfit building facilities all over town. Supposed to be putting people to work."

"These people?" she asked, pointing to all the tents.

"Hope so."

At the grocery store, Robin followed John and Scarlet up and down the aisles. It was her first time back in the city since the attack. As she strolled through each aisle, memories of her family filled her head, and her anxiety increased. She tried to fight back against the burgeoning wave of emotion when she heard Guy's voice playing in her head.

She closed her eyes and breathed three deep breaths, trying to banish him from her thoughts, but he would not go. Instead, his voice became so clear that goosebumps prickled up and down her arms in a shiver. Then came the voices of Flicker, Rowdy, and Crank.

They're not haunting me. They're real, she thought, leaving the cart mid-aisle to search for their source.

"We just don't have it all right now," the manager pleaded. "We need more time."

Four men in black suits loomed over the manger. The tallest one closed in, saying, "If you don't pay us, then we can't give you the protection you need. You understand how this works, doncha?"

The three men behind him tossed nearby shelves, saying, "Oops," and "That's a hazard," as they scooped up bags of chips and drinks in their arms. One of them grabbed some candy bars and shoved them into their pockets.

Robin scanned around, searching for a weapon. She spotted a fire-hydrant on a pole. As she reached for it, John grappled her arm. Robin whipped around, ready to fight, but John caught her hand and whispered, "Are you trying to kill yourself?"

She wriggled away from John and maneuvered closer to the men, trying to survey their faces and memorize little details particular to each one: a severed ear top, a dragon tattooed up the neck, a scar across the face with a discolored eye, and a massive yellow happy face tattooed on the back of a shaved head. The happy face turned to face her, but John stepped forward, blocking the view.

"You need to be careful, Robin," he whispered, snagging a box from the shelf. "Go find Scarlet."

As Robin hurried away, John turned to catch the man, still staring. John gave him a swift nod as he tossed the box into the cart and scooted away.

That night, Robin donned a green hoodie and snuck into the secret arsenal at Sherwood. She fitted herself with a short sword and crossbow, the weapons she had the highest proficiency in thanks to John's training. Armed and dangerous, she ventured into Nottingham alone for the first time in her life. Her eyes blazed red with vengeance as she stalked the city streets, pouncing from rooftop to rooftop, searching for signs of the bastards who changed her life forever.

As she surveyed the haphazard rows of tents, she saw a man in black with a ski mask, dipping in and out of the tents. *Gotcha*, she thought, dropping from her perch and dashing with silent steps toward the shadowy figure.

"Knock knock," the man said, opening a tent's veil. "I got Merriment. Whatcha got for me?"

Crank, she thought. *Maybe.*

Her mind raced and adrenaline pumped. She needed verification, so she crept closer to the tent and peeked inside. The man's back was to her, and a woman's arms wrapped around his waist. Robin shuttered at the sounds the woman made. She reached in and ripped the mask from his head.

"What the—" he yelped, rolling around as he pulled up his pants and buckled his belt. "Quit playing!"

The woman inside grabbed his bag of pink vials and scurried away. He paid her no attention, turning instead toward his attacker. Robin was gone.

"Rowdy? Is that you?" Crank called, peering out of the tent.

From her vantage point, she saw the protruding scar running from his forehead, across one of his eyes, and down his cheek. A bolt sank into his chest.

"Hey. No," Crank yelped, trying to pull out the bolt. "What is this?"

Robin lurched forward, retrieving the short sword from the scabbard.

"Whoa! Whoa!" he cried, turning on his heels and starting to run.

She ran faster, sliding next to him and slicing the backs of his ankles. He collapsed in a heap on the ground, his feet limp and useless. She jumped onto him, holding his arms down. He snarled at her glaring with his mismatched eyes. She leaned forward and pulled her hood back, revealing her face. His eyes went wide.

"You're dead," he murmured with a hard swallow.

"No," she said. "You are!"

The next morning, Guy arrived at the camp in a white NP van. An array of sheriff's vehicles circled the camp, and yellow caution tape stretched everywhere. He ducked through the barriers and headed straight toward the crowd of sheriff deputy uniforms.

Sheriff Bill Lacey shouted orders as Guy broke their huddle.

"What the hell is—" he started to say, but the words died on his lips as he came face to face with Crank's head mounted on a tent pole.

The rest of Crank lay before him. His body splayed out in front of a tent with hands and feet severed. Pink liquid covered his chest, writing out the word KILLER.

"Who did this?" Guy asked.

"We're working on it, Guy. Just go home."

Guy refused. Instead, he spent the next hour interrogating every homeless addict he could find. The only clue he got out of them was someone in a hoodie killed Crank.

"I think we've got a damn vigilante on our hands, boys," Guy said into his cellphone. "Someone's been reading too many comic books. Meet me at the camp. We're gonna set a trap."

A reporter stood at the edge of the camp, talking into the camera, "Another death in the homeless camps, but this time the Sheriff is calling it murder. They could not share if they had any leads, but some folks in the camps say the killer wore a hoodie. Possibly a green one. More to come on this breaking story after these messages."

"Lionheart Industries values life," the commercial began.

John Little clicked the remote, switching off the television and scratching his chin.

In the other room, Robin stuffed the blood-splattered green hoodie into her hamper before heading to the laundry. Other girls were already awake, doing chores and various other tasks around the house.

"Hey, kid," John said to Robin as she passed by. "You're looking a lot better today. You get some decent sleep last night?"

"The best in my life."

257

That night, Robin donned her green hoodie and weapons once again, heading back to the camp. *If Crank had been there*, she thought. *Maybe the others are involved.*

As she stealthily maneuvered through the camp, lights from a van cast her way. She ducked in time, catching the NP logo on the side of the van. *Nottingham Pharmaceuticals*, she thought. *What are they doing here?*

She continued to creep through the camp, picking out familiar voices, but they belonged to her former neighbors, not the killers. *I thought they moved away.*

"You think this'll happen, Rowdy," whispered someone. Her ears perked up.

"Shut up!"

She followed the murmurs, finding two men sitting inside opposite tents and chatting to one another. They both appeared to be homeless, but Robin saw the wisps of dragon fire on Flicker's neck. She circled to the back of his tent and slit an entry, slipping in with great stealth. Other than the man sitting at the entrance, the tent was empty, nothing more than a ruse. She tiptoed toward his back, unsheathing her short sword. Yanking Flicker back by the hair, she sank her blade into his dragon. He yelped in surprise and pain.

A rustle came from the other tents around her, as warm blood sprayed on her and against the tent walls.

"There!" someone yelled, spotting her escape from the tent.

She stopped and faced them, but a few others were already running toward her from different directions. She withdrew the crossbow and targeted her attackers with perfect aim, cracking through skulls and bursting blood out the other side. Then, someone shot at her. She felt the sting of the bullet rip into her shoulder, leaving a gouge in her skin. Blood pumped out with each of her racing heartbeats. She ran, leaving a trail of blood behind her.

"Hey, boss," Rowdy said into his cell phone while staring at the Sherwood Home for Girls. "I gotta show you something."

Inside, Robin whimpered in the bathroom, cleaning her wound.

"What are you doing in there?" asked Mary.

"I'm fine," Robin said unconvincingly. "Go back to bed."

"If you don't let us in," Scarlet threatened. "We're going to have to wake up John."

Robin opened the door, let them in, and told them everything.

"You need to tell John," Mary said.

"No. I don't trust him."

"You can trust him. I promise," Scarlet assured. "After he went to internal affairs about his partner's corruption, thugs invaded his house and killed his family. They nearly killed him too. He helps us because he couldn't help them."

"Now his ex-partner's the sheriff," Mary continued.

"Probably used the same thugs too," Scarlet added.

Was it the sheriff?

Robin agreed to speak to John, and to her surprise, he was not angry.

"We need to prepare," he said with a warm smile as he gripped her healthy shoulder. Then, a flash of light cast across his eyes. He peered out the window at several headlights pulling up to the house. "We may not have time. Wake the others and get ready to fight."

The girls scattered, entering each room and waking the others. Then, they rushed to the arsenal to arm themselves.

Guy and his army of goons sauntered up the doors with weapons in hand. Guy rapped at the door, saying, "Little pig, little pig, let me in!" Then, he waved for Rowdy to blast the door handle off with a shotgun. The men dashed inside to find John standing his ground with pistols in both hands.

"You guys came to the wrooong place," he said before blasting one of the intruders in the head.

As gunshots peppered the house, many of the girls ran away. Robin, Mary, and Scarlet led a small armed group toward the entryway. The barrage of loud bangs rattled the house like thunder. They approached the hallway just in time to glimpse Rowdy and Guy standing over John. Robin started to move forward, but Mary and Scarlet held her back. John glanced over and winked, mouthing the word RUN just before Rowdy blew his face into a red puddle of brains and gore.

Through eyes streaming with tears, the armed girls escaped Sherwood. As they hurried away, their home exploded, bursting into flames.

"We must end this," Robin said, glaring back at the inferno. "You think these thugs work for the sheriff?"

"No doubt in my mind," Scarlet answered. "Let's pay him a visit and find out."

"You know where he lives?"

"John took us once in a while when he surveilled his old partner," answered Mary. "We can take you there."

At Sheriff Bill Lacey's house, several running cars and vans littered his driveway. The girls scurried to the back of the house. Hearing someone inside yelling, they peered through the windows at the sheriff stalking back and forth in the middle of his living room, berating Guy. Robin spotted Rowdy sneaking toward the backdoor, getting ready to light a cigarette.

Smoke billowed behind the big yellow smiley face as Robin took aim. The bolt pierced the back of his neck, ripping clean through his larynx. Blood burbled out of his mouth, but no sound came as two more bolts punctured his back. He faced his attackers, finding Robin rushing him with her short sword. The steel entered him like butter, and his guts fell to the floor with a sickening wet smack before his body collapsed on top of them.

As the girls crept inside the sheriff's home, the phone rang.

"Yeah?" the sheriff said gruffly but quickly changed his tone. "I'm sorry, sir. I didn't realize... No sir. We've developed a slight hiccup with the shipment and delivery." On the other end, the person yelled so loudly everyone could hear even if they could not make out the words. "I'll take care of it... I understand."

"He's working for someone," Scarlet whispered. "We should contact the authorities."

"Like who?" Mary asked. "He's the authority around here... and the mayor."

"We should contact the mayor. He's a nice guy."

"What if he's working for the mayor?" asked Mary.

"Let's find out," Robin said, standing up and loosening two bolts, both hitting Guy in the chest. The other girls rose behind her, training their crossbows on the two men.

Guy fell to a chair as the sheriff peered wide-eyed around him. Robin approached, reloading her crossbow.

"Hello, Sheriff," she said. "Who do you work for? Why did you send these maniacs after my family?"

"Who the hell do you think you are, little girl?" asked the sheriff, stepping defiantly toward her. "Coming in here like this means you have no clue who I am either."

"She's the—"

"You shut the hell up," the sheriff barked, ripping a handgun from his back like a quick-shooter and shooting Guy between the eyes.

Robin didn't hesitate. She launched two bolts at the sheriff, both hitting his right arm. He dropped the gun. She reloaded.

"Why are you putting homeless people into camps?"

"You little girls need to find something better to do with your time. This here's big people work."

"Who do you work for, Sheriff?"

"You wouldn't—"

A bolt pierced into his left side near his shoulder and clavicle. He wails.

Thugs burst in through the front door with guns blazing. Robin dashed for cover. The girls fired their crossbows at the thugs, hitting some, missing others. Robin fired wildly at the sheriff as his thugs rushed to him and pulled him to safety.

"Get out of here," Robin yelled to the girls, trying to scramble toward the backdoor.

Some of the girls hobbled out, and others ran without looking back. Robin, Mary, and Scarlet found temporary shelter not far from the Sheriff's home.

"What do we do now?" Mary asked.

"I think we should go to the mayor," Scarlet urged. "I know him. He is a good man."

"How do you know him?"

"I don't want to talk about it. I just know he's good."

"We need to reach someone outside of Nottingham," Robin said. "Like the governor."

"Leona Richards," Mary clarified. "I think I can help with that. She's a distant cousin."

"Good. See what you can do," Robin said. "In the meantime, Scarlet and I will go to the mayor's office. See if he's clean."

***

They arrived at the mayor's office in the late afternoon, finding security cameras everywhere. Without weapons, Robin and Scarlet approached the front doors, where a guard seemed to be waiting for them.

"The Mayor is aware of the situation and wants a meeting right away," he said, escorting them to his office.

"How is he aware?" Robin murmured.

"Maybe the Governor told him?" Scarlet replied.

They sat in bulky leather chairs in front of a massive redwood desk with intricate carvings throughout. Their feet dangled from the chairs, making them appear much younger than they were. Two guards stood by the door.

A toilet flushed from behind another door. Water turned on and off before Mayor Johnson King entered the room.

"So, what's all this ruckus about?" he asked, strolling toward the girls.

"Hi, Mr. King," Scarlet said, smiling from ear to ear. "Do you remember me?"

"Oh, my dear. I didn't recognize you." He said, brushing her cheek. "You've grown up a lot, it seems."

"I have."

"Yeah, you look so much older and—" he looked her over again, "—used up."

Her smile fades.

"Guards," he said with a wave.

Robin jolted forward, but the guards held them down. Scarlet spit on the mayor. He wiped it away with a wink and an evil grin.

"I trusted you," Scarlet cried. "I ran away for you. I thought you were a good man."

"Oh, Scarlet. We had so much fun back in the day, didn't we? How much of your story have you told your little friend here?" he asked before turning to Robin. "Scarlet here used to be a whore. It is *used to be*, right?"

Scarlet dropped her head as he continued.

"Anyway. She was my favorite. I'd visit her what, like once a week?"

He lifted her face.

"You thought I was a good guy. I was going to take you away from all of that. She was so sweet and innocent. One day she told me she loved me and wanted to go away with me. Isn't that right, Scarlet?"

Scarlet nodded, tears streaming down her cheek.

"I told her that could not happen as long as she was a whore. I was trying to be nice about it. I didn't mean for her to run away. I loved her little body. So sweet and tight everywhere."

Scarlet wailed.

"Leave her alone!" Robin cried. "You sick, mother—"

"Ah ah ah," Mayor King said, wagging his finger. "Good girls shouldn't speak that way."

"I'm not a good girl!" Robin belted.

"I was counting on that," the mayor said with a wink.

An intercom buzzed from behind the desk. "Sir, Sheriff Lacey is here."

"Send him in."

Patched up with bandages around his shoulders and right arm, the sheriff wobbled into the room. "I'm sorry, sir. I've been—"

"Meet our guests, Bill," the mayor said, motioning to the girls. "Remember Scarlet. This is her friend—"

"Robin. Robin Locke!"

"Roland's daughter?" the mayor said, caught off guard. "My God, I thought you were dead. You look like him. Just prettier. Your dad. He was a challenge."

"You had him killed!"

"You're pretty and quick, but you have no clue who your dad was, do you?"

"He was an important lawyer. He fought against the system and corruption like you!"

x

265

Johnson laughed. "He was my partner. Well, one of my partners."

"You're lying!"

"He wanted out. I thought after killing your mom, he would've gotten over the idea, but he decided to go against me once more. If it weren't for him, I wouldn't have all of this. My kingdom. My beautiful kingdom."

"Filled with druggies and homeless?"

"Isn't it perfect? Well, to be fair, I wanted to build a golf course and call it King's Green, but Nottingham Pharmaceuticals paid big money for the land. The homeless are perfect guinea pigs too. What I call a win-win situation."

Another buzz from the intercom. "Sir, a representative of the governor is here."

"Just another busy day at the mayor's office. Let them in."

The girls shared surprised glances.

Mary storms into the office with three men in dark blue suits. As the men enter, they reveal their badges, and Mary runs to her friends.

"Mayor King. Sheriff Bill Lacey. You are under arrest."

"Wait. What? What is this? We're—"

The men draw their sidearms.

"Sirs, if you cannot come peacefully, we will be forced to use violence."

"You don't understand," the mayor said, inching toward a drawer in his desk. He opened the drawer. "We're—"

Smoke rose from the hole in his head as blood and brains splattered against the wall behind him. Scarlet and Mary screamed. Robin looked around, confused.

What is happening?

"Are you coming peacefully, Mr. Lacey? Or do we have to—"

The sheriff raised his arms as best he could and followed the three men. The guards led the way.

"You saved the day," Robin said, embracing Mary.

Scarlet crawled to Johnson King's corpse.

"I can't believe he's dead," she said, noticing something in the drawer. "He wasn't even reaching for a gun. Look."

She retrieved the file, handing it to Robin. Robin flipped a page, finding her father's signature next to Johnson King's signature.

It can't be.

She flipped to a page with Nottingham Pharmaceuticals letterhead and scanned the document.

"Find anything?"

"It says here that Nottingham Pharmaceuticals is a subsidiary of Lionheart Industries."

"Did you say Lionheart Industries?" asked Mary.

"Yeah, why?" Robin said, stuffing the file folder under her hoodie.

"I'm pretty sure that's Leona Richards' company."

"Then, this isn't—" Robin said, swallowing hard. "—the end."

Jared K. Chapman is an author, filmmaker, and educator. He is a native Californian who spent his formative years at school in frigid Alberta, Canada with his father and summer vacation in arid central California with his mother. He holds degrees in psychology & religious studies and is currently a doctoral candidate studying the social psychology of extreme groups. He lives in a little oasis just east of Los Angeles with his wife and three sons. 2HVØRHVNØT is his debut novel. You can find him at: www.jaredkchapman.com

Jack, the Clock, and the Beanstalk

By J. Lynn Hicks

Under a gray sky in a town far away lived a greedy giant who owned all the land and the food in the countryside. From his sky mansion, he watched as the townspeople slaved away with barely enough to survive. But the greedy giant always wanted more. When he learned younger people could work longer, harder hours, he put timers in the townspeople's chests so that when they could no longer work as well; the timer slowed until their hearts stopped beating.

In this gloomy town lived a restless boy named Jack…

***

Sulking down the dark country lane, his pack over his shoulder, even the ticking of Jack's clock, in perfect unison with his beating heart, couldn't ease his troubled mind. The sweat mill where everyone worked would soon speed up production. Jack knew that his mother could never keep up, and that her timer would stop, and she would surely die.

How would he tell his mother? Her ticker might not handle more bad news.

Passing among the shadowed hills, Jack thought about his own time compared with his mother. His life was not the great adventure he hoped for, but his timer was like new because he worked hard. Dear mother's timer hadn't been the same since father's gears stopped, just a year ago.

After his father died, Jack dedicated himself to his mother, as his father had asked him. Jack longed to give his mother the life she deserved. But they had so little. If they wanted to save her, they would have to summon the Clockmaster, who could bend space and time. But it would be expensive to get word to him in the distant lands. So expensive that they hadn't enough money when his father was dying. How would they pay for it now when they couldn't afford milk and bread?

Jack could only think of one thing he could do—sell his grandmother's antique cuckoo clock. Built with hand-struck gears, her relatives forged two clocks a lifetime before, but this was the only one left to them. Dad hadn't let her sell it, calling it her legacy.

Jack didn't know how much the clock was worth, but it was the only thing left. Mother would mourn the loss of her beloved heirloom, but her life depended upon it.

Jack steeled himself against the wind as he moved out into the dreary countryside toward their little house on the hill where his mother sat at the window and waited for him to return from his shift. But when Jack arrived, his mother wasn't there to greet him.

Turning the doorknob, Jack hoped that she just stepped aside for a glass of water. He burst through the door, dropped his pack, and called out, "Mother, Mother, where are you?"

In return, a weak voice called to him from the corner where his mother sat wrapped in her warm shawl. "Jack, I am here."

He rushed to her and pulled the shawl back to look at the clock on her chest. It was still beating, but in an unhealthy rhythm.

"Hold on, Mother. I'll get the clock grease and make you good as new. He fumbled through the bedroom drawer, looking for the salve he hoped would help his mother.

"Jack, look at you," Mother said as the cuckoo popped out silently on the hour and poked his head back in. "You've got so much time, and mine is running out. There's little you can do to stop the final toll."

Jack found the grease and placed it around his mother's gears. "Don't talk that way, Mother. We'll be fine. We just have to believe."

When he finished placing the salve, he pushed his mother's hair back. "You will be fine, Mother."

"Not like this, Jack. The giant has increased production. I will have to work harder, but I won't be able to keep up."

Jack sighed. He wanted to tell her first, but in a small town, news travels fast. Certainly faster than Jack.

"We've got time, Mother. You just hang on, you hear? We have the money father left us. I will use it to get you new gears and springs until I can afford to summon the Clockmaster."

"Son," his mother heaved her chest. "I spent your father's money on your beautiful pack. It was foolish, but I know how you long for adventure. I thought if you could use it to travel to a better land when I am gone—far from the greedy giant. Perhaps, you still can. My days are almost behind me."

Jack wanted to reassure her, but without his father's savings, they would have to find another way for his mother to survive. His shoulders drooped.

"How much do we have left?" Jack asked.

Mother shook her head. "It's gone. I spent the last for milk and bread for your supper."

Jack put on his bravest face and smiled at his mother. This woman, who raised him and set his gears in motion, was at life's edge, and they hadn't a coin to spare.

That night, Jack didn't drink his milk or eat his bread until his mother took half. They were in this together. Each other was all they had, and Jack worried that if he didn't think of something, he would be left alone.

They ate slowly, both of their stomachs growling for more. His mother's clock had slowed again, and the air hung silent. When her ticker skipped a beat, they both looked up, neither knowing what to say. Jack scooted his bowl over to his mother and let her finish his food. She refused, but Jack insisted, "I'm young, Mother, and I can find something tomorrow in the woods. Maybe by some fortune, it will get better."

"No," Mother said. "It's time we made changes. If we continue like this, we'll both perish. I'm old, son. My husband has left this earth, and soon, so will I. But you? You are still young. I know you are down, but you still have your entire future ahead. Don't despair."

"But, Mother…"

"But Jack, I am right. One day you'll have a wife and children of your own, and if you can get away from the greedy giant, there is much left for you to do."

Grabbing her hands, Jack implored her, "But don't you see, Mother? That woman will be a daughter to you, and those children will be your grandchildren. We can't give up now."

Mother laughed. "Give up? I never said anything about giving up. I said we need to make some changes, and the first order is to get money to summon the Clockmaster. Then, we can find a way out of here."

Jack let the air out of his lungs, glad that Mother still had hope.

"The antique clock," Mother whispered. "It's the last one. We must find a buyer and hope the clock brings enough to buy us milk and bread. If there is any more left, we will save to call for the Clockmaster and then leave this town for good. First thing in the morning, I want you to take it into town and trade it for coins."

"I'm sorry we have to sell your mother's clock," Jack sighed, though he was glad she understood.

Mother smiled, and the sadness in her eyes made way for her silent determination. "Nothing to apologize for. My mother would not have us starve for a clock."

Picking up the empty bowls, she turned to him. "First thing in the morning."

Neither spoke another word. Once Mother decided, it would be done.

The next morning when the cuckoo reached five, Jack woke up and got ready for work before remembering what his mother told him. He made his bed and walked to the kitchen table, where no breakfast waited. Mother stared out the window, drinking a glass of water.

"Hitch up the wagon and take the clock at once. We'll need our strength to get through this next part. Any son of mine deserves a hot meal for breakfast, and I won't have another empty table for you. Not on my watch."

Jack nodded at her. "You're a wonderful woman, Mother."

"And you are your father's son. Do hurry and bring home some food for lunch."

Once outdoors, though, Jack's worries multiplied in the dank weather until he remembered his father's charge. He must be brave. His mother had to live, because he couldn't imagine a life without her. With determination, he reminded himself, "I will find the funds to summon the Clockmaster and get us away from here or die trying."

Loading the clock took longer than Jack expected, but soon he grabbed the poles and pulled the cart behind him.

The morning rain was fresh on the ground, and the clouds wept, but as he walked, Jack imagined a brighter future. He pulled the clock and daydreamed down the lane.

Just before he got to town, Jack met a man on the road. Short and squat, he looked to be a salesman.

Jack greeted him. "Good morning, sir."

The small man stopped. "Young man, I have wandered these streets now for many days, and everyone is too overwhelmed with their own problems to greet me as I pass."

"They are probably thinking about the greedy giant," Jack told him.

"And you?"

Jack laughs. "Well, I'm trying to think of a life without him and these horrible timers."

"I see. Nice cuckoo clock, you're pulling there. Does it keep the time?"

"It does, sir. The cuckoo doesn't make a noise, but otherwise my mother has taken excellent care of it."

Putting his hands on his chin, the man walked around the cart. "I used to have the same clock in my house as a child, and my mother treasured it always."

Jack tilted his head, curious. "I'm told mine is only one of two clocks of its kind. Funny that you had the other."

"No, no, young man. There are no coincidences. There is a time and place for everything. And this is our time. Come and look."

From his pocket, the man pulled out a picture, old and bent. Jack looked at it. There, in a small room, was a table with goods. It must be the items the man sold to his customers.

"Now, look in the right corner," the man said. "There you'll find the clock of which I speak. So, you see, our meeting today is not of chance."

Jack squinted his eyes, trying to get a better look, but it was hard to make out any details after years of the photo being pressed in the man's pocket. But if he said the clocks were the same, they must be.

"Thank you for sharing your picture with me. My mother will be delighted with the story."

"You misunderstand, son." The man returned the photo to his pocket. "I have news for you, both good and bad. The bad news is the clock is worthless except for sentimental reasons. It will not bring you any money, but then you probably have all the money you need."

"No, sir," Jack assured him. "My mother sent me to sell so that we would have milk and bread. The rest we are to save to summon the Clockmaster for my mother's heart."

The man took his hat off and frowned. "Oh, that won't do at all."

Jack set the wagon down. What could he do? If he couldn't sell the clock, his mother wouldn't survive.

"Would you like to hear the good news?" the man smiled at him as he pointed his finger into the air.

Feeling there could be no good news that would outweigh the problem of the clock, Jack did not share his optimism. How would he break the news to his mother?

"Here, now," smiled the man. "No use in being down. The good news is that though this clock is worthless to anyone else, it is priceless to me. It reminds me of all the good times with my own mother. I will buy it from you."

Jack looked up, daring to hope. "You would? Oh, my mother and I are in desperate need, and it will help us greatly."

"Not a problem, son. The deal is mutually beneficial. Now, I don't have a lot of money on me at the moment, but I am carrying something of great value. Would you be open to a trade?"

Jack bit his lip. "A trade?"

The man reached into his other pocket and pulled out a black cloth. He unfolded it to expose an ancient gear.

"What is it?" Jack asked.

"It's a magic clock gear."

Jack looked again at the dull surface. "Will that restart my mother's heart?"

"No, no, son. Shine this gear and it will reveal a giant clock that will stop the clocks forever."

His breath slowly deflated, Jack cried, "What good will that do my dear mother?"

"When the big clock is ready. All the heart clocks will stop!"

"But that would be awful. We'd all die for sure."

The salesman laughed. "Why would I want to die? No, starting the big clock again means that we will be immortal. We'll no longer need the heart clocks."

Jack pulled his head back, trying to picture people without timers on their chest, living without fear of the greedy giant, but he couldn't imagine it.

A thought came to Jack. "Why don't you start the clock then?"

The salesman leaned toward him. "Would you give up everything for your mother?"

"Of course!" The insult stung Jack.

"As I thought. That's why I think you are the truest heart, and only the truest heart can start the clock. That's you, Jack."

"How did you know my name? I never told you." Jack eyed him suspiciously.

The salesman held his arms out. "I know many great things, both big and small. If you want to change your destiny, you will make this trade with me."

Giving it some thought, Jack shook his head. "But I need milk and bread for my mother. This will not feed her."

"I have neither milk nor bread, but here's a handful of beans to help you on your way. Eat half tonight, plant the rest, and don't forget to shine the gear. Do as I say and you will live a life immortal.

Jack pursed his lips and stroked his chin. It wasn't perhaps the best deal, but if the old clock was worthless, what choice did he have? At least with the beans, he could get them to grow.

He took the deal. He placed the beans in his pack and polished the gear in his hand as he ran home. And when he entered the house, it surprised his mother to see him so soon.

"Have you sold the clock then, Jack? Did you bring the milk and bread?"

Jack explained. "I don't have milk and bread, Mother. Instead, I have beans to plant for you. And I also got this as well." Jack showed her the now shiny gear.

"That's nice, too," she said of the gear, "but how much did you get for the antique cuckoo clock? Will it be enough to hold us until we can find our way from the greedy giant?"

Jack shrugged. "These, these are what I got, Mother. The old clock was worthless. These beans will feed us, but this gear will make us immortal."

The look on his mother's face was strange for a moment, her brows quirked and her mouth pursed, but it did not last long. A fire lit in his mother's eyes as she turned her head to the side. "You gave your dear grandmother's clock for some beans and a shiny gear?"

The bitterness in her voice made Jack look down at his boots, ashamed. "Yes, Mother."

"Jack, you've been had, and your gullibility will be my death. You have all but put the nail in my coffin!"

"No, Mother. You don't understand…" Jack mumbled.

"No, Jack! It is you who doesn't understand." Mother grabbed the beans and the gear in her hand and threw them out the window. "You've squandered our last chance."

As she rushed from the room, Mother cried.

Jack didn't know what to do. Was it true that he'd been had? But the salesman was so sure. Now, Jack had to wonder. Had he squandered their only chance?

With no actual way to know who was right, Jack stepped out to look for the gear, but he couldn't find it. What he found were the beans. They were all he had left.

Jack thought. "If Mother is right, then we are done for, but if the salesman is right. There's still hope."

Doing what he was told, Jack buried half the beans right where they lay. The rest he made for dinner that night. But his mother wouldn't touch them, and so Jack spent the evening alone.

***

The next morning when Jack awakened, there was a light shining from the window. Confused, Jack rushed over and sprung the sash. In one spot, the cloud had lifted, and the sky was bright blue with ribbons of sunlight cascading over the hill. It was absolutely gorgeous.

Rushing outside, Jacks saw two things of wonder. Where he planted the beans, a thick beanstalk had grown tall and reached into the sky. Jack ran to the gear and looked up to where the light beam bounced off the gear and pierced the stratosphere. His shiny gear, which had reflected the sun and cleared the clouds, lay on the ground in front of a golden clock with a golden pendulum so high Jack couldn't see the top or the clock face.

Jack slid the gear into his pack and hopped onto the beanstalk. He only got a few feet when his mother called from the window. "Jack, Jack, foolish boy. What is this? What are you doing?"

When she came outside, Jack stepped down to try and explain. But his mother was at her wit's end. She put her foot down and wagged her finger. "You are not climbing that beanstalk, my son. You know nothing about it, and it might be dangerous!"

278

"But there is no milk or bread for breakfast, and we've nothing left to sell. Besides, the salesman told me that this would bring immortal life. I have to see for myself, Mother, while I am strong enough to climb. Perhaps I'll find my heart's desire."

Mother shook her head, but there was doubt in her eyes. Jack pounced on the moment of weakness. "I'll be careful. I will. And soon we will have everything plentiful. Just you wait and see."

He blew her a kiss and climbed the beanstalk.

It was a long way up, but Jack only stopped to rest once. Above the pendulum, he saw the clockface was stopped.

After a few hours, Jack reached the top. To his surprise, the salesman made his way through the clouds toward him. "There you are, son. I'm so glad you've come. Follow me. I have something to show you." Jack followed him with many questions, hoping to get answers for his mother. But the salesman wouldn't hold still long enough to ask him.

Jack found the man pointing off in the distance between the clouds. Through the opening, Jack saw the largest house he'd ever seen. This one looked big enough to hold his entire village, perhaps the whole countryside.

"That was once your family's home, and you must take it again from the greedy giant if you ever wish for your people to be free."

Jack turned to ask him just how he planned on setting them free, but the salesman was gone. Jack couldn't find him anywhere.

He cautioned himself. The expansive mansion made him imagine a life free from the restrictions below and a life immortal. If Jack could overtake the giant, he could free his village from the evil reign.

Jack sneaked up to the house, careful to avoid any servants, but he found none. Surprised, Jack crept around to the back entrance where there was a smaller door and entered a large room filled with food.

Spying the giant loaves of bread, Jack opened his pack to put some in when a hand grabbed him and pulled him up through the air. Jack found himself looking at an ugly old ogress.
"What might ya be?" she asked him. "Never ya mind, you'll make a might fine supper." And with that, she put him in her pocket.

Before Jack could poke his head out, a bellowing voice proclaimed. "Tick, Tock. I hear a clock. A human's heart is beating."

"No, no," the ogress patted her pocket, "You hear only the old wood stove clamoring on the floor."

Jack peeked to see the biggest man he'd ever seen. Broad and ugly, with fat cheeks and bloodshot eyes, the giant called to the ogress. "Bring me my dinner!"

But before the ogress could leave the room, Jack jumped onto the table and scrambled behind a teacup. When she returned, Jack peeked around. The ogress looked flustered, probably from having lost Jack. She set a golden serving plate in front of the giant.

The giant said, "I wish for roast beef and mash." He tapped the plate twice and opened the dish to find his wish granted.

Now, Jack was hungry, and he knew he left his mother hungry as well. With that dish, they would never hunger again.

Jack waited until the giant was sleeping, balanced the big plate on his head, and carried it to the beanstalk. Using vines, he lowered the plate down and climbed down below the dark clouds.

Mother was there waiting for him. She hugged his neck. "Oh dear, Jack. I'm so sorry I was cross. I thought the greedy giant might eat you."

"No, Mother. Not at all. And I've brought this dish back for you."

"It's lovely," Mother said. "But will it fetch money for milk and bread?"

"It probably would, but we'll never sell it," Jack told her. "Answer me this, if you could have anything to eat, what would it be?"

Mother furrowed her brow. "Well, I'd wish for a glass of mead and meat pie, but Jack…"

Jack didn't let her finish. "I wish for mead and meat pie" and tapped the giant plate twice.

"Now, look, Jack," Mother started, but she never finished because Jack pulled off the golden dome and revealed enough mead and meat pie for the village.

"Oh, Jack. You've done well, son. Very well, indeed. We will eat our fill and carry the rest into town so that everyone will feast."

***

The golden serving plate did a great service for the townspeople. They fattened up their children and themselves, and it didn't take too long before people forgot what it was like to be hungry.

Jack loved the adventure and was pleased with the food that restored the town's health. But the sky was dark. The people were gloomy and overworked by the greedy giant, and Jack still worried about his poor mother's heart. He decided to sneak up the beanstalk and see what else he could find.

Soon after, Jack stepped on the beanstalk again. But his mother must have known. She called from the window. "Jack, we have enough to eat. What else would be worth the danger of the greedy giant?"

"It is true, Mother. There is plenty to eat, but there is something more. I'm hoping to find it at the giant's castle. And we are not yet immortal."

Mother sighed, but she had seen what good Jack could bring, and dared not stop him.

Jack climbed and used the same small back door. Sliding in, he saw a coin lying on a coffee tin. Jack climbed up to get it when the ogress swept him up and asked, "What might ya be? Ah, never ya mind, you'll make a might fine supper." And she put him in her pocket.

Jack stayed until a bellowing voice proclaimed. "Tick, Tock. I hear a clock. A human's heart is beating."

"You hear only the rattle of the pantry keys," laughed the ogress. Looking up, Jack saw the greedy giant standing there, broad and ugly, with a pocked forehead and hair shooting out his nostrils.

He called to the ogress, "Bring me my money!"

Before the ogress could leave, Jack jumped onto the table and dove behind the candlestick.

When the ogress came back, he peeked around. She looked flustered, but she brought the giant a bag and a great stack of gold.

"Count yourself!" the greedy giant commanded. And the coins called out their numbers and filled the bag with more money than Jack had ever seen.

Now, Jack was poor, and his mother was poor as well. If they had that money, they could summon the Clockmaster, and he could give his mother anything she wanted.

Jack waited until the giant fell asleep, balanced the heavy bag on his head and sneaked it to the beanstalk. Using vines, he lowered the bag and climbed down below the dark clouds.

Mother was there waiting for him, "Oh dear, Jack. I'm so glad to see you in one piece. I thought the greedy giant had caught you."

"No, Mother. Not at all. But I've brought something back for you."

"Will it fill your heart's desire?"

"It probably will," Jack told her. "But first, answer me this. If you could have anything you wanted, what would it be?"

Mother looked at Jack and then at the bag. "Well, I'd wish for an antique clock just like my mother's…"

Jack did not let her finish. He pulled open the bag and revealed more coins than his mother could count. He says, "Mother, it's all the money you could ever spend. Perhaps we can find another clock, but this is enough to summon the Clockmaster."

"Oh, Jack. You've done well, son. We will take what we need and then find someone to summon the Clockmaster. The rest we'll give to the townspeople, so that everyone will be rich and won't have to work like slaves for next to nothing."

Mother celebrated as Jack sent off for the Clockmaster and gave away his riches.

***

The golden coins were a great boon for the townspeople. They built better homes and wore warm clothes in the winter. It didn't take too long before people forgot what it was like to be without.

Jack loved the adventure and was pleased the coins helped to restore their town. Everyone had enough to eat and wear, the homes were spacious and warm, and the people didn't have to work as much. But still the town was dark and gloomy. And Jack worried about his mother's poor heart.

As they waited for the Clockmaster, Jack also remembered the salesman told him he needed to recapture the house as his own. Doing so would bring immortal life and save his mother's heart. Feeling obligated to finish his task, Jack decided to try the beanstalk again.

Late that night, Jack tiptoed to the beanstalk, but his mother must have been waiting. She called from the window. "Jack, we have more than enough food to live on and more money than we can spend. What else could there be that would be worth the danger of the greedy giant?"

"It is true, Mother. There is plenty for all, but there is something more. It's as if something vital is missing—my heart's desire. I'm hoping I find it at the giant's castle. Besides, we aren't yet immortal."

Mother sighed, though she dared not stop him. But this time, she bid him to wait. She exited the house and reached deep in her pocket and pulled out an old pocketknife. "This knife is not worth any money, but is worth more than a treasure full of gold. It's your old father's favorite hunting knife, and it is time for you to have it."

Jack took the knife and wiped a tear from his mother's eyes. "Thank you. Just one more trip to see what the giant has in store."

Mother didn't argue, because Jack was now a man.

He climbed up and made his way to the same small back door he used before. He slid in, and he could see a room full of riches and delicate foods. Yet, there was nothing he wanted.

He was about to leave when the ogress swept him up and said, "What might ya be? Never mind. You'll make a might fine supper."

She put him in her pocket, then thought better of it, dropping him in a hot pot of water. Jack was quick to escape, and he crawled onto the ribbon of the ogress's long apron.

By the time Jack settled, a bellowing voice proclaimed, "Tick, Tock. I hear a clock. A human's heart is beating."

"You hear only the boiling pot, rattling on the stove," she sighed.

Looking up, Jack saw the giant standing there, broad and ugly, with a snarled brow and wart upon his chin. He called to the ogress, "Bring me my joy."

Now, Jack had never heard of joy, but it sounded precious. So, before the ogress could leave the room, Jack jumped out and hid behind the dinner bell.

When the ogress came back, he peeked around. She looked livid, but she brought in a clock with golden gears that resemble the shiny gear the salesman once had given him.

"Sing to me!" the greedy giant told his clock, and he set the time.

Jack waited for the chime and when it came, out popped a gilded cuckoo bird with the most enchanting melody Jack had ever heard. As the music took wing, he understood what joy was. This is what he'd been missing after years of oppression. The joy of being alive, the joy of the cuckoo released.

As the cuckoo bird continued its beautiful song, the greedy giant put his hands on his fat belly and slept.

Jack's town now had plenty to eat and money to spend, but this joy would lift them all. So, Jack crept up to the sleeping giant and balanced the cuckoo on his head. But the cuckoo grew scared and cried out when Jack took him away. The greedy old giant awakened as Jack ran out the big front door and down to the beanstalk.

The giant's heavy footfall pounded behind him. And with no time to let the cuckoo down, Jack set the golden bird free among the clouds to make its song forever.

Jack rushed down the beanstalk, but before he got to the pendulum, he pulled out his father's knife and clipped the vine so he could swing up to the clock. Jumping among the clock's gears, Jack found one missing. From his pack, Jack took the gear the salesman had given him. Jack slid it into place, swung the pendulum back, and the clock started.

Above, the greedy giant was close behind. He put his mighty foot on the top of the beanstalk, but his weight made the stalk bend until the pendulum swung and knocked the giant to the ground where he landed on his big greedy head with a big thud.

The townspeople, who heard the mighty crash, came to see the giant on the ground, but he was not dead. Jack ripped out the clockworks with his father's knife and threw it down on the giant's chest.

"Jump on it!" Jack screamed as he used the pendulum to slide down. At the bottom, he helped the townspeople jump until the clock wedged deep in the giant's chest. Jack set the timer for one second, and as it sounded the greedy giant's eyes grew big and his clock stopped forever and the giant disappeared as the large clock chimed. The clouds lifted, and the sun shined over the land.

Jack looked toward his mother's timer and then his own. Gone. Not only theirs, but all the townspeople were free of the timers. The people stood in awe, all except for one.

Mother ran toward Jack. "Oh, son. I'm so glad to see you in one piece. You should have seen it! I thought the greedy giant crushed you."

"No, Mother. Not at all. But I've finally found my heart's desire. Listen!"

Just then, the cuckoo flew down and sang its beautiful song. The townspeople began to sing, too, and so the birds returned to the town and mimicked the cuckoo's song.

When the song was over, the cuckoo flew back into the clouds, leaving the other birds to continue.

"That song!" Mother smiled. "It's as if I know it from long before. It makes me feel... Well, I don't know a word for it, son."

"Oh, Mother dear, it's a magical feeling called joy, and we all shall know it now the clouds are gone, and we are as free as the bird who sings."

The townspeople shouted and sang, and Jack wanted to join them, but his mother held him back.

"Oh, Jack. You've done well, son. Very well, indeed. And now, you can safely go on your adventure!"

The thought made Jack laugh. "Oh, no. No more adventure for me! Now you are safe, I am ready to start a family of my own."

Jack hugged his mother and turned her around in a great circle. But when he set her down, the salesman appeared. Pulling along a cart with his mother's antique clock, he wore a bright smile.

"Wait, Jack! Your good fortune is just beginning!" He tapped the antique clock on its side as he set it down. "This is for your mother, but there is much more for you."

"What more could I possibly ask for?" Jack quizzed him.

The salesman smiled and said, "I've told you there are no coincidences, my friend. You may call me the Clockmaster."

Jack's mouth fell open. This was the Clockmaster, but now his mother had no timer to be fixed.

"Don't worry about your mother." The Clockmaster raised his index finger. "Since the giant is dead, and the ogress ran away, you can take back your family's mansion in the sky. You and your mother will live there for as long as you so shall wish. The timers are all gone, and now your people are immortal."

Jack didn't know what to say. All that he could manage was, "How?"

The Clockmaster winked. "Why, happily ever after, of course!"

J Lynn Hicks, author of *The Daughter of Rebellion* trilogy, writes young-adult dystopian fiction that empowers teen girls to change the world and fight for justice in the face of adversity.

After ten years of teaching language arts to teens, J Lynn sat down to write and hasn't stopped since. When she isn't writing, she loves theater, fine dining, and riding shotgun. You are likely to find her geeking out on craft books, scrolling through YouTube, and sharing memes and gifs on social media.

All of her books are available through Amazon and Kindle Unlimited. Follow the link for a free story:

http://mailchi.mp/f0be97e8e2ae/facebook

THE PIPER

By Christine French

They say that when you call the Piper he will come, but you'd better be prepared to pay the price. I can't help but feel that whatever the price is, it can't be worse than the one we are paying now.

***

For decades the Ratgebers have been the only thing standing between us and death. When the rains stopped, and the River Wesser dried up, those of us who remained in the town were slowly starving to death. Our once plentiful export grains stopped growing, as did much of the food we grew to eat. Our population was slowly dwindling; not only were people leaving in search of refuge, but people were also dying, and fewer and fewer children were being born. And then, one day, we were summoned to Rathaus by our new rulers, the Ratgebers. They were offering to save us all and they wanted only one thing in return: our children.

We had never heard of these Ratgebers and we weren't sure where they came from. Far upstream somewhere, we supposed, where the River Wesser still flowed and the rains still came. We also weren't sure why they wanted to help us. But they did, and we were too desperate to refuse. They told us our children would be used as guarantees of our good behaviour, as hostages, and even knowing this it was an easy decision to make. It was worth risking those who weren't born yet to save the living, especially since without this agreement we were all going to die anyway. Without the Ratgebers help there wouldn't *be* future children. And so the deal was made.

They say that the first time the Ratgebers came to take a child, they were ripped from their mother's arms as she fought against them, against an arrangement about which her opinion had never been sought. That first mother had to be sedated. Years later, she still never was never quite right. This did not deter the Ratgebers though. They still come time and time again to collect their payment.

289

Now when they come, it is expected and it is quiet and it is startlingly inhuman. The Ratgebers take only our firstborn children because there is no guarantee that any of us will have another. Despite this, our small town is flourishing with children, all second and third and fourth born, and we watch them thrive while pain twists behind our smiles because we know that somewhere there are other children locked away that we cannot see. Children who are the price of our freedom. And, besides, the Ratgebers remind us pointedly, even if no one is ever quite really happy, at least we are not all dying on the streets.

But after all these years, we have had enough. We are no longer willing to pay the price that our ancestors agreed to so long ago. All this pain has led to this moment, to now, when we stand huddled deep underground where we hope that the Ratgebers have no spies, no bugs, no drones. Where we hide and plot to overthrow them. There's an old joke about not telling secrets in a field of corn because there are ears everywhere. There is a truth in that. We make sure that secrets are told deep underground where we hope the ears cannot follow.

"Is this safe?" someone asks in the crowd where they stand with fearful eyes that flick between the entrances to the room. "What about the Ratgebers?"

"Pah, the *rats*," my father, the Mayor, exclaims, spitting in disgust. "We will no longer need to fear them. Not once we hire the Piper." Though he is leading this rebellion, not everyone trusts him. Some fear he is in the pocket of the Ratgebers and will betray us, others resent the benefits his status affords him. They resent him because of me.

I am a first born, the only first born to roam these streets. The Ratgebers let my family keep me as payment for my father's services, services that he is no longer willing to provide. And even though we did not make the rules, even though we are now fighting against them, that resentment still simmers amongst the others. Even now, here, they all avoid looking at me, as if somehow it is my fault.

But it doesn't bother me because I get it. I am a constant reminder of the children they have lost.

"Who is this Piper?" a voice calls from the corner. It is Markus. He stands in the dimness, his arm wrapped around his child. She is fourteen. Some of the older townsfolk claimed that she was too young to be here, but Markus argued with them. It was her future that was being decided in this moment. We could not make decisions for future generations without their say, not the way that it had been done to us. It was hard to argue with that, and so she stayed.

His question surprises me though. I thought everyone had heard of the Piper, but perhaps my father's position also grants me a level of knowledge and privilege that I had not considered before.

"The Piper is an assassin," replies my father. "Though it is usually put more euphemistically than that. 'Problem solver' is the preferred title, I believe." There are nods of recognition around the room. Many who gather here know this, but not everyone.

"And how do we contact him?" It is a different person asking this time, Klaus, a man so old and grey that he claims to remember some of the first takings. I don't find it hard to believe him.

My father is more evasive in his answer this time, but perhaps it is only obvious to me because I know him so well. I wonder what he is hiding and why. "We have contacts that will send a message through."

"What if the Piper says no?" It is another voice, but I do not recognise it and the shadows make it too hard to see them.

"We will make it worth his while to assist us," he says. A titter pulses around the room; a sea of voices, all with a common response.

"With what money?" It is impossible to know who asked this question; it is the question of everyone here, except perhaps my father. While our city has prospered again under the rule of the Ratgebers, we receive our payment in food and water and medicine, while they gather the riches amongst themselves.

"Once the *rats* are gone, we will have plenty of money," asserts my father. "All the money they have stolen from us." This time the murmurs are of agreement, and with this I know that he has convinced all the people standing here that an uprising is worth it. Recover our children, and take back our wealth? What have we got to lose?

***

Days pass and to the outside eye nothing much changes, but behind closed doors there is a hive of activity. We are meeting in another dimly lit cavern that is deep underground. A hooded figure stands in the corner, and even in the wavering light I can see that they wear a cape of dully dyed cloth in a cacophony of colours. My father moves to stand before the crowd and raises his hands for silence. The voices ebb and die away, but before my father can speak the Piper moves forward.

"You have heard my terms?" her voice calls out calm and low.

The Piper is a female? I think to myself. I do not know why it should come as such a surprise, but it does. Here all the women stand docilely by while the world happens around them, numbed by the loss of their firstborn. They take care of their household and the children they were permitted to keep. It had never occurred to me that a woman could change the world around her, around us.

My father glances to the corner where the Piper stands shrouded in shadows with a slightly displeased look on his face, but then he smooths it over and steps to the side, angling his body towards her and inviting her into the space at the front of the room. Either she does not notice, or she does not wish for such honour. She stays where she is.

"We have heard your terms," my father agrees, smiling reassuringly at the people before him. A murmur of voices ripples quickly through the room, and I wonder how many of them would agree with his statement since the rest of us are unaware of the specifics.

"And do you accept them?" she asks almost challengingly.

"We do," my father agrees, his reassuring smile never fading. Beneath her hood, the Piper nods.

"Very well," replies the Piper. "I will take care of your problem. I will be in contact." She gathers her robes around her and disappears further into the shadows. I didn't know there was another entry point to this space. I wonder how she did.

I am trying to see where she went in the darkness and I do not notice the rising voices until one of the people surging towards my father shoves into me. They are all demanding answers, more information. My father has no intention of sharing anything with these people. Information is currency, is power, and he knows it.

"Please," he says in a voice loud enough to be heard over the clamouring crowd. "Please stay calm. You know how this is. It is safer for us all if information is not widely disseminated. I have met with the Piper, as have a selected number of your delegates. She will do what we ask, and the price is no more than any of us are willing to pay, I promise you."

The outraged cries die down into disgruntled rumblings and the people begin to disperse. An odd few here and there shoot discontented looks at my father as they leave, but he pretends to not notice, and soon the room is empty again except for my father, his cronies, and me.

Not long after the room clears, I leave my father with his conspirators. I am already sick of their self-congratulatory ways. It is true that our lives under the Ratgebers aren't our own, but they saved us when not much else could. I felt we owed them something for that, though perhaps our children was taking it too far. Regardless, I believe this is cold-hearted disloyalty. My father would tell me I am too soft, that freedom is hard-won, that it has a price. Perhaps he is right.

I am lost in my thoughts as I wind my way back to our house when I notice someone slipping through the shadows around me. I don't pay them much attention, but then the cloak of the Piper appears right next to me, her steps in time with my own, hiding in the noises I make. I gasp as I realize that she is there. She touches my arm in warning as she gestures to the houses nearby. I am surprised by her attention; she must not know who I am.

Carefully she manoeuvres us so we are both shrouded in shadow and then asks, "The Mayor, he is your father, yes?"

I nod in the darkness. Apparently, she does know who I am and yet, she still wishes to speak to me. Even if we are only talking about father, my heart still flutters. "Yes," I whisper back.

"Is he a good man?"

I do not know how to answer this question. Is anyone truly good in this world, especially when we are forced to live the way we do - secrecy and lies at every point - by the Ratgebers? "He tries to be," I finally manage in response.

"Can I trust him?" I do not know why she is asking me these questions. How does she know if I am trustworthy? Is she going to go to every person in turn and ask?

"I think so," I reply cautiously. "I know reuniting our families and freeing us from the Ratgebers is his priority. There is no reason for him or anyone in the town to betray you."

She stands still for a moment, digesting what I have said. "Good," she replies, and then a ghost of a smile whispers across her face. "But if I were you, I would try to avoid having such questions asked of you by the Ratgebers. Your face," she says as she trails a fingertip along my cheek, leaving shivers in its wake. "It gives everything away."

Her hand drops and she steps back, fading further into the shadows. I can no longer see her, and her departure leaves no sound. Still, I stay peering after her in the darkness, my hand clasped to my cheek where my skin still tingles where she touched it.

***

I am lying on my bed in the darkness when my father returns. My mother stayed home during the meeting in case anyone stopped by, but she now comes out to meet him. I listen to their hushed conversation and I wonder if they even realize I am here.

"Is it done?" my mother asks him.

"It is done," my father responds, his voice a strange mix of triumph and weariness.

"And the Piper?" my mother asks.

"It has been arranged," my father says.

"Good," replies my mother, satisfied.

I find their words oddly troubling, but I cannot make sense of why. I lie there puzzling over it for a while and then let sleep pull at me. There will be time to work it out later.

***

It has been two days since the Piper arrived and nothing seems to have changed. We watch over our shoulders in fear that the Ratgebers will somehow discover what is going on. After what the Piper said I feel even more self-conscious when I am in town, worried that the Ratgebers will read our plans in my face.

***

I am hurrying home from the market when a hand from the shadows reaches out and clasps my shoulder. I jump and whirl around, afraid of what I might see, but it is nothing more than the Piper. She places her finger over her lips, indicating that I should stay silent. "Tonight," she says softly. "Tell your father."

"Tell him what?" I ask quietly, but she is already melting away. This time, in broad daylight, I dare not dally and draw attention to myself. I continue on my route home, the whole encounter taking only moments.

***

When I arrive home, my father is in his office and I knock on the door. The voices inside fall silent as my father calls for me to enter. I open the door and step into the room.

"What do you want, Katja?"

"The Piper came to me in the Village," I say, almost as if I'm embarrassed.

"She approached *you*?" my father asks sharply. "Why you?"

I shrug uncomfortably under the pressure. "I don't know," I answer. "She didn't say."

He stares at me for a long moment before looking away. "Very well," he finally says. "What did she say?"

"She said to tell you 'tonight,'" I reply. He continues to stare at me, his piercing gaze attempting to see through me, but he cannot see what is not there. I have nothing to hide

"Did she say anything else?" he asks.

"No," I reply. "Just that."

He nods and turns away. I take that as my cue to leave. As I am walking through the door, I hear the murmur of voices start up behind me.

"Can she be trusted?" one of them asks.

"Oh yes," my father says dismissively. "What could she do anyway?"

My cheeks burn with shame as I close the door, and it is enough to erase the lingering memory of the Piper's touch.

***

The news passes quickly around the townspeople, though I am never quite sure how it is done. Underground whispers that have been perfected through decades of oppression. No matter how it happens, the instructions are clear: no matter what, stay at home tomorrow. No matter what you hear or what you think you see, stay inside. Something is going to happen. The next morning: chaos. It fills our normally subdued streets with noise and urgency. The sound of running feet is only overpowered by the desperate shouts. The sounds come closer, and then fade slightly, only to be repeated again and again. I edge closer to our front window trying to determine the cause, though I have a sneaking suspicion I already know what it is. I am almost at the window when my father appears in the room. For a large man, he has always been able to move silently when it suits him.

"Katja," he says disapprovingly.

"I just wanted to see," I explain. "Curiosity would be expected, surely."

"We can do nothing that draws attention to us," he says. "Especially not now. Let us pretend that this is normal, that there is nothing they can do that would cause us to question anything."

I let my hand drop from where it had been poised to pull back the curtains enough to see outside. "Very well," I agree.

He nods at my compliance and walks away. I stand there staring at the curtain for a very long time, wondering whether I have the courage to disobey, whether I have the courage to accept the consequences. I do not.

***

We do not dare to meet that evening, not in the numbers that we have been meeting, not until we can be sure that the Piper has finished her job. My father works in his office late into the night; I am not certain he sleeps.

***

The next morning the chaos has been replaced by an eerie calm, as though we are in the centre of a whirlpool. My father asks me to dress in my nicest clothes and I pull them on, puzzled by his edict. When I am dressed, I meet him in our front room. He and my mother are both dressed in finery that I have never seen before. My father guides us outside, and we join the stream of people walking towards the city of Rathaus.

At every intersection we are joined by more and more townsfolk until it feels like we are a giant river flowing towards the sea. As we approach, I see that the gates stand wide open. I have never seen Rathaus unguarded before and a shiver works its way down my spine as I walk carried by the crowd through the gates. The city center stands at the top of a series of steps with a large courtyard below. Many of the townsfolk are milling aimlessly around this large square, and I hear questions being whispered on the wind.

What has happened?

Why are we here?

Where are the guards?

Where are the rats?

My father alone dares ascend the steps, though he is soon joined by his compatriots, Wilhelm and Heinrich, who walk a respectful distance behind him. His slow, measured rise up the stairs soon draws the attention of the people. Before he is even at the top, the square is silent, except for the sound of his shoes clacking on the stone steps.

"People of Hamelin," my father declares once he has arrived at the summit. He stands before the large, iron doors of the main building of Rathaus. Doors that have always been closed to us, in the way that the gates have always been closed to us. "Today, we are free."

For moments his words just hang on the air, then the people catch the sound as they pass it back and forth amongst themselves. *Free, free, free…*

"The Ratgebers – the *Rats*," this word is filled with disgust as it always is. "Have been, let us say … taken care of."

Though I was sure that most of the people gathered here must have been aware of this plan, a sense of shock still seems to reverberate around the area, as though they cannot believe that their audacity has paid off.

"Be assured, the Piper has done her job thoroughly," my father continues. "The rest of the guards have been corralled right here, in the main building of Rathaus, from whence they ruled for so long. And your children, *our* children," here he lets his voice catch with emotion, "have been found and are being cared for by our good medical men and women. Once we are sure that they are all healthy and not in need of any further care, we will begin reuniting families tomorrow."

Tomorrow. Again, the word dances amongst the people who whisper it with awe, with astonishment, with gratitude. My father could say anything now, do anything now, and these people would still revere him. Any lingering distrust has melted away with this news.

While the crowd celebrates their good fortune quietly, with tears of joy streaking across faces and hands clasped tight, too overjoyed to find the sound to rejoice, my mother has ascended the steps and joined my father upon the temporary dais. He reaches across and clasps her hand in his. They nod to me and reluctantly I climb the steps to join them.

"Let us no longer live in fear of the *rats*," my father finishes. "Let us no longer have our families in fear. Let us no longer cower behind closed doors hoping that this time they won't notice us, that this time we will escape their notice, that this time it will be different. From this day forward it *shall* be different. Go in peace, my friends, for tomorrow will be a new day."

At the end of his speech, he looks around the crowd, nodding to those who catch his eye, and then turns to me.

"Let us go home, now, Katja," he says, and as a family we go, leaving those who are not yet whole to watch after us with hope instead of pain for the first time.

***

It is late that afternoon when I hear unusual noises and I creep to the hall to see what is happening. The Piper has arrived and is demanding that my father give her an audience. Her back is to me and her voice is low, calm, but uncompromising.

"You promised me payment, Mayor Veraten," she says to my father, and he smiles. There is a cruelty in it that I have never noticed before.

"Indeed I did," he says as he throws her a small sack. She opens it and glances inside.

"This is not the agreed-upon price," she says.

"No?" says my father in mock-surprise. "Oh dear," he continues. "You must have made some sort of mistake." His gaze flicks aside and from the shadows appear two men who grasp her arms and move her along to a back exit.

"I will go," she states as she shakes the hands of the men off of her. "But remember: those who call for the Piper must always pay the price."

My father laughs softly. "Or else what, Piper?" he asks her. "You will bring all the rats back?"

She glances back over her shoulder, piercing him with her gaze. "There are always new rats to be removed," she says, and there is a threat in her words.

"There is nothing you can do if you have no power," he gestures once again to the men who grip her harder and begin to pull her away. "Place her in the underground tunnels which she loves so much."

"There will always be a price to pay," she says calmly, as if she isn't being taken as a prisoner.

My father obviously does not believe her, though, and he turns his back to her as he re-enters his office. I stay hidden in the shadows until I am sure that there is no one left to see me slip away.

***

The ringing of the doorbell startles me from the reverie into which I had sunk. My heart starts racing, an automatic reaction when normally the only people ringing the doorbell at this time of night have been the Ratgebers. This time, however, my mother opens the door and for the first time in memory my father's compatriots step through, daring to openly visit him. Before today they would never have risked such a thing.

"Welcome," says my mother softly. "Gerhard is in his office." She steps to the side, and they all walk confidently through the house to his office door, as though it is a journey they have made a million times. Perhaps it is, though never this openly.

I am restless after the events of the past few days, and so I throw on a cloak and head into our back garden, hoping that the cool night air will somehow soothe me. I'm not sure why my father has imprisoned the Piper, but I don't dare ask. I wish there was something I could do to help her.

As I walk, I find the curtains to my father's office closed, but the window slightly ajar. Unable to resist temptation I move closer, eager to listen to their conversation.

"Have you met with the doctors?" my father speaks.

"Yes," says one of the men. I think it is Willhelm. "They say that most of the children can be released, but that they'd like to do further tests on another dozen or so."

"Do they have the gene?" asks my father eagerly.

"They believe so. If they survive the tests tomorrow, then they'll know for certain."

"Excellent," says my father in a satisfied tone. "Expedite the tests tonight. We need to know how many families we must prepare for the bad news that their children have not survived. The money we get for pharmaceutical development should keep us well cared for, whether the river flows or not."

"How are you going to explain their absence?" asks the man I think is Hans.

"We'll blame the Piper," says my father, his words sounding rehearsed but malicious. "She must have decided that she could extract more money from us, and when we refused, she killed the children in retribution. That is why we have imprisoned her. We'll have her publicly executed in two days, after we have reunited the families."

I stay frozen where I am for a moment, unable to believe that my father has been arranging all of this behind the scenes. Even without these children he would have been revered by the townsfolk, their official leader for as long as they wanted. This desire to continue to hold some children for testing could only arise from greed, and the idea that my father could leave them and their families to suffer like this sends my belly swirling in disgust. I cannot let this happen.

***

I steal through the dark tunnels to the room where the Piper stays, the room where she is kept. She is a prisoner, now awaiting death, and I wonder if she knows it. I creep to her door, unwilling to risk opening it, and press my lips to the crack between door and wall.

"Piper?" I call in a hushed whisper that susurrates down the shadowy corridor.

"Who's there?" Her voice calls back assured, confident, and I am jealous of her strength.

"They are going to kill you," I respond, my tone still hushed and wary. I failed her. She asked if my father could be trusted and I told her he could. I feel betrayed as well.

"Katja, is that you?" Her voice sounds closer now, softer, as she calls to me.

"Yes, but listen, you are in danger. I was wrong. My father - he intends to kill you."

"Why?" She doesn't seem surprised just in want of more details.

"My father wanted the Ratgebers gone, and the children freed. But not all of them because they still need some for the town to remain prosperous. For my *father* to remain prosperous. More children will go missing. They'll go into the main building of Rathaus and we'll never see them again. You must go."

"Go?" she answers. "How can I go?" Her words are double-edged; she knows as well as I do that she is a prisoner here. But I know that even if she were free, she could not just walk away. Not after all she had done to secure the freedom of Hamelin and its children.

"I will come." I lean forward earnestly, my hands pressed against the door as though I could push my way through it to secure her freedom.

"I will be waiting," she says in response, and somehow there is no hint of irony in her words. "And then we must go far from here."

I nod in agreement even though she cannot see me, and then I slip away, leaving her alone in the darkness with nothing to do but plan.

***

Back in my room, I wait until the household is asleep and then I steal down the stairs to my father's office. I am lucky because there, in the top draw of his desk, are a bundle of keys. I wonder whether he is foolish to be so trusting, or just too arrogant to think I would ever betray him. I take them with me as I slip back down through the garden to the tunnels that take me to the Piper.

Dawn is not far away as I return and release the Piper from her involuntary confinement.

"We must hurry," she says to me, and I agree. We waste no time as we wind our way silently through the underground tunnels to Rathaus.

She opens a door and strides through. She knows these secret tunnels well. I follow her more cautiously, but I freeze in place as I see the room into which she has led me. My gaze sweeps the room, unable to grasp the scene I see before me. Rows upon rows of partially formed bodies – of corpses – float in jars and tanks as far as the eye can see. A wave of horror flows through me and nausea churns in my belly.

I turn to the Piper, revulsion creeping over my skin. "Did you know?" I ask her.

She nods. "I knew."

"But how – why?"

"There's something here, something in your water or your soil – no one knows exactly – but it caused the first genetic mutation. Somehow, malnourished though you were, sickness avoided you. The scientists have been testing, cloning, genetically selecting for what would effectively be immortality. To be perfected and sold to the highest bidder, of course. And in the meantime, all these subjects upon which they can perform any number of tests," she finishes bitterly.

"Why didn't you do anything?" I ask.

"I always stand by an agreement. As I said, there is always a price to pay. You didn't know?" she asks. There is no judgement in her tone, only gentle curiosity.

I shake my head, too many emotions writhing through me to give any other response. The Piper approaches and places a gentle hand on my shoulder, melting some of my tension away. "We had no idea why they wanted the children or what they were doing to them."

"There is nothing you can do for them," she says, nodding towards the scene before me. "But we can still save the others. I need

304

you to stay here, to keep watch. Your father's associates, they will trust you. I will take care of anyone ahead of me, I cannot succeed if more are coming in from behind."

Still numb with shock, I nod.

"Good," she says. "I will return. Be safe, Katja." And with that, she disappears through a doorway to another room.

I try not to look around as I wait for her return. Seconds bleed into minutes and nightmares dance through my head at what she could be doing. Periodically I glance anxiously at the metal ceiling, as though I can see through it to the impending dawn. Anxiety twists in my chest and I force my breathing to slow. My heart rate remains uncontrollable, galloping along as though it can speed the Piper on her travels.

Finally, the sound of a hundred scurrying feet arrives and I step forward, eager for us to be on our way. To my surprise, the Piper has not just brought the dozen or so children that my father had intended to retain, but all the children who had been taken for all those years.

"What-" I begin to ask, but the Piper silences me.

"Not now," she says. And so, though a thousand questions burn in my chest, I acquiesce and we begin our trek out of the tunnels. When we emerge, we are in a place I do not recognise and dawn is lighting the sky in tendrils of silver and gold.

"We must go this way," says the Piper as she gestures towards a narrow path through the mountains. How she convinced the many children to follow her, I do not know, but the sun is creeping towards noon by the time we reach the safety of the mountain pass.

"My father will come for them," I say to the Piper.

She shakes her head. "He will never find them."

"Why?" I ask her, and though the question is abrupt, she does not mistake what I am asking.

"Would you have me leave them there?" she asks me. "Returning to families that they never knew? Families that gave them up? Living in a village ruled over by one such as him?" Then she pauses. "I am sorry," she says. "I know he is your father."

I shake my head. I feel no loyalty to the man I have discovered he is.

"I don't even know your name," I say to the Piper, somewhat irrelevantly, and she laughs. A rich, clear sound that thrills through me.

"Piper. My name is Piper," she says, sounding amused, and I wonder how I could not have realised it before. "You will come with me?" she asks and for the first time in our many conversations she sounds uncertain and I blush even as my heart beats faster.

"I will," I say in a soft voice, and she squeezes my hand.

"I am glad," she says, and there is something in her tone that I cannot identify, but that makes me blush even harder. Then she stands and addresses the hundreds of children who are milling around us.

"It is time for us to move on," she says. "Any who do not wish to come with me may return to the town, but remember all that I have told you."

All the children move forward, except for one young boy, who limps towards us.

"I twisted my ankle on the pass," he says to Piper. "I cannot continue my journey on foot." He looks longingly at her. There is sympathy in her face, but also resolution.

"I am sorry, but in that case you had better return to the town," she states. "Although it pains me to say it."

The boy nods.

"How do you know he won't say anything?" I quietly ask her.

She shrugs. "There is nothing he can tell. By the time he has returned to the town we shall be long gone. They will not be able to find us."

Piper moves to the front of the group and begins the long walk away. I stand and watch the line of children wind along, moving further and further from the one lame little boy who will return to Hamelin to tell his tale. I watch until I can no longer see him, and then I join the tail of children following Piper.

***

They say that to this day the town of Hamelin mourns the loss of its children, the memory of their departure inscribed on the city gate for all to see. A story told of a Piper who stole them away. But I do not know this for certain as I have never returned. Sometimes I think of my father and the town we left behind, but it is not with regret. My home is with Piper now, and the children we saved.

Christine French lives in Melbourne, Australia, where it doesn't snow nearly as often as she'd like, but does have some of the world's best coffee so the trade-off is almost worth it. In addition to the cold and coffee, Christine has a love of reading and writing that follows her nearly everywhere. An avid reader, Christine enjoys mystery, romance, fantasy, science fiction, and dystopia. She enjoys writing the same – except mysteries in which she can never work out whodunit or how.

Christine lives with her husband, daughter, and stepchildren and cannot wait to use them as beta readers. When not reading, writing, or consuming copious amounts of coffee, Christine can be found pottering around the garden hoping that this time she'll beat the various bugs and birds to the vegetable patch. You can find out more about Christine's upcoming works at www.christinefrench.com

The Seven Kids

By Audrey M. Stevens

Seven children wander through the woods. They know not where they are going, but know they can't go back. Each of their skin is a different tone and their features vary like the difference between snowflakes. Not a single one is related by blood, though they act as if they are siblings. All of them are classified as children, forced to use their limited experiences in order to survive. The older ones lead the way in an attempt to keep them all safe. Grayson, Riley, Nikki, and Dexter are all under ten while Emma, Hannah, and Tommy take their role as older children seriously.

"We have been walking for hours," Grayson complains.

"And we will keep walking until we can't," Emma replies, stomping forward through the forest.

"But I'm cold," Nikki whines loudly, slowly falling farther and farther behind the group.

Hannah stops and turns to face the younger, whiny girl behind her. "And you will be even colder if we stop," she hisses in a loud whisper. "Now, keep quiet! We don't know these woods." The unknown forest has thick branches that seem to have no end.

"No one will be out this far from the city," Nikki, the youngest, contests, dragging her feet.

"You don't know that." Hannah shakes her head and pivots quickly on her heels to resume walking.

"Why would they?" Nikki says in a lower tone, still trailing Hannah. "There is nothing out here. We probably will just die out here from starvation and thirst." Hannah doesn't turn around to refute Nikki's words. Nikki sighs loudly, when she realizes she is being ignored. "So, now, instead of a quick death, we will just have a slow agonizing one?"

Hannah stops once again, causing Nikki to bump into her back. She slowly turns around and looks down at the younger girl with anger. "You don't understand what kind of death awaited us," she says through gritted teeth.

"Like we know what will happen out here?" Nikki raises her arms and gestures to the empty forest around them.

"At least we have a say in our future out here," Hannah sneers.

"Not really," Nikki says pushing past the older girl, purposefully bumping Hannah on the shoulder.

"Will you two stop it?" Tommy sighs, obviously annoyed by the juvenile bickering. "We made our decision."

"Not like we really got a say in the matter," Dexter scoffs under his breath, knowing the youngest of the group didn't get a vote.

Riley who is walking beside Dexter hears his soft words. "We never do," she agrees.

"What did you say?" Hannah storms toward them.

"Nothing," Riley and Dexter say in unison, letting Hannah pass.

"Do you always have to pick a fight with the younger ones?" Tommy asks Hannah as she joins him.

"It's like they don't want to be protected!" Hannah scoffs, matching his strides.

"You know we stand a better chance together," Tommy reminds her.

The moon lights their path as they slowly walk through the dim forest. The light wind rattles the leaves on the trees and twigs snap under their stomping feet. Their breaths leave a small fog with each exhale as they silently continue their journey farther and farther away from the city.

"Maybe you are just keeping us all around so you can eat us when you are older," Nikki says, joining in their conversation.

"I will never stoop that low! You know that!" Hannah replies with disgust.

"I'm sure that's what they all say." Nikki shrugs.

"None of us will be that vile. Plus, you will most certainly taste sour," Emma adds nudging Nikki in the arm, making her smile for a moment.

"Maybe we should just walk in silence for a while," Tommy suggests. "Think we can handle that until we find some shelter?"

The younger ones grunt and kick rocks in defiance while the older kids march forward with purpose. Regardless, they all stand united, fighting against the beasts of the world. Unlike the creatures of the wild, the beasts they fear look much like they do now, only older.

Aside from fear, survival keeps their legs moving. It wasn't safe on the outskirts of the city any longer and the limited resources nearby were quickly dwindling, like they are everywhere. The best chance was to escape into the forest and hope to find some sort of food and a water source able to sustain them until it was time to move again. No place is safe for long, no matter how perfect it may seem. Eventually, the adults will come in search of their next meal.

Due to their ages, all the children traveling together are at risk of being the next target. The adults don't go for the younger prey, not enough meat they say. They also try to avoid the older, stronger humans, fearing they will lose in a fight to the death. Instead, the adults band together, three or four of them, and hunt down the adolescent kids. Adolescents are still weak, but have enough meat to fill the stomach.

These adults don't view themselves as beasts. In fact, they have an excuse for every young human they feast upon. The small conscience they have left inside them has been twisted into thinking they are saving the younger ones from a life of hardships that the world has left for its few survivors. But in fact, they are just desperate and hungry, stooping to the lowest of human morals just to survive another day.

For now, the horrors of the city are behind them and hopefully, so are the adults. These kids need to find a place to rest for the day ahead. It's not safe to be outside in the light of the sun. The darkness of night conceals their presence from the adults and keeps them safe.

The sky is slowly illuminating; though the sun has not yet broken over the horizon. "We are running out of time," Hannah says to Tommy as if he didn't already know.

"Spread out," he calls to everyone. They each give a small nod and disperse in a different direction. This tactic has been used many times before and is well practiced. Each of them will search for a place that either works as a shelter, or can be put together as one quickly.

Within moments a whistle is heard in the winds and all the children come toward the sound. Riley and Dexter have stumbled upon a brush pile among a patch of thorn bushes. "Looks like it's already claimed," Grayson notes, gesturing at the compacted bedding inside.

"My guess is it's an old shelter for a deer and her fawn." Some of the other children perk up at the chance for a meal. "There is a very slim chance they are still around, but if they are, they won't bother us when they come back. They will just find somewhere else to sleep for the day," Tommy says examining the makeshift shelter. The little hope the children have for a live animal slowly diminishes.

"It's small, but it will work," Hannah remarks. She quickly crawls inside as if the looming sunlight will burn her skin.

"Gather a few branches to conceal the entrance," Tommy instructs Grayson and Nikki. "This will have to do." While the two youngest find some branches on the ground nearby, the others begin to lick the morning dew off of the leaves of trees. Once they are satisfied, they make their way inside the small burrow.

By the time Grayson and Nikki return, the others have covered the small area inside with their bodies. Grayson stands the branches up on the side of the thorn bushes so that they can be easily reached from inside the brush. Then, Grayson and Nikki make their way into the shelter, climbing over and on top of the bodies already positioned inside. They look like a pack of freshly delivered puppies, making it difficult to tell where one body ends and another begins. They don't mind, though. Once the branches are moved to conceal any presence of an opening among the bushes, rest finds each of their exhausted bodies easily.

***

Even the heat of the day doesn't disturb the children. They all stay asleep, feeling comforted by the tangled web of bodies around them. No one wakes until the loud song of the crickets lulls them out of their slumber.

Dexter is the first to open his eyes. He stretches his body out of its current fetal position and forces his extremities into the bodies surrounding him. Grayson groans as Dexter's foot slowly squishes against his shoulder and Hannah moans as a breath is forced out of her stomach by an elbow. Slowly, the mountain of children stir and shake until Tommy opens up the entrance so that they may flood back out into the wilderness.

The sun has begun its descent, but still shines its light on the forest. "We can't risk leaving yet," Emma says in a soft whisper to Tommy. "Plus, we need to find some food and water if we are going to walk all night again." Tommy nods.

"Go with your partners. No one wander too far," he instructs. "And stay quiet. If you find an abundance of food, gather enough for the group. As soon as the sun sets, we leave."

They all slowly nod their heads in understanding and carefully split off into different directions, hoping to find some sort of nutrition. "I'm real hungry," Grayson admits to Emma. He holds his stomach as if the weight of his arms might alleviate the feeling of emptiness.

"Me too." Emma swallows the small amount of spit that has accumulated in her mouth. It isn't enough to satisfy her body's growing need for substance.

"Will we really have to walk all night again if we don't find anything to eat?" Grayson asks, afraid of the answer.

"I know it feels like your stomach is about to eat itself, but we can go another day or two without eating much and be fine." Emma tries to stay positive for the younger boy, though, she too is feeling weaker by the minute.

Still within eyesight, Nikki and Thomas wander through their part of the terrain. "What are you hoping to find?" Nikki asks Thomas who is keeping his eyes on the ground.

"Mushrooms," Thomas answers.

"Fungus?" Nikki asks in disgust.

"I think you mean, food," Thomas corrects with a smile on his face.

"No. I meant fungus," she states. "I keep an eye out for nuts and berries."

Although they are the largest group, Hannah, Riley, and Dexter stay close to one another, fearing what may be lurking in the forest. They can no longer see the other two groups, but know how to get back to the rendezvous location when the sun sets. "We only have like fifteen minutes to find something," Hannah says in a whisper to the younger children.

Dexter turns his head to find the sun. It is quickly setting and it will be too dark to search for food soon. He picks up his pace and the two girls follow close on his heels.

Suddenly, the forest opens up into a small clearing and Dexter immediately halts, causing the girls to bump into his still body. "What are you…" Hannah begins to complain, but stops when she looks past Dexter and into the clearing. A garden filled with rows of various types of vegetation stands in front of them, begging to be picked and eaten.

A smile forms over Dexter's face as he begins to step into the clearing. Hannah quickly grabs his shirt and pulls him back into the concealment of the forest. "What are you doing?" Dexter asks as saliva forms in the corners of his mouth. "Don't you see all that food?"

Dexter frees himself from Hannah's grasp, but is tripped by Riley before he can make it out of the tree line. His face burns red with anger. He rolls over to yell at the young girl, but notices her staring off to the other side of the clearing. He sits up and follows her eyes to a small cabin sitting in the opposite corner. Smoke is coming out of its stone chimney. The three of them stay in the trees, watching the smoke rise and then disappear into the sky above. The scene looks like an old painting, but there are no rips in this perfect image. The vegetation sways beautifully with the small breeze, wafting simple smells of dirt and growth into their noses. The small plantation looks peaceful and serene. Even as the sunlight fades, the scene stays beautiful, begging to be enjoyed.

Without a sound to alarm them, Hannah suddenly feels a pair of hands grasp her shoulders, causing her to jump. Her sudden movement startles the other two as well and they all turn their back on the unspoiled image. To their surprise, Tommy stands behind them with an angered expression.

"Where in the hell were you guys? You had us worried sick!" he spits at them.

Hannah twists her head, looking for sun. It has completely set and darkness fills the forest. She turns back to the homestead, wondering how the time faded so quickly. Tommy follows her glance and is too, pulled in by its beauty.

"Food," Nikki happily sighs as she pushes past the immobilized children.

"Wait," Tommy says, snapping his arm in front of her to block her forward motion. He nods his head, gesturing to the house.

"So?" Nikki scoffs. "It's dark. We won't get caught."

"We don't know that," Tommy remarks, relaxing his arm to his side. "It's impossible to tell what kind of precautions the people who live here have taken."

"For all we know," Riley interjects, "they have poisoned some of the food so that those who steal some will die."

"You're being dramatic," Hannah mocks. "If anything, they probably have traps set up, just waiting to capture us. There is no way they would ruin good food. Not with how scarce it is."

"It doesn't seem that scarce to them," Dexter adds, still longingly looking at the garden.

"We will be quick, in and out. Plus there are seven of us! I'm sure we outnumber them," Grayson says excitedly.

"There is enough food here to feed maybe… ten grown adults for the season," Emma says. "Plus, they may have livestock somewhere too. It's hard to say how many people live here."

"There is no way more than three adults could fit into that small house," Nikki contests, gesturing to the small shelter.

"And seven of us managed to fit into a deer's bedding," Hannah snickers. "I think it's too risky. We will find more food. We always do."

"We won't take much!" Dexter says in a panicked voice. "And just from the edges! We don't have to go near the house. I promise we won't be greedy!"

"It's not about greed," Tommy sighs, looking longingly at the ripe vegetation. "It's about safety."

"So, it's safe to starve to death?" Nikki asks in a sarcastic tone.

"We don't know these woods or this land. We don't know what kind of people or how many live here. These people could be dangerous and we have no weapons to protect ourselves. It's not safe because there are too many unknowns," Tommy says, annoyed.

"I don't mind sharing a little," a frail voice calls from the dark. The children have been too caught up in their bickering to notice the man who was slowly closing in on them.

They all quickly turn their bodies to face the man. "Stay back!" Hannah yells at the man in a shaking voice.

"Oh I'm sure you all could outrun me if you needed," he says, first chuckling, and then coughing. "I'm an old man out here by myself. You all are more than welcome to take some provisions with you. I have more than I need."

The moon cast only a bit of light on the encounter. The age of the man could not be well seen, but what could be distinguished was his hunched posture balancing on a wooden stick beside him. His baggy clothes and untamed hair seemed to float with the small breeze.

"It's much too cold to be outside tonight," the man adds when the children remain silent. "Come, join me in my cabin. In return for my hospitality, you can help me in my preparations for the winter." The man turns from them and begins scooting his way back toward his home.

All seven of the children stand still, frozen in confusion and dazed by the kindness of the man. Emma slowly leans over to Tommy and whispers, "What should we do?"

"I...." Tommy begins, trying to quickly think.

"I think we fill our stomachs!" Nikki starts to follow the slow man.

"We can't just go with him!" Hannah spits at Nikki, grabbing her shirt and yanking her back.

"He said he lives here all alone and is old. We could easily overtake him!" Nikki pulls herself free of Hannah's grasp.

"And we are going to trust an adult, just like that?" Emma asks.

"He has plenty of food for himself! He doesn't need to eat us!" Nikki gestures to the garden.

"Need and want are two very different things," Tommy adds, still unsure.

"Then let's take a vote!" Grayson suggests catching everyone off guard.

"This is about safety. A vote is juvenile. Plus-" Hannah's words are cut off by Nikki.

"No! We should vote! You older kids always push us around. We should get a say in what we do. We are a team," Nikki says. Before anyone else can say anything, she continues, "Who wants to eat?" Grayson, Riley, Dexter, and Nikki all shoot their hands into the cool air.

"Let's just grab some food and run," Emma suggests. "He said so himself that he couldn't catch us."

"Now you want to steal the food," Nikki rolls her eyes and sighs. "I thought we were 'better' than the adults. Is it really right to steal from this old man?"

Dexter faces the older kids, "You guys always say how morals should stay intact even when it comes to survival. What has suddenly changed your minds?"

"Staying alive!" Hannah says.

"Now you sound just like the adults…" Nikki says in disgust turning away from them. "I'm eating and helping this man. Both parties get what they need and I see nothing wrong with that." Riley,

Dexter, and Grayson slowly follow Nikki and quickly catch up to the slow-moving man.

"What do we do?" Emma asks Tommy and Hannah.

"We stick together I guess," Tommy sighs as he, too, follows the man back toward the cabin. "But keep your guard up. As you both know, we are never truly safe."

***

"This is it," the old man says wearily, opening his cabin door. The old man's hobbles didn't keep a fast pace and the children felt as if he was torturing them as they were forced to slowly walk past all the vegetation without touching it.

The man climbs his front step with effort and invites all seven of them inside. The cabin is only one room holding his dining area, bed, kitchen, and closet. The space is crammed with all of them inside, but with some shifting, they are able to shut the door.

"Please, sit," the man says as he bobs over to his lit stove. He holds his right hip as if it causes him pain.

The children glance around the room, trying to find a place to sit. Emma, Tommy, and Riley sit on the bed. It looks big enough to sleep a few adults, but the mattress is old and stained and smells of sweat. Tommy is too alert to notice the odor as he keeps his eyes locked on the man.

Nikki, Grayson, and Hannah sit at the homemade stools around the small dining table while Dexter leans against the closed wardrobe. "Why do you have three stools if you live alone?" Tommy asks sternly. Riley elbows Tommy in the side and gives a wide smile.

"Don't mind him," Riley quickly states. "He is just nosey. You don't have to explain yourself."

"Oh, it's okay child," the man replies with a shaking voice. He takes the lid off a large pot that sits on the stove and steam wafts into the room. The smell of cooking soup makes the mouths of the children begin to water, even Tommy can feel the salvia accumulating in his cheeks. He swallows it hard, trying to stay focused.

"I didn't always live alone," the man explains, stirring his concoction. "Though, it has been a long time since then."

"Then why keep the seats?" Tommy asks, not letting the man down easy. Nikki turns from the table and gives him an angry glare, which Tommy ignores.

"I just couldn't bring myself to get rid of their seats," the man responds. "Now, I don't have enough bowls for everyone, but between what I have and the cups, hopefully you all get your own serving. I don't have much made as I was unaware company was coming, but I can always whip up more if you stay a while." The man begins spooning the hot liquid into various containers.

"Why did you invite us in?" Tommy asks sternly, still wary of the man's intentions.

The man doesn't stop scooping soup as he says, "I'm an old man and my days are numbered. I am well aware of the wolves that prowl in the city. We have fewer savages out here, but they still exist." The man puts the lid back on the pot and opens up a sealed jar. He removes what looks like shredded purple petals and places them in each of the servings. "I haven't always been so kind to those traveling, even children, but if there is such a thing as the afterlife, maybe I can make up for some of the bad I have done."

"What kind of bad?" Tommy asks, genuinely curious. Riley hits him hard with her elbow before she stands up beside the man.

"Here, let me help you, you have done enough already." She grabs a few of the containers and begins passing them out to the children. Except for Tommy and Hannah, all of the children eagerly accept their servings.

The younger ones don't wait for everyone to be served before they begin slurping their food, not bothering to chew the larger chunks of vegetables.

"Why the petals?" Hannah asks the man as she and Tommy look at each other.

"I'm all out of seasonings, the petals help counter the bitter taste of the vegetables," the man states as he waddles over to the front door. Hannah continues to watch Tommy as the other children happily finish their servings. "You all seem mighty hungry. I'll go pick some more vegetables and another pail of water to get another pot going." He smiles and exits, closing the door behind him.

"See? Nothing to worry about," Nikki says with a smile on her face.

"I'm still not sure," Hannah says poking at the purple petals floating among the chopped carrots and potatoes in her cup.

"Well I am," Grayson says as he takes the cup from Hannah and begins to chug her serving. "What? he asks when she glares at him. "I'm not letting it go to waste. Plus, he said he was going to make more."

"Yeah," Hannah responds as she looks back to Tommy who hasn't touched his cup either.

"Will you two stop it?" Riley yells at Hannah and Tommy. "You are both so ungrateful! This man opened his home to us, fed us, and even left us alone with his things. He obviously trusts us, why can't you trust him?"

"And doesn't that seem odd to you?" Tommy hands his cup to Emma to finish. She gladly takes it and begins slowly sipping the broth. "He says he is old and frail. If you were that vulnerable, why would you allow seven children into your home? We could easily just kill him and take all of his stuff."

"Because he is trying to be a better person," Dexter says with a yawn as he slides down the wardrobe and sits on the floor. "I wish others in this world would act like him."

"That's my point," Tommy says. "No one else in the world is like that and I don't think he is an exception. I don't understand why you are all quick to trust him."

"Because he can't overpower us," Nikki says, laying her head back and closing her eyes. "We outnumber him and honestly, just one of us could overpower him."

"Maybe that's what he wants us to think," Hannah says, agreeing with Tommy. "You know the adults are always coming up with new ways to capture us."

"But he isn't an adult," Emma says, laying down on the bed and looking up at the ceiling. "He is a sad old man who just wants to redeem himself. I'm more than happy to help him with that." Her eyes slowly close as she speaks.

"I think Hannah is right," Tommy states. "You know we have tried to protect you from a lot of things, and we have. There are some things we haven't told you because you don't need to know, but I don't think anyone left in the world has good intentions."

"Like what?" Grayson asks, setting his head on the table.

"Like how death may not come quick if we are captured," Hannah blurts out, frustrated with the group. Tommy gives her a worried expression. "What?" She throws her hands up in the air as she stands. "Obviously they have no clue what true horrors await us if we don't survive this! Maybe it's time we stop protecting them."

"Okay," Tommy sighs. "Maybe you are right. Look guys, the adults don't just hunt you down to kill you, the meat spoils too quickly. What they do is much worse than just cannibalism, they torture you. They chain you up and slowly peel away your flesh until you finally die. It can take weeks for you to die. And that's if-"

"Tommy?" Hannah interrupts his speech with a worried tone.

"What?" he asks, slightly annoyed.

"I think everyone is..." Hannah walks over to Nikki and lifts her arm in the air. She releases her grip as Nikki's arm hits the table with the full force of gravity behind it. "Dead?" Hannah can barely choke out the words.

"No!" Tommy says, quickly going over to Emma on the bed. He violently shakes her, but she doesn't respond. He places his head on her chest. "She's breathing!"

"So is Grayson!" Hannah exclaims as she listens to Grayson's deep breaths. "So what?" Hannah asks. "They are all just asleep?"

"The soup had something to do with this." Tommy looks at Hannah. "I knew that purple flower was added for a reason. This was the only way he could take us all out at once."

"What are we going to do? We can't just leave them and he will be back soon." Hannah begins to panic.

"I have an idea, but you're not going to like it," Tommy says.

***

"I told you I'd get them all," the man chuckles as he enters the cabin once again. He is no longer hobbling or limping, instead he takes large strides and stomps his strong feet on the floorboards.

"And where do you suggest we keep them all?" a woman's voice asks in a low tone.

"I'll take care of it, don't worry dear. Now we will have plenty of food for the winter. You'll be nice and strong when it comes time to push out the new baby." He rubs the woman's swollen tummy.

"What will we tell little Georgey and Ashley when they ask where the meat came from?" she whispers hesitantly.

"We will deal with that when the time comes. All that matters is that our family will be well fed. We can't just live off of vegetables much longer. We are all getting too weak," he sighs as he caresses his wife in a hug. "Now, take the kids to the small shelter south of here and don't come back until morning. I'll take care of everything." He kisses her head and leads her outside to their children who are waiting.

"We are going to let our new friends rest here tonight," the man explains to his kids. "We have done our part to help them and they will be on their way in the morning. Just in case they cause a scene, I want you guys to go with your mother to the little shack by the pond. I need you all safe."

"But what about you, Daddy? Will you be safe?" the young girl asks her father.

"Of course, my love," he says, hugging her. "Now go and protect each other." The three members of his family leave into the night. Once they are completely out of sight, the man goes back into the cabin.

He closes the door and lets out a large sigh of relief. All seven of the kids are fast asleep and won't wake up for a few hours. He cracks his knuckles and decides to start with the small male on the floor. The man grunts as he squats down and places his arms in and around the armpits of the young boy. He lifts with his legs, until he is standing straight up and begins to drag the body, trying to rotate it so he can easily get them both out of the door.

Before he can take his second step, a large object comes down on the back of his head. The man falls to the ground, dropping the body in the process. He quickly gains his composure and stands back up as blood trickles down his forehead. A second blow comes down hard and dazes him as pieces of a wooden stool fall at his feet.

"Grab another!" Tommy yells to Hannah who quickly pushes Nikki's body off of her chair, causing her to thud on the floor.

"Sorry," she whispers to her friend as she quickly hands the stool to Tommy. He lifts the stool high in the air and comes down hard on the man's skull, causing it to crack. The man falls to his knees before slamming face first on the floor. A small pool of blood begins to form around his head.

"Is he dead?" Hannah asks Tommy.

He leans down close to the man to examine him. "No, he is still alive, though I'm not sure how long that will last."

"We need to get out of here," Hannah says, panicking at the sight of the bloody body.

"We can't leave until the others wake up," Tommy says. "Plus, I'm not done with him."

"What do you mean?" Hannah asks with a worried expression.

"Did you hear him speak to his wife? They have plenty of food here and yet, they still wanted to harvest our bodies! He deserves to die and so does his family!" Tommy's eyes are filled with anger and rage.

"No, we are better than them," Hannah says with a stern voice. "We will take what we need and continue on our way. I refuse to eat another human no matter how awful they may be. We will learn to survive off a garden. We can plant seeds once we find a safer place and start our own, safe community. I want to be better," Hannah's eyes fill with tears.

"I didn't say we should eat him," Tommy says with a mischievous grin. "Instead, we should thank him for his hospitality and give him a full stomach just like he wanted."

***

The next morning the mother and her two children return to the cabin. Many of the crops have been picked clean and trampled in the dirt. They quickly run to the front door and notice it is wide open. The place has been ransacked, cleared of most of their limited resources. And there, on the bed sits the man. His head is covered in blood and his stomach has been cut open from the ribs all the way down to his pelvis. His intestines, stomach, and other organs lay beside him. Large rocks fill the empty cavity inside the dead man. No one is around to hear the cries of his family.

Audrey M. Stevens is an Indiana resident who married her high school sweetheart after graduating from IUPUI. Now a stay-at-home mom to a beautiful daughter and rambunctious pup, she continues to write in the hopes of publishing more books. Find all her current works at:

https://www.amazon.com/Audrey-M.-Stevens/e/B087777W7P

Spinner's Song

By Heather Carson

"This song is just for you." Ligeia pulls the newborn baby to her chest. The blood of birth soaks them both and the baby screams until his mother's hum soothes him into a trance.

"Let's finish the process." The midwife digs her knuckles into Ligeia's stomach. She moans against the sudden pressure, but it is nothing compared to the pain that occurred just a few moments ago.

After she's bathed in boiled sea water, the midwife gets Ligeia into bed. The seal skin blankets are tucked around her creating a nest of warmth. The baby wiggles his small body down, sucking skin until he finds the nipple.

"You did a wonderful job." The midwife smooths the wet hair back from Ligeia's face. "He's perfect. You'll heal fast."

"That's good." Ligeia nods drowsily. "I need to get back to work."

"Hush now, child," the midwife croons softly. "The spinners will take care of you."

Ligeia shuts her eyes. "I don't need their pity."

"It isn't pity." The old woman shakes her head. "They want to help. You just had a baby."

"Plenty of women have babies," Ligeia sighs with her eyes still closed. "But not many of them are recently widowed."

"All the more reason to accept the help." The midwife shrugs.

"I don't need help." Ligeia yawns as the newborn baby falls asleep in her arms. The midwife moves to take him so that she can get some sleep. "Leave him," Ligeia whispers. "We will be okay."

***

"Look." Leif mimics the word as he reaches his chubby fingers up toward the seagull flying overhead.

"Look at that baby." Ligeia smiles as she kisses the top of his downy curls. The baby squirms in her arms as he struggles to see where the white winged creature has flown off to. The frustration tenses his tiny body and she can feel the scream that is building in his lungs as they move through the crowded wharf.

She lowers her lips to his ear and begins to sing softly against it. The tantrum fades as he relaxes against her chest. By the time she reaches the fish market, Leif has fallen asleep. His hot breath blows against her arm and mixes with the crisp morning ocean breeze.

"Hello, Anna." Ligeia smiles in greeting as she approaches the young woman at the stall. They used to play together as children behind the wall that separates the cities from the earth, but that was a long time ago. Life took them in different directions as it so often does. Anna's sharp eyes glance over her childhood friend and notice the baby sleeping in her arms.

"Hey. What can I get for you today?" she whispers as she gestures to the catch laid out in the bins.

"I'll take 4lbs of tuna, 1lb of mackerel, and 1/2lb of shrimp if you have any." Ligeia removes her coin pouch from the pocket under Leif's limp leg.

Anna bites her lip as she takes the money. "Do you want me to have someone carry it to your house? Bergah is off from his father's shop today. He's a sweet boy. I know he won't mind."

"I can carry it." Ligeia lifts her chin and shifts the boy's weight to her hip so that she can hand over the shopping bag woven from plastic. Anna lowers her eyes and hurries to fill the order so that Ligeia doesn't have to stand there waiting for long.

***

Leif sleeps the entire walk home allowing Ligeia the chance to wander lazily through the city on the sea. She hasn't taken the time to do something like this since Hamon's boat was caught in a storm and capsized a month before Leif was born. The memory of his warm hands on the small of her back and his beard as it tickled her cheek brings about a hollow ache as deep as the ocean. Ligeia tightens her grip on her son unconsciously.

Their house sits at the edge of the wharf, down the floating docks, and near an outcropping of rocks too sharp and jagged to walk on safely. Behind it is the wall. The rusted metal extends twenty feet high in the air and protects the remaining bit of earth that survived the rising seas and earthquakes.

In another year or two, Leif will be allowed through the gates to spend his mornings playing on the small strip of island just as Ligeia and Anna did. All children are given this opportunity. When they get too big, they won't see the land again unless they choose to retire at the age of 60. The retirees take a ship to the Northern Gate where the land isn't eroding like it is here.

Ligeia looks at her son's rosy cheeks as he snores against her chest. She could never imagine retiring and leaving him behind. No matter how old he gets or how much easier life would be on the land, she could never abandon him. Ligeia closes her eyes as she hums softly to the baby.

"Oh gods, I'm sorry!" Ligeia gasps as she crashes into the back of a watchman. Leif wakes in a confused daze just as the bag of fish spills out onto the metal planks beneath her feet. The watchman turns and Leif begins to cry.

"Watch where you are going…" the man's voice trails off as he stares into Ligeia's startled eyes. "Here, let me help."

"It's alright," she whispers, adjusting the baby on her hip and reaching for the handle of the fallen bag.

"No trouble at all." He squats down, creasing his drab green uniform, and quickly gathers up the food. His eyes never leave her face. Her cheeks flush under the intensity of his gaze.

"I can get it," she insists. Leif's cries grow louder as he sobs against his mother's chest.

"You have your hands full." The watchman smiles. A dimple indents his clean-shaven cheek. "Where are you heading? I'll carry this for you."

"No need." Ligeia holds out her arm for the bag, but he moves it out of reach as he stands.

"This is an official order." He winks playfully.

The color of her cheeks deepens. No one refuses an official order from a watchman. Their job is to protect the wall and keep order in the cities. Those who don't comply disappear. He's only joking, but hearing those words spoken aloud sends fear spiraling into the pit of her stomach.

"I live just over there," her voice cracks as she speaks.

"Then let's get you home," the watchman says gently, wishing the worry on her face didn't tug at his heart that way. "It looks like the boy needs to continue his nap."

Leif's eyes widen and the screaming stops as he studies the man who walks beside his mother. Little hiccups rock his small body.

"Thank you." Ligeia takes the bag from the watchman as she reaches her front door.

"Atlas." He smiles, holding out his hand to shake hers and then realizing the futility of the action. "You really have your hands full," he laughs. It's such a light and carefree sound that the tension eases from her shoulders and even Leif smiles.

"Thank you again, Atlas." Ligeia nods as she opens the door and then locks it behind her.

***

"She's beautiful." Atlas shakes his head to dispel the image burned into his mind and takes a sip of sugar kelp rum.

"You aren't falling for one of them, are you?" Tagart leans back in his chair and laughs.

The loft above the tavern floor where the watchmen come when they are off duty is unusually warm tonight. Atlas rubs a hand across the back of his neck as the smile creeps its way back to his face. "I'm just saying she is beautiful. Can't a guy give a compliment?"

"Which one is it?" Charles leans over the table to scan the crowd below. "The girls that serve here all look the same to me."

"Not here," Atlas sighs. "I've never seen her come in here. She lives down by the sharp rocks and has a baby."

"The widow?" Charles' jaw drops. "Her name is Ligeia I think. She is pretty though."

"She's a widow?" Atlas lowers his face. "That's awful."

"Yeah, I wouldn't want to get mixed up in that if I were you," Tagart laughs. "We only have two months left on this rotation. You wouldn't want to break her heart."

"Do these women have hearts?" Charles chuckles.

Atlas stares sullenly into his mug as he swirls the brown liquid around. The amber tint reminds him of the freckles splashed across her cheeks and the hair falling softly around her face.

***

"There's your girl." Charles nudges Atlas as they make their patrol around the city. Atlas looks over to the pier and sees Ligeia with the boy child strapped securely to her back. The sea breeze blows wisps of long curly hair around her face which she fights to tuck behind her ears.

His feet move him forward without thought until he's close enough to catch the faintest notes of music drifting back to him in the wind. *She's singing.* A wide grin lights up his face and he wants to laugh.

"Hey Ligeia, wait up," he calls. She pauses, unsure of who spoke her name, and scans the crowd.

"Atlas?" Her eyebrow arches as he approaches. "Is there something wrong?"

"Of course not." He cocks his head to the side and smiles. As she stares at him, he quickly straightens his shoulders and coughs into his hand. His voice lowers, "I just wanted to make sure you were alright."

"Why wouldn't I be?" She takes a step back as Charles comes to Atlas' side. Both men tower over her slight frame. The sight of two watchmen standing there causes her pulse to quicken. She glances over her shoulder to make sure no more are coming. When the trouble makers disappear, it is always in the middle of a group of watchmen. She hasn't done anything wrong, but the fear is still real.

"Was there something else you needed?" she musters up the courage to ask. Atlas stands silently watching her face as Charles rolls his eyes.

"No, ma'am. Have a wonderful day." Charles pulls his friend away.

"What is wrong with you, man?" he whispers harshly once they are out of earshot.

"I don't know," Atlas groans. "My tongue got stuck in my throat."

"Get it together." Charles shakes his head. "You have a job to do."

"I know." Atlas runs a calloused palm over his chin as he looks hopefully at Charles. "Did you hear her though? She was singing."

"Oh boy, you are screwed." Charles claps him on the back. "You found yourself a siren. What song was she singing?"

"I didn't hear it well, but the notes were familiar." A grin erases the embarrassment from his face. "I'll have to ask her the next time I see her."

***

Ligeia sets Leif down in the rock circle near her feet as she takes her rightful place amongst the spinners. She reaches into the pile of plastic strips and pulls out a handful. It's the start of a new strand. Three twists and a knot.

A long time ago, before the rising seas and the earthquakes, humans had other material of which to make rope with. That material is gone now, but the ancestors did leave millions of plastic bags behind. To this day, divers recover pounds of plastic from beneath the sea. The plastic is cut into strips and braided into rope that is strong enough to anchor boats but versatile enough for everyday use.

All around Ligeia the spinners sing the song of a woman meeting her sailor home on leave. It's an ancient song, one Ligeia knows by heart. The music lulls the mother and child into a calming state as they continue about their business. Ligeia spins while Leif plays with rocks and seashells under her careful eye.

"Sorry I'm late," Margaret says breathlessly as she takes her place next to Ligeia. She is younger than Ligeia by a few years, but they sit closest together so the women have formed an easy friendship.

"Did the midwives keep you?" Ligeia asks.

"I don't know what I was thinking." Margaret twists her long red hair into a bun and fastens it at the base of her neck before grabbing her bag of plastic strips. "I wish you would have talked me out of the apprenticeship."

"You're a natural," Ligeia reassures her. "It's where you belong." Margaret laughs as Leif reaches his chubby arms up to her and she leans over to tickle his belly.

"Is that a new dress or something?" she asks as she sits on the rock beside Ligeia.

"No." Ligeia looks down at the tanned hide dress. The color fades near her knees. "Why do you ask?"

"Something is different." Margaret gives her a long look.

Ligeia lowers her eyes and focuses on her work as she ponders her friend's words. "There is a watchman named Atlas that startled me today."

"Are they watching you?" Margaret's voice drops to a whisper. The other women cast worried glances at the girls. Up on the docks, a single watchman walks by. Margaret motions with her eyes in his direction. The spinners take notice and raise their voices so the song will cover the sound of their conversation.

"I don't think so." Ligeia chews her lip as she watches the watchman pass. "It seems like this one just wants to talk to me."

"Is he cute?" Julie leans forward and interjects herself into their discussion.

"I don't know." Ligeia shrugs. She hasn't looked at a man in that way since Hamon was lost at sea eleven months ago. She struggles to recall the watchman's face. He had a strong jaw that was cleanly shaven and a dimple on his cheek. His eyes were playful and kind. "I guess he'd be considered attractive."

"There's no harm in playing around. We still have two months left before their rotation." Julie winks.

"Stop it." Margaret glares at the girl.

"What?" Julie asks. "I'm only saying that if she wants to, and is ready to, then she should go for it."

"I don't think I'm ready," Ligeia whispers before inhaling a deep breath and joining the spinners' songs.

***

"What are you doing?" Ligeia gasps as Atlas steps from the shadows of the market stall. "Are you following me?"

"No. I…" He pauses to look around. "Yeah, this looks awkward, doesn't it?"

Once her heart rate returns to normal, a smile teases the corner of her lips. She's never met a watchman who acts this silly before.

"Yes," she laughs. "It's a little uncomfortable."

"My apologies." He places a hand over his heart. "Allow me to make it up to you. I was just heading to the tavern to meet up with my friends. Can I buy you some dinner?"

The smile fades from her face just as quickly as it came. "No, thank you. I need to get Leif home."

"Of course." Atlas twists his boot across the plank as he lowers his eyes. "Well, do you mind if I walk with you for a while? I'm off duty now and don't have any plans besides meeting up with the guys."

Ligeia glances at the empty walkways. Everyone not heading to the tavern has gone home to be with their families. Leif needs some dinner before he melts down. Then she'll sit alone by the light of the whale oil lantern and get some stitching done. Atlas gives her a hopeful smile.

"I suppose that will be alright." She smiles back. "You already know which way I'm going."

***

"What's it like being a watchman?" Ligeia asks as they pass by the open doors to the tavern. The laughter from the customers drifts into the cool night air like a warming breeze.

335

A cloud falls over Atlas' face. "It's alright. I wasn't really expecting things to be the way they are, but I only have another two years until I'm done."

"Where will you go then?" She steps gingerly over a rotted plank. The welders haven't fixed this portion of the walkway in a few months.

"Home." He shrugs.

"And where is home?" The teasing of her voice sounds foreign to her own ears.

"Down South," he answers mechanically.

"Near the watchmen training center." She nods. "I've always wondered why all the watchmen seem to come from that area. I've never been to another city. Is it nice there?"

"Not really for young men." Atlas looks away as he speaks. "There aren't a lot of jobs for us to do there and most of us join the watchmen."

"Not even fishing jobs?" Her brow furrows as she studies his profile.

"The older men have a monopoly on those." His smile doesn't reach his eyes. "But enough about me. I want to know about you."

"There's not much to know," Ligeia giggles as she nears the docks. "I used to love to sail. Now I'm just a mother and a spinner who does seamstress work on the side."

"But you like to sing." Atlas moves slower as they near her house.

"I'm a spinner." She smirks. "We sing a lot."

"You were singing on the pier yesterday. I only heard a note or two." It doesn't matter how slow he walks; they reach the door of her house anyway. "The song sounded familiar to me. What's the name of it?"

"You've probably never heard it." She shakes her head. "It was a song that was passed down for generations in my family."

"Will you sing it for me?" he blurts out the question as her hand touches the doorknob.

"Maybe some other time," she laughs awkwardly.

"Please." His eyes widen as he begs, standing on her walkway with his hands in his pockets. He looks so sad that she can't help but smile.

"Alright." She begins to sing. The notes drift sweetly through the air between them.

"What's wrong?" She stops abruptly when Atlas takes a frightened step away.

"Do you know what that song means?" His words are cautious and guarded. The sudden change confuses her.

"Yes." She eyes him warily. "It would be too hard to explain to you though. Just think of it as a pretty song."

"I don't understand," Atlas whispers as he moves closer to her. "That shouldn't be possible."

"There's nothing to understand." Ligeia grips the doorknob tightly in her fist. "It's a song for a child. Nothing more. Forget I even mentioned it."

"How can you know this?" He places a hand on her arm to keep her from disappearing into the house. The touch sends a jolt of lightening down her skin and the intensity of his eyes causes her pulse to race.

"You're scaring me." She glares at him as she pushes his hand away. Leif wakes crying and Ligeia uses the distraction to open the door quickly and slip inside before slamming it in Atlas' face.

"Ligeia, wait!" He knocks against the door. "We need to talk about this."

"You need to leave," she states firmly through gritted teeth as she unties Leif from the pack.

"Okay." The word shatters like broken ice. "Listen. I'm sorry. I didn't mean to frighten you. I've heard that song before and I know the meaning of it. But I don't think you should sing it anymore. Does anyone else know it?"

Anger makes her skin crawl and Leif cries louder as he clings to her chest. "I said you need to leave."

"I will." There's a soft rap on the door as he rests his forehead against it. "Just promise me that you'll never sing it again."

"I said go!" she screams to be heard over the baby. Tears streak her cheeks and dampen the top of Leif's head just as his tears soak her shirt.

"I'm leaving," Atlas whispers. "I'll find a way to keep you safe."

***

"What's gotten into you?" Charles asks as he jumps down from his coffin rack on the ship and begins to straighten his blankets. Atlas sits on the edge of his mattress lacing up his boots.

"You didn't come to the tavern and you haven't said a word to me all night," Charles continues. "Don't tell me you're still thinking about your wharf wife."

"Don't call her that." Atlas grabs Charles' shoulders and slams him into the bulkhead.

"Hey man," Charles says wide-eyed. "Want to tell me what's going on?"

"I'm sorry." Atlas releases his grip on the starched fabric. "I just don't know what to do."

"Do about what?" Charles brushes off the wrinkles on his uniform and takes a steadying breath to calm his anger.

"Ligeia," Atlas whispers her name like it's a delicate artifact.

Charles places a reassuring hand on his back. "Don't let a girl make you feel this way. There are plenty of fish in the sea as they say. You'll find yourself another."

"It's not that." Atlas rubs his fingers through his short hair as he stares at the floor. "You can't tell anyone, but I figured out what song she was singing."

"A song?" Charles studies his friend. They've served together for four years now and he's never seen him act this way. "Why does a song have you so worked up?"

"It's not just any song," Atlas sighs as he begins to hum the tune.

"Oh, shit." Charles punches him in the arm. "You have to go report this."

"No." Atlas' eyes are pleading. "She can't know what it means. It's probably just a song to her. She has a baby and a dead husband. She's been through enough. It wouldn't be right to cause any more problems in her life."

"That's not for us to decide," Charles states. "We are told to report stuff like this. If they find out you knew and didn't say anything, you might get years added to the watch bill or worse."

"I can't." Angry tears fill Atlas' eyes. "I can't risk hurting her."

"You have to. It's our job." Charles edges himself to the door.

"You don't understand," Atlas puts his head in his hands. "I care about her."

"And I care about you, man." Charles sighs. "I'll do it. I can't let you get punished for this."

"You can't!" Atlas raises his head, but Charles is already gone.

Ligeia hurries to the spinners as Leif sleeps tied in the pack on her back. Every turn she takes down the wharf, she glances over her shoulder waiting for Atlas or the other watchmen to appear. The city goes about its day lazily, impervious to the pounding of her heart. She reaches behind her back to touch Leif's cheek for reassurance that he is still there.

Foolish. The word rings in her ears so loud it drowns out the sound of the sea. Her mother told her to never sing the song to anyone. But her mother and father retired to the land after her marriage to Hamon. She'd sung her new husband the song and taught the meaning to him, just as her parents had done for her. Now Hamon was dead and Leif was all she had left to sing to. Why had she sung it to a stranger and a watchman?

His words scared her. He wanted her to be silent. There is something so important about that song that it stopped a grown man in his tracks and brought fear to his eyes. *And he said he knew what it meant.* The full weight of what she'd done in a foolish moment when she tried to open her heart came crashing down on her head. She had to find a way to fix this. Leif needed her to be okay.

The spinners were just arriving as Ligeia breathlessly made her way to the rocks.

"Sisters." The tears flowed freely down her cheeks. "I need your help right now."

The women paused, unsure of how to respond to this request when they'd never heard it spoken from her lips before from her.

"Whatever you need." Margaret reached for her hand and the rest of the women nodded in agreement.

"I just need you to sing," Ligeia whispered.

***

Atlas marched sullenly with the group of watchmen who were tasked with retrieving the girl. The baby was to be left behind, preferably with the midwife in training named Margaret. Atlas wrestled with what he would do for the entire walk from the ferry to the spinners' caves.

When she saw his face in the crowd of watchmen, she would hate him forever. If he could figure out a way to make a stand, to somehow sacrifice himself for her, maybe she could understand that this wasn't his fault. The hours spent begging the commander to spare her had only bought her half a day and added a year to his watch. He needed to do more, and fast.

The music drifted over the waves before the singers came into sight. The spinners' voices in their flute-like melody called to the men from afar. Such a simple song, sung so sweetly, brought forth so many emotions that the watchmen paused to look at each other.

The commander continued to approach cautiously. Before him, on the rocks with their hands busy twisting plastic into rope, sat the hundred women with their angelic voices drifting to the clouds.

"You there." He pointed at Margaret. Ligeia's shoulders stiffened as the girl stood.

"Do you know the meaning to this song?" he asked.

"It's just a song for babies, sir," Margaret answered innocently. "It has no meaning."

"Very well." The watchman turned on his heel to leave, giving Atlas a nod as he passed.

Ligeia let out a sigh of relief and lowered her face to hide her smile. They'd have to take them all now. A hundred women would disappear if this song was as dangerous as Atlas implied it was. There was no way the city could lose all of these women, all of these mothers. The spinners didn't hesitate. They all agreed to help and picked up the tune easily. Each of them sang loudly with the truest part of their hearts. The melodious notes drifted over the sea breeze and followed the watchmen back to their ship. *"A, b, c, d, e, f, g…"*

Heather Carson is the mother of two feral boys by day and author by night. *Spinner's Song* is a short story prequel to *The City on the Sea (City on the Sea Series #1)*. To find out more about this series visit:

https://www.amazon.com/gp/product/B08P2D94R2

Dear Reader,

We sure hope you enjoyed the stories within this book! This anthology was made possible by Dystopian Ink. If you love dystopian fiction as much as we do, come join us on Facebook at https://www.facebook.com/groups/dystopianink/ or find us on TikTok and Instagram @dystopianink.

Before you go, could you leave us a review? Tell us what your favorite story was or let us know what we could have done better. Reviews would mean so much to everyone who contributed to this anthology and we'd really appreciate your feedback!

Thanks for reading,

Dystopian Ink

Printed in Great Britain
by Amazon

36234518R00199